Wallace Breem (1926–1990) entered the Indian Army Officers Training School in 1944 and later joined a crack regiment of the North West Frontier Force. After the war, he joined the library staff of the Honourable Society of the Inner Temple, where there is a Memorial Award in his honour. Breem wrote *The Legate's Daughter* in 1974. His other novels include *Eagle in the Snow* (1970, republished by Weidenfeld & Nicolson in 2003) and *The Leopard and the Cliff* (1978).

By Wallace Breem

The Leopard and the Cliff
The Legate's Daughter
Eagle in the Snow

The Legate's Daughter
A novel of intrigue in ancient Rome

WALLACE BREEM

PHOENIX

For Rikki, who made the map and guided
Curtius through the streets of Rome

A PHOENIX PAPERBACK

First published in Great Britain in 1974
by Victor Gollancz Ltd
This edition published in 2004
by Weidenfeld & Nicolson
This paperback edition published in 2005
by Phoenix,
an imprint of Orion Books Ltd,
Orion House, 5 Upper St Martin's Lane,
London WC2H 9EA

1 3 5 7 9 10 8 6 4 2

A CIP catalogue record for this book
is available from the British Library.

ISBN 0 75381 895 7

Typeset at The Spartan Press Ltd,
Lymington, Hants

Printed and bound in Great Britain by
Clays Ltd, St Ives plc

www.orionbooks.co.uk

CONTENTS

AUTHOR'S NOTE

The naval battle at Actium in 31 BC that destroyed the power of both Marcus Antonius and Cleopatra of Egypt left Octavian the undisputed master of the Roman world.

There followed years of consolidation in which the scars of war healed slowly and every effort was made to revive the traditions and the virtues that had made Rome great. On the surface there was apparent calm: the Republic had been ostensibly restored. Certainly the legions and the ordinary people – the plebs – supported Octavian; but political expression was silent. Ardent Republicans of the aristocracy who resented a one-party state endured political impotence with smiling faces. Their thoughts were their own.

Never in his lifetime, and he ruled for over forty years, was Octavian regarded as emperor in the sense that Napoleon was Emperor of the French. In 27 BC he received the appellation of Augustus, a title hinting at veneration and for which there is no modern counterpart. For himself he selected a title that conveyed most satisfactorily his own views of his constitutional position, Princeps, which may for convenience be translated to mean 'the Chief'. It was as first citizen and, in his relations with the Senate, the first among equals, that he wished to be regarded. Thus, by limiting his own power the fiction was maintained, the opprobrium of being named dictator avoided. In fact his position was not dissimilar to that of the President of the United States of America, though the comparison should not be pressed too far.

Augustus and his second wife, Livilla, produced no children.

He had a daughter, Julia, by his first marriage; and Livilla by her first marriage had two sons, Tiberius (whom Augustus detested) and Drusus. The question of a political heir became acute when in 24 BC, after a three-year absence in the provinces, Augustus returned in ill health to Rome. Augustus may have thought he had solved the problem when he married his daughter to her cousin, Marcellus, the previous year and thus marked the young man by his favor. Not everyone, however, agreed with his choice.

At the time of Augustus' return Marcus Primus, a senator of unknown persuasion, was Proconsul of Macedonia; Marcus Aelius Gallus, Praefectus of Egypt, had just concluded an unsuccessful invasion of Arabia; and Terentius Varro Murena, a senator and successful soldier, was in Rome, shortly to be appointed joint consul with Augustus for the following year. Also in Rome were Augustus's two chief lieutenants, Marcus Agrippa, the soldier, and Gaius Maecenas, the diplomat; the latter related to Murena by marriage if not ambition. In Rome, too, was Fannius Caepio, an ardent Republican, of whom little else is known. Across the sea Juba II sat on the throne of Mauretania, where Augustus had placed him two years before. Juba was married to an exotic link with the past – Cleopatra Selene, the only surviving child of the liaison between Marcus Antonius and Cleopatra of Egypt.

Augustus's health failed to improve and the year 24/23 BC became a year of great crisis for the party of Augustus and the State of Rome, but the outline of the story is hard to trace (Cassius Dio, who gives the fullest account, misdates some events to the wrong year) and the details if known were deliberately suppressed. Only two facts are clear beyond dispute: the sickness unto near death of Augustus, which was to precipitate a constitutional crisis; and the apparent exposure of a conspiracy against his life by two men, one of whom he had the right to trust absolutely.

Novelists are permitted to conjecture about matters on which historians must remain silent. It is with the events of this year, therefore that this story is concerned.

HISTORICAL CHARACTERS

This list includes all named characters known to history and living 23/24 BC.

Agrippa (Marcus Vipsanius)	senator, statesman, and friend to Augustus
Antonius Musa	physician to Augustus
Augustus (Gaius Octavius, afterward Gaius Julius Caesar Octavianus)	first citizen of Rome
Bathyllus	a celebrated mime
Caepio (Fannius)	a patrician
Calpurnius Piso	a senator
Cassius	a physician
Cleopatra Selene	daughter of Cleopatra VII of Egypt and Marcus Antonius, the triumvir; wife to Juba II
Gallita	wife to Lucius Seius Strabo
Gallus (Gaius Cornelius)	first Praefectus of Egypt
Gallus (Marcus Aelius)	Praefectus of Egypt
Hyginus (Julius)	Librarian to the Palatine library
Juba II	King of Mauretania
Julia	daughter of Augustus by his first wife; wife to her cousin, Marcellus
Labienus (Titus)	an orator
Livilla (Livia)	second wife to Augustus, her second husband; mother of Tiberius by the first
Maecenas (Gaius)	diplomatic adviser and friend to Augustus
Marcellus (Marcus Claudius)	son of Octavia by her first husband and nephew to Augustus
Melissius (Lucius)	a librarian
Messalla (Marcus Valerius)	a senator, former consul, and distinguished statesman
Murena (Aulus Terentius Varro)	a senator and consul-elect of Rome
Octavia	sister to Augustus, widow of Marcus Antonius, and mother of Marcellus
Pollio (Publius Vedius)	a freedman's son of great wealth
Proculeius (Gaius)	a friend to Augustus
Pylades	a celebrated mime
Sestius (Lucius)	a senator
Strabo (Lucius Seius)	a praetorian tribune
Terentia	sister to Murena; and wife to Maecenas
Tiberius	son of Livilla by her first husband

PART ONE: ROME

CHAPTER I

He had been susceptible to headaches ever since the brawl in the wineshop at Tomi. It was there the Sarmatian horse trader had flung the beer mug that scarred him above the right ear. Now, when the traffic woke him as it always did in the still time before the dawn, the pain returned; the result, no doubt, of too much wine the previous evening. The heavy shutters across the windows creaked as the October wind blew hesitantly against the tenement block in which he had lived for the past year.

He lay tensed beneath the worn blanket and tried, as always, to shut out the noise of the rumbling carts that, empty now, having deposited their loads at the warehouses south of the Aventine hill, were moving up to the Aemilius bridge. But he found it impossible to sleep and, presently, went to the window to cool his head and watch the torches of the night patrol blowing gustily in the narrow street as they went off duty.

The street began to flare with torches and movement. The baker's assistant opposite began to pile fresh loaves onto a handcart, watched intently by two barefoot boys. When it became overloaded they would pick the spoiled bread from the gutter without fear of being charged with theft. A murmur of voices came from below as men filled the street on their way to work. Over all, he could hear the din of hammers as the metalworkers in iron and bronze who occupied the next street commenced their day.

His feet grew chilled on the bare floor. Half closing the shutters, he took the pitcher from its place in the corner and splashed his face with stale water, swallowing a mouthful to rid himself of the taste of wine, almost as an afterthought. Then he sat on the end of the bed, carefully avoiding the place where the webbing was frayed, and warmed his feet on the stained mat. A baby cried suddenly, a woman laughed, and he could hear voices in the passage as two men who shared the room at the end passed quickly by. They were auctioneers, people of no account, and he rarely spoke to them, though he knew their names well enough. The walls were thin, they made love in the night, and they did not seem to mind who heard them. From the room opposite came an occasional cough. It was occupied by a young seaman from Puteoli, now sick and out of work; but the girl whose father was a stonemason, and who lived on the second floor, brought him food now and again. The Greek doctor on the third floor might have cured him easily enough, but without money he would do nothing. He did a better trade in abortions.

Curtius Rufus took a fresh tunic out of the chest that contained all his possessions and examined it carefully to see that it was clean. Feet sounded on the stairs, climbing to his level. That would be Criton, the Macedonian, who wrote indifferent verse no one would buy. He made a meager living as 'client' to a lawyer who practiced before the Centumviral Court but when in funds was inclined to generosity. Perhaps he had remembered that old debt. The two men had loaned each other money upon occasion.

He put on his tunic hastily and was tying his sandal thongs when Criton knocked at the door.

'Come in.'

The Macedonian entered, looking anxious. 'I have the tickets I promised for the Circus Maximus. See! I even remembered to get one for your girl too.'

'Thank you. I was hoping—'

'It is nothing. You know I can always get them for you.'

'It is very generous.'

'It costs him nothing. That is why.' The Macedonian smiled

4

nervously. 'I hope your girl is generous too and thinks the same way.'

Curtius Rufus laughed. 'Pero is a little devil.'

Criton sniffed at the bleakness of the room. 'My dear Curtius, I know it is not fashionable to sleep in comfort, but you must buy some furniture. That chest looks as though it was made by a Gaul with ten thumbs. And this stool now – is it safe?'

'Try it and see.'

'You will be late for work.'

Curtius Rufus smiled. 'It would seem likely if you intend to stay for long.'

The Macedonian said gloomily, 'It will probably rain and I shall get wet.'

'We shall all get wet,' said Curtius Rufus lightly.

The Macedonian dropped his eyes and said hesitantly, 'I have to attend my patron. He has so many clients. My toga' – he swept a fold aside – 'has a hole in it.'

'True,' said Curtius Rufus gently. 'You need a new one.'

'Yes. The trouble is, I have already worn one out this summer.'

'As have I. Even good togas wear out, and ours are not the most expensive.'

The Macedonian nodded impatiently. 'It is the wool. The material is not what it was.' He paused. He said in a low voice, 'He is very fussy, and that new chamberlain of his is – is difficult. Full of self-importance. He prefers to remember new faces.'

'Ah! You wish to borrow mine?'

The Macedonian nodded. 'Please.'

'Is it so important? Yes, of course it is. You will find it in the chest. But be careful, mine is also worn.'

'Could I keep it for a while, until—?'

'Why not, dear friend? I, as you know, seldom attend official functions. Here, let me help you. Now, that is better. You look yourself again.'

5

'You are sure?'

'Of course. I have my old cloak. They are used to the way I dress. No one will mind.'

The Macedonian looked at the oiled hair, unfashionably long at the nape of the neck, the saffron tunic, the close-fitting cap that matched it, and at the silver earring in the left ear. He said disapprovingly, 'You like to upset people. You are a fool, dear boy.'

'I upset no one except myself. I remain what I am.'

'And what is that, pray?'

'A free man. No man hires me to clap bad speeches or swell his self-importance by being a paid hanger-on, dancing attendance like a slave.'

The Macedonian flushed. 'Your cloak is thin enough.'

'But not yet ragged.' Curtius Rufus paused and then said gently, 'Do you attend him at court today?'

'No, today we go to the baths.' The Macedonian bit his lip and then said with a curious pride, 'I am invited to dinner.'

'But you have been before. You are always dining out. You get depressed if you have to eat at home.'

'This is a special occasion. Fannius Caepio is coming.'

'The Republican.'

'And that is not all. They say that Murena may be there also. He will be consul next year.'

Curtius Rufus laughed. 'You keep good company. Your patron has powerful friends. The governor of Macedonia is one of them.'

'Yes, I have always wanted to meet Primus. An introduction to him would be invaluable.' Criton blushed. 'Perhaps when he returns to Rome—'

'Of course, Criton. You must tell me all about it afterwards.'

'I will, I will.' The Macedonian could not conceal his excitement and his pleasure. 'You laugh at me.'

'No, only with you.'

6

Criton went to the door. 'I must hurry now or I shall be late. Do not worry. I will repay you at the Saturnalia, if not before. I hope to receive a present then. My patron can be generous when he chooses.'

'Of course. I will share your hopes with you, if not the dinner.'

The door closed and the footsteps died away. Curtius Rufus ran a comb through his hair and prayed that he would not meet the landlord on the way out. He had been a fool to gamble so heavily at the races. The Reds had gone through the card against all expectations, and he was never lucky at the Flaminius. Now there was rent owing on the room and he had no means of paying it unless he starved. Still, it had been worth it. He would not have met Pero otherwise. He went to close the shutters. The sky showed thick clouds, and drops of rain fell upon his face. To the north a scattering of red-tiled roofs, the houses of the wealthy, came into view among the woods and groves that covered the Aventine.

It was then that he remembered. It was his birthday. He was thirty years old.

On his way to work he joined the crowd streaming up the Tiber embankment to the city gate, and then paused for a snack of bread and olives at a cookshop inside the Servian wall. It was close to the Circus Maximus; he always ate there after the races, and the proprietor knew him well and would allow him to run up credit in a bad month. This morning he marked the tablet as usual and said cheerfully, 'You ought to go back to sea. There is no money in working for the government, only in trade.' He patted his stomach affectionately and chuckled.

Curtius Rufus said, 'One needs capital to buy a ship.'

'I know a freedman who might put up the money. But he would require a good return on his investment.'

7

Curtius Rufus nodded. 'Then I should be working for him and not myself.'

'Why not think about it?'

'You need more than a ship. You need confidence. I would have the guild against me.'

The proprietor roared with laughter. 'It is only their daughters who have confidence in you. Keep away from them and all will be well again.'

Curtius Rufus smiled. 'Don't worry. I have a girl.'

'You have too many. Watch out that this one does not get the better of you.'

The streets were full and Curtius Rufus pushed his way slowly through the crowds that thronged the markets of the Velabrum. He paused at the junction of Tuscan Street and the New Way, where there was a crossing, while a closed litter swept by borne by a team of Galatean slaves; turned left up the side of the Basilica Julia; and crossed the western end of the Forum behind the New Rostra. He nodded briefly to the guard on duty outside the Tullianum prison. 'You have an easy time,' he said cheerfully, for the Tullianum was a two-roomed prison occupied only by the condemned. He had been shown inside it once by a friend and the remembrance made him shiver.

'Not now. We're full up.'

'Oh!'

'Two men.' The soldier dropped his voice. 'They say one was once a slave to the new consul. The other I don't know. They were brought from Macedonia under arrest.'

'What are the charges?'

'It's a state matter.'

'Have they been here long?'

'Four days. They've been questioned.'

Curtius Rufus said bleakly, 'When?'

'They go down to the lower room tomorrow.' The man hesitated and then said in a whisper, 'I heard my centurion talking to the tribune. They say that Primus is being recalled from Macedonia before his tour of duty as governor is up. It's odd, that.' He raised his voice suddenly as a senator escorted by his secretaries came toward them. 'No, I don't want any tickets, thanks. I've got two already. I'll see you at the circus. Thanks for the tip.'

Curtius Rufus smiled and moved on. Behind, he could see the tiled roof of the Tabularium, the official record office of the central government, rising behind the prison. He climbed the steep steps leading to the Temple of Juno and so came to the small rectangular building where he worked – the temporary head office of the city water supply. The gatekeeper on duty grinned and held out a hand, the thumb and index finger extended. He twisted his wrist with the motion of a man turning a water glass and then passed one finger rapidly across his throat.

'I am always late,' said Curtius Rufus softly. 'They are used to it.'

They were. None of the six draftsmen bent over their tables so much as looked up, though one of them said in a low voice as he passed, 'He is in a bad mood today.'

He went through a second room and a clerk looked up from an abacus board and said coldly, 'He is waiting for you. A message came through from the Curator of the Palace Water Supply and he has been in conference with the Praefectus.' He crossed the room, hesitated, knocked on the door, entered, flung his cloak over the rail provided, and said cheerfully, 'Well, we shall not be short of water today.'

The Inspector of Aqueducts said sourly, 'You would be in a better position to judge if you had arrived on time to read the reports on your table. There is one from the Surveyor's Department that must give us considerable concern, particularly since there is to be a state dinner on the Palatine in two days' time to celebrate the commencement of the Games.'

'I will read it.'

'If it is not too much trouble.'

Curtius Rufus opened a wrapped bundle that lay on his desk. 'They've sent us the wrong papyrus again. Not even a goat could avoid tripping over the fibers on this Egyptian muck.' Mechanically he took a roll and began to smooth the first page with an ivory blade. Then he picked up the reports and looked them over. An inquiry was called for into an accident that had taken place at harvest time when a weakened arch in the Julian aqueduct had collapsed, injuring not only the repair gang but also a wagon belonging to an influential fish merchant. Now the driver had died and a sharp question had been asked in the Senate about responsibility and compensation. A proposal to extend an existing aqueduct to the Capitoline hill was being blocked by the landlord of a valuable apartment block, and he was being supported by the merchants of the adjacent market, who complained that it would ruin the entire site. There was a protest about drainage from the Praefectus of the Fourth Region, and a request from the Praefectus of the Second for more street fountains because of the population increase in his area. None of these concerned him directly, but he was responsible for checking them against the records to ensure that the basic facts were correct, adding any data that might assist his seniors in reaching satisfactory decisions. Finally, he read the surveyor's report, frowned, wrote a note below the signature, appended his initials, and passed it to the Inspector. 'This is urgent.'

'I will pass it to the Praefectus for consideration by the Water Board.'

Curtius Rufus said, 'This is his third report in three months. It concerns' – he paused – 'the Marcian Aqueduct. He claims the section mentioned was incorrectly sited and that the piers have settled badly. The consequent cracking and leaking has worsened in the last week. He recommends an immediate major repair, involving the rebuilding of three arches.' He paused. He wondered why the report, which had been dated three days previously, and which he had not seen before, had not been shown to the Praefectus at the morning meeting. But the Inspector said nothing.

When the hourglass had been turned over six times Curtius Rufus yawned and put down his pen. The Inspector looked up. 'Have you finished?'

'No, but it is time for a drink.'

'I suggest you complete your work first.'

Curtius Rufus said patiently, 'I have annotated the reports. The facts about the inquiry are clear. All that is needed now is the approval of our masters for an opinion by the legal department. It is for them to say what happens next. The complaint by the landlord has validity, but less than that of the merchants. Again, this is a matter for the lawyers, and if the landlord wins, as he must, since he has connections with the Senate, then the region will be as badly off as ever. Their complaints will continue. The drainage problem is important. It would seem to be reasonable. Our own inspector confirmed this in the summer. The street fountains, however, are another matter. There is some justification for the Praefectus' complaint, but his statistics are wrong. I am checking them now. In any event, if we meet even half his demand it will make nonsense of our budget for next year.'

'Very well, but don't be long.'

'I am going to the races next month. Would you like me to place a bet for you?'

'You know I do not bet. I cannot afford it. I am a family man. I have four children.'

'Neither can I,' said Curtius Rufus. 'But I forgot. You prefer the fights. It is always preferable to watch blood spilled when it is not your own.'

'Be careful what you say.'

'I am always careful. Come, let's not quarrel. I know a good team and the odds are likely to be reasonable.'

'Waste your own money then, not mine.'

Curtius Rufus shook his head, smiled, and went out. On the steps, between the pillars, he paused and blinked. The rain had stopped, the clouds had cleared, and the sun was casting soft shadows on to the damp ground. It was going to be a fine day after all.

There was a booth just behind the colonnades in the Lautumiae, much frequented by junior officials from the state departments. The wine was cheap, but Curtius Rufus liked it as a place where one could hear all the gossip, some of it grounded in fact yet much of it malicious. Piso, a clerk in the Censor's Office, was already there, sitting in his usual corner. A copy of the Acta Diurnia, the official gazette containing state intelligence, lay on the table before him.

Curtius Rufus sat down, touched the surface of the liquid in his cup with an extended finger, and then traced a half circle on the table. He watched it until it dried.

Piso said, 'Are you short of luck today?' He was a fat man and his second chin quivered as he spoke.

'I am always short of luck, but especially today.'

'Another quarrel?'

'Not yet, but there will be one soon.'

'Arrange a transfer.'

Curtius Rufus smiled. 'I like the job – I think. But transfers are not easy.'

'I worked with him once. The man is a pig.'

'You are unfair to pigs who are friendly creatures.'

Piso said sharply, 'What is it this time?'

'Trouble with the Marcian Aqueduct. He is worried should the Palace water supply give out at the wrong moment and that he will be blamed.'

'Oh! I have heard something of that.'

Curtius Rufus looked at him questioningly, but Piso nodded

12

toward a praetorian who stood by the counter, talking to a street girl from the Subura district. 'Not now. Do you wish to see this?' Piso picked up the news sheet.

'My eyes are tired. You read it to me.'

'Well, there is an abstract of the Senate's report to magistrates on court procedure. That is lawyers' business. Very dull.'

'Go on,' said Curtius Rufus, his eyes on the young girl.

'Oh, two magisterial edicts: one about the salt tax and the other amending the harbor regulations at Ostia.'

'The passenger boat that sank on the evening run from Puteoli?'

'Yes. A list of appointments, but no one very interesting. A little about our First Family. Marcellus and Julia have returned from the Campania—'

'That should please Augustus and the Lady Livilla.'

'I doubt it. Augustus perhaps, but not his wife. Everyone knows that Marcus Agrippa wanted to marry Julia, and Livilla is concerned for her sons, particularly Tiberius.'

Curtius Rufus said, 'Whenever I contemplate marriage I remember the Lady Livilla.'

Piso laughed. 'Aelius Gallus is on his way to Rome.'

'To explain away the failure of his Arabian expedition, no doubt.'

'Of course. And the Senate held a special meeting in the Temple of Juno yesterday to hear a report on the Hispania war. Attendance was very low.'

The soldier touched the girl's cheek. She had beautiful skin. Curtius Rufus said absently, 'It always is at this time of year. They are still on their estates.'

'True, but Augustus was not pleased. I hear he made some sharp remarks.'

'I can guess. If we who have spent three years in campaign tents for the good of the state and without holidays—'

'Precisely.'

13

'How does he look? Still sick?'

'I did not see him, but those who did say that he walked to the Senate with his arm on Maecenas' shoulder. He seemed very frail.'

Curtius Rufus said casually, 'Any news of my old legion in Hispania?'

Piso paused and put down his cup. 'I will see if I can find out. A dispatch boat docked in Ostia yesterday. There was a tribune on board with messages. He is at Agrippa's house.'

'On the Palatine?'

'Yes, but his escort are quartered with the third cohort. I know one of the centurions. I will find out what I can.' Piso wiped his mouth and said casually, 'Tell me, how is the great affair going?'

'Pero?'

'Yes.'

'She smiles, and I pay. She is grossly extravagant.'

'Slave girls to great ladies usually are. They try to imitate their betters.'

'She amuses me.'

'But does not surrender,' said Piso shrewdly.

Curtius Rufus shrugged. 'She will.'

'Do you hear any gossip about the Lady Terentia or her husband?'

'None that would interest you. Pero's mistress and Maecenas go their own way.'

'Is it true that she and Augustus—?'

'Very probably. But it is all women's gossip that Pero passes on.'

When the office closed for the day he stayed on alone to finish his work. Then he walked up the Esquiline to Maecenas' house and spoke to the doorkeeper. The man knew him slightly, and smiled. 'Not a chance. An important visitor has arrived. The place is in an uproar. You'll not see your girl today. The Lady

14

Terentia has them all running six ways at once.' A small coin changed hands. 'I'll give her your message. Tomorrow at the usual time and place. Do my best.'

Curtius Rufus nodded his thanks. Disappointed, he returned to the tenement and collected his washing things. Criton had recommended a new bathing establishment, recently opened by a middle-aged Syrian. It stood a little way off the Long Street, not far from a desolate area of brick rubble, old houses, and decaying empty blocks. The whole district was due for redevelopment, and the Macedonian, whose gossip was often reliable, said that Augustus had announced plans to build a new forum there but was held up by the owners of a number of properties, which they had stubbornly refused to sell. The Syrian, with his eye on the main chance, had built on land that was going cheap and was only waiting until the forum went up to find himself close to a thriving area in which, otherwise, he could never have afforded to operate. When that time came the profits would be enormous and the ground rent, should he wish to sell, would be worth a small fortune.

Curtius Rufus approved of the baths, was charmed by the Syrian's politeness, and, having fallen asleep in the warm room, awoke feeling hungry. He ate in the cookshop attached and then, clean and contented, asked for a girl. In this matter also the Syrian was efficient, and it was close on dusk when Curtius Rufus set off for home. On the way he stopped at a tavern, carefully choosing one where he was not known. Here, in return for a drink, he showed a soldier on leave how to play dice. When the tavern had filled sufficiently and he was sure of a crowd, he borrowed three drinking cups, produced three ivory flats from his tunic (identical except that one had a black spot on one side), and introduced the visiting countrymen to the mysteries of Three Men in a Row. It was late when he reached his room and the aching envy that he had felt that morning when he awoke and which had made him sick to his stomach was now gone. He had avoided a bad quarrel at work, he had been lucky in the girl of his choice, no one had robbed him in the streets or picked his purse clean while he slept; he had drunk a good deal of free wine and had made a little money into the bargain. He was contented. On the whole it had been a good day.

CHAPTER II

The next morning he had a headache again so that he noticed every sound. the beat of the rain against the colored glass above his head; the clatter of a clerk's sandal in the next room, and the squeak of the Inspector's pen coming from the corner table. He worked slowly, concentrating with difficulty upon the documents before him. It seemed to be the morning for complaints, the chief one being from a senator about the quality of the water coming from the aqueduct that crossed his estate and which he had the authority to tap for his own use. He wrote his commentary, signed it with his name, and then coughed.

The Inspector looked up. 'Yes.'

'This one has no substance either. Everyone knows that the senator complains twice a year as a matter of habit because he has nothing else to do.' He pointed to a closed press. 'There is a file of them there. We have tested this stretch of aqueduct three times in the past six months. The results have been negative.'

'We shall have to do something.'

'Of course. I have attached a note suggesting – politely – that he should check his own pipes, commencing at the point from which they leave the aqueduct. He is a miser, and he used too much lead when he had them built. He should have used copper. He can still do so, but there is no reason why the state should pay.'

The Inspector smiled. 'But we cannot word it like that. A senator is entitled to proper respect.'

'I am merely stating the facts, Inspector. Reword them as you please.'

'It is your report. You must do as you think right. You know your own business best.'

Curtius Rufus said in surprise, 'I had thought it was our business.'

The Inspector smiled – protruding eyes in a bald head. He discarded his pen, now quite blunt, and picked up another. He did not speak.

On his return from the booth Curtius Rufus found that the daily reports had arrived. They lay there, a heap of rolled tubes upon his table. He said politely, 'I think some of these are yours.'

The Inspector said, 'I, as you can see, have enough work to do with the half-yearly accounts.'

'I thought they had been passed to the Board.'

'No. There was a clerical error which the assistant curator discovered. Two names had been entered twice over on the pay sheets. It was gross carelessness.'

'That new clerk?'

'Yes. I dismissed him immediately.'

Curtius Rufus looked at the Inspector but said nothing.

The Inspector began to tidy his table, meticulously laying his pens in rows, the sharpened ones on the right, the used ones on the left, as he always did at the end of a day.

'I see you are going home.'

'Yes,' said the Inspector. 'I had a message while you were out. My wife is sick. She is pregnant. I cannot leave her—'

'With four slaves in the house. Or is it five? No, of course not.'

The two men stared at each other.

Curtius Rufus said, 'Well, I will do what I can before we close.'

'You will see that I have added the report from the Surveyor's Department.'

'Another one!'

'Yes. We shall need two copies for tomorrow's meeting.'

18

Curtius Rufus said slowly, 'I am not a field hand who must work until sundown.' He paused and said coolly, 'I have an appointment to meet a friend at the stables. It is important – to me.'

'I am sorry. We are hard pressed as you can see. Work for the Department must come first, as always.'

'I will do what I can – as I said.'

'Have you no loyalty? No sense of vocation?'

'None. I work for money, as do all who work in Rome.'

The Inspector pulled his cloak from the rack and flung it round his shoulders; his head was shining with sweat. 'Every day you are late. You left your last post because of a scandal. But not even that was sufficient warning, oh no.'

'Well, it was certainly not my fault that the centurion's wife had green eyes.'

'You see! You make jokes. You think because you are a citizen and I am a freedman, you can do what you please. You are my subordinate. Understand?'

'We are both subordinates, like the wretched clerk you dismissed. It was a new job. He was nervous. Everyone makes mistakes.' Curtius Rufus paused deliberately. The Inspector looked at him, his face quite white. 'Be careful what you say.'

'I am always careful. You don't have to be, because your mistakes are always covered up for you.'

The Inspector stared. He said, 'I have had enough, do you hear?'

His headache worse, Curtius Rufus stood up suddenly. He said, 'You remind me of Vedius Pollio.'

'Ha! Who is he?'

'One of the vulgar rich. He is reported to feed his slaves to the fish in his ponds.'

The Inspector said angrily, 'I will recommend to the Board that you be dismissed. I have had enough.' He slammed the door and went out.

Curtius Rufus sat down again and carefully unrolled the first report. The settlement tanks of the Julian Aqueduct, built only nine years before, were giving trouble again. He sighed, pulled out the last roll of quality papyrus, and began his work. In the next three hours he paused only once – to grind fresh ink – but at last it was finished. His wrist aching, his fingers numbed from holding the quill, he sprinkled the sheets with cedar oil to protect them against the damp, and then when they were dry put the documents into a press and locked it carefully. If he hurried he would still be in time to meet Lucius at the stables and have a close look at the new team his friend was boasting about.

He was putting on his cloak, preparatory to leaving, when the door opened and a voice said sourly, 'Does nobody do any work round here? I must see the Inspector – someone in authority – immediately!' He shook his cloak in exasperation and wiped his face.

'We are just closing for the day,' said Curtius Rufus politely. 'May I help you?'

The man said, 'My name is Crispus. I am the surveyor in charge of the Ager section of the Marcian Aqueduct. I wrote a report about the condition of the arches.'

Curtius Rufus said, 'I have it here.'

'I wrote that three days ago.'

'I know. I have only just seen it. I have marked it for urgent attention.'

'But it is still on your table.' Crispus paused and said coldly, 'The arch is cracking now. If I am any judge it will have given way by nightfall.'

'I see.'

'What are you going to do about it?'

Curtius Rufus said, 'There is no one in authority here. They have all left.'

'The Praefectus?'

20

'He is probably gone to his villa beyond the Subura. Or he could be at the law courts. There is a case involving the department in which he may have to give evidence. I am only an assistant inspector.'

'So?'

Curtius Rufus hesitated. Then he smiled. 'I was going to the barber's for a shave, but it can wait. Tell me the exact trouble.'

'The river runs at this point in the shape of an S. The aqueduct crosses the lower curve at an angle of thirty degrees to the line of the main flow. The river in flood has been widening the bank where the right-hand pier stands. The pier was poorly constructed and is crumbling at the base. Cracks have appeared higher up and in the arch itself.'

'Can it be shored up?'

'I imagine so. But you need an engineer for that.'

'There isn't one available. We are very short-staffed at the moment.'

Crispus said in exasperation, 'We must do something now.'

Curtius Rufus said suddenly, 'I will get authority. I know a little of these matters. But you must help me. We shall need a gang of men; wagons, food and wine, ropes, scaffolding, timber, carpenters' tools, and lots else besides.' He was walking as he spoke.

Crispus followed him out onto the portico, flooded now with the early-afternoon sunlight. The square was empty and their sandals scuffled the dust as they crossed the road. The Temple of Juno soared above his head, white against the blue sky, and the sentry nodding on his heels outside the praetorian station watched their approach with a flicker of interest.

The duty centurion, irritable at being disturbed during his siesta, rubbed his eyes and said angrily, 'What in the name of Hades do you want?'

Curtius Rufus said quietly, 'I am the duty officer at the City Water Supply. I need your help on a matter of great urgency.'

'Oh! You do, do you?'

'Yes.'

The centurion blinked.

'You will put yourself under my orders.'

The centurion said incredulously, 'I will, will I?' He reached for his staff of office, while the soldiers in the orderly room grinned expectantly. The surveyor's face went white and his hands began to tremble.

Curtius Rufus said, 'I am a citizen of Rome.'

The centurion said coolly, 'And on whose instructions, may I ask?'

Curtius Rufus said, 'I speak in the name of Marcus Agrippa. Will that do for a start?'

It was midafternoon when Curtius Rufus and a half century of the city cohort reached their destination, some five miles outside the city. By this time the yellow-brown water had broken the lower bank and flooded the open fields behind, so that the damaged pier could not be reached except by wading knee-deep through mud and grass and the inevitable debris that swirled about the cut-stone foundations of the pier.

'What are its measurements?' asked Curtius Rufus.

'The piers are about thirteen feet wide and fifteen feet thick. The span of the arch is fifteen. The superstructure of the pier is built up, as you know, in sections. Here, they are three feet nine inches high. You can see the crack from here in the springing of the arch. There, where the course of cut stone is.'

'What else can you tell me?'

'There's a bad crack in the base of the pier below the water-line. I'm inclined to think it was there when the whole section was built. There are a lot of signs of careless workmanship. The force of the current at various times has widened the crack and eaten into the foundation.'

Curtius Rufus nodded. 'We can make a temporary repair and

hope that holds till the water goes down. Let's get on with it. What's the height of the duct? To the top, I mean.'

'Twenty-nine or thirty feet. What do you suggest?'

'Ferry the soldiers across on a raft and get them to build a protective wall across the flooded ground in front of the pier, so as to take some of the force of the current off it. They'll need timber to drive piles in. I'll show them how. When that's done we shore up the face of the pier with balks of timber. That ought to hold it.'

'How do you get the timber across?' said the centurion angrily. 'Swim with it?'

'Get the viaduct gang to build a hoist on this side' – the foreman nodded agreement – 'then carry it across the aqueduct. The width is probably three feet. They should be able to manage that.'

The foreman said, 'I'll organize the men.'

'Why not? Let's get started, shall we?'

By sundown the scaffolding for the hoist had been cut and lashed into position and the first balks of timber lifted to the top of the duct. On the far bank the work had progressed more slowly. A platform had been erected above the floodwater and the piles had been ferried across on the raft, but that was all. The sun vanished swiftly, and the men, wet and exhausted, broke off to eat a meal. Curtius Rufus, crouching by one of the fires they had started, yawned and said sleepily, 'Can we wait till dawn to finish the work, or is that too great a risk, do you think?'

Crispus said, 'It is my opinion that the arches have suffered considerably from wind stress. We have had three bad winters running.' He shivered at the remembrance.

The centurion said, 'There has been a lot of erosion of the far bank.'

Crispus said, 'Show me that sketch you drew.' He looked at it carefully. He said, 'It is more serious than I thought.'

'What do you suggest?' asked Curtius Rufus.

He shrugged. 'I am only a surveyor. I have had very little experience of building work.'

Curtius Rufus said, 'But I have. I think we need very heavy buttressing of the piers on both banks, and we must underpin the arches.'

They looked at him.

He said, 'If the men rest for an hour can they go on?'

'For how long?'

'All night if necessary.'

The foreman said, 'My men will do what they're told.'

'They certainly work hard.'

'The Jews and the Iberians are the best. The Mauri and the Greeks are the laziest.'

The centurion said stiffly, 'You can rely on my men, though they are new to this kind of work.'

Curtius Rufus smiled. 'We shall need torches. Centurion, get one of your men to wake up that farmhouse over there. They should have plenty of oil.'

'What we need is pitch.'

Curtius Rufus stood up. 'I had a date with a girl.' He thought fleetingly of Pero waiting in the late-afternoon sun by the Temple of Portunus, where they usually met, tapping her foot impatiently and then hurrying off in a rage when it was obvious that he would not come. 'I had forgotten all about it till now.'

The foreman said, 'Never mind. She will learn to dry her tears. Think of the money you saved.'

The centurion was looking at the sky and at the thin light of the moon, then entering its last quarter. He said, 'The Pleiades will set in two days and then we shall get cold and frosts and after that bad weather.'

They worked all night by the flare of the torches. At about the third hour the wind got up and the sky darkened and it began to rain. The men cursed as they labored to tie wet ropes around the streaming timber. A section of scaffolding collapsed as the damp

24

cords tightened and then gave way under the strain, but the soldiers working waist deep in the water, holding the piles as the sledgehammers drove them into the mud, were too intent to notice the outcry of voices across the stream. Torches spluttered in the rain and then went out, and precious time was spent in getting them lighted again before the high-level men, squatting precariously on stone and timber, could recommence their work. Once, a man slipped on the top of the duct and only saved himself at the expense of the trimmed pole he was carrying. This fell with a great splash into the stream, and was swept through the arch by the current until it drifted aground half a mile further down the bank. As the night progressed the men grew more tired and tempers became uncertain. Two fights broke out between factions of the viaduct gang, and these had to be broken up with whips. Accidents became more frequent. A saw slipped in a tired hand and its owner gashed his foot badly as a result. A pile of timber slid sideways in the mud and pinned a man who was too slow in his efforts to jump clear, while a soldier nearly drowned in the stream through cramp, though roped between two comrades at the time.

A little after midnight the outer wall of the dam was finished and the easier task of strengthening it on the shore side was under way. An hour later the rain stopped and the sky began to clear a little. The men took heart at this and renewed their efforts, for the end was now in sight. By cockcrow the buttressing on both sides was in its final stages and the task of underpinning the arch was in progress. Daylight came, the torches were doused, and men who had finished their tasks huddled in exhausted groups seated against the feet of the piers, too tired to talk, too exhausted to sleep. And then suddenly, as it seemed, there was silence. The incessant sound of hammering, of voices talking, of orders being given, of feet squelching through the mud, the clatter of wood upon stone – all had gone, and only the wind beating against the

25

walls of the viaduct and the stream rushing angrily past the dam could be heard by the men on both banks.

Curtius Rufus wiped his hands on his tunic and said, 'Is it really done now?'

Crispus said hoarsely, 'Yes, if you are satisfied at last.' He sneezed suddenly.

'You have a cold.'

'Are you surprised?'

'No, not really.'

The two men looked at each other and then the surveyor laughed. The centurion and the foreman came up to where they stood by the carts.

The foreman said, 'I have six men hurt, but only two badly; one has a broken leg.'

The centurion said steadily, 'I have two men injured.'

'It might have been worse.'

'But it is worse. A third man died. He was hit by the timber that fell from the aqueduct. We have only just found his body.' He paused. He said deliberately, 'I shall have to report this.'

Curtius Rufus nodded. 'I – I understand. I, too, will make a full report when I return. I am sorry about your man. Your soldiers worked well.'

Crispus looked at him curiously. 'Are you worried? No need to be. We all share the responsibility. It is work well done. Perhaps we shall all get a bonus.' Curtius Rufus did not speak. 'Besides, you had the authority. No one will question that.'

The foreman said, 'I should hope not. Marcus Agrippa values his slaves too well to let them be wasted unnecessarily. It was a fine job all right. Anyone could tell from the way you handled things that you know all about engineering.'

Curtius Rufus said slowly, 'I think I feel sick.'

Now that it was all over the sense of elation had gone. He remembered the excitement he used to feel when they worked all night to load one of his father's ships so that it might catch the morning wind, and then the sense of desolation that set in afterward when the ship had sailed and he was alone on the empty quay with nothing to do but return to the warehouse and the long day that stretched ahead, counting bales of goods and entering figures into a ledger, dull, hateful, necessary work that he loathed because it brought him into contact not with people but only with things. Now, he had the same feeling and with it a sense of apprehension that, he was convinced, must show upon his face for all to see.

On their return to the city he parted from the others at the Viminal Gate and walked hurriedly down Patrician Street, conscious all the while of the curious glances his appearance must attract. It was the first day of the Games, the Ludi Victoriae Sullae, and the city was packed; people poured in from the suburbs and the outlying farms, to make money or to lose it, but all determined to enjoy themselves. He shouldered his way through the crowds in the narrow streets of the Subura district, past brothels, taverns, and shops. Hucksters thrust their wares in his face; two boys stumbled against him as the cat they chased fled between his legs, to be lost behind a pile of boxes, while an elegantly perfumed pimp, leaning against the wall of the shop where they sold the executioners' whips, sniffed pointedly as he passed. A girl who knew him from a previous encounter cried his name from a doorway, but he shook his head and walked on.

The crowd thinned as he left the houses behind him. Skirting the stagnant lake at the foot of the Esquiline, where few cared to walk after dark, he looked up to the villas that were beginning to crowd the southern slope, and wondered briefly what it would be like to be rich, to be a Maecenas and have power and security and everything you wanted. Augustus was probably there now and not at his house upon the Palatine. They always said he stayed with Maecenas when he was sick. The spiteful were inclined to make more vicious jokes. Passing the western end of the Circus Maximus he could hear the rumble of chariot wheels

27

and guessed that some of the teams were undergoing a training session. His pulse beat faster at the thought. The races at least made life endurable. Perhaps he would be in luck this time. He had a good eye for the horses. It was in the blood, he supposed, remembering his father with a flicker of affection.

Upon reaching the tenement where he lived he paused to eye a pretty girl who was offering a prayer at the shrine on the corner. He went in by a side door and crept quietly up the stairs, collecting his key on the way from the stonemason's daughter. He always left it with her when he was out of funds. He changed his clothes hurriedly, washed at a nearby fountain, and then went straight to his place of work.

The Inspector listened to his story in silence and then said mildly, 'Well, you must make a report on the matter. When you have finished, go home. You look tired out.' But when the report was written he could not face a return to the tenement and risk a meeting with the landlord. He would have liked to talk to the Macedonian, but that must wait until later. Well, there was always the baths. He cheered up at the thought, practiced a smile at a heavily jeweled lady who was watching him speculatively through the gauze curtains of a passing litter, and walked rapidly in the direction of the Campus Martius.

The chamber was full of noise as men exchanged greetings with their friends. Curtius Rufus put down his cup and smiled as Piso sat down beside him. Sitting on a nearby bench was a young boy with an older man for companion. He caught Curtius Rufus' eye and grinned. He had fair skin, blue eyes, and dark brown hair, and wore a gold chain around his neck, from which hung a medallion. Curtius Rufus said suddenly, 'Do you come from Mauretania?' He spoke in Berber and the boy, astonished, grinned, showing beautiful teeth. 'Yes,' he said. 'You know my country?'

'I know Tingitana a little. My father used to trade there.'

The boy grinned again. 'Rome is very beautiful. Its people are beautiful also.'

'Some are more beautiful than others.'

Piso said, 'When you have quite finished—'

'I have.'

'That's as well. His friend thought you were trying to steal him. By the way, the governor of Macedonia has been recalled. He reached Rome this morning and went straight to Murena. There is a big row brewing. Murena is said to be furious.'

'Well, have you ever known two consuls to be on speaking terms?' He laughed. 'Shall we eat here or elsewhere?'

Piso said, 'I thought you said this place was respectable, or are you changing your habits?'

'Neither the one nor the other,' said Curtius Rufus gloomily. 'I was misinformed.'

'You were. I must go home. We are having neighbors to supper. I will leave you to dream of your fortune.'

He thought of the shabby rooms in the tenement block, the noise, the dirt, and the squalor. He thought of the drudgery of performing a job that he loathed, of the strain of working for a man he despised and who hated him. He thought of Pero and of the meanness of his pay.

'Oh yes, my fortune! I shall go for a walk among all the expensive shops in the Campus Martius and choose all the expensive gifts I shall never buy.'

In the dressing room he saw the boy again with his companion. The older man had a strong face and an indolent manner. Two slaves wearing livery were arranging his toga while he fussed at their not getting the folds right. The toga gave him a dignity he had not seemed to possess in the bathing rooms and it bore, to Curtius Rufus' surprise, a narrow purple stripe that designated its owner as a member of the lower nobility. Watching Curtius Rufus dress he said, disapprovingly, 'You have forgotten your toga, dear boy. You really should come properly dressed. One may think that some of our laws are absurd, but it is up to every one of us to do our best to observe them.' He spoke with a faint Etruscan accent, and though his voice was gentle the note of authority was unmistakable.

29

Curtius Rufus said, 'I am sorry, sir. I do agree. Unfortunately—' He spread out his hands and smiled.

'I understand. Well, at least you have the grace to apologize. Very handsome of you.'

Curtius Rufus held his smile.

The man's eyes dilated slightly. 'I will admit that your costume is becoming – as I am sure you are aware. Are you from the east, Parthia, perhaps?'

'No, sir, but my father was. I am a citizen myself. I know only Rome.'

'And you are unattached, no doubt?'

'I am not married.' Curtius Rufus paused. He said delicately, 'I find that the costume of my race attracts the ladies.'

There was a short silence while the Mauri boy flirted with his eyes at Curtius Rufus.

'Do you often bathe here?' The stranger, dressed now, was on his feet, one hand on the boy's shoulder. The fingers of his hand showed the tightness of his grip.

'When I can afford it, sir.'

'But the cost of the entry is a mere nothing.'

'Oil is very expensive, sir. It is the customs tax.'

'Yes. We must try to do something about that, one of these days.' He pulled the boy's ear affectionately. 'Some of us forget that the baths cost more than we think, if one is to enjoy oneself properly.' He smiled maliciously as he spoke.

Curtius Rufus said dryly, 'It is the same for all of us then.' He bowed politely and followed the stranger and his friend from the building. The doorman, seeing their approach, clapped his hands. 'Fetch Gaius Maecenas's chair. Quickly!' Curtius Rufus picked his way carefully between the squatting slaves who patiently waited with their masters' sedan chairs, and then paused to wipe the sweat from his face. The baths, he decided, had been warmer than he had expected.

*

30

It was a dry day and the streets were partially filled with strolling couples enjoying the warmth of the late-afternoon sun. The Tiber was crowded with a long line of barges coming up from Ostia to the warehouses below the island; a group of idlers were playing backgammon in the doorway of a closed shop; a cake seller with an empty tray was shuffling home, counting his takings as he did so, while a group of small boys were watching fascinated as a man repaired a roof under the scolding eye of his wife. The cattle market was deserted except for the penned oxen that had been bought and sold that morning. They watched him with flickering tails as he declined the cries of a vendor of fresh water. He winced at the sight of a convoy of sick slaves being carried on litters toward the temple on the island in hope of a cure, and remembered his own mother fleetingly as he did so. From the Theatre of Pompey, as he passed it, came the roar of the audience. Pylades was performing that day and the place was packed. The streets widened slightly. He was in the fashionable area now, where the wealthy bought elegant trifles for their wives or mistresses, where the furniture in a shop was made of ivory and citrus wood, selling at a price that would have kept all the poor in Rome fed for a month without effort, and a necklace with earrings to match might have filled the pay chest of a legion for half a year. Here, young men made assignations with pretty girls. Heirs to the aristocracy that had destroyed the Republic, they gossiped in clear, high voices about a pampered world whose members lacked nothing save personal distinction. Subsidized and secure, they lived a life of ease. It was the one thing they could do supremely well. Walking among them he felt uncomfortable, though he tried hard not to show it. His clothes, which had seemed to him smart enough at the baths and in the tenement, now felt cheap and their colors gaudy when set against the expensive fabrics of those who could afford to buy the same garments ten times over and still have no cause to worry about the rent.

31

A chair passed him and was put down. The passenger inside got out and went into a perfume shop, followed by her maid. He paused and waited. Presently the girl came out. She was fashionably dressed and wore her dark hair piled in intricate curls upon her head. Married, he decided, watching carefully the remote expression upon the painted, exquisite face. Her maid whispered and she smiled, looking straight through him. A young man came up whom she evidently knew. They spoke together, the maid fell back and the girl showed him her purchase. He laughed, and Curtius Rufus heard him say in a clear voice, 'Let us go. The streets are full of peasants today. It is the festival. They spoil even one's shopping.'

The girl wrinkled her nose. 'Yes, I even envy Valeria now, visiting her father in Tarraco.'

He said, 'I, too, am waiting news from Tarraco.'

'Poor Lucius. You know your father will never agree. Never mind. Perhaps a letter is on the way.'

They moved off past him. He could have put out his hand and touched her as he had touched so many women, but she was as far from his world as a princess in one of the legends. He might work in the city, but it was they who owned it. He grinned ruefully, felt the ache in his stomach, and decided that he would feel more comfortable in his own haunts. Besides, it was getting late and the young boys were already returning from their exercise in the fields beyond. He turned and made his way back to the cattle market where he and Pero usually met. It was always bad to think on an empty stomach. It made one feel sad.

She was crouched at the foot of the steps leading up to the Temple of Portunus, her turquoise skirts spread about her, her eyes large with delight as she watched a tiny kitten staggering uncertainly in the sunlight, trying to catch the ribbon she trailed in the dust.

Curtius Rufus saw her and slowed to a walk. He was late and

she was probably furious again, but it would not do to let her think that he cared too much. Pero heard his step and looked up, her chestnut hair shining as though it had been polished.

'Do look at the kitten, Curtius. It is very young. Do you think it has lost its mother?'

'Very probably. This area swarms with stray cats. The fit live and the weak die, just as it is with us.'

'Don't say that. You will bring it bad luck.' She looked at the kitten. 'It is very strong. See!' She held out her hand and he saw the tiny red marks on the wrist.

'They all have claws like needles. I had one when I was a boy. This one will live, I think, if it scratched you and survived.'

She laughed, fondled the kitten for a moment or two, and then stood up and faced him. She was nearly as tall as he.

'Well?' she said.

He smiled. 'I am sorry about yesterday. It was not my fault.' The tiny bottle of perfume that he had bought with his winnings at dice, and which was a peace offering, lay inside his tunic, but he did not give it to her.

'I waited an hour. A whole hour. Was she prettier than me? Now that you have come you can tell me.'

'I will go if you talk like that.' He turned away.

'Curtius.'

'Yes, Pero?'

'Don't go. What happened? Tell me.' She smiled and held out her hand. He took it and smiled back. 'Well,' he said. 'It was like this—' And he told her. When he had finished they were on the promenade by the Tiber, just below the Agrippa bridge, the open meadowland of the Campus Martius stretching away to their right. Pero clapped her hands and said, 'They will promote you for being so clever.'

'I doubt it.'

'Poor Curtius. You must have been tired. Anyway, now you owe me a present.'

33

'What for?'

'For keeping me waiting.'

'I will buy you one when I have some money. I like that dress. It goes well with your hair.'

'Thank you. Do you like my perfume?'

He sniffed, noting with pleasure the looks that Pero was attracting from passersby. 'I have not yet had a chance to get close enough. But I think it is the same as you wore at the Circus.'

She nodded approvingly and glanced at him quickly. 'Why did you talk to me that day?'

He said lightly, 'Because you laughed at me when I tore up the tickets.'

'Did you lose a lot of money?'

'Too much.'

'Did I bring you bad luck?'

'I don't know yet. Let's sit down and you can tell me what mischief you've been up to. I tried to see you the other day.'

'I know. We had an important visitor. No, I cannot tell you. I will be beaten if I do.'

'I might guess.'

'Guess then,' said Pero tartly. She plucked a piece of grass and bit it thoughtfully. 'There was a dinner party,' she said. 'The great Murena came, and Marcus Agrippa. He is very attractive. But I would not like to cross him.'

'You are not likely to have the chance.'

Pero spat out the grass. She sighed theatrically. 'No. I am only a slave girl. There is a young boy, a year older than myself, who likes me. Perhaps I will live with him, since we cannot marry. My children will be slaves too and be taken away from me. That is all that can happen.'

'You can save your tears and your tips – then buy your freedom.'

'Lady Terentia gives little. I worked it out once when I was bored. I would be too old to marry if I waited till then. Her husband is kinder, but he never looks at us.' She giggled. 'Only at Bathyllus.'

'The mime! I did not know that.'

'He may be an actor but he is better at other things.' Pero laughed. 'Perhaps if I spoil my Lady's hair before an important dinner, she will sell me, and I will go to a household where there is a young son.'

'He might not fall in love with you.'

'This one would. I should make him. Fannius Caepio's son is very handsome. I saw him at the dinner his father gave. I went with the family.'

'Did he look at you?'

'They all look at me,' she said carelessly. 'I am used to it. But I think he was just practicing. He is in love with a legate's daughter who is out of Rome. There was bad feeling between father and son. I expect he has other plans for that boy.'

He took her hand and held it tight. In the distance a group of youths were throwing spears at a straw target, watched by two men on horseback. Pero looked at him and smiled, and he smiled back.

'Perhaps I might have plans for you,' he said gently.

She glanced at the sun. 'It is time I was going,' she said. 'I must not be late getting back or I shall be in trouble again.'

They stood up, close together and face to face. 'Are you often in trouble, Pero?'

'Always,' she said. 'But I smile at the steward and escape my punishment.'

'How do you smile?'

'Like this.' She raised her head and looked at him inquiringly. 'You must tell me your plans, Curtius.'

He bent and kissed her. 'I will,' he said. 'I will indeed.'

They turned and walked back, hand in hand, toward the bridge.

CHAPTER III

The Macedonian said impatiently, 'Must we eat here? And after last night too.'

'Why not?' said Curtius Rufus. 'It is cheap enough unless you care to pay for us both.'

They ate, then the Macedonian pushed his plate away. He emptied the jug into his cup and said contritely, 'I forgot. It is I who had the pleasure, not you. Tell me again, do you think there will be trouble for you over what you did?'

'I would as soon jump into the arena while the mixed pairs are performing as forget what he can be capable of.'

Criton looked worried.

'I do not know what he is, but there is little left to choose from. Never mind. Tell me about your dinner. Did they all come?'

'Yes.' Suddenly Criton was calm and his face resumed its normal look of permanent anxiety. 'It was a wonderful dinner. We were not close, of course, to the main couches, but we could watch them.'

'Were there ladies present?'

'Oh yes, a number came with their husbands. Fannius Caepio brought his lady. A plain woman, I thought, but she wore a wonderful hair net sewn with pearls.' He added eagerly, 'And Maecenas came also. That was awkward, because the Lady Terentia was there with her brother. They scarcely spoke to each other, and when they did they addressed their remarks to Murena. It was very uncomfortable for those around them.'

Curtius Rufus grinned. 'Well, you know the story. The Lady

Terentia was dressing for dinner one afternoon when Maecenas minced into the room, wearing women's clothes, his face made up, jewels in his ears. Terentia said, "My dear Gaius, you know I don't mind what you do when you entertain your friends but – must you wear my robe?" And Maecenas said, "Of course. How else can I hope to attract Augustus?" '

Criton said severely, 'I do not believe it. That sounds like one of Pero's stories.'

'I hoped you might laugh. Was the dinner a good one?'

Criton sighed and pushed his plate further away. 'Yes, excellently cooked, but nothing vulgar. As for the wine, it was—' He picked up his cup, sighed, and then put it down again. 'It was excellent.'

Curtius Rufus grinned. 'I once drank a flagon of Mamertine – but that came from a wreck we helped to salvage.'

Criton raised his hands. 'That is good enough for public banquets. We, however, had Alban, both the sweet and the dry.'

'So you enjoyed yourself. Have another drink.'

'Yes, I did. No dull recitations, no vulgar dancing. A compatriot of mine played the lyre between courses. He was quite good, for a Theban. One cannot have everything.' He hesitated. 'There are times – other occasions – other houses—' Criton paused, his face pink with remembered embarrassments.

'I know. One gets the second quality food, the servants are of the clumsiest, and the wine is inferior. I endured it once; never again. I have not the talent to be a client.'

The Macedonian said, 'This was different. Why, at the end, we were invited to take away what was left in our napkins. And there were no sniggers when we did.'

'You should have invited me. What of the conversation? I am always curious to know what the rich talk about when they are not discussing riches.' Curtius Rufus leaned back on his stool and glanced round the room. Two soldiers were getting quietly drunk in a corner; four men – they looked like merchants from

Illyrium – were telling each other bawdy stories, while a servant girl wearing a silver girdle was deftly fending off hands as she went along the benches, pouring wine for the customers. 'Do they relax as we do here, or talk with pebbles in their mouths like Demosthenes?'

Criton said tartly, 'Well, we did not spend all our time talking of the future of the soul.'

'I should hope not. I had to do that once when I was a private tutor to a family in the south.'

'You did not tell me. I do not believe it.'

Curtius Rufus said, 'I have tried everything. I start well, I have good intentions, then I get bored.'

'Whom did you seduce that time?'

'Oh, the wife, of course. I was young and she was not. I was even paid – though that I did not expect.'

'Really!'

'Yes. So, no gossip, no scandal.' Curtius Rufus smiled. 'I have wasted the price of a dinner.'

Criton shook his head. 'No, no. There was gossip—'

'But no politics of course.'

'No. We are not in the Republic now.' Criton paused. He said slowly, 'There was a little talk about the marriage of Marcellus and the Lady Julia. The Lady Livilla apparently is furious.'

'So I have heard. But why? A suitable enough match: the daughter of Augustus marrying his sister's son. The girl is fifteen and the boy a little older. Surely!'

'They say the Lady Livilla had other – did you know that the boy has been appointed aedile for next year? Everyone thinks he is marked out for the succession.'

'No, but it is common knowledge that Augustus dislikes his stepsons.'

'Only Tiberius. Drusus is too young to count.'

'Old enough to admire a pretty girl's legs when he sees them.'

'Perhaps, but Tiberius is so morose. He has no gaiety.

Whenever one sees him in public he scarcely bothers to smile. He could take a lesson from you in that.'

Curtius Rufus grinned. 'I show my face and Tiberius shows his. Come, I don't believe that Augustus's lady could be angry or anything else. I doubt if she has feelings. Those patrician women spend most of their time trying to avoid tripping over their own noses. When she looks at a crowd I always feel she is holding her breath to keep out the stink.'

Criton said, 'But it is true. The marriage was arranged in secret and then Augustus was afraid to come back from Hispania and face her.'

'Nonsense. He was ill. No man would stay away from his only daughter's wedding.'

'Murena was asked if he knew if the marriage pleased Julia. He said, "Well, when they broke the news she clapped her hands and swore by Diana that never again would she touch another spinning wheel." '

Curtius Rufus laughed. Then he broke off and said quietly, 'I wonder what the great Agrippa thinks of it all. What would you think if you were the second man in the state and—'

'Hush!'

'Well, what other news did you learn?'

Criton was silent.

'Any news from Hispania? I am sure the fighting is not finished over there. They are a tenacious and ferocious people. I wonder how my old comrades are getting on.'

Criton sat still, looking at the empty jug and the wet rings on the table.

'What is it, Criton?'

The Macedonian looked up. 'I heard something curious.' He wrinkled his nose. 'The rich are so heartless.'

'Tell me.'

Criton said, 'It was towards the end when many were drunk. We were all on our feet and the ladies had gone to get their cloaks. My host – I was right behind him, waiting to catch his eye and say goodbye – my host said suddenly, "I hear there is bad news from Hispania. Some girl has been kidnapped by pirates." He spoke in a low, sneering voice and winked at Fannius Caepio, who looked uncomfortable. Then my host said, "Poor bitch, to think that for fifteen years she's been taught to sit with her knees together and now she must learn to lie with her legs apart. I hope she enjoys the lesson." Another man said, "Don't worry. Legates' daughters are taught to obey orders." A third man said, "Perhaps Augustus will pay the ransom," and Fannius Caepio said, "I hope so, I do hope so." He seemed uneasy. Another man, whose face I did not know, grinned and made an obscene remark. Then Varro Murena saw them and came over. He heard them speaking. He knew what it was about. I am sure of it. He looked at them and then said in that voice of his, "You should always walk softly in the presence of the gods." It was as though he had thrown a pitcher of cold water over them. They fell silent and then he said, "Here is a guest come to say his farewells." And they turned and I said all that a guest should.'

Curtius Rufus said quietly, 'I am sorry for the girl, if it is true. It will certainly cause trouble here in Rome. To kidnap a slave girl is one thing, but not a girl of the aristocracy. Pirates used to raid that coastline when I was out there. They came from Mauretania.'

Criton said, 'They were quite heartless.'

'The pirates? They will not harm her. It is usually a matter of ransom.'

'No, I mean those men of wealth. It was their indifference; they were obscene.'

'They were only men who had drunk too much.'

Criton sniffed. 'You Romans have no imagination.'

'And you Greeks are the fathers of all the vices,' said Curtius Rufus amiably.

Criton laughed gently.

Curtius Rufus said, 'I wish I felt like laughing.'

Criton put a hand on his arm. 'Do not worry. Your job is safe enough. You did your best.'

'I wonder.'

The Sub-Curator said, 'I have read your report. It is admirably concise. I have also received reports from the others involved.' He paused and looked at Curtius Rufus. 'Have you anything you wish to add?'

Curtius Rufus swallowed. 'No, sir.'

'Very well. I shall, of course, await the findings of the centurion engineer I have sent to inspect the repair.' He paused again. Curtius Rufus did not speak. 'On the face of it you seem to have behaved either very intelligently or very irresponsibly. Eight men were injured and one – a soldier – was killed. There will have to be an inquiry into that.'

Curtius Rufus clasped his hands behind his back. The palms were sticky with sweat. The Sub-Curator went on speaking. 'There is also the question of your general conduct. There is a serious complaint from the Inspector. That I cannot ignore.'

Curtius Rufus licked his lips. 'How long, sir, will it be before the engineer makes his report?'

'About two days. Lastly, there is the fact that you exercised an unlawful authority which you did not possess. You deliberately misled both the centurion and the foreman of the gang.' He paused and stared coldly at Curtius Rufus. 'You lied to them. Two of the slaves are critically ill. I will not be so tactless as to inquire for how long you actually succeeded in tricking them. For less time, I suspect, than they maintain.' He bent to the table, picked up his pen, and signed the sheet that lay before him. 'For the time being you are suspended from duty. Report here three days from now and you will learn the date of the inquiry.'

Curtius Rufus said, 'I am sorry, sir, but – could I have an advance on my wages?'

The Sub-Curator looked up in surprise. 'You are paid quarterly, I believe.'

'Yes, sir.'

'Quite impossible. You should learn to manage your affairs more carefully. If you are reinstated you will be paid at the Saturnalia. If not, you will be paid up to the date of your suspension – that is today.'

'But I owe rent on my lodgings, sir.'

'I suggest you stay with a friend then.'

'But, sir—'

'That is all.'

Curtius Rufus turned and went out. The clerks in the outer room looked at him curiously as he passed. He flashed a smile and nodded to them cheerfully. Never be angry with the crowd, his father had said. You lose the race when you should have won; a trace breaks at the wrong moment; you crash and it's not your fault, and they scream abuse and blame you for letting them down. Take no notice; just smile as though nothing had happened. Ignore the pain in your broken wrist. Bear it and go on smiling. They hate a bad loser. Don't make excuses. Go on as though nothing had happened, because nothing has happened that can't be made good tomorrow or the next day or the day after that. He remembered standing in the stables of the White faction, scarcely able to peer over the top of a chariot wheel, watching his father come in from an unexpected defeat, covered with dust and sweat and grinning while he talked to his son, and nursing a broken arm at the time. It was not till he had grown up that he realized what that afternoon's disaster had meant: the loss of a season's racing; the putting off for another year of the chance to buy freedom with the much needed prize money; the postponement of all plans; the loss of a promised partnership in a venture on which his father had set his heart; the facing up to another year in the circus when you risked your neck every time you drove round the track for the pleasure of an audience who could roar applause one moment and spit hate the next. It was advice that was easy to give but so very hard to practice. His father had mastered the lesson as he never would, however hard he tried.

He walked through the portico into the autumn sunlight, and then paused uncertainly. He had grown to hate the job with its fixed hours of attendance, the constant pressure of overmuch work upon too small a staff, and the conflicting aims of a service that, as the Curator had designed it, was intended for all, yet which was subject to unreasonable demands by a handful of people who, knowing themselves to be politically impotent, sought to save their pride through the exercise of social influence alone. Often, on a warm day, he had wished passionately that he might be free to walk the streets, to hear the gossip, to drink in the bars, and to be able, even for a moment, to pretend that he was a man of leisure, and one rich enough, therefore, to live in the shade. Now, he was free, and the day was warm. He could idle in the Forum with the best of them, and watch all Rome pass by. The very thought made him sick.

He turned left and headed toward the river, pausing for a drink in the wineshop behind the cattle market where the dealers met to fix the prices before the auctions began. Then, on the embankment opposite Tiber island, he bought a fresh crust off a passing vendor and looked at the yellow, swirling water. A small sailing barge drifted slowly downstream, moving cautiously toward the jetty that had recently been erected by the newly formed Oil Masters Guild at the confluence of the Petronia with the Tiber. The sailing master shouted instructions, a crane was wheeled forward from the shade of a warehouse, and two men descended the jetty ladder and took the skiff upstream to meet the incoming barge. As they passed her a line was thrown from the skiff and tied fast to the barge's stern. Men moved on the deck, the sail was furled, and the skiff, rowed into the stream, turned the barge sideways into the crosscurrents. A second rope thrown from the jetty was fastened forward of the single mast and the barge slowly pulled toward the jetty. It was a difficult operation, made easy only by constant practice, and Curtius Rufus, watching, was filled with a moment's envy for people who could still live usefully by their hands instead of by their wits.

On a sudden impulse he walked down the ramp that led to the jetty and spoke to the sailing master, who was now watching his cargo being swung ashore. 'Do you need any crew?' he asked.

The sailing master looked him up and down. 'You! What do you know about boats?'

Curtius Rufus smiled. 'Enough to do what you did just now. I have sailed a ship, bigger than this, as far as Byzantium. Though I did once sink a skiff in the harbor at Rhodus.' He grinned at the memory. 'I was a boy at the time.'

The sailing master shook his head. 'I don't want another navigator who will spend all his time trying to teach me my job, and I have all the crew I need.'

Curtius Rufus turned away. He spoke to a clerk inside the warehouse but there were no jobs there either. He walked back down the embankment and headed for the granary area, where the barges tied up and the foreign merchants gathered and the sailing masters haggled for the hire of their ships. Everywhere he met with the same response. He was too old and spoke too well to be regarded seriously when he suggested a job as a deck hand, was too inexperienced or lacking in practice to be trusted with a senior post. Some thought him a runaway slave, others a debtor trying to leave Rome and dismissed him hurriedly when he spoke to them. Always there were excuses, evasions, and sometimes lies. A Jew would not engage him because he did not belong to the faith; an Egyptian worshipper of Isis rejected him for a similar reason. The river people were a community who made their living from the sea and, whether merchants or sailors, resented the intrusion of strangers. They sold their goods to all but kept their work for their own kind.

Presently he made his way back through the street where the commercial agents had their offices. These were the middlemen who hired ships and organized fleets for the rich who wished to invest in mercantile ventures without personal involvement or effort to themselves. The fat man, scratching himself under his tunic, had as client a Capuan factory producing bronze vessels for export; the Greek opposite specialized in buying the best of the vineyards in the Padus valley, and it was no accident that his brother was agent to a great estate in the north. The thin man from Rhodus, sitting at the table in the doorway, had lost a fortune twenty-five years before when the conquest of Gaul had destroyed the export of pottery, but was doing well out of the sale of Numidian horses to the army. The man from Tuscania with the scarred face, talking to him idly, was in constant touch with Memphis and knew the seasonal demand for linen almost down to the last bale. These men had known his father and he had avoided this street for years as a result. Now, only an inner sense of despair had brought him back.

Achillas, gray-haired now, who had handled everything in his time and whose agents in Parthia organized spice caravans from the east, recognized him first and whistled softly in surprise. 'What brings you here, boy?'

Curtius Rufus smiled. 'Curiosity,' he said. 'It's been a long time. I thought it no harm to see how you all were. The same faces, I see. Trade still good?'

The man spat. 'Not with me. If they can get their differences settled with Parthia things might pick up a bit. But the breach over those accursed lost eagles is a running sore still. I can hardly get a caravan through to Antioch these days.'

'Bring it round by sea.'

'Too expensive and too slow. We've had trouble with pirates off the coast whenever we've tried that.'

'How about copper and tin? There's a good market and good prices to be had, provided you've got sailing masters who know the Scythian coast.'

'Aye. But you lose your profits in tax at Byzantium.'

'Not if you know Byzantium.'

Achillas looked up at him. 'You sailed there once, I remember.'

'More than once.'

There was a pause while they regarded each other.

'Are you buying or selling, boy?'

'Neither.'

'What's your interest then?'

Curtius Rufus said lightly, 'None, really. I have a good job. It pays well and I am content.'

'Scythia, eh! Well, that's not a bad idea at that if one could get the right man. You always had a head on your shoulders, boy. I will say that for you. Pity you couldn't control your eyes.'

'That was a long time ago.'

'True.' The old man rubbed his chin. 'You want to sail again?'

'I'd be willing to think about it.'

'How much?'

'A fair wage for the job and two percent of the profit on the cargo if I bring it home.'

Achillas said slowly, 'You must want the job badly if you price yourself so low.' He stared hard at Curtius Rufus. 'Down on your luck, boy, is that it?'

'Not at all. Just modest.'

'You – modest. Don't lie to me. You never knew the word. Scythia, eh! I wonder. It's a long time since I cast a net there. We'd need a backer, of course. I might find one though. Plenty of folk on the Quirinal, and all greedy for more. Have a drink with me and talk it over.'

46

'No!' said a harsh voice.

Curtius Rufus turned. 'I beg your pardon,' he said.

The old man was suddenly silent.

A thickset man with dark hair and heavy features stood by him, his eyes cold, his face angry. 'You should have begged years ago. It's too late now.'

'I don't even know you. I'm sorry' – Curtius Rufus spread out his hands – 'there must be some mistake.'

'But I know you. And you don't sail any ship down the Tiber to Ostia and beyond while I'm a member of the Guild.'

Curtius Rufus stared.

The old man said, 'Now come, Labienus. Let's be reasonable about this, boy.'

Labienus said furiously, 'No, Achillas, this is my business.'

Achillas put his hand on the younger man's shoulder. 'Come inside, boy. Virinia's here, waiting for you. Let's talk it over. A good offer.' He glanced at Curtius Rufus. 'Never quarrel in the street. It's bad for business.'

Labienus hesitated.

'Virinia will come to no harm talking to him now.' Curtius Rufus stood suddenly very still. 'She's the mother of your son, remember. Your son, not his.'

Labienus said curtly, 'No.'

Curtius Rufus said coolly, 'I shan't rape her in the street, if that's what's worrying you.'

Labienus turned and hit him across the face. Curtius Rufus staggered back, lost his balance, and sprawled in the gutter. Then he got slowly to his feet. He shook his head like a dog coming out of water and wiped the blood trickling from the corner of his mouth. The back of his hand was smeared. A tooth felt loose. He explored with his tongue and then mumbled to the old man through cut lips, 'Don't worry. There are other men who can sail to Byzantium. It was just an idea.'

Labienus said, 'Get out of this street and keep away from her.'

47

Curtius Rufus spat blood.

'Wait!' Labienus put his hand in his tunic and then tossed two coins into the gutter. 'For you,' he said. 'My guild is charitable to the poor.'

Curtius Rufus hesitated. Common sense overcame his sense of pride. He was desperate and the other knew it. Why else would he have come back? He bent and picked up the coins. 'I will keep them in memory of you both,' he said savagely. 'The coins represent what the memory is worth.' He turned and then moved away down the street. The pole of a chair poked him in the side as he stepped off the pavement to avoid a laborer carrying a wine cask; a man with a pile of timber on his shoulder caught him in the back as he paused to give way to a group of women returning from the public fountain; he stumbled and knocked a pitcher to the ground, where it smashed into fragments. He walked dazedly on while the women screamed abuse. He took no notice. He was looking for a side alley where he could pause and be sick in peace.

Presently he came to a tavern frequented by sailors. He went inside, sat down in a corner by himself, and bought a drink. His head ached, his face was swollen and his clothes filthy. He ordered a second drink and then a third in an effort to quell the panic he felt rising inside him. Achillas, who had been his father's friend, had been his last hope. Now he did not know what to do. The shops had closed for the midday meal, the offices were shut, and business was at a standstill. The day stretched ahead of him, a long and endless passage of hours that he could not bear to face. He had all the time in the world and he did not know how to fill it.

The stonemason's daughter said briskly, 'He is in his room. He was away for three nights. I gave him the key this afternoon. He is probably asleep.'

Criton said, 'I am worried about him.'

The girl nodded. 'Me, too,' she said. 'But he's had bad patches before and he gets through them. Lives by his wits, I reckon.'

Criton said dryly, 'We all do that, one way or another.'

'Well, you know what I mean.'

He nodded and went on up the stairs. The door was shut but not locked and Curtius Rufus was lying on his bed, one arm flung across his face.

Criton said, 'I have been worried about you, my dear fellow. Are you all right?'

Curtius Rufus moved his arm and opened his eyes. He said thickly, 'Forgive my voice. I have lost a tooth.'

'You look as though you had lost a fight,' said Criton disapprovingly.

'Oh, you should have seen it three days ago. It was worse then.'

Criton said, 'I have searched the city for you.'

'I have searched the city for work.'

'Oh!' Criton sat down on the stool. 'You have had no luck then.'

'No. I tried for a tutor's post, but the boy's uncle came in just when it was about to be offered to me. It seemed he knew the brother of the senator for whom I worked some years ago. My name was remembered. It is curious, that. They do not mind their wives having a favorite slave as a lover, but a teacher who is not a slave touches their pride.'

'Was there a scene?'

'I left as it was starting.'

'You had bad luck,' said Criton primly.

'I was offered another post, this time as assistant to a horse dealer I met in the cattle market. But he was dealing in stolen horses and I thought it too risky to accept. Then I tried my father's patron. By this time I was frantic, or else I would not have gone to the house at all. But he was out of Rome. There was a young girl there, some kind of relation, and an old lady

49

who disapproved of me. The girl was charming. Very sympathetic.'

'But the old lady was not.'

'She had a face like the Medusa. I could see at once I was wasting my time. So I left. I went to an inn by the Capena Gate and played games of hazard for three nights. I made a lot of money.'

'What happened?'

'A young man was there. I discovered, too late, he was entitled to the gold ring of the Equestrian Horse. He was amusing himself in low company, it seems.'

'And?'

'He accused me of cheating.' At the remembrance of the boy's voice Curtius Rufus sat up. 'As if I needed to cheat.'

'Only when the luck is against you,' said the Macedonian with a malicious smile.

'Of course. There was a dispute, then a riot, and then soldiers were called. I escaped out of a back window. The landlord's daughter is an old friend of mine.'

'That was fortunate.' Criton shifted on his stool. 'Well, what now, my friend?'

The two men looked at each other. Curtius Rufus stood up and went to the window. The light was beginning to fade and the streets to empty. From a tavern further down came the sound of laughter. 'The carts will be moving in soon,' he said. Criton did not answer. He went on in a low voice, 'It is a great city, full of people, some rich, some poor. What makes it so hard for a man to earn a living, to get a job, to make money even?'

Criton said gently, 'You have no Latin blood?'

'My grandfather was a Parthian horse trader's son, captured by brigands when his caravan was attacked on the way to Byzantium. He was bought and sold, and ended up on a ranch in Sicilia. My father was born there – married a girl of your race. He was manumitted; and I am a citizen, just as that stonemason downstairs is a citizen. It should make no difference, and yet it does.'

Criton said, 'Why ask me the difference? You know it as well as I. They are a hard, industrious, and clever people.'

'So are many others.'

'True, but where Rome goes, she conquers, and all obey her.'

'Anyone may conquer who is strong enough.'

'Anyone indeed, whether he comes from Athens or Parthia. It is all the same. But where else than in Rome may a slave become free by law, and his son the equal of his father's conqueror? These people do more than conquer: they know how to rule.'

'And we?' asked Curtius Rufus quietly.

'We remain what we were. Blood does not change in a generation.'

'Meanwhile I still seek work, and you a patron for your verses.'

Criton smiled. 'Forgive me. I talk too much.'

'You do, indeed.' Curtius Rufus fell silent. Then he glanced at the Macedonian, who had pulled a piece of linen from his pouch and was trying to read the writing on it. 'Light the lamp; you'll tire your eyes.'

The Macedonian obeyed him gratefully. 'I had some luck today,' he said presently. 'I was introduced to Pylades. He is a great artist, that one. He was most kind.'

'Did you show him your verse?'

Criton hesitated. Then he said, almost shyly, 'Well, yes, I did.'

'And what did he say?'

'He said—' Criton paused and then gathered his courage. 'He said they would do well enough for a recitation at a rich man's table, but that – that was all. He said – however – that I had talent and offered me work. He wants me to – to rewrite some scenes from old plays for him.' The Macedonian paused and said mournfully, 'I don't know if I should be pleased or angry.'

Curtius Rufus laughed and clapped him on the shoulder. 'Be pleased then. It is good news. We must celebrate. Well done. If Pylades uses your work you will be made.'

'You think so? I had hoped—'

'Then you are too like me. You dream of gold and ignore the silver at your feet. It is better to write for money and know your work is used than to do so for pleasure, while your friends yawn behind their hands.'

'But it is not literature.'

Curtius Rufus drained his cup. 'It is what you make of it that counts; not what others merely think they think.' He lapsed into silence, staring out through the window at the flicker of lights as the night patrol crossed the end of the street. He said, almost dreamily, 'I built a bridge once in Hispania. It was a beautiful bridge. I was proud of it.' He turned and Criton saw happiness in his face. 'Perhaps one day I shall see it again, and then it will seem very small. But to me then it was the biggest bridge in the world. And the best.'

CHAPTER IV

Curtius Rufus slipped into the water and closed his eyes. He had been on his feet all day, and his body ached. Now that he could relax he suddenly felt exhausted, and his head began to throb, as it always did when he was tired.

A voice said, 'We thought you had given up coming to the baths.'

He opened his eyes and saw Piso smiling at him through the steam, the sweat glistening on his too-white skin. He forced a smile. 'I have been out of the city on business.'

'Indeed. I am glad to hear it. I had heard rumors. I was concerned.'

'I went to Ostia.'

'You look tired. You must have been working too hard.'

'I have.' Curtius Rufus grinned lopsidedly to conceal the gap in his teeth. He ducked his head and then ran his fingers through his wet hair. 'It was an important matter.'

'Yes? One that concerned the Sub-Curator, no doubt?'

'Correct.'

'Then the stories—' Piso looked puzzled.

'What stories?'

The two men eyed each other warily. Piso puffed his cheeks.

'My wife wants another slave.' He shrugged and splashed water over his arms. 'Women!' he said. 'She goes on at me still because I did not get a promotion. A new slave would keep her quiet.'

Curtius Rufus smiled. 'Not too quiet, I hope.'

Piso laughed coarsely. 'Not in my house. I leave that to the rich and idle. We are respectable.' He heaved himself out of the water and sat, dangling his fat legs. 'And how is your frienship with the little Pero?'

'Well enough. Why?'

'I saw her yesterday in the arcade of Octavia. She was with Fannius Caepio's son. They were very interested in each other.'

'Yes, I saw her too. It was a commission for the Lady Terentia.' Curtius Rufus grinned. 'I have missed your – gossip.'

Piso said crossly, 'Oh, I have no news that is not as cold as the water in the next chamber.' He paused. He said grudgingly, 'She is a pretty girl. Be careful she does not lead you on a ring.'

'Thank you for your concern.' Curtius Rufus wiped the water from his eyes. 'She is the Lady Terentia's slave, but no one else's.'

'That I wondered.'

'I will tell you when she becomes mine. Are you coming? I am going to the gymnasium to meet a friend.'

Piso laughed. 'I dare not. I am for a massage. My wife thinks I am too fat.'

'Then I will see you later. Try to get the Syrian boy. He has good hands and knows his job.'

As he had expected, Criton was in the exercise area having a match with one of the bathing establishment's professional wrestlers. A small crowd had gathered, and the two men, their bodies coated with oil, were circling each other warily in the opening moves of the first bout. Criton's approach to gymnastics was as humorless as that of any Greek, but he was an excellent wrestler. He did not come here often, and the professional was new to the staff. Curtius Rufus smiled with joy. The omens were too good not to be taken advantage of. 'Who will take a wager?' he cried.

'What odds?' asked a young man with a Cretan haircut.

'Twenty to one against the Macedonian,' said Curtius Rufus. 'He cannot win against Macro.'

Two water clocks later he was the richer by several thousand coins and had to carry his winnings to the changing room in a hired towel. 'It was a close call,' he said cheerfully to Criton. 'When you slipped in that last bout I thought he had you.'

'You made me nervous,' said the Macedonian disapprovingly. 'I have told you before, I do not like to wrestle while my friends make wagers. That is not the purpose of exercise. It spoils the concentration of the mind.'

'I hope it will not spoil your concentration on the dinner I am going to buy you you.'

Criton stared at him. 'Where did you get those clothes? And what is that boy doing? Have you gone mad?' He pointed to a slave who was carefully unfolding an elaborately embroidered tunic.

'Hush! Here comes Piso.'

Curtius Rufus adjusted a silver bracelet with care while Piso looked at him, breathing heavily.

'Did you enjoy your massage?'

'Massage?' said Piso blankly. 'Oh, yes. Yes, indeed.'

'I must lend you my new slave next time we meet here,' Curtius Rufus said. 'He has even better hands. Are you ready, Criton? We must not keep our guests waiting.'

'You are giving a dinner?' said Piso with blunt incredulity.

'Why not? I have hired a room at the Winged Mercury.' Piso breathed more heavily. 'I would have invited you, but I know that you always dine at home.'

Piso said weakly, 'My wife—'

'I understand. Come, Criton. Boy, take the towel and handle it carefully.'

Outside in the street two sedan chairs were waiting. Curtius Rufus took the first and Criton the second. Two blocks further on the chairs halted and Curtius Rufus got out and paid the slaves for their hire. 'We walk now,' he said. 'Where would you like to go?'

Criton said wistfully, 'Could we not have kept the chairs? It is not often—'

'You wanted to see me?' Criton nodded. 'Well, I will still buy you your dinner, but it is early yet.'

'I have earned it, I think,' said Criton with dignity. 'But why—?'

'My credit had run out. Someone at the department talked and Piso heard. It was the only way to reestablish myself. I spent the last of my pay. It was worth it.'

'You should pray for your luck to change. Where are we going?'

'I do. I tried for jobs in Ostia. It was no good. The new walk by Agrippa's Baths is a good place. It's quiet, and you don't get many people there at this time except poets and philosophers. If anyone sees us we have been to look at that carved lion everyone is talking about.'

They sat on a stone bench under a cypress tree. They could hear the water lapping the bank as the wind blew in sharp gusts and dead leaves from a nearby shrub scuffed along the ground.

Criton said, 'You remember, I told you about the girl who had been kidnapped?'

'I remember.'

'Later, I attended at my patron's house. He took me into a corner, apart from the other clients, and asked me to wait behind till they had gone. I did so and when we were alone he said, "You are a man I can trust, I think." I replied that I hoped I was and that he might have every confidence in me. He took my hand and said, "Faithfulness should be rewarded." Then he handed me a leather bag. "Wine makes for much foolishness." Then I went home. When I got to my room, I opened the bag. It contained a great sum. More than I have ever owned.'

'Well, you are in luck. I could do with a patron like that.'

Criton twisted his hands nervously; the good looks his sallow features always acquired after exercise had quite gone. He

56

moistened his lips, touched them with a finger, and then put the finger to his ear.

Curtius Rufus noticed the gesture. 'What is troubling you?'

'It was a bribe. I am sure of it.'

'To keep quiet. About what? The kidnapping?'

'Yes.'

'What of it? Perhaps you did hear an item of news you were not meant to hear; something they do not wish published in the State Gazette.' He smiled at Criton. 'In this restored Republic there is less talk of the serious, more talk of the frivolous. We know that.'

Criton said, 'A dispatch boat from Tarraco reached Ostia this morning.'

'Well?'

'They knew.' He paused and looked at Curtius Rufus, his lips trembling. 'The dispatch boat came in great haste. The courier went first to Augustus' house on the Palatine and then to the house on the Collis where Valerius Messalla lives. The news was round the Forum within the hour. It was Messalla's niece. Both her parents were killed.'

'I am sorry. He is a good man. The legate was too. Now there will be a storm – a senator murdered and his daughter stolen. Phew!'

Criton said, 'They knew before anyone else did. It was in their faces. They knew and were glad.'

'You are being fanciful. How could they know?'

Criton said, 'They talked of it ten days before the news reached Rome. Almost as though—'

'Now you are being absurd. They were drunk at the time. The official news was obviously held up for state reasons. It is often so. Why, in my own department—'

'But he gave me gold. Why else did he give me gold?'

'What!'

57

'Yes, gold. I am so afraid. I wish I had never gone to that dinner party.'

Curtius Rufus leaned forward. 'Just how much did he give you?'

Criton told him.

Curtius Rufus opened his lips and then closed them again. 'You are like a Byzantine housewife,' he said. 'You see a double meaning in every utterance. Have dinner with me and let us forget the matter. Tell me, how did you achieve that last hold? I thought he had you. You moved so fast I couldn't follow your attack at all.'

Criton mumbled a reply. Curtius Rufus said, 'By the way, I would like to borrow my toga for tomorrow. I have an appointment for which I must dress up.'

Criton nodded. 'Of course. I had it cleaned. You will find it in good order.' He spoke without thinking.

Curtius Rufus looked at him and then shrugged. They lapsed into silence.

They dined at the Winged Mercury and had the best table in the room, but not even the food and the wine could completely allay the Macedonian's fears. When two soldiers, off duty, came in for a drink, he trembled and went white in the face. Curtius Rufus could stand it no longer. 'You are a fool,' he said brutally. 'You have done nothing wrong. It is not a crime to accept a present from one's patron. I am taking Pero to the Circus. Will you come? She may have heard something. All these families are connected.' He looked at Criton but the man was trembling still. He leaned forward. 'Would you feel better if you got rid of the gold?'

The Macedonian nodded. 'I am a fool,' he said. 'I cannot help it. I am sorry. Please do what you think best.'

'Very well. Let's go home. We must get rid of that bag. A pity, but there it is. And when that is done you and I will forget we ever had this night's conversation. You will feel better about it in the morning.'

The two men went out into the darkened streets and did not speak again until they reached the apartment block where they lived. But the fear was infectious. And all the way Curtius Rufus kept his hand on the dagger inside his tunic and without which he never walked through Rome by night.

Pero stood under the arcade, by the pillar to the left of the cookshop, close by the stall where a one-eyed man sold gaudy trinkets and souvenirs to tourists and visitors. The street swarmed with hucksters crying their wares, and she was delighting in the bustle of the crowd and the looks she received from the passersby, many of whom were hoping to obtain tickets at the last moment by illegal purchases from those who possessed them.

'The prices asked are outrageous,' said Curtius Rufus. 'If people do not wish to go, why do they accept tickets in the first place? It is not fair to those who genuinely enjoy the racing.'

'Fairness does not enter into it,' said Criton dryly. 'Only money counts here.'

Pero watched them approach. Curtius Rufus looked tired and dejected, but his expression changed when he saw her. 'I am not late,' he said firmly. 'It is you who are early. This is Criton, my friend. He will see that you are looked after when I lay the bets. Afterwards he will be discreet and disappear when we tell him to.'

The girl laughed and gave her cheek to Criton, who kissed it cautiously. 'I approve of the perfume, if not the sex,' he said shyly. 'You are a lucky man, Curtius.'

Curtius Rufus said cheerfully, 'I hope to be luckier still before the day is over. Let us find our seats.'

Pero said, 'I nearly couldn't come. My lady was in a difficult mood. But I will tell you about that later.'

They climbed the passage steps leading to their block and Pero's eyes widened as she came out onto the terrace and saw the arena stretched out before her, the sand of the track golden in the sunlight.

She said, in a voice tinged with awe, 'I have never seen so many people. It is frightening.'

Curtius Rufus said, 'My father thought that too.'

'Your father?'

Criton said, 'You are in the presence of the shadow of greatness. Curtius's father was the leading charioteer of his day. He was quite famous and the crowds – the ladies in particular – adored him.'

Pero turned an excited face to Curtius. 'You never told me.'

'You did not ask.'

'Is he still alive?'

'No. He was the champion for ten years and then he bought his freedom. Later he died. He drove for both the Whites and the Reds as they all do. But he was the only man, the experts said, who could steal three lengths on the turns, when all seemed hopeless, and still come from behind to win. I saw him do it myself as a small boy.'

Pero said, 'You were very proud of him.'

'My mother loved him,' said Curtius Rufus with a grin. 'That is enough history for one day. Criton, catch that fellow's eye and hire cushions, or you and I will be sore with sitting on these benches.'

'Why not me?' said the girl indignantly.

'You have a better covering than we.'

'I am not fat.' She appealed to Criton. 'Am I?'

'I did not say you were fat,' Curtius Rufus retorted.

'But you meant it.'

'Here is a cushion. Rest your argument on that.'

Pero looked round with interest at the rapidly filling block. 'What happens?' she asked, adjusting the skirts of her cloak.

'Oh, as at the Flaminius, the size of the teams varies. The race may be between two, three, or four horse chariots. It depends on

60

the conditions laid down for each race. The first race is usually for apprentices in their first season.' He went on to discuss the merits of African-bred horses, and when he paused Criton said calmly, 'When the lecture is over, may we buy some water? It is going to be a hot day.'

The girl dissolved in laughter as Curtius Rufus grinned ruefully. 'I am sorry. Horses, I find interesting. They are less intelligent than people, but more beautiful and better mannered. They do what they are told without argument.'

Pero said tartly, 'You should have given your ticket to a horse. I like it here. No one to give me orders or pull my hair if I am clumsy.'

Criton smiled. 'That is what we all feel. The crowd is the holiday.'

Curtius Rufus said, 'We have no responsibilities, no worries. We give those to the charioteers instead.'

The sun rose higher, the crowd began to grow impatient, and there was a stir of interest and loud cheers every time an official or one of the staff walked out onto the course. The two soldiers on duty below the President's box began surreptitiously to play noughts in the dust with the butt ends of their javelins. Curtius Rufus watched them and guessed what they were at. He had done the same himself when on sentry duty in the heat of summer.

'Hush now. The procession will begin at any moment.'

'The family have arrived – all except Augustus,' said Criton.

'I have never seen him,' said Pero. 'Are his statues a good likeness?'

'I don't know. I have never seen him either,' said Curtius Rufus. 'Forgive me. I must go to lay the first bets.'

'Is he there yet?' said the girl again to Criton.

The sudden roar of the crowd, all standing, gave the answer. The gates at the Tiber end opened, a trumpet sounded, and through the archway filed the procession that had come from the Capitol. It was led by musicians and dancers, and followed by

61

priests from the sacred colleges, and young men bearing images of the divine gods. Finally, the chariots of the competitors came into view and the crowd roared again for the teams, each faction attempting to outshout the other. The procession wound itself round the arena, partially concealed from view by the Spina that divided the course, and then dispersed. There came a lull while slaves smoothed the sand, and Curtius Rufus returned, bearing a fistful of tickets. 'The Whites should win this one,' he said cheerfully.

'Which faction should we support?' asked Criton anxiously. 'We are surrounded by partisans of both.'

'I like the Reds,' said Pero, her face flushed. 'I have a feeling they will win the day.'

'Then you are in good company. The Reds are supported by Augustus and the populace, while the Senate and the aristocracy, who are against the restored Republic, back the Whites. But no one takes it too seriously unless they find their team is losing.'

'And you?'

'I am a professional gambler. I vote for the charioteer with the best horses.'

A fanfare of trumpets sounded and the presiding magistrate, a flash of scarlet and purple, rose from his seat. He held an ivory baton, crowned with a golden eagle that winked in the sun. The teams for the first race came out from the stables, paraded before him while an official checked their harness and equipment, and then returned to the stalls. When the noise of the crowd had subsided a little, the magistrate raised his hand and threw down the white flag. The rope dropped and, amid the sudden thunder of hooves, the rumble of wheels, and the flash of white and scarlet, a dust cloud erupted from behind the starting line and rolled at tremendous speed down the track. The last day of the Games had begun.

At midday there was an interval. 'What about eating?' said Curtius Rufus.

'I am stiff and thirsty,' said Criton. 'I can see there is real skill but the sport lacks that harmonizing of the elements that makes gymnastics its superior.'

Curtius Rufus said sharply, 'You need wrists of iron and the coordination of an acrobat. Shift your weight at the wrong moment and you will overturn the chariot and kill yourself. These gymnastics win you money.'

'Have we won much?' asked the girl. 'Please let us go out. I feel cramped.'

'Four out of six,' said Curtius Rufus. 'We could have made it five if you, Pero, had not changed your mind on the last race.'

'I am sorry, but the Reds' horse looked so nice. I adore chestnuts.'

Curtius Rufus said patiently, 'Their color has little to do with their form.'

At the end of the eighth race Curtius Rufus said, 'I am going down to the stables, Pero. The next race is the main event. Come with me and look at the horses. But put your hood up first.'

The stables were behind the starting stalls and the familiar smell of horse sweat, fresh dung, and oiled leather made him remember his childhood. The stable guards knew him and let him through with a coarse jest. They ducked beneath the pole of a chariot whose wheels were being checked by a blacksmith, paused to watch a veterinary surgeon applying a bandage to a gray that had strained a fetlock, and continued, weaving their way between a crowd of grooms, stable boys, bundles of hay, and water buckets. A short, thickset man who was watching four horses being exercised in a tight circle saw them and flicked a hand, his eyes never leaving the horses under his care.

'Come to see the best as usual, Curtius. Steady now, steady. Ever seen a finer team?'

'Not since my father's time, Lucius. These are from Libya, aren't they?'

'That's right. Cost the management a fortune. But worth it. Mark my words. Don't you agree, madam?'

'They are beautiful,' said the girl. 'Will they win, do you think?'

Lucius laughed. 'If they don't, I'm out of a job.'

'Who's driving?' asked Curtius Rufus quickly.

'Pompeius.'

'Hmm. I'll think about it. Come on, Pero.'

They moved on to a stream of terse comments from Curtius Rufus. 'No good, sweating too badly. Crack up at the third, I don't wonder. That trace horse has his tail set too high. Now these' – he pointed at four grays – 'beautiful runners, but no staying power. Look at that leader – not broad enough in the chest. I'd as soon put my money on a pack pony.'

'Still teaching me my business?' said a strange voice.

Curtius Rufus grinned, and the girl noticed that for the first time that day the strained look had left his face. She wondered what was worrying him.

Curtius Rufus said, 'Pero, this is Scorpus, who trained the horses my father won with. He used to carry me on his shoulder so that I might see better. Well, Scorpus, whose race is it now?'

The old man smiled through broken teeth and scratched his gray hair. 'It will go to the best,' he said in a gentle voice. 'It always does.'

'Not always.'

'No, not always. Well, for my money, go and look again at those chestnuts.'

'The Libyans!'

'Go and look hard. Forget the odds and look at them as a professional would.' The old man turned to the girl. 'If he had been shorter he would have made a fine charioteer.' His eyes twinkled. 'He has good hands for a horse or a woman.'

Pero stood very still and looked at him questioningly. He nodded and she shook her head. 'Thank you – for the warning.'

She heard him chuckle as she turned away and followed Curtius Rufus back to the starting stalls. 'I am going to lay a big bet,' he said. 'I am in a reckless mood. That is your fault, I think. Wait here by the pillar till I return. We will watch the race from here. You see less but you feel a greater excitement.'

Pero waited, watched the charioteers in their bright livery and their leather helmets mount the light-framed boxes and carefully adjust their balance, the reins knotted round their waists, feet apart as they crouched with knees bent a little; saw the horses, restless, nervous, and excited, moving like dancers as the teams lined up in a confusion of shouts, orders, and oaths; felt the roar of the crowd vibrate against the stone tufa of the arches; shut her eyes at Curtius's order as the rope dropped; was choked momentarily by the dust thrown back by the chariot wheels; and saw, as through a mist, the taut backs of the charioteers, red and white in the sun, dwindle into the distance.

Curtius Rufus held her close, his arm round her waist. 'If I win,' he said, 'I will buy you a white gown and slippers to match, and you will wear gold in your ears and a gold torque, and Criton will write you a poem that men will sing still when we are dead.'

Pero caught his mood. 'If I win,' she said, 'I will live in a villa by the sea and I will be rich and beautiful, and I shall marry a senator's son and he will have a great career, and when we die our tomb on the Appian Way will be the finest in the land, while our love will be remembered to eternity.'

He tightened his grip. 'Let us settle for happiness instead. It is so much easier.' She did not answer and they stood there in the arch, silent, among the stable staff, waiting tensely for the horses to reappear down the straight.

Criton said in a dazed voice, 'We have won how much?'

'That is the third time you have asked me. We won on seven races out of twelve. Am I not a judge of horses?'

'Horses or women. How did you get such odds?'

'I spread it around in the early races and then found a banker for the ninth. I will collect it in the morning. But we have this to be going on with.'

Criton said, 'Be careful. Do not lose it.'

Curtius Rufus grinned. 'I worked too hard today to be cheated of it now by any footpad.'

Criton looked at the girl, who was tidying her hair. The street was beginning to empty and the attendants were closing the entrance doors to the Circus. They clanged hollowly in the gloom.

Criton said, 'I think I am dreaming.'

'We shall wake up.' There was an edge to Curtius Rufus's voice that Criton had not heard before. 'What is wrong?' he asked.

'I did not tell you before – I did not wish to spoil the day. The inquiry was held yesterday. Things did not go well.'

Criton stood silent.

Curtius Rufus said, 'I can appeal to the Curator himself if I wish, but I do not think he would reverse the decision. Two of the slaves died. I killed three men that night so that a dinner party might be held on the Palatine for Augustus and his friends.'

'But—'

'Marcus Agrippa values his slaves and Augustus values his soldiers. That is all there is to it.'

'I am sorry, Curtius.'

'Do not be too sorry. I did not like the job anyway. We are now going to have that dinner I promised you. And afterwards I will take Pero back.'

'It was – it was respectable.'

'That is something I have never been – though I tried once or twice. I may go back to horse trading. I like shoes that are comfortable.' He raised his voice. 'Come on, Pero. I am hungry and so is Criton. Let us go and make magic and talk the stars down from the sky.'

They parted outside the inn, tired from sitting in the

November air all day, and a little drunk from the wine that Curtius Rufus had ordered with a defiant disregard for the cost. 'A good dinner deserves good wine,' he said, and in honor of Criton ordered a large jug of Chian, taking care to see that Pero's cup was well watered. Criton said, 'I shall go home and write verses that even Pylades will not scorn to declaim. I am in the mood.' He disappeared down the street, and Curtius Rufus said, 'Well, I must see you home. It is late and you will be in trouble.'

Pero looked up at him, her face shadowed by her mantle. She said, 'My Lady Terentia has gone out of the city to visit a sick aunt. She will not return until market day.'

'And your master?'

'He dines out with a friend and will be back late. Those of us not on duty may do as we please. He is an easy man and his steward will not mind.'

He could not read her expression. He said coolly, 'When the cat is away—'

'I am not yet a mouse, but if I did wish to be taken home late there is a side door and the night watchman will let me in. He has done so before.'

He said, 'I understand.' He turned and began to walk hurriedly down the street so that Pero had almost to run to keep up with him.

'You are angry,' she said breathlessly. 'Why?'

He did not answer.

'Why?' she repeated. 'Why are you angry?'

He stopped and faced her. 'We have our faults,' he said. 'Mine are that I gamble too much and that I do not care. At least I thought I did not care—' He broke off suddenly.

Pero said, 'You are angry because I have stayed out late before. Is that it?'

He said, 'When I drive a carriage I do not care to find that my horse has run away with me.' Even as he spoke he felt ridiculous and this made him angrier still.

The girl pushed back her hood and began to laugh. She saw

67

his expression and stopped. 'I am sorry,' she said. 'I should not laugh. It is wrong of me. I should be grateful for the fact that you noticed me. I should be grateful that a citizen of Rome wished me to accompany him to the Circus. It is a great honor for a girl who should be content with the attentions of a kitchen boy.' She broke off suddenly and then said quietly, 'I had a lovely day. You expect me to show my gratitude. I show it. And you do not like it. What do you like?'

Curtius Rufus said, 'I am beginning to think that I do not like you.'

'Then you had better decide. It is cold, standing here in the street.'

He said, 'I will take you back.'

'As you wish. It will still have been a nice day until our dinner ended.'

They walked side by side. Presently he took her hand. He said, 'How old are you?'

'I am sixteen, old enough to be married and to have children if I were free.'

He did not answer.

She said, 'You have not told me where you live.'

He remained silent.

She went on: 'Is it because I might ask you to take me there and you would be ashamed of me?'

He said savagely, 'I live in one room in a bad district of the city. It is all I can afford.'

'That I guessed. When I told him about you, the steward said that I would do better to go walking in the Campus Martius at the fashionable hour. Then I might meet a senator's son or a young knight who would like my face well enough to buy me and set me up in an apartment – that I was a fool to go out with a man as selfish as you.'

'He must know a great deal about me.'

'He does. If you dress to please yourself, as you do, then do not be surprised if others—'

He said roughly, 'You talk too much.'

'This is not the way back. Where are you taking me?'

'To another inn that I know of. It is discreet and quiet.'

'Suppose I do not wish to go?'

'Then you may do what you wish.' He stopped and they looked at each other. Pero tilted her head and there was a faint smile on her face. She said, 'You have not asked me, Curtius?'

He said, 'Then I will ask you now. Will you come, Pero?'

'You have not asked me my price.'

He laughed. 'There was once a consul who lived on the Palatine. When asked he said that a rich man was one who could afford to pay for the upkeep of a legion. Name your price, Pero.'

She said, 'I do not want a legion. I will have one former centurion instead.'

He bent and kissed her and she put her arms about his neck. It was not until the next day that he began to wonder how she really knew the things about him that he had never told her.

Later, the wind rose and it began to rain. The wind rattled the locked door, and the wooden shutters, which had a faulty catch, blew open and he woke and had to close them. The noise disturbed her too and she sat up in bed, the blanket round her shoulders for warmth, and saw him standing there in the dark, looking out across the city toward the Temple of Jupiter. The inn stood in a side road, just inside the Naevian Gate, and the sound of the carts was muffled by the intervening houses.

She said, 'It is cold. Come back to bed.'

He smiled. 'The rain woke me. Will you have a drink?'

'You have some. I can drink from your cup.'

He poured a little out and then sat on the bed and put his arm round her. Gently he stroked the long hair that flowed down her back. She shivered, but not from cold. 'Was everything all right?' he asked. She did not speak but bent her head and kissed his arm. He drank the wine and put the cup back on the table. Then he lit the lamp.

'Why are you doing that?'

'So that I can see you.'

Pero pushed her hair forward so that it covered her breasts. 'Like this?' she said. She smiled and raised her arms so that her hands were behind her head in the pose adopted by the dancers she had seen at a banquet given once by Maecenas for his friends. 'Is this better?'

His expression changed. She saw that he was looking at her left arm where she wore the silver bangle that the steward had given her the day she entered the house. 'I would like to take that off,' he said. 'I would like to throw it away and give you one of my own.'

'Will you buy me then? Perhaps I might not wish it.'

He said, 'No, I do not wish to buy you.'

She said, 'And I would not let you.' She touched the bangle with slim fingers and said hesitantly, 'Why should I mind? He is rich and the house is quiet and has beautiful things in it. My Lady gives us material she does not want to make dresses with, and I like pretty things. There is a garden with a fountain where I can sit when I am free and wish to be alone. In summer when it is hot we go to the Campania. It is lovely there. I enjoy coming back to the city, and going out on errands to the shops, and visiting the fashionable places.' She stretched voluptuously at the memories she had conjured up. 'Could you buy me that dress or take me to the places I go to when I attend my Lady?' She mocked him because he had been kind and gentle with her. She did not realize at first the effect of her words. He sat silent, not knowing what to say.

'Did I make you happy?' she asked. He nodded. 'Then I am glad. Even though it was a mistake and I should not have come.' Her voice sounded amused.

'Why do you say that?'

'Because now you will not want to bother with me again. You can tell your friends that you added Pero to the list.' She was crying now, but he knew that it was not altogether from unhappiness.

The wind rattled the shutter again and the tiny flame of the oil lamp flickered wildly. She said, 'I like it here. I feel so safe. No one to say to me: do this or do that.' She raised her head and her eyes smiled at him. 'I share a room. Always I share a room. I have never been in a room before with a door you could bolt on the inside.'

He knew that she was lying to please him, but he knew also that she meant the emotion even though the words might not be true. He had been born in a room with no door and for a long while had lived as she did now. The difference between them – if there was a difference – lay only in the fact that he had been lucky. Not everyone had a father who had skill with horses, so that he might become a charioteer and earn more gold in a single race than most men saw in a whole lifetime.

He thought of the room where he worked and which he could not go to again; he thought of the appeal to the Curator that he would never make; and he thought of this city with its stifling streets, its fevered activity, and its rich opportunities that slipped through his fingers like wine whenever he tried to grasp them. He thought of the horror that lay beyond sunrise when he must move among men who had jobs; he thought of the efforts he must make, steeling himself to ask for work, facing the shake of the head, the condescending look, the flash of pity; and smiling as he did so to show that he did not care – a pretence that would deceive no one. He thought of the hours he would have to pass in shabby cookshops and noisy taverns, drinking slowly and carefully in a corner by himself, while the rain poured outside or the sun shone and he rested his aching feet, thinking of names, recalling faces, trying desperately to plan what to do next, whom

71

to see, how best the approach might be made. The smell of failure was something he could not shake off and it seemed to precede him wherever he went.

The girl stirred and stretched out her arms. 'You look sad,' she said softly. 'I have never seen you look like that.'

He smiled. 'I was remembering what you said. With the money I have won I could buy you a dress made of silk that has come all the way from a land where the people look like this.' He pressed the skin outward at the corners of his eyes.

'I do not believe you,' Pero said. 'No one could look like that.'

'It is true,' he said. 'I am not lying.'

'Do it again,' she said, and giggled. Then she said gravely, 'But could you buy me such a dress – I saw one once on a girl who came to dine. She was very beautiful and the men could not take their eyes off her. She had been married three times and – But could you buy me another at the Saturnalia, and another when the festival of Ceres comes round?'

'If the horses run well,' he said lightly. 'And I am in luck.'

She laughed. 'It does not matter,' she said. 'You have given me something you cannot buy.'

He said, 'If I could learn the right spells, then my horses would always win.'

He sat close beside her and she heard the sudden sharp intake of breath as her hands moved. 'Let me weave the spells,' she said softly. 'We can make our own magic.'

The rain fell upon the roof as a fresh gust of wind hit the walls of the inn, and the lamp flame leapt sideways and went out.

He dreamed of his father, who had bought his freedom and become a merchant. He might now have been a rich man, a leading member of his guild, but the luck that preserved him through his years in the Circus deserted him in the end, as he knew it must. He gambled everything, as the poor always did, on a single voyage, and the gods in their anger at his presumption sent a storm that destroyed his fleet and left him a broken man who died in poverty, desolate and without hope. The dream was ugly and frightening and he moved restlessly and then woke up. The girl woke up too and he felt her shape and knew who she was. He said, 'Pero,' and she laughed because she knew why he had touched her. 'Yes,' she said, 'What is it?'

He said, 'I was dreaming.'

'You twitched and snorted like a dog,' Pero said. 'Was it a nice dream?'

'No,' he said, and took her hand.

They lay in silence and then she turned her head and he knew that she was smiling, though her eyes were now closed.

'I am luckier than that poor girl,' she said. 'It must be terrible to be touched by someone you don't like.'

'What poor girl?' he asked drowsily.

'That niece of Valerius Messalla's.' Pero shivered suddenly.

He put his arm round her. 'Why think about it? It is not our business.' He closed his eyes again, but she went on talking. 'I went yesterday to Fannius Caepio's house with a message for his lady.' She paused and prodded him with a finger. 'Wake up. I'm talking to you.'

'I know,' he said.

'It's a lovely house, but smaller of course. Only eight household slaves.'

He grunted and buried his face in his arms.

'I had to wait by the sundial till they finished. There was a quarrel going on.' She giggled. 'They always think you're deaf.'

He began to stroke her arm gently. 'What was the quarrel about? Gambling debts?'

'I don't think so. The son was accusing his father of having heard from the family and of keeping back a letter. She had promised to write to him. His father swore that he'd had only one since the legate and his family arrived in Hispania. Fannius Caepio produced the letter and said, "Look at the date; it was written the day I dined out and met Murena. I received it five days later." '

'Perhaps her father wouldn't let her write.'

'That's what I thought. But you know what boys in love are like.' She laughed softly. 'Still, I felt sorry for him. It must be awful, wondering, and not knowing.'

He was wide awake now. He said, 'Is the boy's name Lucius?'

'Yes.'

'And the girl's name Valeria?'

'I think so.'

'And are you certain that's what his father said, about the letter, I mean?'

'Oh, yes, but I can't remember the exact words.' She touched his face with her hand. 'It's like sand,' she said crossly. 'You need a shave. Why do you ask?'

'Nothing. I just wondered.'

'Do you like the name Valeria?'

'I prefer Pero.' He turned and put his hand on her breast. He said, 'It will be dawn soon. I will see you home before I go back to my rooms.'

'Please,' she said. 'Don't talk about it now.'

He said, 'You talk too much.' He began to kiss her throat and she clung to him and they were happy. But afterward when she had cried a little he found it impossible to sleep. He remembered what Criton had told him and he remembered the boy he had seen that day in the Campus Martius. And slowly he began to feel afraid.

The second half of November was cold and wet and Curtius Rufus grew apathetic as his sense of failure increased. The landlord had been paid and was no longer hostile, but he dreaded the coming of the Saturnalia, when rents would become due again. His winnings dwindled, the days shortened, and he began to hate the long nights when he must lie on his bed in the dark with nothing to do but think his own thoughts until eventually sleep overcame them.

One evening he returned late from an unsuccessful visit to a farm near the Sabine Hills. He lit the oil lamp, poured himself a cup of sour wine, and began to practice with the worn dice that had so often helped him through bad periods in the past. Presently, he tired of this and knew that he could keep his news and his fears to himself no longer. He went out of the room and knocked on Criton's door.

The Macedonian was at his table writing, the linen laid out between two oil lamps. 'I hoped you would come,' he said. 'I am trying to work, but I cannot find the words.' He threw down the pen and looked up. 'Well?' he said. 'What do we do now?' He looked tired, his face was strained and his hands trembled.

Curtius Rufus sat down on the stool opposite and began to play with the dice.

Criton said, 'I have a brother in Smyrna. He teaches rhetoric in the schools. I am thinking of going back there. With his help we could both get work.' He paused. In the silence Curtius Rufus could hear him breathing heavily. The dice chinked softly. The room seemed suddenly very dark and very small. He tried to smile but he felt as exhausted and as beaten as his friend. 'Why?' he said.

Criton said hopelessly, 'I, too, was down in the Forum today. I heard the news there about Primus.'

'That the Proconsul of Macedonia has been arrested on a charge of making war against Thrace without authority. It's absurd.'

'Yes.' Criton licked his lips. 'But the offense is treasonable.'

'And that it is rumored Murena is angry about it and intends to speak for him at his trial?'

The Macedonian nodded. 'I am afraid,' he muttered. 'Primus is related to Fannius Caepio and both are my patron's friends. I

75

do not like it. There is a connection.' He clasped his hands together. 'I am sure of it. Tell me that I am wrong.'

Curtius Rufus was silent.

'Perhaps – perhaps you are right. There is no connection.' Criton looked up and tried to smile. He was breathing heavily.

Curtius Rufus shook his head. 'No. I was wrong. Pero heard something. She did not know what it meant. Then I remembered something else that I had heard by chance. These things confirm your story.' He paused. He said casually, 'We must get out of Rome.'

Criton stared at him blankly. 'But—'

Curtius Rufus said brutally, 'Your patron has been put under house arrest. He went to the Palatine this morning to attend the first reception. He bade Augustus good morning. Augustus looked at him and said, "And I bid you farewell."'

'Oh, no.' Criton rubbed his hands together and shivered. 'Leave Rome, did you say? Is that wise?'

'I think so.'

Criton said, 'But there is no evidence.' Sweat shone on his face.

'Are you sure? Was there no slave within earshot to hear your conversation when he paid you the gold?'

'You are right. Forgive me for being stupid. What shall I do?'

'Take half my money. If you are careful it will get you to Brundisium. I will follow you.' Curtius Rufus smiled. 'First, I need more money. I must use these—' He rolled the dice in his hand. 'There is our sea passage to pay for. And I must see Pero.'

Criton put his head in his hands and shivered again. 'My head – it hurts. A pity we did not keep the gold.'

'There was too much of it to be explained away by a dismissed clerk with a grudge, and a penniless client who lives off charity.' Criton flinched. Curtius Rufus said savagely, 'How would they get that much gold – or any gold?'

'You might have kept a little,' said Criton doubtfully. 'It was mine after all.' He shivered violently.

'Too risky.'

Criton said uncertainly, 'Are you sure this is the best plan?' His face was flushed and he was breathing badly.

'Do you know a better? They have taken his slaves. Three at least. If I were in the Lautumiae prison, and they asked me, I would swear that the sun rose in the west. How long before they begin to question those who frequented his house?'

Criton raised a flushed face. 'That is logical.'

'You will not be safe in Brundisium for long.'

'How long shall I wait for you, and where?'

'If I do not join you in ten days, then look to yourself.'

'But—'

'Go to bed now and sleep. We can settle the details in the morning.' Curtius Rufus hesitated. He said suddenly, 'You do not look well.'

'I feel cold.' Criton shivered again. 'I will do as you say.'

He went to bed but not even two rugs and Curtius Rufus' best toga could keep him warm, and when his friend visited him at dawn the Macedonian said hoarsely, 'I have a fever. I cannot go today.'

'Never mind. As soon as you are well.' Curtius Rufus hurried from the room and spoke to the Greek doctor who lived on the third floor and who took nearly all that was left of their journey money before he would consent to look at his new patient. Criton he left in the care of the stonemason's daughter. 'Look after him,' he said. 'Don't let anyone in.'

'Must you go? I have shopping to do.'

'Yes,' he said. 'I need money for food and I shall need more for the doctor.'

'I cannot wait here all day. My father—'

'I shall not be long,' he promised. But he was wrong. For once the dice did not run in his favor and he had to work hard for his luck. It took much longer than he had expected and when he returned to the tenement it was to find Criton's room empty and the entire block in a panic of excitement and mingled fright. Feeling sick, he went to his room. The door was open and the girl was lying on the bed, crying.

'What happened?' he asked quietly.

'They came for him in the early afternoon,' she sobbed.

'They!'

'The city guard,' she said. 'He was too ill to walk. They took him away in a litter.'

'Do you know why?'

'No. But he – he gave me a message. He said, "Tell Curtius Rufus I will do my best to remember that the sun rises in the east. But if I do not, ask him to forgive me." I don't know what he meant. Do you?'

He knelt by the bed and stroked her hair. 'Yes,' he said. 'I know. But I wish with all my heart that I did not.'

CHAPTER V

The dawn light shone faintly on the prisoner's face as Marcus Agrippa received the reply to his last question. 'Take him back,' he said, and bent over the papers on his table as a slave moved noiselessly round the room, extinguishing the candles one by one. The prisoner turned and went out to where the guards waited, and a secretary laid a set of fresh documents on the table. 'These require your signature, sir,' he said softly.

'What are these?'

'Two orders for repairs to aqueducts together with estimates, a report from the Senate Planning Committee about the business for the week, and a schedule for the entertainment of the Parthian ambassador.'

'Has Maecenas checked this? Tell the guard commander to wait. I want a word with him.'

'Yes, sir. He has and approved it.' The secretary spoke over his shoulder. 'Ask the tribune, Seius Strabo, to come in.'

'What else have we?' Marcus Agrippa looked up.

The secretary consulted a wax tablet. 'You have a meeting with the Praefectus of the City about the processional route to the Circus—'

'Why?'

'There was a delay at the last Games because of the repair wagons blocking the way on that building project.'

'I remember. There was a great muddle. Go on.'

'You have another meeting with the naval commanders at Misenum and Forum Iulii about fleet dispositions. They both arrived yesterday.'

'What else?'

'There's a third meeting with the military pensions board to discuss the grants to the Hispania veterans. Four hundred are due to retire next month.'

'Will a representative from the Senatorial Treasury be there?'

'Yes, sir. Here is a memorandum on the subject.'

'Good. I'll see the naval commanders first. Tell them to be here in an hour. I'll hold the pensions meeting at the Temple of Saturn, as usual, and I'll meet the Praefectus in the Temple of Jupiter. I have to discuss the ceremony of the Epulum Iovis with the College priests.'

A slave brought a brass tray with a jug of wine and a plate of bread and honey. Marcus Agrippa poured himself a cup. The door opened and the tribune came in. 'I won't keep you a moment, Strabo. Any problems at the reception this morning?'

'No, sir.' The secretary consulted a second tablet. 'There will be a senator with a complaint about the delays in the post service to Gaul; two other senators are seeking permission to go overseas—'

'For good, I hope.'

'No, sir. One has a sick son; the other has business affairs. The aedile responsible for the Games has matters to discuss, and the Consul, Norbanus Flaccus, wishes to discuss the Primus trial.'

'Ask the last two to wait and walk with me to the Temple.'

The secretary said, 'I'm sorry, sir, this is making a great deal of work for you.'

'The Senate does that; a useless body of old women, like all self-perpetuating oligarchies. As always their ability is in inverse proportion to their self-importance. Still, I am used to it.' The secretary smiled discreetly. 'Strabo, come here.'

The young man approached the table and stood rigidly to attention.

Marcus Agrippa said, 'Well, what did you make of the Greek's story?'

'You mean the Macedonian, sir.'

'Answer my question.'

'He hasn't changed it, sir.' The tribune hesitated. His face was carefully devoid of expression, but there was a note of anxiety in his voice. 'He seems to be honest but he may be mistaken. He is a man of imagination.'

'What about the money? Would you throw that much gold away? If it was gold. Don't answer that.'

'He says he gave it to a friend.'

'Who conveniently disposed of it. Why didn't he report the matter in the first instance.'

'He says he was frightened and that he had no evidence.'

'Exactly. There is no evidence. A drunken client's story.'

'But would he make up a story like that, sir, to impress a friend?'

'Why not? We all love scandalous stories.'

The tribune's hand relaxed slightly. Marcus Agrippa noticed the gesture. Strabo said, 'You are right, I am sure, sir. It was ridiculous of him to mention – to mention the consul-elect.'

'You may be right. However, in view of the slave's testimony, we will have to look into it further. The Macedonian mentions a slave girl of Maecenas. I forget her name. Have her brought here but don't make a fuss. I don't want an armed guard of six men knocking at the door. Get one of your centurions into ordinary clothes. Tell him to contact the house steward on – on a matter to do with fraudulent shopkeeping. Say the girl is wanted to make a statement as a witness. Something like that.'

'I don't know where she shops, sir.'

'Find out then. Have her brought here by the seventh hour. Don't frighten her.' Marcus Agrippa paused and looked at the shorthand writer. 'Have you transcribed the Macedonian's statement yet?'

'It's not quite finished, sir.'

'Hurry up with it then. Seius, get me the names of

everyone who's visited Criton's patron since he went under house arrest.'

The tribune saluted and turned on his heel.

'One more thing, Seius. You are, I believe, related to Terentius Varro Murena?'

'Yes, sir, our wives are sisters.'

'Then remember – this matter touches the state. You will talk about it to no one. Do I make myself clear?'

'Yes, sir.' The tribune saluted again and the door closed behind him.

Marcus Agrippa said to his secretary, 'It's time for the morning reception. Are there many?'

The secretary smiled. 'You have a full atrium as usual, sir.'

'I shall not be a moment.' Marcus Agrippa picked up a document. 'This aqueduct inquiry. The man didn't appeal, did he? What is his name?' He peered at the file closely. The secretary stood behind him. 'Curtius Rufus, sir,' he said.

At the mention of the name the shorthand writer looked up to find his master staring at him.

'Is that the same man as the Macedonian mentioned?'

'It could be, sir.'

'Then find out. This man' – he tapped the paper with a blunt forefinger – 'I want to know everything about him. Get me his record sheet from the Tabularium.'

There was a knock at the door and his steward entered.

'Very well. I'm coming.' To his secretary he said: 'Find out where he lives. I may wish to see him. Where's my toga? Ah, thank you.' Marcus Agrippa stood up while his body slave dressed him for the reception. A hum of voices came from outside, where his visitors – officials, friends, and clients – waited. Through the thickening crowd of his household staff he saw the gleam of metal where a centurion waited. He beckoned to the man, who came forward.

'Yes,' he said. 'What do you want? Is it urgent?'

'My news is, sir. I'm in charge of the guard on duty at the house of—'

'Quieter. Go on.'

The centurion dropped his voice and spoke in a whisper. 'He took his life, sir, just before dawn. His lady came out and told us. It was too late to prevent—'

'I understand. You did right to come. Withdraw the guard.' Marcus Agrippa smiled. Primus, at least, had not escaped him, but this was no time to think about such matters. He began walking toward the Atrium, his secretary by his side. 'Well, that simplifies our speculations a great deal, though not our actions. Draft a notice for the State Gazette. Hint that the arrest was to do with an inquiry into the bribery of court witnesses. You know what to say.' He gripped his toga firmly with his left hand. 'Now, let us get on with the real business of the day.' His hand outstretched, a smile on his face, he moved forward to greet the senior among his visitors as one of his staff called out their names. 'Ah, Calpurnius. You do me honor. A good morning to you.'

It was a day of dark clouds and cold winds and the streets were wet with rain, but not even bad weather could entirely thin out the crowd that waited on the Palatine below the steps leading to Augustus' house. The day had not gone well for Marcus Agrippa. A meeting with a senatorial subcommittee over the vexed question of customs tariffs had had to be adjourned when it was discovered that the schedules supplied by the department concerned were inaccurate; a torrential downpour of rain and two funeral processions had delayed his chair and made him late for a meeting with the City Praefectus at the latter's office near the Temple of Tellus; and the latter part of the morning had been spent in making a second inspection of the city's oldest sewer, the Great Drain. The boat had leaked so that his feet had got soaked, the smell had seemed worse than ever, and the swollen waters had made the return journey as hazardous as his staff had predicted. They had returned damp and dirty and even Agrippa, who cared little what men thought of him, had abandoned his original arrangement to accompany a friend to a private bathing house much patronized by the senatorial order. He went hurriedly to his house on the Palatine for a quick bath and a change of clothing, for he had an appointment with Augustus' wife. Dinner in her company was always a formal affair and she seldom forgave a lack of punctuality. Now, hungry and tired, he stepped out of his chair and walked up the steps to the plain door with the civic crown fixed upon it. The solitary soldier on duty saluted him as he entered; a secretary, waiting in the vestibule, greeted him politely, and led him down a covered corridor, across a yard filled with bushes where the rain fell mournfully on to a small pond stocked with fish, through a larger yard lined with the busts of family ancestors, and then under a portico of white stone, off which opened the entrances to the winter dining rooms.

The secretary paused. 'In the Minerva Room, sir. You have not seen it, I think, since the redecoration. The Lady Livilla is particularly pleased with the paintings.' He hesitated, hearing voices. 'I did not know the senator was still with her.'

Marcus Agrippa grunted. He recognized the voice. 'I will be my own messenger,' he said and stepped inside. Household slaves were preparing a table around which were arranged three couches, while others busied themselves at the sideboard and lit the lamps on the bronze standards that stood at each end of the room. The Lady Livilla, seated upright in a high-backed chair, was talking in a low voice to a gray-haired senator who stood at her side. She had been married to Augustus now for fourteen years and her devotion to his cause and to her two sons by her previous marriage was such that no breath of scandal attached to her name, while even her bitterest enemies could find nothing of which to accuse her. Agrippa had known her for a long time. He admired her for the many qualities that made her so suitable a wife, respected her for her intelligence, and resented the fact that she was the only woman who could make him feel afraid. She was thirty-three years old.

He coughed and she looked up and smiled. 'You are early,' she said quietly. But not even her smile could warm the coldness of her beauty. What charm and warmth she possessed she reserved entirely for her husband.

Agrippa said, 'Your slaves always call the time to flatter the late guest.' He bent and kissed his hostess's cheek.

The senator, Valerius Messalla Corvinus, straightened and turned an almost expressionless face toward the newcomer. He inclined his head, but did not speak. Agrippa said, 'I share your grief.' To the Lady Livilla he said, 'How is he? I had hoped—' He paused and glanced at the senator briefly.

'No, Marcus. He is not well, and I will not have him bothered unnecessarily.'

'It would only take a moment.' Again he glanced toward the senator.

'Your moments are other men's days.'

'It is a state matter.'

'It is always a state matter. Gaius wishes to be fit to attend the Epulum Iovis, and he will be – if he rests; not otherwise.'

'But—'

Valerius Messalla said smoothly, 'It is a poor state that will collapse while you at least are on your feet. The Lady Livilla is right, Marcus Agrippa.'

Agrippa said, 'Then I defer to her judgment. The Lady Livilla is always right.'

'Certainly in matters of this kind, Marcus. Excuse me – Yes, what is it?' She turned as her steward approached, and spoke to him in an undertone.

The two men looked at each other. Agrippa's face was hostile. He said, 'Are you dining also?'

85

'No, I came on business and it is nearly concluded. I waited only to see you.'

Agrippa said, 'I am sorry about your niece.'

Valerius Messalla said, 'I am even more sorry. But that is another matter. I am disturbed about Primus.'

'I cannot help you.'

'I am disturbed for a number of reasons.'

'The affair is not in my hands. It is a matter for the Senate.'

Valerius Messalla raised his chin and said coldly, 'That I would appreciate if I thought it was true.'

Agrippa said, 'I do not understand you.'

'It seems to me that only six senators, apart from yourself, of course, have been chosen to command armies in recent years.'

'I have not kept count, but three years ago the Senate supplied the proconsuls for nine provinces.'

'Eight.'

'Eight then, if you insist on being precise. And Africa was added to the Senate's care.'

'But not Numidia, not Egypt.' Valerius Messalla paused while Agrippa frowned, and then said smoothly, 'Posts of importance for my order shrink year by year. Since Actium, the fleets have been commanded only by – by men like Cornelius Gallus.'

'His was an unfortunate case.'

'I could not agree more. That is why I am concerned for the prestige of the Senate. Too many new men—'

'Times have changed,' said Agrippa brusquely. 'We do not live in the days of the bearded ones. New times require new talents.'

'As I remember it there was always room for talent.'

Agrippa said, 'It seems we are not talking of the same things.'

'No. You are speaking of influence, and I of power, which the Senate lacks. It seems to me that Octavius—'

Agrippa said coldly, 'You are speaking of the uncle of Marcellus, I think.'

'Forgive me.' Valerius Messalla inclined his head. 'I always think of him as Octavius, though naturally I did not know him as a boy.'

Agrippa stared at him. In the silence the Lady Livilla paused in her conversation with the steward. She turned and looked and Agrippa saw the thin lips tighten. 'You must not talk like that,' she said in a clear voice. 'We are not in my father's world now. We are in my husband's house.'

He turned. He said, 'I was talking to Marcus Agrippa and I was dealing in facts. I am sorry indeed if the truth startled you. The Valerii have been in Rome a long time.'

She looked at him. She said, 'We are all old enough to have faced realities. I did so fourteen years ago, as you did also – after Philippi.'

He stood quite still, his face expressionless. 'You are quite right, for surely one may assist the state on whichever side one stands. I served Marcus Junius Brutus and his fellow liberators, then Marcus Antonius, then your husband.' He spoke quietly, as though he were addressing himself. 'I waged war against Sextus Pompeius and, sharing the consulship with Octavianus, saw another victory at Actium. I believe I was also a proconsul in Gaul and I celebrated a triumph in the year of the eight senatorial consuls.' He paused. 'I have always acted as I thought right, but that is something of which no man can be certain.' Then to Agrippa he said, 'Can I be certain that I live in a restored republic?'

Agrippa glanced at his hostess, who sat quite still with her hands in her lap. He grunted.

Valerius Messalla said, 'If I am wrong, please correct me.' He waited but no one spoke. 'I think that all authority lies here in this room and in one other, lacking only Maecenas to make it complete.'

Agrippa said stiffly, 'Augustus is only the first among the senators.'

Valerius Messalla raised an eyebrow. 'Of course, as the deified Julius, his uncle, was only the first among his generals. What a pity that I cannot remember their names. Well, you reassure me. I may speak on Primus's behalf with an easy mind.'

There was a long silence while Agrippa and the Lady Livilla looked at each other and the ex-consul watched them both in turn. Then he said gently, 'I understand that Terentius Varro Murena intends to speak also.' He paused. 'That makes two – almost a party.' He smiled and kissed Livilla on the cheek. 'I have overstayed my time. I keep you from your dinner while my own grows cold. Thank you for your hospitality. I will pray for your husband's recovery, as does all Rome. Will you walk to the door with me, Agrippa?'

'If you wish.' By the door he stopped. 'Well?' he asked. 'Let us be brief. We are all hungry.'

Valerius Messalla said, 'I am concerned about my niece.'

'It was a most unhappy accident,' said Agrippa shortly.

'And reflects credit on no one.'

'Efforts have been made to trace her.'

'Routine inquiries only. I have examined the report of the incident that you were kind enough to send me. I do not believe that she was kidnapped by accident. No goods were stolen except trifles, and – apart from the murder of her parents – no one else was harmed. Nor was anyone else taken captive.'

'It is thought that the alarm was given sooner than expected.'

'Do you believe that?'

Agrippa said, 'I am still making inquiries. I do not know what to believe. Perhaps she was kidnapped for ransom. It is possible.'

'No demand against her return has yet been received.'

'Well then?'

Valerius Messalla said, 'I am not a man of action like yourself. I am, however, the head of an ancient house and I have a pride in my family's achievements. As the victor at Mylae, Naulochus, and Actium you will understand that?'

'Yes.'

'I am glad. There at least we are on common ground.'

Agrippa grunted.

'Very well then. I do not wield power, as you know. But I understand power and how it operates. No one man can ever rule successfully alone. Power is always in the hands of a faction, however small. Power also functions solely upon success.'

Agrippa nodded. 'Like generalship.'

'Yes. There have been too many misfortunes recently to too many in authority for the good of Rome.' He dropped his voice and added ominously, 'We do not want any more. I care about Rome, as well as my family.' He wiped his mouth with his handkerchief. 'Primus is not a friend of mine, you understand, yet his situation disturbs me.'

Agrippa said mechanically, 'The Senate will——' but Valerius Messalla ignored him. He said, 'Perhaps I am wrong in my views as to Primus' culpability. It could be so. In which case I may leave his defense in the hands of Murena. The consul-elect is a powerful advocate. It is a matter I must think over carefully. Perhaps you would care to advise me at a more suitable time?'

'I shall be pleased——'

'I am glad to hear it.' Valerius Messalla smiled. 'But I want my niece returned to my house. Is that clear?'

Agrippa said, 'You make yourself very clear. The one matter depends upon the other.' He spoke bluntly, hoping to shock, for he was very angry, but he did not succeed.

Valerius Messalla spread out his hands. 'Oh, no,' he said. 'You are quite wrong. These are entirely separate matters. In my mind there is no confusion, none at all.' He nodded and went out, and Agrippa stared after him in silence. Presently he became aware that a slave was standing by his side, offering him a cup of wine. He took it without a word and came back into the room. Livilla was walking up and down, her hands clasped in front of her, a faint flush on her cheeks.

'Forgive me,' he said awkwardly, 'I – I could not trust myself to speak.' And then, curtly, 'I do not like him.'

She said, 'I think that must be obvious. Your views that paintings and sculpture should not belong to individuals but to the state are too well known. Yet he is an interesting man to talk to and I enjoy his conversation. We discussed the fate of his poor niece.'

'He dreams of a world that is dead. He lives in the shade.'

She looked at him. 'I seem to remember that when we invited him to live in the sun again it was we who got scorched.'

'He laughed at us.'

'Perhaps, but not out loud. He is usually polite. It was not until you arrived, my dear Marcus, that he became so – so outspoken.'

'He insulted us both. Why did he come?'

She said calmly, 'I have told you. He came by appointment. He wished to see my husband. It would have been – unwise to refuse him.'

'He dared suggest—' He broke off. Then he said angrily, 'Next time—'

'I would not bother. The Valerii have a habit of saying the last word. If I do not mind, why should you?' She hesitated and then said quietly, 'He is genuinely worried. The family means much to him. That, I at least can appreciate.' She added slowly, 'My husband thinks highly of him.'

Agrippa took warning from the note in her voice. He said carefully, 'As we all must do. He has great influence.'

The steward entered and spoke to her. 'Come, Marcus, another cup of wine? Gaius Maecenas has been detained but will be with us shortly. Do you wish to be serious still or shall we wait till he joins us?'

He said, 'Is it true that Augustus intends to speak at the trial? It should not be necessary. His presence will be sufficient. The Senate will understand.'

'He has not discussed the matter with me. I told Valerius that, merely hoping it might persuade him to change his mind. Was that wrong of me?' She sipped her wine. 'This is excellent. Did you add your persuasions also?'

'I tried but he would not listen. He might not be bothered to speak if we would undertake to find his niece.' He grunted. 'It would be an impossible task and, in any event, would take too long.'

She said thoughtfully, 'He is a man of his word.'

'But that still leaves Varro Murena.' Agrippa clenched his hand. 'I do not like it.'

'You mean you do not like him; a man who is as blunt and outspoken as yourself.'

He look disconcerted. 'Perhaps. But there must be no controversy over this matter. If no one speaks for him, then Primus is a dead man. Murena must be stopped. Perhaps if we asked Gaius? He is after all married to Murena's sister. The Lady Terentia—'

'Has great powers of persuasion,' said Livilla calmly. 'She tried to charm my husband once, as you know, and succeeded. I bear no grudge. That would be foolish. Men are always so. They are like children, always wanting a new toy. Well, ask him then.' She smiled. 'You do not like Gaius Maecenas, do you?'

'No,' he said vehemently. 'He represents everything that I loathe. He is effeminate, extravagant, and interested only in pleasure. Besides, I distrust men who do not seek office.'

'He has been a good friend. He has great talent. He is a most skillful diplomat, and popular with the people.'

'I must allow him that.'

'Then why not tell him so. Here he is. Come in, Gaius, and welcome. You are late but I will forgive you this once if you will but try and take the scowl from Marcus' face.'

Maecenas, scented and swathed in silk, moved elegantly

toward them. 'Dear Lady, a thousand pardons. You ask of me, as always, the impossible, yet I will do my best.'

'And you will succeed.' Livilla clapped her hands and then turned toward the dining table. 'Let us eat, shall we? I am famished and though I cannot offer you donkey flesh – which, I understand, you have recently tried to make fashionable – Gaius, I do not think you will go hungry or complain. Will you sit here, and you, Marcus, here.'

'And how is your daughter, madam?' asked Gaius pleasantly.

Livilla, arranging her dress, paused before replying while Agrippa grunted and looked quickly at Maecenas.

'Very well,' she replied. 'Julitta is happy in her marriage. But at the moment she is distraught with grief over a pet cat which has gone astray, and blames poor Marcellus.'

'But why?' asked Maecenas with interest.

'It seems the cat scratched Marcellus and he put it outdoors in a rage and it did not return.'

Agrippa said, 'Animal bites can be dangerous. I hope he is taking good care.'

Livilla said, 'Indeed, yes. Antonius Musa was sent for at once. He is an excellent physician.' She looked across at Agrippa and added slowly, 'Marcellus is – he is a fine boy and my husband is proud of him.'

Maecenas said, 'And, with good cause. His life is very precious to the state, since he is now marked out to be the heir.'

There was silence and he glanced from one to the other, a smile on his face.

Livilla said, 'Gaius, I know of no arrangements, no plans – nothing. It has not been discussed even.'

'Why else should one so young and so inexperienced be made an aedile? The writing is not upon the sand, it is carved, dear friends, upon the wall.'

Agrippa said, 'If I thought that—' He broke off quickly.

'But Marcus, you have thought of nothing else.'

Livilla turned to Maecenas. 'Gaius, this conversation is point-less as well as in bad taste.'

'I accept your reproof, dear Lady, but you should know – must know – that it is a conversation taking place at every dinner table in Rome.'

She said coldly, 'You listen to gossip and rumor.'

'Of course. It is what makes me a diplomat. I keep my ear to the ground.'

Agrippa said angrily, 'And what else does this gossip say?'

Maecenas hesitated. 'Oh, some are blunter speakers than others.'

'Go on.'

'They say that if Marcellus were to die, then Augustus must make Agrippa his son-in-law, or perish.'

Livilla said calmly, 'Then for my husband's sake I must do my best to see that no harm comes to that boy.' She smiled.

Maecenas, watching, saw the smile fade as she raised her eyes and found Agrippa looking at her. He sat quite still but he was not smiling and Maecenas had little difficulty in reading his thoughts. Outside, the sky darkened and it began to rain.

In the middle of their meal the rain stopped. Later the wind dropped a little and the sun appeared, its diffused light illuminat-ing the paintings on the walls while casting watery shadows across the decorated floor.

Maecenas put down his cup and watched the slaves clearing the table. One of them, a dark-haired boy, smiled nervously under his gaze. Livilla's eyes flickered a little and she paused in her conversation. 'No, Gaius,' she said sharply. 'He is not for sale.'

Maecenas spread out his hands. 'But of course not. I merely admired your taste.'

'I leave such matters to my steward.' She turned her head. 'Well, Marcus, tell Gaius what you have told me.'

'But I can guess at it, dear Lady. Let Marcus save his breath. I can count the eggs in the Circus Maximus as well as the next man.'

'You know then that I questioned one of your slave girls?'

'I have trembled for my own safety ever since. Yes, I know, and I questioned her in my turn. I only trust she told both of us the same story.' Maecenas played with the gold ring on his index finger.

Agrippa said, 'Well?'

Maecenas smiled. 'We have two problems. The first is the support Primus may obtain at his trial; the second concerns a group of men who knew of an event before it took place. They are linked by two common factors: one is Valerius Messalla and the other is Varro Murena.'

Livilla said, 'It may be coincidence. Valerius Messalla is a man of honor. He would scarcely—'

'Connive at the kidnapping of a relative? No, of course not. It is as unthinkable as the suggestion that he would violate the sanctity of the Temple of Vesta.' Livilla flushed. 'On the other hand, I do not believe in coincidences.'

'On that I agree,' said Agrippa. 'I smell trouble of some kind. But what have we to go on? The stories of a slave girl who may be seeking self-importance and a Macedonian scribbler of verse who is half-witted.'

Livilla said thoughtfully, 'Neither came forward to tell their stories voluntarily. That may be in their favor. What about the other man, their friend who threw away this bag of gold. A doubtful story.'

Agrippa said, 'I will know about that when I have seen him. If he is the man I think he is, and the reports are correct, he has a curious and unsatisfactory history.' He wiped his hands with a napkin. 'However, if he corroborates their story I may have the evidence I need.'

Maecenas said in a flat voice, 'And what will you do with your – evidence?'

'Arrest Fannius Caepio on a charge of conspiracy. His son's testimony – if the boy does not lie – will hardly tell in his favor.'

'You are a fool then, Marcus. You will play into their hands.'

'Why? Who are they?'

'Gaius, what do you mean?' said Livilla anxiously.

Maecenas sat up. 'Dear Lady, certain things can never be proved, so I will not offer you proof but only suppositions.'

'Go on,' said Agrippa impatiently.

'I think there is a plot to embarrass this government – this party.'

'You mean Augustus?'

'I said this party, for no one can rule without a party.' He smiled at Livilla. 'I mean no disrespect, dear Lady.'

She said, 'I understand you, Gaius.'

'Augustus is ill. He has governed for fourteen years, yet the memory of the Liberators is not dead. You have told me what Valerius Messalla said. Others are saying it too.'

Agrippa snorted. 'He lives on dreams.'

'Perhaps, but he is of the Valerii. He is no trousered senator from Gaul.'

Livilla said, 'Go on.'

'The party of Augustus has suffered many embarrassments recently. Consider: there was the case of Cornelius Gallus, Praefectus of Egypt, who committed suicide two years or so ago. The same year Valerius Messalla was offered the post of Praefectus of Rome, accepted, and resigned after six days.' Maecenas sighed, almost in envy. 'Can you think of a better way to insult a man of whose government you disapprove?'

Agrippa said, 'It was explained that he did not understand the full nature of the new office.'

Livilla said sharply, 'That he told me, certainly, but—'

'But, dear Lady, that was not how the people in those narrow streets down there interpreted his actions.'

'If you are right—'

'Don't reach for your dagger, Marcus. You know I detest sharp instruments. Valerius Messalla is no traitor, only an over-honest man like the Liberator he served. Now, we have the failure of Aelius Gallus' expedition into Arabia and, finally, the curious behavior of Primus, arraigned of all things on a charge of treason. How many failures can be endured before a party loses the confidence of those stinking streets out there?'

Agrippa said harshly, 'I cannot accept—'

'My interpretation. You must. Only the elderly and the pompous, the self-satisfied and the righteous – your brother senators – cannot bear the truth. You do, dear Marcus, for why else are you worried also?'

Livilla said, 'If only he were not ill.'

'But he is and the dogs are beginning to growl.'

'And who is the chief dog?'

'That I do not know,' said Maecenas carefully.

Agrippa rose from the couch and the others followed him. He went out onto the balcony. Below lay the Circus Maximus, huge and empty. In a few days' time it would be filled to capacity and the crowd would roar the name of the man who had destroyed their most feared enemy, returned peace to the provinces, and restored the republic. But the mood of the crowd could change. A favored charioteer might be applauded one day and howled down the next, should his luck change for the worse. Agrippa shivered. Even parties and rulers needed luck if they were to survive, Valerius Messalla had warned him. Maecenas too had seen the writing on the wall.

He turned and said, 'We have done so much. Augustus has repaired the Flaminian Way, Cornificius has rebuilt the Temple of Diana. Look at Messalla's work on the Latin Way; and then there is the Taurus Amphitheatre. Don't they remember such things?'

Maecenas said, 'It is men who make a city, not houses nor walls nor marketplaces, empty of men. Of course we have achieved a great deal. You, especially, with your work on the aqueducts.'

Agrippa shrugged impatiently. 'But there is so much more still to be done. We cannot be stopped now – in the middle of it all.' He turned to Livilla, a look of impatient bewilderment on his face.

She said, 'I understand. He, too, feels as you do. And he gets impatient. He wishes to reorganize the city's administration, the four regions being much too large. He has plans, too, for Hispania and Gaul. They must be surveyed, he says, organized and taxed. There are roads to be built, new ports to be constructed, and his veterans to be provided for. Oh, the catalog is endless.'

Maecenas said sardonically, 'Is there a tree that the wind has not shaken? Come, I think we wander from the point. To return to it, I suggest that the kidnapping of the girl was done to add to our embarrassment. Valerius Messalla's pride and influence are known. At worst he prods us with a fork; at best – their best – he responds to a rallying cry of the disaffected. For how safe are the provinces if the daughter of a legate may be kidnapped by pirates with impunity? Where now is the boast of peace, of law and of order? I do not say these things – but they will.'

Agrippa nodded. 'I had thought as much myself, but there can be no connection with the business of Primus. They could not have known about the Proconsul of Macedonia. That must be coincidence.'

Maecenas looked at him.

Livilla said, 'I think I agree with Marcus. They could not know that he would act so or that Valerius and Terentius would be willing to speak for him.'

Agrippa said brusquely, 'About Murena – I was going to ask you if—'

'I am coming to that now,' said Maecenas gently. 'Terentius Varro Murena is an honest man – sometimes too honest. He shouts where others whisper. If Murena intends to speak it is because he believes there is good reason.'

Agrippa said harshly, 'And what is his good reason?'

Maecenas yawned and reached for his cup. 'I understand from Terentia – and she had it from her brother – that Primus will state on oath that he acted on the orders of Augustus and Marcellus.'

There was silence, and Maecenas could hear the fountain in the courtyard drip into the pool. Agrippa frowned and rubbed his chin nervously; Livilla stood still, her eyes on Maecenas.

'He told that story when first questioned and no one believed him.'

'He has told it again under house arrest and someone does – Murena.'

'Why?'

'He – Primus – has said that the instructions were contained in a letter.'

'Which is now lost, of course, and which cannot be found.'

'That is correct.'

'Do you believe this?' Livilla was flushed with anger. 'How dare he suggest that my husband—' She broke off suddenly.

Agrippa said, 'Well, do you believe it?'

Maecenas smiled. He said carefully, 'The question of belief would not arise if the letter could be produced and then shown to contain what it is said to contain.'

'Gaius.'

'Dear Lady, be patient. It is an interesting problem. There are three possibilities.'

'Does it matter what he says?' There was contempt in her voice. 'Let him bring charges. My husband will deny them.'

'It is serious, Lady. As you will remember, no man of substance has betrayed Augustus since Salvidienus.'

A sandal scraped the floor as Livilla sat down in the high-backed chair. Agrippa moved his arm suddenly and the sleeve of his gown knocked a tiny statue of a faun from a table. Livilla said wonderingly, 'I remember him. We played together as children. He had red hair.'

Agrippa said tonelessly, 'And he was a consul designate.'

'So is Murena. But Salvidienus had reason to negotiate with – with the enemy. The outcome in those times was uncertain and he had the army of Gaul at his back. Salvidienus' case is not the same as that of Primus. Or is it?'

Agrippa said coldly, 'I have served Augustus—'

'As long as I have,' said Maecenas smoothly. 'We both enjoy his trust as he enjoys ours.' He paused and put down his cup regretfully. 'It is just possible, of course, that if Primus is not lying, then the letter was forged.'

Livilla raised her eyes and blinked with surprise. Agrippa started to breathe heavily. He said stubbornly, 'Who would dare to forge a letter like that? It is inconceivable.'

'That I cannot say. Marcus, you are an engineer. You know that a pebble dropped in the wrong place may start a landslide. All plots and conspiracies begin in the heart, not the head.'

Livilla said, 'That, I suppose, is your third possibility?'

'Yes.'

Agrippa frowned again. 'What do you advise?'

'Drop the case against Primus, my dear Marcus. There will then be no spark that others can ignite into a flame.'

'I cannot.'

'You mean you will not. Then at least find that girl and for the same reason. It is fortunate that Valerius Messalla prefers prestige to power. As I do.'

'Do you?' Livilla asked gently.

'Oh, yes. The extravagancies and absurd ceremonials of a senatorial life are far too fatiguing. I prefer comfort and security.' Maecenas smiled. 'You look disbelieving.'

Livilla said, 'If your third possibility is true, then someone is seeking power who has not got it.'

'Perhaps it is someone who wishes for more.' Maecenas inclined his head. 'Do not look at me so. It is not I who have red hair.' He glanced at the steward still standing patiently in the corner of the room. The steward raised a hand and Maecenas' body slave entered, bearing his master's street shoes.

Maecenas said, 'I have dined well as always. Thank you, my dear Lady. I look to see you at the Games.'

'Remember me to Terentia.'

'But of course. You are often in her thoughts.'

'And she in mine.'

Agrippa said, 'I will find those responsible, whatever happens.'

'I am sure you will do your best. Yet though you search for Hylas, my friend, I think you will never find him.'

Agrippa touched his lips and then put his finger behind his ear. He seemed suddenly disturbed. Livilla rested her chin on her hand and said nothing, her face a mask, empty of all feeling.

By the door, Maecenas turned. 'We are all his friends and his lieutenants and we all share his purpose.' He paused. He said, 'Yet the fingers of one hand even are not alike. It is as well to remember something so small and so obvious.'

He went out, his body slave following, and presently the sound of his feet in the corridor quite died away.

CHAPTER VI

The centurion, who had been standing patiently against the wall of the tenement in an effort to keep the rain off his back, saw the figure of a man lurching drunkenly toward him along the opposite pavement, and smiled with relief that his long watch was nearly over. The man crossed the road noisily and the centurion waited until he had almost turned into the entrance to the building, where a torch spluttered upon the wall. 'Just a moment,' he said in a thick voice, and tapped with his stick upon the pavement. At the sound the man swung round, his face ghastly in the light.

'Yes.'

'Are you Curtius Rufus, a former clerk to the Water Board?' The centurion sneezed suddenly.

The man swallowed and his eyes flickered sideways as though he contemplated flight. 'That's right. What do you want with me?'

The centurion put his hand to a pouch at his belt. 'I have been trying to deliver a message to you for two days.'

Curtius Rufus steadied himself against the door post. 'Why — why didn't you leave it with the landlord?'

'I was told to deliver it to you, not to your landlord. Where, in the name of Mercury, have you been? I missed our burial club dinner on your account.' He put his fingers against each nostril in turn and blew into the darkness. 'And picked up a running nose instead. I'm wet through.'

'Oh, getting drunk, my friend. And dicing too much. Shall I show you?' Curtius Rufus rolled the dice from hand to hand.

The centurion said huskily, 'A man in your position should have – more . . .' His voice trailed away and he sneezed violently.

'Pride is the word you want.' Curtius Rufus gave a weak grin, shook his head to clear the wine fumes, and grinned again. 'Well, give me the letter.'

'Don't lose it as you no doubt lost your staff.' The centurion shivered and pulled his cloak about him. 'It is from Marcus Agrippa. Get some sleep. You will need it.'

'Have a drink first. There's a tavern across the way that's still open. It's been a long time.'

'Sorry. It's late and I must go. My woman is expecting me. I shall be in trouble as it is.'

'Have a drink and—'

The centurion shook his head, his face bright with rain, and strode off into the darkness. Curtius Rufus let his hands drop to his side, the rain falling unheeded upon the parchment. 'Only wanted a chat about old times,' he muttered.

Upstairs in his room he lit the lamp, his hands shaking, broke the seal, and read the few words quickly. The letter had been dated three days previously and the message was an order rather than a request. He was to report to the house of Marcus Agrippa on the Palatine at the second hour on the morning after the letter's receipt. The last sentence above the signature was as short as the others – 'if you do not attend, you will be sent for.'

He put the letter down while a feeling of sickness grew inside him. He licked his lips, drank a mouthful of water, and then lay down on the bed and shivered as the inevitable pain started again behind his right eye. He thought about Criton and Pero and himself, and he wondered who had talked and what had been said. Presently he fell asleep and did not stir until the sound of the carts woke him as usual in the still-time before the dawn.

He had never visited the Palatine before, save once to attend a ceremony at the Temple of Victory on an occasion when attendance had been compulsory for all who worked for the Curator of the Water Board. Consequently he approached his destination, without thinking, from the west end of the Circus Maximus and found himself faced with a steep, unrelenting climb up the Caci steps. In this he was alone but for a slave or two, carrying letters from one house to another. It was a cold day but he was wet through with sweat by the time he reached the gate at the top. Pausing there to rest and rearrange his toga, he walked slowly past the Temple of Apollo. In the distance a crowd of women slaves were drawing water from a cistern. Threading his way through a growing body of senators and their clients, who had concluded their morning calls, he reached the house with difficulty, and then only by a process of repeatedly asking the way of every passerby that he met. Once inside he gave his name to an attendant and joined a crowd of men thronging the anterooms. Many knew each other and were exchanging greetings in overloud voices; all were well dressed. Even the minor officials and the craftsmen, hoping for work on commission, were neat and tidy; and he felt shabby and ill at ease in his worn toga. The crowd began to thin slowly, as in groups or singly the visitors answered their names and were led forward and out of sight.

Presently an attendant came up, polite, servile, and knowing. 'If I have your name I will see that you are not kept waiting.' He extended his hand, palm upward, as he spoke. Curtius Rufus shook his head; the man shrugged and moved off. The last comers, hurrying out, cast curious looks at him, sitting alone now on a marble bench. An old man, a naval pensioner, wounded in a skirmish with Sextus Pompeius, paused by his side. 'You'll never get in without tipping. They see to that.' He nodded to two elegantly dressed men, lounging against a column.

Curtius Rufus looked up and tried hard to smile. 'I don't wish to go in. I am not here by choice.'

The old man shook his head wonderingly and limped out.

The room was empty now. One of the lounging men said in a loud voice, 'No use waiting. Some of them never learn. He won't see anyone now.' The other laughed.

Curtius Rufus stood up and walked toward them. He said politely, 'I am not a client. I am here on business.' He paused and added gently, 'Here is the letter. Centurions aren't usually employed as messengers unless the matter is important.'

The attendants stared at him. Then the elder one said quickly, 'Give me the letter. I will take it in.' He returned at a fast walk. 'I am sorry, sir,' he said hurriedly. 'Had you shown me this earlier . . . This way, please, if you will follow me.' He returned rapidly the way he had come and Curtius Rufus followed him, his face and hands cold with sweat. Unlike his father he had always been afraid of the unknown.

Marcus Agrippa pushed the papers on his desk to one side and signaled to the clerk who had been taking shorthand notes. The man rose and left the room.

Curtius Rufus said, 'May I go, sir.' He spoke in a tired voice, exhausted by the ceaseless questioning he had endured for the past hour. His legs ached and he would have liked to sit down, but he did not dare.

Marcus Agrippa said, 'You may when I have finished with you.' He paused, put his arms on the table, and frowned. He said, 'I believe your story as I believe that of the Greek and the girl. There is no evidence for my belief, but it is all too stupid not to be true.'

Curtius Rufus swallowed. 'Thank you, sir.'

'There is nothing to thank me for – yet.'

'I – I am not under arrest then?'

'That is another matter.' There was a long silence while Curtius Rufus looked at the pattern on the mosaic at his feet and Marcus Agrippa looked at Curtius Rufus. Presently the harsh voice spoke again. 'You have an unsatisfactory record.

Your father's talents and the state both gave you good opportunities. But you have wasted them. I acquit you of responsibility for the accident that terminated your career in the centurionate. That was unfortunate. Since then you have tried a dozen jobs and lasted at none of them. You pursue women out of all moderation; you drink, you gamble, and you are content to float like scum through the gutters of Rome. You live by your wits, I believe, which are not as great as you think, and will probably end your days knifed in a tavern brawl. Well, that will be no great loss.'

'I had bad luck.'

'Bad luck! We all have bad luck. Do you think yourself the only one to have had bad luck in his life?' Marcus Agrippa stood up. 'All Rome asks where I come from, who my grandfather was, and what my father did. None of that matters. It is what you do that matters. I know your world better than you think. I was born into it. But I control myself and I make my own luck, Curtius Rufus. I make it work for me, as your father made it work for him. But he had courage.'

Curtius Rufus said quietly, 'Have I permission to go, sir, I must attend to my mules.' The words, dating from the days of Marius, were the centurionate's stock formula for ending an interview when an officer had said too much, and Marcus Agrippa recognized them. He stopped frowning and smiled. 'At least we understand each other,' he said. 'That is more than I can say for half the conversations I hold with my brother senators.' He tapped irritably with his fingers. 'The girl knows nothing. Fright made her impertinent. Well, you did not talk to her. That at least shows discretion. Your friend, however, knows a good deal. But he had the good sense to consult you. I doubt if he spoke to anyone else.'

Curtius Rufus said, 'No, sir. He spoke to no one else.'

'As I thought. Now we come to you.' Marcus Agrippa hesitated. 'I know what you have said. I do not know what you think.'

'There is a difference, sir.'

'It is all one to me. We are concerned with a matter that is highly confidential. It touches the security of the state.' Marcus Agrippa paused and adjusted his toga. 'It is unfortunate that you, on your own admission, get frequently drunk, and that you are generally held to be unreliable. Even the girl does not trust you overmuch.' He hesitated, biting his lip. He added casually, 'You know too much.'

Curtius Rufus stood quite still, his fingers curled stiffly against the palms of his hands. He felt his tired legs begin to shake and could not control them. The moment that he had feared and dreaded had come at last. He remembered the soldier on duty outside the Tullianum, to whom he had spoken that day, and the man's words came back to him — 'They go down to the lower room tomorrow.' A muscle in his cheek began to twitch uncontrollably. He licked his lips with a dry tongue and tried to speak, but the words would not come; and all the while Marcus Agrippa stared at him coldly as though he were looking at a dead man.

In the silence a slave's voice in the distance cried the hour and a dog barked shrilly in an adjoining courtyard.

Marcus Agrippa said abruptly, 'Fortunately for you there is no evidence against you that is not equally in your favor. No magistrate would convict you in the courts. I am, therefore, going to send you out of Rome. If you are wise you will accept the commission I now offer you.'

Curtius Rufus stared at him. 'May I sit down, sir?'

'Yes. Now, listen to me carefully. I know that Valerius Messalla's niece has been kidnapped for reasons I do not propose to discuss. It is important, however, that she be returned unharmed. This is a matter of prestige, you understand. She comes of a great family.'

Curtius Rufus nodded in bewilderment.

'We know she was taken by Mauri pirates and believe she is in the hinterland of Mauretania. Who has taken her I do not know, but the man responsible will not be the captain of the ship that carried her off. Nor do I know where in that vast country she is concealed. You will leave Rome in ten days' time, as an accredited envoy to the court of King Juba. But first you will sail from Misenum to Carthage. The Proconsul of Africa will give you advice and supplies, as well as a military escort. You will then proceed to the king's palace at Caesarea.' Marcus Agrippa smiled. 'It used to be called Iol, but has been tactfully renamed. Ostensibly your mission is to offer the king assistance on many matters that are dear to his heart. He needs men who can train his people to build roads, aqueducts, and bridges; survey the countryside; advise on administrative matters. You will supply yourself with the economical and technical assistants you require, and you will do all in your power to assist him, so that the expense of your journey and stay may not be wasted. Gain his confidence and the king and his advisers may be able to help you. But remember, after you reach Caesarea it will be your responsibility as to how the affair proceeds.' Marcus Agrippa paused. 'Well?'

'Why – why choose me, sir? I have no experience, no qualifications.'

Marcus Agrippa said dryly, 'I am not overimpressed by formal qualifications. I saw this city and its provinces brought to near anarchy and ruin by men who believed they had the right to rule because they alone possessed the qualifications to do so. The result was twenty years of civil war. Qualifications, unfortunately, are not a substitute for talent.'

'But, sir—'

'You underrate yourself. You have sailed in those parts; you speak a little Berber and some Phoenician, so I understand; you get on with people – oh, yes, I know all about your freedman inspector – it requires patience to endure the incompetent and the lazy; you have some engineering ability; and you showed

107

initiative over the business of that aqueduct. You were also of the centurionate; that itself is a recommendation. Those are reasons good enough for me.'

'But—'

'If I send some tribune with a Janiculum accent he will make everyone bristle like a porcupine within the hour and learn nothing. In any event there is no one of rank suitable whom I can spare, and I do not wish too much weight to be given to this matter in the event of failure.'

'I do not know if I can do it. I—'

'I doubt if you will succeed, but at least we can be said to have done our best.'

Curtius Rufus said desperately, 'I cannot. I would not know how to begin.'

'You can try.' Marcus Agrippa leaned forward. 'I learned for myself how to win battles at sea. No one taught me. King Juba is a good friend to Rome. Do your job well and if I receive favorable reports you will be suitably rewarded.'

Curtius Rufus said miserably, 'I shall only let you down.'

'Let me be the judge of that. If you fail, I shall have failed too.'

Curtius Rufus stared.

'Of course,' Marcus Agrippa said gently, 'I, too, am a gambler. How often have you staked all on the dog? Do so again. Remember, this is an age for new men. Don't waste the opportunity I give you.'

'Very well, sir.' Curtius Rufus hesitated. Then he said, 'Sir, there is the matter of Criton. He is a friend.'

'Your loyalty is touching. Come here tomorrow, attend the first admission, and I will give you the written authority of Augustus Caesar concerning your commission; also a letter regarding your friend. Take that to the magistrate and he will write the order of release. On all matters regarding the duties of an envoy Gaius Maecenas will instruct you. On all other administrative matters consult the chief clerk of the Senatorial Treasury.

'One last thing. Your troops will be an escort for dignity, not a show of force. Rely on tact, diplomacy, argument and reason. There must be no bloodshed, no violence. Is that clear?'

Curtius Rufus nodded.

'Very well. You may go. I have important matters to see to now.'

Curtius Rufus turned and went out in silence, feeling cautiously for the few coins that lay in an inside fold of his toga. At that moment what he desired most in the world cost very little, and he could make the purchase with a free mind. It was an amphora of wine.

Criton said again, 'I do not believe it,' and sat there on the edge of his bed as he had sat in the wineshop two hours before, his face pale, his eyes huge, and his hands trembling each time he tried to hold his cup.

'Was it so very bad?'

Criton said, 'It was the waiting and the uncertainty.' He shivered again.

'Go on.'

'I was with two men. One was a runaway slave who had been with a gang of brigands. The other was a boy who had conspired with his sister to kill their father. He told me so himself. We were together for two nights.' He stopped speaking and put his head in his hands.

'And then?'

'They – they took both of them away for questioning. The slave first, the boy second. I heard their screams in that room down the corridor where – where they asked the questions.'

'What happened?'

'They did not come back, and I was alone. I kept on waiting, wondering when they would come for me. Each time I heard footsteps in the corridor, I thought—' He licked his lips nervously. 'I lay awake at night, waiting.' He swallowed and looked at Curtius Rufus with dilated eyes. He said, 'I was so afraid of the pain.'

A hand touched his arm. 'It is all over now, as I have been telling you since this morning. Tomorrow you will feel better.'

'Perhaps.'

'Of course you will.' Curtius Rufus added slowly, 'Pylades gave your task to Cleon. He could not wait.' The hurt look in Criton's eyes startled him. He said hurriedly, 'But he would like to have you back. He said you were the only person who understood what he was trying to do.'

The Macedonian said hopefully, 'You went to see him? For me?'

Curtius Rufus said, 'Yes, the moment I knew all would be well. You will be all right. I am sure of it.'

Criton held his cup in both hands and smiled suddenly. 'Did Pylades really say that? Oh, I am so glad to be back. I feel safe again.'

Curtius Rufus glanced round the room, seeing in it everything that he himself wished to escape from: the peeling walls, the short bed, the marble-topped table with the crack across one corner, the single clay lamp with the smoke-blackened rim, and the old chest with the broken lock that Criton had never been able to replace. He looked at the little statues he had given Criton as presents at the Saturnalia and other festivals: a clay figure of Hercules, a bronze of Apollo, a plaster of Leander, and a hermaphrodite in marble that Criton admired best of all. They were clumsily executed because they were made for the poor and sold cheaply in the Sigillaria market. They were the best he had been able to afford, and they stood there, chipped, discolored with damp, a permanent reminder of his poverty.

He picked up the paste seal-ring that lay on the table beside an earthenware basin and turned it over in his fingers. His father had given him a gold one once but it had been big for his finger and he seldom wore it. Later he had lost it at a time when the horses were running badly. He had never had another.

He said, 'Come with me as my secretary. I shall need a good one, and who better as an adviser than a friend?'

'I am a poet, not a secretary.'

Curtius Rufus picked up the tiny amphora that contained all the oil Criton could afford to buy. 'It is a good opportunity.'

'For you,' said Criton shrewdly.

Curtius Rufus put the amphora into his friend's hands. 'That is all you can afford,' he said brutally. 'You will never be able to buy more at one time. You will go blind, working by that tiny flame. And what can Pylades pay you?'

'It was almost enough. I do not gamble like you.'

'Who will pay the doctor's bills next time you are sick?'

'Yes, you spent a great deal on me,' Criton said, remorse in his voice. 'I am sorry I was ill. But now everything will be all right.'

'You have not answered my question.'

Criton said indignantly, 'Who threw away my gold? It was worth a great deal.'

'Eight thousand sesterces to be exact. The doctor's bill was less.' Curtius Rufus grinned. 'So it is I who owe you money.'

Criton shook his head. 'I did not mean that. I am sorry.'

Curtius Rufus looked round the room. 'I envy you. You are happy with little.'

'I do not try to pull down the stars, that is all.' Criton smiled happily. His hands had stopped shaking. He was back again in his small room, where, at night, he could write and dream that one day his poems would make him famous. Meanwhile there was Pylades, who liked him. It was enough, he was content.

Curtius Rufus said, 'Listen, I am to receive a salary of twenty thousand sesterces. That is more than I would have earned as a chief centurion, if I'd been lucky enough to get that far.'

Criton said, 'It sounds like a great deal, but there will be expenses. You will need slaves, clothes – oh, so many things. A successful tradesman earns far more.'

'Yes, but I am to receive allowances for food, wine, servants, lamp oil, firewood, and clothes, so I shall be nearly as well off as old Lepidus. He was the tribune of my cohort.'

Criton put down the amphora. He said, 'I do not know what to say.'

'But I do. Come with me. You must throw your dice at the right time. Look at that chest of yours. "Chewed by barbarian mice" was your expression for it. Stay here and they will chew everything you have. Remember the rats last winter?'

Criton shivered.

'There is nothing for us in Rome.'

'Except opportunity. Pylades told me—'

'Forget what he told you. No one climbs on his shoulders. He takes care of that. All these actors are the same.'

'You think so?' Criton frowned.

'I do. You will get half my salary and allowances, if you come.'

'But if I stay—' Criton hesitated. 'Cleon could get sick. He has a weak chest. He is often ill in winter. Then Pylades will have me back.'

'Did he pay you a secretary's salary?'

Criton shook his head. 'You know what he paid me.'

'And you have no patron now. Well then?'

'Please, I don't want to go.'

'Why not?'

Criton did not answer.

Curtius Rufus said, 'We receive half our salary before we go, the balance upon return. We can manage without difficulty and live well.'

There was a long silence. Curtius Rufus crossed to the window and looked out at the Tiber wall. He said quietly, 'The only poets who succeed are those who sing songs in honor of Rome and who catch the eye and ear of Maecenas. I received a letter from him today, delivered before I went to meet you. I am to dine at his house tomorrow. He said I might bring one friend.'

Criton sat quite still, his face averted.

Curtius Rufus said, 'You do not understand. I need your help.' He paused and added in a low voice, 'I cannot manage without you.'

Criton looked at him.

He turned his head and smiled faintly, 'You see, I am not so self-reliant as you think.'

CHAPTER VII

Maecenas, as was his custom, dined always at the hour when the courts closed, and Curtius Rufus arrived ravenously hungry, anxious about the quality of the embroidered tunic he had bought hurriedly upon credit, and already regretting the cups of wine he had drunk in self-protection against the magnitude of the occasion.

Criton had no fears. Accustomed to the indifferent manners of the rich he relaxed under the politeness of his host and was able to enjoy the occasion with critical pleasure. He approved the gold and ivory that decorated the couches, the silver standards that held the torches, and the rose-tinted marble of the columns, but deplored the wall paintings, executed by an artist from Delos, who was generally esteemed for the subtle indelicacy of his works. He sniffed appreciatively as, in the warmth of the room, the scent from the stacked flowers mingled with the smell of pine from the braziers, but thought the execution of the flute players who performed while the first table was being served poor in the extreme. Seated with the secondary guests his main contribution to the conversation was a well-timed question whenever silence fell. He had long since learned that to be popular it was only necessary to encourage others to talk. Good listeners were always prized.

Verrius Flaccus, the court tutor, discoursed on education, but shook his head with a smile when questioned about the children under his care. 'They grow up,' he said cryptically.

Labienus, the orator, who had spoken with warmth and gentleness of a visit he had recently made to Rhodus, was less discreet. Asked his opinion of the first lady in Rome he said brusquely, 'She is a woman who seems to be permanently undergoing the change of life.'

Arruntius, a Palatine doctor who was reputed to earn a quarter of a million sesterces a year, plied Domitius with questions about missile wounds. Domitius, a centurion of the palace guard, who had served in only one minor campaign, answered with difficulty and was relieved when Maecenas' secretary intervened. 'Is it true that you recommend almonds as a prevention against getting drunk?'

Arruntius said cautiously, 'It has not been proved, though in certain cases—'

'There is more money in recommending the wines of Surrentum to invalids for their improving qualities,' said the centurion with a smile.

'Especially if you own half the vineyards there,' added Labienus maliciously.

Maecenas' secretary said smoothly, 'I will put you a question, Labienus. Which is the greater crime – to poison a man's body with noxious liquids, or his mind with evil words?'

Arruntius chuckled. 'I will reply when our orator has spoken.'

Verrius Flaccus said to Criton, 'You have a brother in Smyrna, I believe. Is it true that there is a new method of teaching in the schools?'

A plump young man, a jurist by profession, turned to Domitius with a grin. 'Let us return to Rome. Is that gossip about our new senator's wife really true?'

Domitius said cautiously, 'The sentry outside the house was not one of my men, but – yes, I think it may be. Certainly guard duty there is always popular. Tell me, that man at the table facing our host – is it really the charioteer's son? I should like to meet him.'

Curtius Rufus, cautiously eating shellfish, hardly noticed the flute players. He had already made the mistake of addressing his fellow diners as 'sir,' until Maecenas said gently, 'Dear boy, we are all friends here. Do not make us older than we feel.' He dreaded the moment when conversation would start for he knew that he had nothing to say that could be of the slightest interest to those around him. Facing him was his host, cool and amiable, outrageously dressed in scarlet silk and with a single pearl dangling from one ear. Next to him was the Lady Terentia, a slim, dark woman in a blue gown. She wore no ornaments except a gold bracelet on her left wrist, and was conversing in a low voice with her neighbor, Proculeius, a man with a thin face who was a close friend of Augustus. He was also a half-brother to Murena.

When the first table was removed Curtius Rufus noticed with growing embarrassment that everyone else, anticipating this, had taken their cups and were holding them up for more wine. Then, to his horror, he heard Maecenas speak and realized that a toast was about to be drunk. He moved and his leg touched his neighbor on his left. A cool voice said softly, 'Bring another cup,' and there was movement behind him, a slave knelt, and a fresh cup was in his hand.

Maecenas was still speaking. Curtius Rufus saw that all were looking at the guest of honor, on Maecenas' left, a brown-haired youth with a fleshy nose, a heavy chin, and a thin mouth that denied him good looks, save when he smiled. Now he was listening gravely to his host, eyes downcast, the cup in his hands quite still. Claudius Marcellus, nephew to Augustus, had the mannerisms already of one long trained to expect a lifetime of adulation.

'. . . to our new aedile, and may fortune smile upon his house and upon the Lady Julia.'

The guests drank, then Marcellus replied briefly; there was a pause when he had finished, and Maecenas said genially, 'Tonight we honor the Muses by our number. But first let us do justice to my chef. For here comes the second table. I can recommend the lobster, but for those who prefer meat there is bear with truffles.'

Proculeius said, 'No donkey? I was hoping to enlarge my experience.'

Maecenas smiled. 'Then try this wine. It bears the name of a good consul.'

There was laughter, conversation broke out, and Curtius Rufus stirred, trying to find a more comfortable position.

A voice said dryly in his ears, 'I am used to men who use a couch for amorous advances, but you, sir, are merely violent. If you kick me again, I shall have much to explain to my husband.'

Curtius Rufus turned, startled, to the girl on his left. In his embarrassment he was conscious of red hair and green eyes. Then he saw that she was smiling. He said, 'I am sorry. I have been clumsy. I have not dined so formally – for a long while. Forgive me.'

Her eyes widened slightly. 'I am relieved to hear it. I thought perhaps it was because you found me unattractive. I began to worry.'

He smiled. He said, 'I am in your debt also as regards the wine cup. This is not my world, as you have guessed.'

Her eyes danced. 'Well, I am good at riddles. You must tell me about your world. That is what good dinner parties are for, to meet old friends and make new ones; to meet all worlds, not just the same one, time after time. But let us introduce ourselves again. I have a bad memory for names.'

He said, 'I am Curtius Rufus.' He paused and added lightly, 'A man of no account.'

Her eyes widened again. 'I am Gallita and there, on the end of the couch to your right, talking to Julia, is my husband – Lucius Seius Strabo.'

Curtius Rufus said awkwardly, 'Yes – I recognized him – we have met before – on business.'

'You are a friend of Gaius?' she said casually.

117

He shook his head.

She looked puzzled. 'Of Terentia then?'

The dark-haired woman looked across the table. 'But, of course, Gallita, my love. Curtius is a coming man, as my husband will tell you. We expect great things of him.' She raised an eyebrow and there was a faint smile on her mouth.

Curtius Rufus said quickly, 'I fear I shall be a going man soon.'

'You are leaving Rome?' asked the girl.

'But you will return,' said Terentia gently. 'Your friends, old and new, will miss you.'

'I am going to the court of King Juba. It is an economic mission.'

Terentia said, 'You remember, Gallita, that nice boy with such beautiful manners? Even Octavia approved of him.'

Gallita laughed. 'That was praise indeed.' She saw that Terentia was still watching Curtius Rufus. She said rapidly, 'Terentia, have you seen those wonderful silks in that new shop in the Portico? Wildly expensive, but such beautiful colors. I am trying to persuade Lucius but he is so old-fashioned.'

'Yes, I have just bought some. The prices are outrageous, but so is the result. They would suit you. Show yourself to him in them. He will change his mind then fast enough.'

The Lady Julia, fair-haired, blue-eyed, and restless, said impatiently, 'Must I drink watered wine, Claudius; I am not a child now.'

'It might be best, Julitta. It is stronger than you think.'

'You sound like father. Gaius, doesn't he sound like father?'

Maecenas said gravely, 'I think that perhaps Claudius is right. See, I, too, am having mine watered. Let us be wise together, my dear.'

Marcellus said, 'I still think that statue of Cleopatra should be removed. To keep it there in the Temple of Venus is – is monstrous.'

118

Maecenas put down his cup. 'It is a very beautiful statue.'

Marcellus, his face flushed, said, 'But what has that to do with the matter? She was an enemy of Rome and – and a harlot besides.' He looked round the table. 'Surely, you must all agree on the principle?'

Proculeius wiped his mouth with a napkin. 'I always considered it a fine example of the Rhodian school.' He paused. 'But – oh, yes, I agree, naturally. I have often said so.'

Maecenas did not smile.

Seius glanced at his wife. 'And I agree, as everyone must; yet it is certainly attractive – as a work of sculpture, I mean.'

Terentia smiled. 'I have not been to that particular temple for some time, but I remember I found it difficult to imagine what *he* saw in her.'

Marcellus flushed.

Gallita dropped a piece of lobster shell delicately onto the floor. 'She used to look at it every time she was allowed out shopping in the Sacred Way. I used to see her there, poor child, standing in the shadows, quite still, as though she was praying. Perhaps she was.'

'Who?' asked Maecenas casually.

'Oh, Selene – before she married young Juba. It was quite natural, I suppose. I thought the resemblance between them remarkable.'

Proculeius said, 'She would have been just about her mother's age. It was executed when her mother was still very young.'

Marcellus said, 'Did you report the matter? I am sure that my mother never realized – You see! If that is not a harmful influence, what is?'

'Have some more wine?' Maecenas nodded to the waiting slave. 'Selene is young and is now safe in Mauretania under her husband's care and protection. Yes, Gallita told Seius and he told me.'

The tribune's clenched hand relaxed slowly and Curtius Rufus

119

heard a quick intake of breath beside him. Maecenas' eyes were fixed steadily on Marcellus' face. 'As for the statue, that has been a matter for the Senate, dear boy, and for Augustus, any time these past few years.' He paused, and his eyes were half closed. He said, 'I saw her once. The statue is very like.'

There was a hush of attention, for he spoke of a world that had vanished beneath the splash of Agrippa's oars in a quiet bay where the wind blew at noon from the northwest onto a sandy shore.

He said, 'Discuss it with your uncle, dear boy. It touches him most.'

Julia giggled. 'Can we play knucklebones later? I adore games of hazard.' She glanced sideways at her husband. 'Father prefers people to gamble after dinner – and then only for money.'

Terentia smiled. 'And so you shall tonight if you wish, my dear. Fortune always favors the newly married, so we will resign ourselves to losing.'

Marcellus smiled back while Maecenas waved to the steward to set the third table before them.

Seius turned to Curtius Rufus. 'I believe you know something of horses. Can you advise me?'

Curtius Rufus said cautiously, 'I know a horse breeder outside Apuleia. He has a fine strain developed from Libyan thorough-breds he imported several years ago. You could not do better than go to him.'

Gallita said, 'Perhaps you can forecast whether Sabinus will win again at the next games with those chestnuts of his. He's absolutely marvelous, but I hate it when he drives for the Reds, don't you?'

He smiled. 'I have no views on the factions.'

'But you must, you must. It is no fun otherwise.'

He said lamely, 'No, really. I have no preference. I try to back only the team that will win. It's hard enough to do even that.'

*

Dinner had been cleared away, the Syrian tumblers had been applauded, and the conversation flowed easily.

Maecenas, his olive wreath giving him a curious dignity, said out loud, 'I have a special entertainment which I have kept as a surprise. Afterwards we will play hazard at the Lady Julia's request. But first let us rearrange ourselves.'

Terentia raised her eyebrows. 'Do you wish us to retire?'

'No, my love, not unless you are tired. There is something for everyone. Will you move to the right so that Curtius Rufus may take your place next to mine. Gallita, my dear, I offer you Caius Proculeius as a hostage. Be kind to him.' To Marcellus he said, 'You must try this Mamertine; your drinking it will be recommendation enough. No, Gallita, I do not water the bushes in my garden with wine. You must not believe all the malicious stories you hear about me. Yes, Seius, it is quite true that I do invent tales about myself. It is the only way I can be sure that at least some of them are amusing.'

Curtius Rufus said diffidently, 'We met at the baths, I think?'

Maecenas said, 'Quite right, dear boy. I visit Rome as seldom as I can, but even I go there occasionally. I had a very dear friend with me. You were kind enough to speak to him in his own language. Now, to business for a moment. If you wish information about Juba, see Lucius Melissius, who works in the library in the Censor's Office. They were friends. For information on Selene, visit the Lady Octavia. I will arrange it for you; but do not mention a word of Gallita's story to her. That has come as a shock to all of us tonight. Valerius Messalla will wish to see you to discuss his niece. He has a cameo that he will give you. It is a good likeness. You will need to take presents – expensive ones. There is a jeweler's shop on the Sacred Way, next door to that of Obelius, who is an exquisite worker in gold. They have been advised of your coming, and the state will pay. The Mauretanian court has an official envoy here. He has a small

121

office in the Forum just behind the Rostra. He is a pleasant and helpful man, but a good liar. Do not believe all he tells you. If you wish further information visit Julius Hyginus, the Palatine librarian. He is from Hispania and once traveled in western Mauretania as far south as the Atlas mountains. He will supply you with maps. If there is anything else do not hesitate to come and see me. Now, have some more wine.'

Curtius Rufus said slowly, 'You are very kind.'

Maecenas said somberly, 'No, I am not kind at all. It is a luxury that few in my position can afford. The only people who will cry at my death will be those to whom I shall leave no single coin.'

Curtius Rufus said, 'I may not suceed.'

'You must. There is a small wind blowing that may turn into a great gale that will sweep us to the ground. I sit too high on the tree and I can feel it already.'

Curtius Rufus nodded. He sipped his wine cautiously. He did not know what to say.

Terentia turned to him, her face so close that he could smell the perfume she wore. 'You see how we depend on you. You may be sure that we shall be grateful.' He thought for a moment that her eyes held more than one promise. He could not be certain. Already he was a little drunk.

Maecenas clapped his hands, the steward gestured, a curtain trembled, and a flute sounded softly in the distance.

He had seen it before when he had taken Pero to the theater and she had been enthralled, her eyes never leaving the stage. It was the old story of Paris, the shepherd boy who was a prince, and the three goddesses who asked him to judge which was the most beautiful among them. In the theater there had been an attempt by the professional company to maintain a degree of dignity in the mime and the dance as befitted the narration of an ancient and hallowed legend. The music had sounded sad and noble by turns, and the performers had sketched a light characterization only, thus creating a sense of style by which they could seem to represent ideas rather than recognizable gods and humans. This production, however, was very different. It did, as Maecenas had said, contain something for everyone.

There was no scenery, it would have been superfluous, for the performers were professionals. The actor playing Paris was beautiful without being effeminate and drew murmurs of admiration from the ladies present. Wearing a golden tiara and an animal's skin he conjured up Mount Ida, his flock of goats, and the charm of his innocence by mime alone. But the music changed and the dance became languorous and sultry, hinting at hidden yearnings and desires that even he could not wholly comprehend. Mercury was a slim, fair-haired boy and Maecenas watched him greedily. Juno, carrying a scepter, had a mature charm that reminded Curtius Rufus forcibly of the woman who lay on his right. Minerva, goddess of wisdom, wearing a bright helmet, was dark and had fine eyes. The actress playing her gave her beauty a touch of dominance that made Proculeius think of a certain lady he knew who offered curious services in a small house below the Aventine. Then Venus entered. She was a tall, dark girl with a white skin that looked like ivory in the candle-light, and she was naked, save for a gold torque round her neck and a transparent blue silk pallium tight against her hips.

Juno, dancing with Castor and Pollux, offered sovereignty over the East with herself as queen-consort; Marcellus' face was beaded with sweat, while Julia smiled in contentment. Minerva, escorted by half-naked boys, danced a dance of strange rhythmic steps that offered wisdom in exchange for something more sinister, as the boys writhed in subjection about her. Gallita watched fascinated, while a pulse beat strongly in Proculeius' cheek. Last of all, Venus entered alone; a drum beat rhythmically in the background and she danced, inviting not Paris but the entire audience. It was a dance of promise, but it was not Helen she offered but herself. Sometimes she undulated her body,

123

shaking her hips and her breasts – Curtius Rufus guessed that she came from Gades. At other time she seemed scarcely to move at all, only the muscles on her body rippled, and again there were moments when she stood quite still, hands clasped in front of her, dancing only with her eyes. Paris offered her the golden apple, Juno and Minerva danced scorn and anger and rage, and Venus, triumphant, smiling, and seductive, beckoned with her eyes and led the shepherd boy through the darkness of a curtain as the flutes died away into silence.

For a moment no one spoke and then the guests applauded. Maecenas smiled, 'Well?'

Marcellus said thickly, 'If I were not a married man I would give a hundred thousand sesterces for that girl.'

'But you are, my love,' said a cool voice by his side.

Terentia said thoughtfully, 'She has a face not even a woman could criticize. Her dancing – and I know something about that – is excellent, if not in the best of taste. I preferred the Paris.'

Gallita shook her head. 'I do not think taste has much to do with it. She danced to entertain the men – not us.'

Maecenas emptied his cup. 'Did you like her?' he said to Curtius Rufus in a low voice.

Curtius Rufus blinked. 'Yes,' he said.

CHAPTER VIII

Criton paused to wipe the sweat from his face. 'What is the hurry? Why walk so fast?'

'It is late,' said Curtius Rufus. 'We have an appointment.' He paused to allow a water carrier to step off the pavement at the crossing and then strode on. Criton found his way blocked by a plump woman, whose expensive gown did nothing for her except display to the world that she was fat and rich. Standing on the pavement, she was examining a length of dyed cotton and complaining bitterly at the price. The shopkeeper stood by, saying nothing. He knew, as did the slave who accompanied her, that she would pay in the end for the privilege of being able to boast to her friends how exquisite the material was and how much it had cost her. Criton caught up with his friend and said breathlessly, 'But where are we going?'

'To meet the officers who will assist us.'

'Did you enjoy last night?'

'No.'

'But why? What was wrong?'

Curtius Rufus said savagely, 'I dislike being patronized by those whose only charm is their money.'

'You are being unfair and you know it.'

'Perhaps I am. Oh, yes, they were very kind in their well-bred way; but conversation was impossible. We had nothing in common. Maecenas I liked. He thought them as foolish as I did.'

Criton said gently, 'It was because that tribune was there. You are always like this when you remember you were once in the centurionate.'

Curtius Rufus did not answer. He stopped and sniffed, looking in the doorway of a perfume shop. 'I must buy Pero a present before I leave.' He turned his head to watch a girl walking along the far side of the road. 'She tried to eat me. I was terrified.'

Criton said, puzzled, 'Who? That girl?'

'No, I mean the Lady Terentia.'

'I don't believe it.'

'She told me she had heard I was a good tutor. She knew the story.'

'Did he hear?'

'Maecenas? No, he was listening to Marcellus talking about his theories of government, and too busy trying not to laugh to notice.'

Criton shook his head in bewilderment. There was a crowd ahead, blocking the street, and they were forced to slow down.

'What is it? A fight?'

'No, I think it's some of the aedile's staff raiding that cookshop on the corner. The man who owns it is a fool. I told him once that he was bound to get caught if he allowed his clients to gamble in daylight. Let's slip down this alley here. It will be quicker.'

They emerged on the Sacred Way by the jeweler's shop that Maecenas had recommended, paused to make way for a crowd of professional mourners in their long, buttoned black cloaks, and joined the throng walking down the incline to the Curia. Criton stopped to speak to one man who greeted him, and nodded to another who waved his hand in passing. He said happily, 'I like it here. There is such atmosphere. You are at the center of the world and something exciting is bound to happen.'

'Does it?'

'Not always.'

Curtius Rufus grinned, paused, and stepped suddenly to one side. The crowd had parted to make way for the praetor, who, preceded by his lictors, was walking gravely up the center of the road. The praetor paused to exchange a greeting with an elderly man in a chair; the crowd's murmurs grew suddenly quieter still, then silence fell. The praetor looked up quickly and stopped speaking in midsentence. A woman wearing a mantle of white wool and carrying a pitcher on her head was coming down the Sacred Way, followed by an attendant. She walked slowly, with immense dignity, and her unpainted, middle-aged face, smooth like a child's, had a curious quality of calm. The crowd who lined the Way stood absolutely still as she passed. Opposite the praetor she turned to the left, the lictors lowered their axes, the praetor inclined his head, and she nodded in answer to his salutation. She continued her way along the passage that led past the Regia, the official residence of the Pontifex Maximus, and disappeared from sight. Beyond stood the Temple of Vesta.

The crowd moved again. Curtius Rufus said thoughtfully, 'It is a long walk from the Camenae Fountain outside the Capena Gate. They do it every day, I believe.'

'Yes, I have never seen them before.'

'Nor I. I always envied the people who could spend their morning idling in the Forum. Now, when I am here, we have business to attend to.'

The steps of the Basilica Aemilia were crowded with businessmen. They pushed their way through a group discussing a banker's draft, held unrolled under the chin of a slave; stepped round a couple who were witnessing the signing of a friend's will; and Curtius Rufus eyed with interest a fashionably dressed girl who had her hand on a young man's arm.

'Lovers,' said Criton with a sigh.

'Yes, at a price, which she is now settling. She comes from the Campus Martius, though from the way she speaks you might think she lived on the Aventine.'

'You know her?'

Curtius Rufus laughed. 'I know of her. You may buy it straight for two gold pieces, or have it made more interesting for ten.'

'I do not have to pay for my pleasures,' said Criton primly. 'I am wanted for myself.'

'No doubt. Which is why you avoid those pretty Alexandrian boys you so often sigh after.'

'I do not sigh after them. They rob with one hand while they play with the other. But they are amusing, Curtius.'

'I will take your word for it.'

At the foot of the steps leading to the Basilica Julia two officials of the courts were standing behind a long ash spear with a silver gilt head, held upright by a wooden block into which the butt was sunk. On the higher steps stood groups of litigants in consultation with their lawyers. Criton's face went pale at the sight of the spear. 'I had forgotten – for a moment. I used to meet him here and wait on him when the court was in session. I cannot believe he is dead.'

'The court still meets and you are alive. That is all that is important.'

A voice said from the steps in a loud voice, 'He is still talking and has used five clocks.'

Another voice said derisively, 'Yes – and still declaiming the history of the war with Carthage. What has that to do with the fraudulent sale of my friend's house?' There was a roar of laughter and Criton shook his head. 'They don't understand oratory,' he said disdainfully.

Curtius Rufus grinned. 'Oh, yes, they do. The longer a man talks the greater his price.' He shouldered his way through a group of slaves waiting for their masters and started to cross the Forum. Even in the thin sunlight of winter the marble of the statues, the columns, the temples, and the basilicae blazed, a mass of white that dazzled the eye.

Facing the Curia, where the Senate met in full session during the summer months, stood three trees, a fig, an olive, and a vine. Together on the pavement in what little shade they provided sat four men, playing backgammon. They were so intent on their play that they did not notice the two men in the uniform of the

Praetorian Guard who stood behind them. The elder, a burly man with a cleft chin and pale blue eyes, tapped one on the shoulder with his centurion's staff. 'If you must, at least don't cheat on your friends.' He turned to say something to his colleague, a younger man with fair hair, saw Curtius Rufus coming toward him, and whistled under his breath. 'Just our luck,' he said savagely. 'A freedman and his oily boyfriend. And we must take orders from them. Which is which, I wonder. Perhaps they don't know themselves.'

Curtius Rufus stopped, looked from one face to the other, and then grinned. 'My credentials,' he said politely.

The centurion took the folded parchment, examined it carefully, sighed, handed it back, and then saluted slowly, his eyes contemptuous. At the casualness of the gesture Criton, ill at ease, bit his lip.

Curtius Rufus smiled pleasantly. 'Perhaps you will introduce yourselves. You know me – or think you do. This is my secretary, Criton. He is also a friend.'

The younger soldier nodded, his face expressionless. 'Of course.'

The centurion said in a growl, 'I am Marcus Pedius of the Second Cohort, stationed in the Campus Viminalis, outside the gate. This is Vatinus, optio of the Third, stationed in the Campus Esquilinus. He will be in charge of transport. The escort optio, Attius, is at the headquarters of the Fifth on the Janiculum.' He paused and looked round at the crowds. 'We cannot talk here. Have you an office?'

'No.'

'I see. I am billeted in a house near the Marcian Aqueduct. It is hardly convenient. Perhaps at your house?' He looked inquiringly from Curtius Rufus to Criton.

'No.' Curtius Rufus frowned. The two soldiers waited patiently. There was silence. The optio shifted his feet while the centurion whistled under his breath.

Curtius Rufus looked at Vatinus. 'Have you any ideas? We cannot stand here all day.'

The optio shrugged. 'None,' he said in an indifferent voice.

'I can see that you are going to be a great help to me.'

The centurion's eyes flickered but he said nothing.

Curtius Rufus grinned. 'I should have asked for an office. I did not think of it. But I will. Meanwhile, let us go to a wineshop. I know of one near here which is quiet. There at least we can make a start.'

Marcus Pedius said, 'I do not drink on duty.'

Curtius Rufus said, 'I never knew a praetorian who did not drink. Duty or no duty, you are going to drink now. It will at least help us to know each other better.'

'It is against regulations.'

'But not against mine.' Curtius Rufus tapped the parchment in his hand. 'This will protect you, if you are afraid.' He turned without waiting for a reply and said cheerfully, 'I know of an empty shop near that disused necropolis just up the Sacred Way. We can use that.'

The centurion stared.

The optio said, 'You mean the brothel?'

'Yes.'

'But, the landlord has a lease,' said the centurion, following slowly. 'It's used by—' He broke off suddenly.

'Everyone,' said the optio thoughtlessly. He added hastily, 'The prices – it is expensive – the rich—'

'We shall have it closed. Four of the girls are not registered. That is against the law. It opens each day before the eleventh hour. That is also against the law. Either he closes it or he goes before the magistrates. I think he will close it. He can have it back afterwards. We shall only need the house for ten days.'

Marcus Pedius said, 'We shall be in trouble.'

Criton said in anguish, 'Curtius, the clients will complain. Some of them are most influential.'

'Let them. The College of Vesta will be on our side. They have complained also.'

Criton said, 'We may have the gods on our side, but I need a drink.'

The centurion glanced sideways at Vatinus who was gazing in fascination at the figure in front of them. He said suddenly, 'You know, I think that's a good idea after all.'

The oil lamp flickered as Curtius Rufus turned the tablet in his hands and smoothed over what he had written with an impatient gesture. Criton, busy checking figures, did not notice. 'Fifty-three pints of oil and one hundred and forty wine rations for three days – that is, let me see – eight hundred and forty pints – that makes a total weight of one five six two pounds. Curtius, it's right. We can definitely get all the food and drink supplies into two large freight wagons.'

Curtius Rufus yawned. 'Well, I still make it forty-nine civilians, if we include those ten camel drivers.'

'You have forgotten my two clerks.'

'That only makes it fifty-one.'

'Let me look.' Criton clicked his teeth. 'I thought so. You need four slaves, not two. You cannot expect the water carrier to do the bath attendant's work.'

'Why not?'

'It is not customary,' said Criton reprovingly. 'And you've omitted the wheelwright, the blacksmith, and the veterinary.'

'Vatinus is responsible for recruiting them when we reach Africa.'

'True, but they must be on the list. Ah! Here's the mistake – seven craftsmen, not five. Again you have forgotten the wall-painter and – and – that mosaic worker. That makes the total correct – sixty, excluding the women.'

The door opened and the centurion entered. He said wearily, 'It is after trumpet call. Do you never sleep?'

131

'Never, when I am alone. What is your news?'

'I have organized the escort, taking ten men from each of five cohorts. Vatinus tells me the majority of the equipment is ready and stacked in the Campus Viminalis. We are still short on medical supplies, tents, cooking gear, olive oil, salt, lard, candles, and water jars. One mule is lame – it was kicked – two of the wagons need repair, one medical orderly has not yet arrived, and the chests to hold the jewelry and presents are still being made. Otherwise everything is fine.'

Curtius Rufus tried not to laugh. 'When can we move?'

'Vatinus will start for Misenum the day after tomorrow, taking one section as escort for the sixteen wagons. Attius will follow with the five cavalrymen, nine horses, and forty-eight mules. They will embark on arrival. I have sent a messenger ahead to see that the port authorities have suitable gangways for getting the animals on board the transports.' Marcus Pedius paused and then said quietly, 'And you?'

'I have maps, information, and four of the seven craftsmen that I need. I had six this afternoon, but two of them changed their minds. I have an engineer from the Highways Department and also a surveyor on loan from the Public Works. But no architect. The man I had in mind has turned out to be ill.'

The centurion snorted his disbelief.

'No, it is genuine. I have had a letter from Maecenas and tomorrow we shall add four women to our party.'

'Women!'

'Yes.' Curtius Rufus smiled and then shook his head. 'Not for me, my friend. I choose my own. I am taking a girl as a diplomatic present – possibly for King Juba – who knows? Criton and I have searched the slave markets but without success. It is a bad time of year.' He paused and looked at the centurion. 'So I spoke to Maecenas and he has helped in this as in so many matters. The girl will have two companions and an elderly woman will be in charge.'

He twisted the silver bangle on his wrist – he had bought it that morning and was not yet used to it – and said steadily, 'When we commence our journey there is to be a sentry on duty outside their sleeping quarters each night between dusk and dawn. He is to admit no one except in the case of sickness.'

Marcus Pedius narrowed his eyes. 'I will see that it is done and your instructions obeyed. You include yourself? I ask only that all may be clear.'

Curtius Rufus picked up a pen. He said in a low voice, 'I include all officers and all in this room. You see, the girl is very beautiful.'

She had been standing by the window, looking out at the crowds in the street below, but she turned as he came in and inclined her head respectfully before moving aside. She wore a white gown with jeweled clasps on the shoulders and a silver chain around her waist. Her hair was drawn back tightly and held by a white ribbon, her only jewelry the pearl drop earrings he had chosen himself the previous day. Her lips had been darkened and her eyelids painted green, yet her face seemed colorless for there was no expression in her eyes. On the floor by her side stood a wickerwork birdcage.

He sat down on a stool and watched her. She stood motionless, her hands clasped lightly together, waiting for him to speak, but he did not know what to say. He knew, from what his father had told him, that the change of ownership was always an unsettling time for a slave, however experienced. Even those born in slavery required time to adjust. Their health was guaranteed – it was always cheaper, he knew, to feed and clothe a slave well than to buy a new one – but their culture, their education, and their personal contentment were in the hands of their master, as were their hopes of a constructive future: money and freedom. In return he put himself, as did all men who owned

133

slaves, in the hands of his servants. Their loyalty might be earned; it could not be purchased.

She broke the silence first. 'I am Urracca,' she said in a voice devoid of all expression. Still he did not speak. It was eight nights since he had seen her but her face was not that of a stranger. She had never once been out of his thoughts, and had he possessed the skill he could have drawn her likeness from memory, as he could never have drawn that of the girl to whom he had once given a child.

She said coolly, as though to an equal, 'I have seen you before. I do not know where. I am sorry.'

He moistened his lips. He said, 'Where do you come from?'

'From the house of Maecenas.'

'No, before that.'

'The slave market.'

'Where were you born?'

She widened her eyes. 'In Hispania,' she said in a low voice.

'Near Gades?'

She shook her head. 'Everyone thinks that – because I dance. But I did not know how to dance, once.' She paused. She said, 'I learned to do that later.'

'Later?'

'After I was taken in the fighting.' She dropped her eyes and looked at the floor. 'I never wished to dance.'

He said, 'You do it very well. As though you were born to it.'

'No,' she said. 'I was a princess.'

He grinned. 'Of course you were. We are all kings and queens the further we get from our own lands.'

Her eyes flickered but she did not answer back.

He stood up. He said, 'We are going on a long journey to Africa. We leave tomorrow. You will have two girls as companions. And the woman who was here when you arrived will be in charge of you.'

She said, 'May I ask a question?'

134

'Yes.'

'To whom do I belong? Are you the steward?'

'You belong to me. My name is Curtius Rufus,' he said brusquely.

She looked astonished. 'I am sorry. I did not know. You see, Maecenas' steward said I would not be sold.'

He said, irritated, 'Nor have you been. You have been given to me as a present. Your master is a generous man. I saw you dance at his house.'

She gave him a speculative look and then dropped her eyes. 'I understand.' He knew then from the tone of her voice that she was smiling. He looked round the room. 'It is not very comfortable, but it is only for one night.' He saw the birdcage then. 'Is that yours?'

'Yes, I brought it with me. May I keep it?'

'If you wish.' He paused. 'But you have no bird.'

She opened her hands a little and he saw the green head and the yellow beak of a tiny bird between her fingers.

'Be careful. The window is open. You may lose it.'

She said, 'When you came in I was thinking of letting it go free.' She smiled slightly. 'But if I did that would be cruel. It is used to being watered and fed. The wild birds would mob it and it would soon die. It is safer in a cage. That is where it was hatched.'

He nodded. 'You are probably right. I know nothing of birds. Does it sing?'

'Yes, indeed.' Her voice was husky. 'All birds in cages learn to sing. Some do it very well.' Her eyes were amused. 'You do not mind? I hope.'

'If I do I will tell you.' He walked toward her and then stopped. He put his hands behind his back and said, 'You have not asked what your duties are in my household. Aren't you curious?'

A faint smile showed on her face. 'I am your slave.' She bent

135

down gracefully and returned the bird to its cage. Then she stood up and looked at him. 'And you are my master. You will tell me when you wish to tell me.'

He said, 'Are you always so polite, so – so malleable?'

'When I am asked, then I dance.' She paused. She said delicately, 'I know my place.'

He was angry now. He grinned. He said, 'I will rest your mind on one point. Your place is not my bed.' He turned and left the room, the door quivering against the frame with the force of his departure.

Urracca smiled.

They met in the small square near the Capena Gate, where there was always a gathering of coaches and litter bearers waiting to pick up travelers entering or leaving the city. While he waited for her Curtius Rufus looked at the line of wagons that would be loaded at sunset for their night's work, and listened idly to the gossip of the drivers.

Pero came at last, but from the direction he least expected, and they held hands a moment and laughed before falling into step and pacing side by side, suddenly shy and not sure of what to say.

He glanced sideways. 'You hair is wet.'

'I know. I came early and went out through the gate to look at the tombs. There was a juggler by the roadside and I forgot the time. I went under the water arch before I realized.' She laughed softly. 'It is overfull today and everyone was cursing. The road was flooded. Look, I got my feet wet.' She touched her hair. 'It will soon dry and I so wanted it to look nice.'

'It does.'

'You are a liar.'

He grinned. 'What would you like to do? We have eight hours. I must be at the cohort camp by midnight. We leave at first light.'

Pero said sadly, 'Only six hours then. I cannot be so late. I am sorry.' She bit her lip. 'We must not waste our time.'

'I don't intend to. Well, then?'

'It is a lovely day. We could walk in the park on the Esquiline but it is too near home.'

'Then let us walk on the Aventine instead and look at all the fine houses of the rich. You may choose which one I shall buy. Afterwards we can go down into the city and find a wineshop and talk. And afterwards—'

'Afterwards it will be very late.' She looked at him gravely. 'It sounds a fine program, but the wineshop will have to be respectable. You look so different now.'

'That is because I cut my hair. Criton insisted.'

She said critically, 'I prefer it long. You look much nicer.'

'It will grow again.' He smiled. 'Unfortunately I feel just the same.'

She smiled faintly and then frowned.

They strolled slowly in the winter sunlight, past the Circus and up the slopes of the hill, through quiet roads where the few houses stood back behind high walls and the only passersby they met were liveried slaves, jog-trotting down the road, bearing a message from one family to another. Once a litter swept by and the sun shone on the oiled backs of the pole-bearers while a plump face looked out indifferently from behind scarlet curtains; a dog barked behind a blue painted wall, and an elderly door-keeper watched them pass, assessed their value and position to the last coin, and then spat contemptuously.

They chose first one house and then another and presently came to the crest where the hillside dropped to the river and, in an open space no one had yet built upon, they could watch the Tiber and see Janiculum and the open country beyond. A string of barges came down from the sea, and they watched the horses towing them along the bank. Beside them the head of a river god grinned from a gray wall and a stream of liquid sprang from his mouth and fell lazily into a basin.

'I would like to live here,' he said. 'It is quiet and you can smell the air, not dirty bodies and cheap food cooking in the next room.'

Pero glanced at him sharply. 'Where exactly do you live?'

He pointed. 'Down there, beyond the granaries, in a tenement where the roof leaks after every storm and in a high wind all the doors fidget like gossipy women.' He paused. He said savagely, 'You would hate to live there after the Esquiline.'

She ignored the remark. She said, 'Are you worried?'

'Yes. I want to get out of there. And I'm afraid that I never shall.'

'Curtius.' She touched his arm. 'Don't worry so. I heard my Lady talking to Maecenas yesterday about you. They're quite certain you'll succeed.'

They walked on, descended the hill, and strolled back past the Circus, along the New Way behind the now almost empty Forum and then on through Fountain Gate toward the Temple of Isis, where, in the late afternoon, the rich who were not respectable gathered to gossip about themselves and their friends. He pointed out the actress who was now living with the tribune of the Third cohort, identified an elderly man with white hair and the manners of a senator as the owner of the largest pleasure house in the Tuscan quarter, named a young man whose profile might have been modeled by Praxiteles as a fortune-hunter who had already tried to run off with three heiresses. 'And you see that man there. He comes here to escape his wife. His only pleasure is in being rude to his friends, who are too polite to answer back. I once worked for him. If he praises you it is only because he dislikes someone else the more.'

Pero said amused, 'You know everyone.'

He shook his head. 'I only repeat the gossip. It amuses me.'

She smiled.

He looked at the Temple. 'Do you come here with the Lady Terentia?'

'Oh, yes, often. Inside we are all the same.' She hesitated. Then she said shyly, 'I have asked if I may come tomorrow. I will pray that you have a safe journey.'

He did not answer and they walked on, turning back to Tuscan Street, now crowded with late shoppers, men who lived alone, and harassed women with children at their skirts. 'This is where I come shopping,' he said, waving his hand at the fruiterers and fishmongers who nodded as he passed. They stopped at a pet shop to look at the caged birds, sniffed a heady mixture of perfumes and frankincense, fingered a bale of diaphanous silk from Tyre, and paused at a bookshop. Pero said in awe, 'Can you read?' and fell silent when he said, 'Yes.' And all the while, despite the noise and bustle and the girl's happy face, the sickness he had lived with since morning grew and grew. It was the old feeling, a sickness that was compounded of fear and uncertainty. He tried to pretend that there was nothing wrong, but the feeling grew until it engulfed him and his hands trembled and his skin felt cold with sweat.

In a quiet wineshop he drank with a shaking hand and then left the room in a hurry.

When he returned Pero said, pretending not to notice, 'You have been fortunate. I am so glad.'

He nodded, not knowing what to say.

She said, 'You will be away a long time. I shall miss you.'

'Yes,' he said. 'And I will miss you, Pero.'

She almost laughed then. 'You tell lies so very badly. You will be too busy to miss anyone. You have work to do; you will be traveling, which is what you most enjoy, as well as meeting people all the time. And you will have your slaves to amuse you in the evenings.' She smiled brightly as she spoke.

He said, 'What do you know about my slaves?'

'I know about Urracca. The steward told me.' Pero looked

139

down at the cup in her hand. She said, 'It is getting dark. We have not much time. I know you and I know Urracca. There is nothing more to say.'

There was a long silence between them. Then she said quietly, 'I hate Urracca. I know why she is going and I am glad she will not be coming back.'

He said, 'I have a present for you.'

Pero opened the parcel carefully with shaking fingers. Her face was all the reward he could have wished for. She picked up the bracelet and said in an awed voice, 'Is it really gold? Is it really for me?'

'Yes,' he said. 'It is for you.'

'Thank you.' She leaned back in her seat and looked at him. 'Why did you buy it for me?'

He did not answer.

They held hands across the table. He said, 'I feel sick.'

She shook her head. 'You mustn't feel like that. You'll be all right.'

He ran his tongue across his lips. 'I meant to suggest going somewhere else. But I don't think—'

She tightened her grip. 'I understand. I don't want to go either. This afternoon I did. Curtius, I wanted you then. Oh, so very badly.' She tried to smile, and failed.

He stared at the wet table. He knew then what was coming and now that the moment had come, that he had dreaded all afternoon, did not know what to say. He had faced it before with other girls and there had been little problem. An easy grin, a flashing smile, and the glib phrases practiced over the years, all had eased the way. He had a great talent: he knew how to escape without causing pain, but the talent was to fail him now.

She loosened her hand and put the bracelet on her wrist. She said in a low voice, 'What will happen, Curtius, when you come back?'

He did not answer her. To his horror he found that he could not lie. And for him this was a new experience.

She said slowly, 'If – if you are successful it will mean a new start for you, a new job – perhaps a good one; money too. I have been thinking – you will be able to marry. You can have someone better than me.'

'Don't be silly, Pero.'

'I'm not.'

'Suppose I fail?'

'Then you will not care.' She paused and dropped her eyes, watching his hands move restlessly upon the table. 'There will be other girls. The steward was right. For you there will always be other girls. I don't want to live in that tenement, having your babies, waiting each night for you to come home drunk, your money all lost on the dice, and no food and the rest owing.'

'You would rather stay on the Esquiline?'

'Yes, Curtius, I would rather stay there.'

He tried to smile. He said, 'I don't know what to say. This this isn't how we should end – quarreling.'

Pero looked at him, her face white and set. She had not cried when Agrippa questioned her and she did not do so now. 'It had to be said, Curtius. We could not go on pretending.'

'At least wish me luck.' He put out his hand and then checked himself.

She blinked and put her hand to her cheek. 'Of course. You sail at a bad time of the year. I will – I will still offer that prayer for your safety.'

'And I for yours.'

They left the wineshop then and walked back through the narrow streets, slippery with rain, but they did not hold hands and they did not talk on the way. When they reached the side door of the great house on the Esquiline she paused and put back her hood. He turned his head and said, 'Write to me of Rome and yourself. The clerk at the—'

'I do not know how to write.' The door opened and she slipped inside and was gone. He stood there, his hair wet, staring at the closed door, wondering what had gone wrong between them, wondering too how much he was to blame. Then he turned and walked away into the darkness toward the gate and the camp. It was still raining when he reached the camp. It went on raining. It rained all night.

PART TWO: AFRICA

CHAPTER IX

They walked through the streets of Carthage in silence, dazzled a little by the light, the hard blue of the sky, and the white walls of the shabby shops and even shabbier houses that crowded about them. The streets were full: children begged for coins at every corner, women sat in doorways, suckling their squalling babies, shopkeepers cried their wares from under the shade of awnings, and donkeys loaded with panniers of fruit and vegetables picked their way through the refuse that lay beneath every window. At times the street widened a little and Roman-style houses could be seen in the distance, covering the slopes of Byrsa Hill. Then would come open spaces upon which no one had built in years, great areas of rough ground covered with coarse grass, and then the streets would start again as suddenly as they had stopped. Once they glimpsed the aqueduct that carried water to the city's eighteen cisterns from Ziqua in the south, and at the familiar sight Curtius Rufus cheered up a little. He heard traders speaking in Greek when they passed through the great market and had their first sight of camels squatting by a wall on the far side, while light-skinned men with blue eyes and brown hair, wearing a strange dress, unloaded the bales and spoke to each other in a dialect he did not know. Then they were ascending the hill and the worst of the noise was behind them, except for the bawling of dogs that roamed the open spaces in search of food.

Ahead was the palace and he strode toward it impatiently, slowing a little as he crossed a forecourt that was strangely empty. Outside, he paused a moment, wiped his face with a handkerchief, and glanced at Marcus Pedius, who raised an eyebrow inquiringly. 'Wait here,' he said. 'I will soon find out what has gone wrong.' The centurion grunted but said nothing.

Inside the palace Curtius Rufus said in exasperation, 'No, I was told the governor would be here.' He glanced round the bleak anteroom, staring helplessly through the curtained doorway at the smooth rose-colored marble columns beyond, and noticed the fine dust that covered the mosaic of the inner court. The official residence of the Proconsul of Africa had the forlorn appearance of a Roman house in summer when the family had moved out to their country estate, leaving behind them only a handful of servants.

The secretary, who had met him, said apologetically, 'I am sorry, sir, but you have come at an awkward time. We have only a small staff here, enough to carry on the day-to-day business: no more.'

'But why?'

'Sir, there has been much trouble in the mountains with the Musulamii. Normally, governor comes north in winter to join his lady, but this year, alas, he has had to take command in the field.' He spoke almost fluent Latin but with traces of an accent that Curtius Rufus could not identify.

'Where are they stationed?' Curtius Rufus asked. He was dazed from lack of sleep, and was beginning to be aware that anxiety, his principal feeling since accepting the appointment, was the most exhausting emotion of all.

'At Ammaedara, sir.'

'A seven-day journey by carriage.'

The secretary smiled. 'A little longer, sir. There are no paved roads such as you are accustomed to.'

Curtius Rufus rubbed irritably at his unshaven chin. 'I shall have to see him. Who is in charge?'

'Sir, the Procurator. But he has had to go to Thabraca on business. A taxation dispute. He sailed yesterday.'

'Well, can you arrange transport and an escort?'

'I can try. The governor has all available horses.' He rubbed his ear. 'Garrison here is very small.'

'Is there no duty cohort?'

'It was moved south on governor's orders.'

Curtius Rufus said politely, 'Never mind. I will arrange transport for myself. Meanwhile, I need lodgings for my staff and escort. I have a secretary, two officers, four women, forty-five civilians, and fifty-nine soldiers.'

The secretary began to look worried. He said, 'I have no authority to open the residence and there is little room elsewhere. The town is crowded.' He added apologetically, 'It is a festival, you see.'

Curtius Rufus said, 'I am sorry, I don't see. My men have spent half a day unloading. They cannot stand on the quayside all night. Did no one get the letters that were sent from Rome? My transport officer, who came on ahead, tells me he left messages. He has been sleeping in the empty granaries in the harbor area for two days.'

The secretary smiled and spread out his hands as though a gesture could explain all. 'I am sorry, sir. I was away ill – the doctor – my stomach.' He looked down as though to reassure himself that he was still whole. 'Ah, an excellent idea to sleep in the granaries. No one will mind so long as you are careful not to start fires.'

Curtius Rufus said carefully, 'That is unlikely. There is no one I wish to roast at the moment. I thank you for the offer. It will be much appreciated by the men and women in my party.'

'If you will excuse me, sir? I am most busy.'

Curtius Rufus nodded. 'Of course. If, by any chance, I am needed you will find me among the grain sacks.' He turned and went out to where Marcus Pedius stood waiting, his face impassive, a crowd of small boys around him, admiring his uniform and the short sword he wore on his belt.

Curtius Rufus said, 'It is quite hopeless. No one knows anything, and the governor is away.' He explained as they walked and the centurion, his face set, said nothing. Presently he spoke. 'I might have expected it. I'll organize things myself.' He wrinkled his nose at the garbage in the street and said reprovingly, 'It's a typical native city, all mud and plaster except for the buildings on the hill. We shall have to watch the stores, or these people will thieve the lot.' He added, as an afterthought, 'My father was interested in history, used to tell me stories about the old wars. You'd never think Hannibal came from a place like this.'

They organized billets in the granaries and sent out parties of soldiers to buy food. Criton was incredulous at Curtius Rufus' story of his reception. 'My dear friend, we should have gone to my homeland instead. We Macedonians know how to receive and entertain visitors. We treat them as guests.' Vatinus was relieved. Until now the centurion had refused to believe his explanations as to why he had failed to secure billets and organize their reception. The technicians in the party sat huddled against a wall out of the wind and were full of complaints.

Probus, the architect, said bitterly, 'You can never trust anyone who works for the Water Board. They live off bribes and lies.' His friend, Crescens, the surveyor, nodded agreement. 'My wife told me not to come. I should have taken her advice. If Juba's capital is like this rat hole, it will take ten years of work to improve the place.'

Fronto, the engineer, shivered and pulled his cloak around his shoulders. 'Our envoy is a Parthian by birth. I might have guessed it. Oh, I agree, you can never trust a race of horse traders.'

The four women complained most of all. The eldest, Felicia, who had a strong, ugly face, kept up a string of abuse at the absence of what she regarded as essential amenities. 'How can I do my job if we have no hot water? These girls have not bathed in five days. The salt water is bad for their hair. I need fresh clothes and you tell me we cannot have them because the baggage has been wrongly stacked. Get the soldiers to move it. They are too idle for their own good. We need a good fire. It is too drafty where you have put us. The youngest girl has a cold and if it turns to a fever it will be your fault, but I shall be blamed for it.' Criton attempted to calm her, but she seized him by the arm and was only diverted by two soldiers who had strolled up, hoping to get a glimpse of the girls. 'Clear off,' she shouted. 'Only the blind would take you for their lovers. Keep to your own quarters or I will tell the centurion.'

When she had gone Criton said in awe, 'Where did you find her?'

Curtius Rufus, who had abandoned all efforts to shave in cold water by the light of a fire, wiped his face with a towel and slipped on his soiled tunic. 'Oh, down in the Tuscan quarter. She claims she was once mistress to a senator who freed her in his will. Then she became partner to Vividus, the Cappadocian slave trader who died last year. Used to boast he never sold a girl for less than fifty thousand. He specialized in beautiful girls for those with unorthodox tastes. Claimed he trained them himself. That was a lie. He liked them really young.'

Criton looked down his nose. 'A charming creature.' He put down the reed he had been pointing and splitting with a knife, and rummaged in the box at his feet.

'Oh, Felicia's all right. She'll look after them. I told her I'd cut her throat if she didn't.'

'That is not the language for an envoy, dear boy.'

Curtius Rufus said grimly, 'I neither look nor feel like one at the moment.' The patter of rain upon the warehouse roof made him look up. 'We have got off to a bad beginning. That centurion thinks me a fool and is barely polite. The men laugh at me behind my back and call me the horse trader. It's true, isn't it?'

Criton nodded silently. He had spread out a book roll and was spacing lines with a ruler.

'Tomorrow I shall go and see the governor.' Curtius Rufus stopped and stared. 'What are you doing?'

'I am keeping a daily record of events. We shall have to present a report when we return and it will be easier to write if we have noted the facts. I am your secretary and I earn my new living.'

'I had forgotten.' Curtius Rufus looked past the oil lamp into the darkness of the shed. 'We used to sleep rough like this when we traded horses. Well, I have my old job back now. I come to sell, to buy, to exchange. I was a good horse trader. Perhaps I shall be again.'

It was cold and drafty in the warehouse and when they awoke in the night they could hear the rats scuffling in search of grain. Just after dawn it began to rain and the wind that rattled the warehouse doors made the fires smoke badly.

Curtius Rufus swallowed his wine and said hurriedly, 'Criton, do something to get the women into billets. There are supposed to be over five thousand veterans settled here. So someone must be able to speak Latin besides ourselves.'

Criton nodded, his face sharp with the cold. 'I will practice using those ciphers,' he said. 'I still don't understand them properly.'

Marcus Pedius said bleakly, 'And what do you wish us to do?'

'Whatever is usually done by centurions in charge of temporary camps.'

Attius, the escort optio, coughed nervously. 'Excuse me, sir,' he said, 'but half the unit is due to be returned to Rome by the next transport.'

Curtius Rufus put on his cloak. 'Well, they will have to wait until the detail from the Third arrives.'

'How long will you be away?' Criton asked.

'That depends upon the roads.'

'You will miss the Saturnalia.'

Curtius Rufus touched him on the arm. 'There will be others. Do your best to organize something here and see that the men enjoy themselves.'

Marcus Pedius looked at the sky. 'It is a bad start to a journey. I hope you are a good horseman.'

Curtius Rufus said coldly, 'If your escort can keep up with me I shall know that they are.'

He left an hour later in the pouring rain. They rode through a countryside of bleak, brown earth, occasional orchards of olive trees, soaked black by the rain, and fields sown with autumn grain that stood empty, awaiting the coming of spring. The farm buildings stood out like oases in a sea of mud and grew fewer and fewer as they journeyed inland, moving steadily, heads down against the wind, from one muddled, white-roofed village to the next.

They made thirty miles the first day and spent the night at a post inn, run by an old soldier with one eye, who had served the deposed triumvir, Lepidus, in Hispania. There they had changed horses and the next day forded with difficulty a swollen stream that cut the road in half. It was late afternoon before Curtius Rufus, wiping the rain from his face for the tenth time in an hour, remembered what day it was – the Saturnalia. He thought of Rome with longing. On the third day the wind shifted a point or two to the west and the rain eased and then stopped altogether. The bleak landscape was broken only by a series of tiny villages, all much alike, consisting of a narrow street with a dozen houses on either side, tall circular storehouses for grain, and a water cistern and fenced enclosures for cattle and sheep. Dogs nosed the refuse in the street, and children played in the dirt, while goats wandered casually through open doorways in search of food. On the fourth day a horse went lame and they had to leave its rider to follow on as best he could. The following night, tired and dirty and stiff from saddle sores, their animals caked in mud to the withers, they reached the camp at Ammaedara.

The governor was a thickset man with heavy eyebrows and a permanent expression of sardonic amusement. He said, 'I am sorry you have been put to this trouble but in this country – as I

151

have discovered – it is the unexpected which always happens. I sent a letter by dispatch boat but it must have reached Misenum after you sailed.'

'You have had trouble yourself, sir.'

'A little. The Musulamii are a desert tribe who seem to have had a bad year with their trading. They are now trying to make up for it by raiding across our southern frontier. They have burnt three villages and destroyed one of my outposts. I am determined to stop it before they concentrate in strength.'

Curtius Rufus nodded tiredly.

'You certainly look drier now than when you arrived.' The governor chuckled. 'Have some wine. I'll call the orderly.'

'No, really, sir – I need a clear head.'

'As you wish. Well, I shall have some. In six months I've learned one thing: to live out here a clear head is the last thing you need. Well, what may I do for you?'

Curtius Rufus said, 'I was told to report to you, sir, before proceeding to Iol.'

'Yes, Marcus Agrippa wrote to me. Very proper, I'm sure. But my dear fellow, there was no need to travel a hundred and fifty miles to do just that.'

Curtius Rufus swallowed. 'May I sit down?'

'How long did you take?'

'Five days.'

'Then sit down carefully. Hmm! That was punishing work for the horses.'

Curtius Rufus said carefully, 'I need your authority to obtain supplies and stores.'

There was a long silence while the governor frowned, his eyes never leaving the young man's face. Then he said, 'But I—' and broke off suddenly. He bit his lip, leaned forward, and said carefully, 'I hope you have been well looked after at Carthage in my absence?'

Curtius Rufus said politely, 'Very well, thank you. My men

are bivouacked in an empty granary on the quayside. I slept there myself the first night to see that all was well. Your secretary could not have been kinder. But in your absence he has not your authority for things I need and need to be done.'

The governor's eyes narrowed. He said slowly, 'That you can have. I will give you a written instruction in the morning. Anything else?'

'I was told, sir, you would supply an escort and an officer who knows the country.'

'How many men?'

'Between twenty-five and fifty.'

The governor shook his head. 'If the present trouble had not occurred – quite impossible in the circumstances.'

'Marcus Agrippa, sir—'

'Is not in command here. I have only six thousand Gaulish soldiers to protect the entire province.'

'But, sir!'

The governor said, 'You will have to manage as best you can. Do you realize just how important this province is? Two-thirds of Rome's wheat is shipped from these ports.'

Curtius Rufus stared.

'Oh, you are thinking of what you have seen. Well, the roads are appalling; irrigation methods are primitive; the majority of the native population don't live as we do; and Carthage is a little shabby, like all the towns. Yet, there are big estates along the coast, and inland; it's a rich farming country; and the olive will do well here. Plans are on foot for developing the interior. We are creating new colonies all the time, and we hope to absorb thirty thousand retired veterans within the next few years. This is a province with a future.'

'Yes, sir.'

'That is why I cannot spare men.' The governor paused and poured out more wine. 'Well?'

'I must have an officer, sir.'

'Must!'

'Yes, if I am to have any hope of finding Valerius Messalla's niece.'

The governor stared in his turn. 'So! That is why you are here. Wait a moment.' He thought, staring hard at the walls of the room. Then he said quietly, 'I have heard nothing. It does not surprise me. We are too far east. But Juba may be able to help you.'

'I was told that you would, sir, with advice.'

'I can tell you very little. The country is quiet and, on the whole, peaceful. This, of course, is the old Africa that Carthage ruled. Africa Nova – the old Numidia – is another matter. It is much less well developed. Trouble with the tribes in the south and in the mountains is what we expect. Juba is an able and most scholarly young man. I like him and I trust him. I think you can trust him, too.'

Curtius Rufus said, 'But his father, I have been told, was a supporter of Pompeius.'

The governor said dryly, 'Juba was a child then. He owes his present position, his wealth – everything, to Rome.'

'And his loyalty?'

'That is to Rome also, or I am no judge of any man's character.'

Curtius Rufus said, 'Perhaps I might accept that drink, sir.'

'Of course. You will also find Cornelius Silius most helpful. He has been accredited as an adviser to Juba's court. He knows the city and the people well. The king trusts him.' He turned, wine cup in hand. 'Are you looking for plots here or in Rome?' The governor spoke quietly and casually, but there was a stillness in his manner, as he awaited the answer, that reminded Curtius Rufus of the sudden concentration that cloaked each gladiator, as he faced his opponent in the arena and drew his sword for the first blow or parry.

Curtius Rufus said with a tired grin, 'I am looking for no plots, only a girl. But I am expected to find her quickly.'

The governor nodded and seemed to relax. 'A pity you cannot stay. On the whole the weather is good and the climate delightful. You must try to see the marble quarries at Simitthu before you leave. They are our great tourist attraction.'

Curtius Rufus said, 'Do you approve, sir, of Juba's wife?'

The governor smiled. 'I always approve of beautiful women. She is charming and also intelligent.'

'And loyal to Rome, sir?'

The governor paused. He said, 'She is a young wife, and obedient to her husband's wishes. Is that sufficient answer?'

Curtius Rufus said, 'It is the reply I will give to Marcus Agrippa as being your testimony, sir.'

The governor clenched his fists. 'Be very careful, young man.'

Curtius Rufus said, 'Forgive me, sir. I am very tired.'

'Of course. I understand. Now you – you want an officer, I believe. Well, I will make the sacrifice and spare one. Let me see – yes, Lucius Eggius, centurion of the Third, is just the man. He came out with the legion and was here previously, about a dozen years ago, when he conducted a survey of southern Mauretania as far as the Atlas mountains. He knows the country as well as anybody.'

'That is kind of you, sir.'

'It is not kindness but necessity. We must help in any way we can. Lucius Eggius is on outpost duty. I will send for him tomorrow. Now get some sleep. You need it and I have work to do.'

Curtius Rufus yawned, nodded, and went to bed. As he turned the handle of the door on leaving he glanced back. The governor was sitting back in his chair, a half-empty cup of wine in his hand. His face had been drained of all amusement and all arrogance. He looked tired, old, and very frightened.

Curtius Rufus slept late and when he awoke it was to find an orderly by his bed, requesting him to take a ride with the governor at the third hour. A little before time he went to the headquarters building and walked through it to the small white-washed room where the Eagle and the cohort standards were hung in a rack upon the wall. He looked at them for a long time but the feeling of regret for a lost career, which he knew to be at its keenest when he had drunk too much wine, was strangely dulled now that he stood in a military camp again. So much, not all of it bad, had happened since.

A voice said dryly, 'Do you miss the service as much as you thought you did?'

He turned and saw the governor standing in the doorway. He said, 'I am not sure. If I do it was because my dreams were clear then; they are muddied now.' He paused and took a breath. He said steadily, 'I used to think, sir, that it was good to be ambitious, like my father, that success came if you were honest, if you worked hard, if you were loyal, if you gave your best to a job.'

The governor smiled. 'And what have you learned since?'

'That I was wrong. Honest men, if they live in Rome, do so — by accident.'

The governor nodded. 'You may well be right. Shall we go? I would like to show you something of the countryside. You are not too stiff, I hope?'

Curtius Rufus smiled.

They rode out past the town and up onto some high ground overlooking the camp. Below them was a small boy, trying to round up half-a-dozen goats with the aid of an enthusiastic but inexperienced dog. On the slopes opposite, sheep were grazing among the rocks and short grass, while down on the dirt road by which they had come a group of men from a nearby village were lazily repairing the bridge over a stream.

The governor signed to his escort to fall back and then reined in his horse. 'It looks peaceful,' he said. 'But it's not.' He pointed toward a distant range of hills. 'Over there are the Musulamii.' A light flickered in the distance as the sun caught the polished surface of a shield. On the shoulder of the hill above them the sentry on picket duty saw the signal and held up his shield in reply. Curtius Rufus could see a column of troops from the camp spreading out in a straggling line along the flat ground to the north.

The governor said, 'Road building – the first job, as always.' He paused and then, with no change in his voice, said, 'I did not tell you last night in camp because I have servants I do not trust. No, don't look towards me. We are being watched. Pretend to admire the view. The governor's movements are always of interest. Now, your coming was known and talked of in the markets of Carthage days before the official letter arrived.'

Curtius Rufus said, 'Does it matter? I have worked in government departments. It is impossible to keep anything secret for long.'

'You keep an open face and a closed mouth, I notice. I will leave you to judge whether it matters. When I heard, I wrote to my secretary, asking that all arrangements be made for your reception and comfort. I sent letters, giving you sufficient authority to obtain what you required. Did you get the letters?'

Curtius Rufus stared in front of him. 'No, sir, I did not.'

'Precisely. I think the messenger was killed on the way and the letters stolen and read.'

'But I am not important.'

'I think you are. I am sure Juba will welcome your mission. But there are others at his court who may not do so.'

Curtius Rufus said, 'I don't understand.'

'My secretary is from Egypt. There are some who still dream impossible dreams.'

'But why delay me?'

'You can answer that better than I. If you are in a hurry to accomplish something, then you have lost, even with your excellent riding, at least twelve days.'

Curtius Rufus looked at the boy, who was now following the goats down the track up which they had ridden. 'There is no proof,' he said quietly. 'Will you get rid of him?'

'Who? My secretary? Oh! No, he is far too good at his job. Besides, I like the fellow. And there is no proof as you say. I must observe the law. Shall we ride on? I wish to show you a rather splendid view.'

The governor said jovially, 'Come back to my quarters. Let's leave the others to relax.' He grinned. 'It's always better when I've gone.'

Curtius Rufus looked behind him. Through the half-closed doors he heard the scrape of benches as the younger officers got to their feet. There was a roar of drunken laughter and a voice cried, 'Balance it on your nose, man, not your head.' Another voice, less blurred, said quite clearly, 'You were a fool to challenge him to a race. I could see he had the look of a man sired by a centaur.'

The governor said, 'Come in and make yourself comfortable.'

Curtius Rufus sat down and the governor clapped his hands and called for wine. Then he said, 'Are you warm enough by that fire? It gets cold at night here.'

'Yes, thank you.'

'Good. Well, you made yourself popular, winning that race. It cheers them up to see a new face and hear the gossip from Rome. Gets a little monotonous at times. I'm glad you didn't take a wager. Might have created bad feeling. Decent of you.' The governor paused and added shrewdly, 'A professional?'

'No, but my father was.'

'So you're one of the new men, eh! I wouldn't worry about that. Rome has been filled by new men. There's always a Cato to grumble that times aren't the same anymore. Lucius Eggius should be here soon. I've asked him to join us.'

Curtius Rufus said, suddenly nervous, 'I hope he will get on with my officers. The praetorians can be' – he smiled – 'difficult.'

'I know what you mean – all shining metal and no brain. Don't worry. He's a rather exceptional man. Here, let me fill your cup.'

Curtius Rufus heard a faint chink of sound and was suddenly conscious that there was someone standing behind him, though he had not heard the door open. He turned slowly and found himself looking at a slim man, a little below middle height, with gray hair, quiet eyes, and tanned skin.

Lucius Eggius looked at him with an expression of cool appraisal, standing absolutely still, relaxed and yet totally alert, like a cat. Curtius Rufus rose to his feet. He knew now what the governor meant.

Lucius Eggius said quietly, 'Good evening, sir.' He spoke to the governor. He had a low voice that sounded as though his throat were full of gravel, but the voice was that of a man educated from birth, not self taught – the difference was always obvious – and Curtius Rufus knew that some time in the past he had belonged to the equestrian order.

He said, 'I hope you had a good journey.'

Lucius Eggius said gravely, 'Yes, I thank you, though I did not travel as fast as you.'

The governor smiled. 'Sit down and have some wine – that is, if you are satisfied with your entrance?'

Lucius Eggius said, 'I am sorry; it has become a habit.'

Curtius Rufus said, 'I did not hear the door but you should not carry coins in your pouch when you wish to move silently.'

Lucius Eggius nodded in appreciation. 'I had hoped you might think they were your own dice rattling. You have good ears for a civilian.'

'You need good ears if you wish to walk the streets of Rome at night in safety.'

'Now that is something I am not practiced at.'

159

The governor rose to his feet. 'I will leave you to talk amongst yourselves. I have letters to write. My wife is very disappointed that I have had to postpone her visit.' He paused and then said quietly, 'So am I. It has been a long year without her company.'

Lucius Eggius held out his hand. 'I have your dispatches,' he said. 'I met the courier on the road and escorted him here.'

'When did the dispatch boat reach Carthage?'

'Two days after he landed.' Lucius Eggius nodded toward Curtius Rufus.

The governor went over to a writing desk and lit a lamp. He bent forward and peered short-sightedly at the documents, opening them one by one. The two younger men waited in silence, Lucius Eggius warming his hands before the fire.

The governor looked up. 'I have news that may interest you,' he said, and his voice was expressionless. 'Primus was arraigned on a charge of treason against the state and tried at a meeting of the senatorial court.' He paused. He said, 'Murena defended him with – with considerable eloquence. However, a certain letter on which the defense hinged its whole case could not be found. Accusations were made – of – of a wild and improbable nature. Primus was found guilty and has been executed.' He paused and blinked. 'I knew him well. Augustus was present at the trial and gave evidence also.' To Lucius Eggius he said, 'Tell the others tomorrow that Augustus's health is better. I will – I will hold a parade and announce a half-day free from duties as – as a celebration. All officers and myself will attend at the temple. I will make the arrangements later. Good night to you both.'

When he had gone the two men sat and talked for a long time but not once did they speak of the news from Rome.

CHAPTER X

Three days later they set out on the return journey to Carthage, traveling more slowly this time at Lucius Eggius's request. 'There is not the same hurry,' he said in his quiet voice. 'I have managed to persuade the governor to give us the escort originally planned so that your draft may return to Italia as promised. But they are being drawn from the coastal colonies in small detachments and will be slow in coming. Besides, I have a boil on my thigh – oh, it is nothing. I always get them when I am near leave-time, but it will be more comfortable to go slowly.'

'You were going on leave?'

'Yes'

'And my coming stopped you. I am sorry.'

'It is nothing. I have been out here four years now. I like the country, you see.' Lucius Eggius smiled slightly.

'Where do you live?' asked Curtius Rufus.

'I have an estate north of Apuleia. It is good for sheep farming. We think our wool is the best, though the blackest fleeces come from Pollentia.'

'I know little about farming; only horses.'

'That I can see.' Lucius Eggius hesitated. 'It is not my business to ask questions,' he said. 'Only to answer them. But is your mission likely to take long?'

'It all depends on Juba, and how much help I get. Six months at our present rate of progress. Why?'

Lucius Eggius said, 'I have an aunt who bought an estate in Picenum. The farming has been unsuccessful. I intended to visit her on leave and put her affairs in order. It seems they will have to wait.'

On the afternoon of their return Curtius Rufus walked down the mole that protected the outer harbor from the sea. On the way he passed Lucius Eggius, who was talking to the praetorian officers. 'The fifth detachment is at Thabraca on the north coast. That's where they ship the beasts for the arena in Rome. At the rate they're doing that there soon won't be any wild animals left in Africa.' He heard the officers laugh at Lucius Eggius' joke and leaned against the wall and looked at the grain ships tied up for the winter. The harbor was filled with them, but no one moved on the sunlit decks. The crews had been paid off and would not be signed on again before the season began in March. He felt the wind on his face and looked toward the north. Beyond the cape lay home. He thought of Rome and of the great house on the hill and he wondered idly if Pero still possessed the bracelet he had given her. It was unlikely. She had probably sold it by now to buy a new dress.

He heard a step behind him and smelled perfume. It was Urracca. Out of the corner of his eye he saw the two younger women laughing together, Felicia by their side. He said politely, 'I hope you are more comfortable now in your new quarters?'

She smiled. 'Yes, we are, thanks to the efforts of Felicia and your secretary. We walk up here each day for exercise. Felicia insists on it.' She pushed her hood back and looked out to sea. 'That was my first voyage,' she said.

'I am sorry the weather was bad.'

'It was exciting. When we left Hispania we went by land. It was a long, slow journey. Not at all comfortable. When do we sail to Iol?'

'As soon as arrangements have been made for hiring ships.'

'It will not be long then before I have a new master. They say the King is a young man. Is that true?'

'Yes, I believe so.'

162

Felicia called her name. She waved and said, 'I must go. Thank you for answering my questions.'

He turned. 'Just a moment.' He looked at her then. He said steadily, 'The King has a wife. He is newly married. Do not assume too much.'

She said, 'I know why I am here. Either I will have to poison his wife or she will have to poison me. Have you thought of that, O, my master?' She smiled and walked away and he stared after her, a look of anxiety upon his face.

Three days later they sailed, moving out of the mercantile harbor under oars a little before sunset. The wind was from the south and as soon as they had cleared the lighthouse on the mole and were in the bay, they raised sails and headed for the cape. Standing a little off from the shore they hugged the yellow-brown cliffs, making a steady six knots their first night. In his sleep Curtius Rufus dreamed of his mother for the first time in years, and when he awoke it was to find the ship quiet and hardly moving. They were at anchor when he went up on deck, lying close to the beach, the sterns of the convoy swinging a little in the current.

'We could make more speed if we rowed by day,' said the master. 'But we should leave the transports behind and that might be dangerous. The weather is uncertain and I think it best that we keep together. We shall reach Thabraca about midnight if all is well.'

Curtius Rufus said, 'We are in a hurry. I am behind my shadow already.'

The master grinned. 'Don't worry. We shall be there in two days and two nights, so long as we get an offshore wind and not too much sea.'

'You must be about due to retire?'

The master spat over the side. 'That's right. I've done thirty-five years. I could have taken my pension before; but what would I have done at anchor all this while? Things have changed a bit though. I used to have command of a quinquereme once. We had two hundred and fifty on board all told, including one hundred and fifty rowers. Five men to an oar and each one thirty feet long. We could do four knots for two hours at full speed before the men got tired. But Agrippa changed all that.'

'Were you at Actium?'

The master nodded. 'He had these smaller ships built. He wanted them in a hurry to deal with Sextus Pompeius. He was a great seaman, that one, so we needed better ships to beat him. We used green timber for some and got them built in thirty days, but the average time was forty. Still, I have a hankering for the old ships, all the same. These are faster, but too much like rowing boats.'

'What was it like at Actium? You must be proud to have served there.'

The master scratched his head. 'It was just a skirmish; not a real battle. They had no intention of fighting once they realized they'd been outmaneuvered on land. Just broke through and ran for the south. A pity. We might have won. Agrippa was no sailor.'

Curtius Rufus looked at him.

The master's face was expressionless. 'Still, I had my orders, though it went against the grain. I remember him coming on board and sitting there with his head in his hands, not saying a word. He knew it was the end. He wouldn't even talk to her. I felt sorry for them both.'

Curtius Rufus stared.

'Oh, yes, I'd changed sides. I was never good at picking the winner.'

The weather held, though the wind freshened a good deal and they continued to make good sailing time. Criton stayed below and, with a pale face, kept his daily record of their journey. The women came up on deck for short intervals but soon tired of watching the brown, scrub-covered coastline slide slowly past them, while the wind blew their hair about their faces and the sea birds quarreled in their wake.

In the darkness Curtius Rufus would come up on deck. Leaning over the side he would watch for phosphorescent fish and stare across the black waters before looking upward to pick out the stars his father had once taught him to recognize. Once, Lucius Eggius joined him on the pretext of not being able to sleep and the two men stood together, listening to the wind in the rigging above their heads. Then Lucius Eggius said softly, 'You will be glad when we arrive and you can begin your real work. The preliminaries are always tiresome.'

Curtius Rufus said doubtfully, 'Yes, I shall be glad.' But it was a lie. He felt totally uncertain and was appalled at the difficulties that lay ahead. The technical side of the mission did not worry him at all. The task of finding the girl, however, was another matter; and he wondered why Agrippa had not selected someone like the man who stood beside him. Lucius Eggius belonged to Agrippa's world, he possessed assurance, knowledge, and education. He had an understanding of how power operated and what levers had to be moved to get it turning in your favor. He knew, far better, how to talk to and deal with men like Juba. It was he who should have the task, not a jobless citizen who had failed in everything he had ever tried to do.

He said, 'I feel like a seaman who sets out on a voyage through waters he has never seen before.'

Lucius Eggius said calmly, 'We all feel like that when we start a new job. I will give you all the help I can, if I am asked, but on all matters of policy the decision must be yours, for you have the authority; not I.'

Curtius Rufus said stiffly, 'You are very kind.'

Lucius Eggius shook his head. 'No,' he said. 'I am merely doing my duty. I do not envy you. It is not a task that I would ever wish to be given.' He said good night then and went below. Curtius Rufus was left alone. He pulled the hood of his cloak

165

over his head and watched a faint flicker of light on the coast to his left; a fire most likely, lit by a shepherd to keep jackals and foxes away. Very softly he began to whistle and a gull, balancing on the deck-house behind his back, woke up, squawked once and flew off toward the shore.

The weather worsened and the convoy was caught by a rising wind and heavy seas while the oars were out. By the time the master had given the order to ship them, two oars on the seaward side of the bireme had kicked back and four men were badly injured; one dying of chest injuries within the hour. The wind shifted to the south, it began to rain and the bad weather slowed them down considerably, so that it was not until the sixth day when the sun passed into Aquarius that they sighted a merchant ship, hull down over their bow.

'Just out of Iol Caesarea,' said the master. 'She's about five miles off. We shall be there within the hour if the wind holds.'

The wind held, the master signaled the dispatch boat, an order was snapped out, and the dispatch boat altered sail and moved ahead to carry the news of their coming so that protocol might be observed.

It was midafternoon when they reached the octagonal harbor that had been newly built and which was now crammed with merchant shipping. Along one quay were moored six biremes, while twelve more lay at anchor, side by side in the center of the harbor.

'The Africa flotilla,' said Lucius Eggius, who had come on deck and was shivering a little in the cold wind. 'The King is very proud that Augustus has given him personal responsibility for guarding the coastline. That includes, of course, the suppression of pirate raids on Hispania.' He gave the envoy a quick look.

Curtius Rufus said, 'I did not know that. It is certainly a point worth remembering.'

They anchored in the harbor and almost immediately a small boat put out toward them.

'How soon can we get ashore?' asked Marcus Pedius, looking anxiously at the sky.

Curtius Rufus closed his eyes, trying hard to remember everything that Maecenas had told him. He licked his lips and said slowly, 'Presently. Including today we have five days of official ceremonies to endure. Only after that shall we begin the talks and the work.' He stopped, wiped his mouth, and looked down at the boat, which was now coming alongside. He added under his breath, so that only those about him could hear, 'In the world of diplomacy, as Maecenas has said, nothing happens at speed, and sometimes nothing happens at all.'

Criton said, shocked, 'But we have got to succeed.'

Curtius Rufus saw the gangway shake as the occupants of the boat began to climb aboard. He said in a whisper to Criton, 'I know. At this moment it is as important to see that the legate's daughter is safely returned as it will be tomorrow to recover the standards and the Eagles taken from Crassus and Marcus Antonius by the Parthians. The one shame is as great as the other.'

The voice was his, but the words were those of a middle-aged man, who had uttered them with tears on his cheeks as he talked to Curtius Rufus in a quiet garden on a hill in Rome.

CHAPTER XI

He rode in a gold and ivory chariot with the second chamberlain beside him and an escort of the King's Numidian light horse riding ahead to clear a way through the white-robed crowd that packed the streets. Behind, in a second chariot, rode Criton, resplendent in a new toga, and behind him again marched his officers at the head of an escort of twenty-five soldiers.

The chamberlain said, 'The King is eager to meet you. This is a great occasion for us all.'

Curtius Rufus smiled in reply, nervously going over the speech he had prepared the previous night with Criton and wondering if the presents they carried would prove acceptable. His eyes flickered from side to side, and the crowd cheered whenever he remembered to wave his hand in salutation. 'It is a large city,' he said politely.

The chamberlain smiled. 'It is not as large as Carthage, your Excellency, yet it will be more beautiful when the rebuilding has been completed upon which the King has set his heart.'

'I shall do my best to offer him every assistance.'

'If there are difficulties I trust your Excellency will remember that his friends will do much to smooth the way. In this I shall be ever at your service. There is no difficulty that may not be overcome if the correct approach is made.'

'I do not doubt it. I will remember your words with – with more than gratitude.'

The chamberlain smiled. 'Your Excellency is most understanding.'

The street widened and there before them was the palace. They drove through the open gates in the high, whitewashed walls, through an outer courtyard, flanked by palm trees, to where a crowd of dignitaries stood at the foot of a flight of steps. He was introduced to the principal secretary, to the senior chamberlain, and to a dozen others whose names he could not recall afterward except that their faces were dark and that all, without exception, had beautiful white teeth. Then they walked slowly between marble columns toward great doors that opened onto the Throne Room, whose sides were packed with men and women, some dressed in the Roman fashion, others in the style of the country, wearing silken tunics that fell below the knees, the women jeweled and with mantles over their elaborately coiffured hair. At the far end, on a raised dais, were set two thrones of gold and ivory. He walked toward them slowly, his hands wet with sweat, and in the profound silence with which the King awaited his coming, he could hear even above the rasp of his sandals the beating of his own heart.

The chamberlain cleared his throat and began to speak in slow but measured Latin. During the preliminaries the two men looked at each other with impassive faces. Juba was very young, very dignified, and had the good looks of his father. Criton, standing on the envoy's left side, thought him the most beautiful young man he had ever seen. It would be his turn to reply when the chamberlain had finished. The King sat motionless while the speeches were made, the documents read, and Curtius Rufus's staff introduced. He accepted the letter from Augustus with a grave face and read it in silence, while the audience waited and the only sound was the rustle of silk as his queen moved one gilded sandal, leaning back a little in her chair to avoid the sun, now coming through a latticed window. Curtius Rufus glanced at her. She seemed to look straight through him, her face equally remote as that of her husband. He thought then how like she was to the statue Gallita had spoken of that night at Maecenas's house and which he had visited before he left Rome.

Then the presents were brought and presented one by one: a gold cross belt and a ceremonial sword for the King, together with a dinner service made of elaborately worked silver that drew a murmur of admiration from those nearest to the throne; while for the Queen there was a gold torque and a gold bracelet, jeweled earrings and a silver mirror with a carved handle of ivory. The King smiled his thanks and it was as though the sun shone upon his face. The Queen did not smile but she inclined her head in acknowledgment. The King rested his hands upon the carved arms of his throne, while Curtius Rufus looked fixedly at a point between the two thrones. His feet ached and there was a tickle at the back of his neck which he did not dare to scratch.

There was a rustle of silk as the King moved. Then he spoke, not in Latin but in Punic so that his court might understand. 'I bid you welcome to my country and I hope that your stay as my guest will be a most happy one. The representatives of Augustus are all my friends.' His voice was light and he sounded cold, though this might have been due to nervousness.

Curtius Rufus said, 'I am honored by your kindness and I thank you.'

The King rose to his feet to signify that the audience was at an end, and Curtius Rufus bowed and retired from the great room.

They returned to the residency in the same manner as they had come, though this time the chamberlain did not accompany them. Once inside Curtius Rufus stripped off his finery and pulled on a loose robe. It was near dinnertime and he was hungry. In the inner courtyard he found Criton and his officers, lounging in the sun. A burst of laughter greeted his arrival and he wondered anxiously for a moment what it was they found so amusing – himself perhaps.

Criton, on the edge of the group, turned and smiled. He said,

170

'It went very well, dear boy, except that I left out a sentence of your speech. However, no one noticed.'

'I think the King did. Well, no matter. Thank the gods that is over.'

Lucius Eggius said gravely, 'It is always worse the first time.'

The tribune, a dark man with a plain face that was made ugly by a scar across the cheek, said bluntly, 'He is very changeable.'

'The King?'

'Yes, Excellency.' Cornelius Silius used the address without affection. He came of a good family and his father had been a friend of the triumvir, Lepidus. Marked out for a brilliant career, so it was whispered, he had drunk himself into a state of debt and had disgraced himself in a camp brawl with a brother officer, of which the scar was a permanent reminder.

Lucius Eggius said curiously, 'He has altered then since I first met him. I thought him a pleasant young man, a little too scholarly for my taste, but reliable and always good-humored.'

'He is still that,' said Cornelius Silius. 'But he is a man of moods these days. Today was one of them.'

Curtius Rufus said, 'If you are a king in your own country, I suppose it is hard to be reminded that your rule is dependent upon the will of another man.'

'Of that I know nothing.' Cornelius Silius frowned.

Lucius Eggius said, 'He would have had no throne, nothing, but for the kindness of Augustus. He is a fortunate young man.'

Curtius Rufus glanced at Criton, who shrugged his shoulders.

Silius said, 'Still, he is pleased your mission has arrived. He has talked of nothing else since the first letter came.'

Criton said, 'Was the Queen also pleased?'

'Yes, I think so, though that is hardly a woman's business. When the city has been enlarged, and if her husband's plans are successfully accomplished, there will be more trade, more shops, more people, more entertainment. She will enjoy that.' Silius frowned again. 'All women do. It is what they live for.' He stared moodily at the ground.

Curtius Rufus said, 'Let us have some wine. I'm thirsty, if no one else is.'

Silius looked up. 'I will join you in that, Excellency, and you can give me the latest news from Rome. Is it true the Whites have had a successful season?'

Later, in the small room that had been allotted to him as a private office, Curtius Rufus sat at the table, a map of the coast set out before him, and said, 'Well, what do we do now? I don't even know how to start.'

Criton said, 'It is a difficult problem. We must take first things first. The King is known to be pleased that you have come – a good sign.'

'He conceals his feelings well. He may be less pleased when he learns the real reason. He may feel tricked, humiliated.'

'Perhaps. All in good time, dear boy. Silius tells me he has a passion for learning—'

'About which I am ignorant.'

'Half ignorant. But I will fill in the other half.'

Curtius Rufus laughed.

Criton said indignantly, 'You hurt my feelings. Never mind. He has also this passion to build a great city.'

'And then?' Curtius Rufus put his hands under his chin.

Criton said, 'Then you commence bargaining.'

'He may know nothing.'

'He is the King. He has spies and informers. He must know something.'

Curtius Rufus said slowly, 'You may be correct. I will tell you if you are when I know him better.'

There came a tap on the door, and Silius entered. He was more than a little drunk but he smiled good-humoredly. 'You wished to speak to me in private, Excellency.'

'Yes.' Curtius Rufus smiled pleasantly. 'I wish to thank

you for making us so comfortable and at the expense of your-self.'

'I am glad to have the company.' He swayed a little on his feet. 'Usually I have to rely on the news of merchants and sea captains.'

'How often does the dispatch boat run?'

'Normally, once every six days.'

'What if you are in a hurry?'

Silius looked startled. 'In time of need there are two merchants. They have always proved reliable. I can get messages away within twenty-four hours in the sailing season. Out of season, as now, it takes longer.' He thought for a while, his brow furrowed like a badly ploughed field.

Curtius Rufus asked quietly, 'Have your dispatches ever been interfered with?'

Silius hesitated and then put down his cup. 'It is curious you should ask that. The Syrian merchant's house was robbed recently and some dispatches were taken with other documents. They were not important. In any event the Phoenician merchant had duplicates.'

Criton exchanged looks with his friend. 'Is that the only instance?' he asked.

Silius shook his head. 'We have a courier service, linking us with Carthage along the coast road. One of the messengers was killed by bandits about twelve days ago. They stripped the body of everything.'

'Was that dispatch important?'

'Yes, but not secret. It was in reply to an inquiry by the Proconsul.' Silius gave the envoy a sharp look as Criton said mildly, 'You had better advise your messengers to take special care from now on.'

'I see,' he said. 'I will do as you suggest. Now, if you do not need me I have an appointment with a lady.' He winked. 'She will be furious if I keep her waiting.' He turned to the door.

173

Criton looked quickly at Curtius Rufus and nodded. Curtius Rufus said in a clear voice, 'Please don't go yet. I have something more to say. It concerns us three alone at the moment.'

Cornelius Silius came back to the desk and it was as though the drunkenness had been wiped from his face with a sponge. 'I can guess at it,' he said quietly. 'I am sorry that to date my spies have brought me no news of any interest.'

They attended the banquet in the palace and there were, Criton estimated, over two hundred guests present. He said, in a low voice, as they were led to their seats, 'The King is determined to show that he is for Rome whatever others may think.'

Curtius Rufus nodded. He hoped that the King would be in a better mood and that the wine would at least be drinkable. But he was wrong as to the King, for Juba wrapped himself in formality as though he wore a cloak against the coldness of the night air, and did not relax, talking little and then only as politeness demanded. He seemed, Criton thought, to be under a strain of some kind. Cleopatra Selene, wearing a white gown, discoursed politely to Lucius Eggius during the first course, smiled at the jokes of Cornelius Silius during the second course, and kept her thoughts to herself. Criton noticed that she and Juba barely spoke to each other, but this might have been the etiquette of the occasion. Curtius Rufus, at whom she never looked directly, thought that she cared nothing for any man.

At the conclusion of the fourth course, when the dishes were being removed, the King asked Curtius Rufus if his voyage had been a pleasant one. 'Yes, indeed, Highness, both swift and safe.' He added pleasantly since the King had not answered, 'It was very different in my father's time. A sea voyage was a hazardous matter.'

The Queen turned her head. 'You have brought peace to both land and sea, and we have much to be thankful for, even though some think the price to be high.'

Juba said, 'Yes, indeed. But I remember my tutor taught me that one cannot have both liberty and peace. His reasons were convincing though I do not remember them now.'

The chamberlain said, 'And his Highness, too, has done much for peace. We are honored that Rome has entrusted to us the guardianship of the sea coast from Carthage to Tingis. It is a great trust.'

The Queen's eyes flicked across the envoy's face like a silken lash. She said, 'I do not think our guest has been speaking the truth for I believe the journey was a stormy one.'

'Indeed, madam, it was, but it was most pleasant because each minute brought us nearer to the country we shall do all in our power to serve.'

The King said, 'That is a fair answer.'

The Queen raised her chin. 'You will admit, however, that there is a limit to the power of the most powerful.'

Juba sat suddenly still and his eyes went blank.

Curtius Rufus smiled and inclined his head. 'Madam, even Rome is ruled by men.'

'Who may be seasick and die?' she suggested in a soft voice.

'Very often, I fear. We rule the seas who cannot rule the skies.'

'I am glad to hear it, for then you would be gods and I might fear to sit at the same table with you.'

The chamberlain said smoothly, 'We have nothing to fear from our friends.'

The Queen said gently, 'Particularly when they come from Parthia,' and turned to speak to the guest on her left. Juba said, in a voice so quiet that Curtius Rufus could hardly hear him, 'Men are too often blamed for their accidents and praised only for their luck.' He relapsed into silence but Curtius Rufus saw sweat on the King's face and wondered what it was that had made him so afraid. His attention, however, was diverted by a troop of sword dancers who entered, and he settled back in his

175

chair to endure the entertainment, and thought no more of the matter.

The following day they attended a play by Plautus, given in the open air – 'excruciatingly acted' was Criton's comment afterward – and admired the new lighthouse and the basilica.

Then, on a day when Curtius Rufus was suffering from a headache after a bout of drinking the previous night, they watched a display of horsemanship by a chosen squadron of Numidian cavalry. Asked his opinion of their prowess by a court official, he said shortly, 'The horses are very fit.'

The King frowned and in the silence that followed the chamberlain remarked softly, 'They are superb, sir. It was their ancestors who destroyed a Roman army at Cannae.'

Criton held his breath, Lucius Eggius said nothing with great eloquence, and the Queen smiled.

Curtius Rufus, irritated beyond endurance by the King's impassive dignity, said coolly, 'Any man on a horse may do as much. My father's people have demonstrated that.'

The King leaned forward. 'Your father's people?' he asked.

'Yes, they hold Roman standards to this day. He came from Parthia, as the Queen has already observed.'

The King looked at him and there was the dawning of a faint interest in his eyes. He said, 'I see. It was you, then, who made that ride to Ammaedara.' He raised a hand, a courtier nodded, an order was given, and the squadron reformed, saluted, and rode off.

The King said, 'The Queen considers that I concern myself too much with books, too little with people. She may be right. But I was taught that the words must always follow the sense. I hope they do so in your case.' He nodded his dismissal and departed, his Queen following him in her litter.

Marcus Pedius said harshly, 'Our client king is beginning to grow teeth at last.'

Criton said, 'But why?' and looked helplessly from the

176

unsmiling faces of the officers to Curtius Rufus, who stood there with the defiant grin on his face that the Macedonian knew well. He had seen it often when his friend had lost the last throw of the dice.

They returned to the residency in silence. That evening Curtius Rufus, walking alone on the flat roof and watching the sun go down behind the hills, saw a deputation approach him, led by Cornelius Silius. The tribune said angrily, 'I have troubles enough of my own. Your Excellency has ruined two years' work in as many minutes. I shall have to report on this when next I write to the Proconsul.'

Lucius Eggius said calmly, 'If you have a reason, please tell us. The story has spread. A fatigue party of two legionaries has already been stoned in the bazaar. The captain of the Numidian regiment has complained of the insult to his men.'

Criton said, 'Dear boy, have the gods made you mad? We are diplomats, envoys; not barbarians fighting in a tavern.'

Curtius Rufus clenched his fists nervously, his hands hanging by his side. He said, 'Let us stop being polite. In short, let us speak truth for once – that is if you can bear to hear it. Let us use blunt words that men of breeding and imagined breeding prefer to avoid.' He looked contemptuously at the tribune. 'Do you think I don't know what you think of me behind my back and what your soldiers have nicknamed me?' He flicked a look at the escort centurion. 'If you fine Romans think this, then ask yourselves with your education what the King must think.'

Criton said hastily, 'Curtius—'

'No, Criton, we are not in the schools of philosophy now, playing with abstract ideas. The people who can afford to do that are those who have retired from life.'

Lucius Eggius said coolly, 'You have ruined this enterprise before it began.'

'Then if you really think that you are a fool.' Curtius Rufus smiled a thin smile, but his blue eyes had darkened with anger.

'You know this country. But I know Juba. I understand him as you never will. Do client kings not unbend in friendship to envoys? Of course they do. But not this man; and why? Because he feels insulted that his patron hasn't sent him a tribune of good family, who will trip over his nose every time he walks and whose perfume precedes his coming round every corner.'

'Your Excellency!' Cornelius Silius turned his back. 'I have heard enough.'

'And you will hear more so long as I hold authority in this matter from Marcus Agrippa. I, too, write reports.'

Lucius Eggius narrowed his eyes. 'Well?' he asked.

'For four days the King, a pleasant and charming young man, thoughtful, polite, scholarly, and sensitive – those are your words, not mine – for four days he has behaved as though I scarcely existed. This could not go on. He has scarcely smiled.'

Criton said, 'He will hardly do so now.'

'Oh, you fool, of course he will. He is a Numidian and I – I am half Parthian. We have a great deal in common. My father was a slave and I know everything about poverty, as you, and you, know everything about being rich. Juba was a prisoner and he had to walk in chains at a triumph when he was a boy. Do you know what that means? Can you imagine what that was like?' He looked at Lucius Eggius as he spoke.

The centurion said hesitantly, 'I don't understand.'

Criton said cautiously, 'Are you certain?'

'I am certain of only one thing – that someday we shall all die. Yes, he and I will understand each other very well from now on. The best bargaining is always done by men who respect each other.'

The tribune turned round. 'I hope your Excellency is right. These people riot easily and they do not love us over much. Our lives are in your hands.'

Curtius Rufus smiled. 'Then we, too, have something in

common, for mine is in yours. Let's open an amphora to celebrate, shall we?'

The King smiled nervously and rolled up the map. He said, 'I think that is enough work for one day.' He rose from the table and walked out on to the balcony overlooking the gardens, where a group of children, the sons and daughters of his staff, were playing on the edge of a pool of blue water. Curtius Rufus glanced at the other table, where Probus was carefully marking elevations on a plan. He said, 'Has Crescens marked the route for the water from those springs?'

The architect nodded grimly. 'Yes, but I reckon there's been an error on the siting of the middle section. The gradient for the piles should be a quarter of an inch in every hundred feet. It's not.'

'I'll see him about it later.'

The King said, 'Please join me,' and Curtius Rufus walked out on to the balcony. It was warm in the sun after the cool room they had left and the two men stood side by side, the King watching the children and Curtius Rufus watching the King. Juba's face was tense and his eyes unhappy. Curtius Rufus said nothing for a while, feeling the winter sun on his face and listening to the murmur of the city beyond the walls. It was, he thought, like standing on the Janiculum and watching the bustle of Rome beyond the Tiber. He began to wonder idly how soon he would see it again; he thought of Pero and tried to guess what she was doing at that precise moment. Inevitably his thoughts turned to the women lodged in the residency under Felicia's care. They kept to their own quarters, they went out once a day in closed litters and under escort, and they gave no trouble. He had seen Urracca twice to speak to since that day on the quayside in Carthage and each time she had remained aloof and impassive, answering his questions with meekness and a humility he knew to be deceptive.

He wished he knew what she was thinking and the fact that he did not was a constant irritation. It had been a long time since Rome and he found difficulty in sleeping at night. He had no difficulty in knowing why.

Juba said boyishly, 'I have great plans for this city, very great plans. I want it to be the finest city in Africa. I want a new theater and a new palace.'

Curtius Rufus said, 'It will be expensive. You realize that, sir? The cost of paving with stone blocks will be two sesterces per square foot – so sixteen miles will total nearly two million. The handling facilities in the harbor need to be enlarged first.'

Juba frowned. 'Yes, yes. More trade will bring more money and we need money to pay for the building. Your secretary has been a great help. I have written to the ateliers he recommended. They have accepted. The dispatch boat brought their letters this morning. They will create fine statues that will stand in the new forum and in the palace. The first will be of Augustus.'

'Naturally.'

The King laughed. 'I know when you are making fun of me, but I do not mind. Yes, and we have need of a great library too.' He looked out across the garden and over the flat roofs of the city toward the sea. 'I miss books most of all.'

'But – you have a library here.'

'It is only a beginning. That is what I missed most when I came. To be cut off from books is to be cut off from life. I hated it at first. I felt an exile.'

'You miss Rome, sir?'

'Yes, don't you?'

Curtius Rufus smiled. 'Yes, a little. But I am grateful for the opportunity that enabled me to visit your kingdom. It is a wonderful land.'

Juba glanced at him. 'And I am grateful for whatever it was that brought you here. Your officers, your technicians, your craftsmen have been wonderful. They work so hard. It was what

I needed to make a start.' He paused and said shyly, 'I intend to show that Augustus' trust is well founded.'

'No one but a madman, sir, would doubt that.'

Juba said anxiously, 'You won't leave too soon, will you? My people are slow to learn, I know. It takes time to master a craft and without your instructors we should be lost.'

'I am here only to assist you. Those are my instructions. I cannot do so if I leave.'

The King laughed. 'No, of course not. It is two months now since you came. Yes, what is it?' He turned as a servant appeared in the doorway.

'Letters, sir, brought from the residency. They are for his Excellency.'

'Will you excuse me, sir?'

'Yes, of course. Ah, there is the Queen. I told her it was a warm day and that she should not walk so far. I was right.'

Curtius Rufus broke the seal and unrolled the parchment. It was a letter from Marcus Agrippa. '. . . I am pleased to have received good reports of the work you have so far performed on the King's behalf. He speaks highly of you and I am glad my judgment has not been proved wrong . . . please do not forget the true purpose of your journey, however. Matters are far more serious than when I wrote to you before . . . I am instructed to inform you that you must take any action you may see fit that will hasten the recovery of the niece of Valerius Messalla.' The letter ended as formally as it began.

Curtius Rufus rolled it and tucked it into his tunic without a word.

The King said anxiously, 'You have had bad news?'

Curtius Rufus nodded. 'Augustus is still unwell.'

Juba turned pale. He said, 'I – I am sorry to hear such news.' He paused. He said, 'But he has been unwell before. I – I will pray for his recovery.' He hesitated. He said, 'Perhaps I should tell you—' and broke off suddenly. His hands began to tremble.

He looked over the envoy's shoulder at a group of people who came into the Library at that moment. Among them was the Queen. The King turned and went to meet her, a smile on his face, anxiety in his eyes.

Curtius Rufus touched his lip and put a finger to his ear. He felt disturbed. It was not until later when he was back at the residency that he began to wonder what it was that the King had intended to say.

For Criton it had been another day of continued interruptions. Vatinus had been first, complaining that they were low on animal fodder and that the groom was irritable because he hadn't been able to exercise the horses. Probus, the architect, had asked to share his room with anyone but Crescens, for the surveyor snored and kept him awake at night; and how could he draw accurate plans if he was always tired and nervy from shortage of sleep? Felicia had been next, demanding to see him alone, which meant that the clerks must leave the room and so waste valuable time. She was worried about the girls, who were irritable at being confined to their quarters; they were too pale from lack of exercise. When Criton protested that he could do nothing and that the bad weather was not his fault, she had said bluntly that the trouble was due to their having so little to do. Criton then said sharply that he was a secretary and not a house steward, whereupon she swore that she had never met a man who understood the obvious, and departed, slamming the door violently. Lastly came Marcus Pedius, dripping water from his cloak and grumbling about the weather. 'I have had to postpone all building work and all fatigue parties. Two of the men have had an accident down at the harbor – oh, nothing serious.' He paused and then unleashed his complaint. 'The surgeon is nowhere to be found – probably drinking in a tavern as usual! Well, do you know where he's hidden the key to the medical chest?' When he had gone, Criton said wearily to the senior clerk, 'Make two copies and then hand them to the Tribune. He will see that they are dispatched.' He shivered and wished he had put on a thicker tunic. Outside it was still raining and he could hear the cold wind that had blown for four days now, driving through the oleander bushes in the courtyard. He bent again over his daily journal, anxious to ensure that he had transcribed accurately the envoy's account of his last meeting with the King. Presently his hand grew tired and he paused, his thoughts turning pleasantly to the memories of the previous night. The Syrian boy he had met in the market place the previous day, and who was almost certainly a spy, had proved surprisingly accommodating. Criton wondered if he would return this evening as promised.

The second clerk, who was preparing the food allowances for the month, said anxiously, 'We are nearly out of ink and pens, sir. Shall I try to get some in the town?'

'Yes, but make sure the reeds are made from a single joint. I don't care for the others. We need parchment too. I never imagined that the mission would involve so much writing. I could have copied the collected speeches of the Senate twice over by now.'

Curtius Rufus returned in the late afternoon from the palace, tired and exasperated. Without waiting to change his riding clothes he went to his study and sent his slaves to fetch wine and hot water. Criton joined him, followed by Cornelius Silius, who had just come from the harbor. 'Another dispatch,' he said.

Curtius Rufus opened it and passed it to Criton.

Cornelius Silius said, 'Did you have a profitable day?'

Curtius Rufus shook his head. 'I saw the King and we discussed little except pleasantries, the health of his family, and rebuilding. The King is fascinated by the craftsmanship of the tessellated floor worker. I think he wishes to learn how to do it himself. Then I attended a council meeting; they discussed trade about which I know very little, being the son of a man who failed in it. And you?'

Cornelius Silius said, 'I have little to report except one curious thing which I learned by chance, and that from the officer in charge of the Africa flotilla.'

'Go on.'

'In early September a bireme stationed at Portus Sigensis went on a short training voyage. The crew consisted of one hundred and eight rowers, all natives to this coastline, twenty-five sailors, of whom only three were in Roman service, and thirty soldiers, all belonging to the King's levies. The ship put in at Russaddir, further along the coast, for minor repairs. Three days before Messalla's niece was kidnapped the bireme's captain put to sea and was last seen close in shore, following the line of the cape – that is in a northerly direction.' He paused and sipped his wine.

'You said "last seen".'

'Yes, sir. The bireme never returned. In November the officer at Portus Sigensis reported the ship as lost at sea to his senior officer here. There was no wreckage and no survivors. The senior officer reported the matter to the palace and the Chief Counselor ordered the building of a replacement. The new ship was built in great haste in twenty-eight days. They must have employed over two hundred men to get the work done so fast.'

Curtius Rufus said, 'Well? It could have been a genuine accident.'

'Sir, the weather was good at the time, and the captain an experienced man. It is just possible that the bireme met the pirate ship returning with the abducted girl and was sunk in a fight.'

'You may be right; but that doesn't get us anywhere at all.'

Cornelius Silius said in a relentless voice, 'We have no proof but it is a possible straw in the wind. I think the new ship was built in a hurry to conceal the loss of the old one. The order for rebuilding was signed by the King.'

'But, surely – there were Roman naval personnel on board. Their absence couldn't be concealed.'

'No, sir. Their deaths were reported to the authorities at Misenum.'

'Well then?' Curtius Rufus shrugged his shoulders.

'That was nearly three months later. The report – I have seen a copy at the harbor record office – says they died in a sea accident when their landing boat was overturned in the surf off the beaches to the east of Portus Sigensis.'

'Are you sure of this?'

Cornelius Silius grinned. 'I have obtained eyewitness reports that the three men were on the bireme the day she last sailed. I have checked the dates of the report of their deaths. Name me a man who despises money and I will call him a fool. My contact is not a fool.'

'Very well, someone has lied. We want the girl, not the con-cealer of embarrassing accidents.'

Cornelius Silius said softly, 'If the signature is not forged, then it is the King who has lied.'

Curtius Rufus said, 'Pour me some more wine, but spare the water. Yes, Criton?'

'Here is your message, Curtius.' Criton looked troubled and his hand trembled.

Curtius Rufus took the parchment and read it. 'There is need to trade as well as build. The good merchant must catch the wind at the right time or he will lose his market. It is better to be forgiven than forgotten.' It was signed in the name of Maecenas's secretary. He looked up at the two men. 'Another warning that we must hurry.'

Criton said, 'But one cannot hurry in matters of this kind.'

Curtius Rufus turned to the tribune. 'What about your spies in the palace?'

'Nothing, sir. I am sorry.'

'Not even from your mistress, that dark girl, Naida, who attends the Queen and who is always smiling?' It was Criton who asked the question. 'Or do you never give her time to talk?'

Cornelius Silius went red in the face. He said stiffly, 'She gives me little except court gossip, and I give her gossip in turn. I think she spies on me for the Queen and receives silver from us both.'

Curtius Rufus ran his fingers through his hair in irritation. He felt tired, harassed, and anxious. He said, 'It is no use our losing our tempers. We have been here – how many weeks? – and we know no more than when we arrived. Time is not on our side in this matter and we cannot delay any longer. Silius, will you arrange an audience for me with the King? I cannot risk, for his sake or mine, our conversation being overheard. It would be best if we go riding together.'

Cornelius Silius said, 'Then we must wait for the rain to stop.'

Criton said, 'And what if he knows nothing, and cannot or will not help us? You will be worse off than before.'

'That I must risk.'

'If Juba turns against us you risk all our lives,' said the tribune.

'I have the authority of Marcus Agrippa.'

'It might be repudiated,' said Criton in a warning voice.

Curtius Rufus said stubbornly, 'I know the risks.' It was getting dark in the room now, the rain was still pouring outside and his face was in shadow. He said, 'You remember your lives, but I have not forgotten that girl. I spoke to Valerius Messalla about her. You did not. She has been in their hands – the hands of a barbarian people – for months now; and each day and each night that passes she is still there; and we – we do nothing. I promised him that I would get her back. I swore an oath before the altar of his household gods, and I intend to keep my word. Let come what may.'

CHAPTER XII

The bad weather continued and each day Cornelius Silius would shake his head and say, 'We had better wait. It is not a day for riding. When Arcturus rises we shall see clear skies again.'

On the fourth day of waiting Curtius Rufus felt unwell. The residency seemed even more draughty and damp than usual, and he suffered, despite the presence of a brazier, from alternating bouts of cold and heat. Criton, visiting him in his study after dinner, took one look at his face and ordered him to bed. He went without protest of any kind, the surgeon was called, and for a week he lay ill with a fever which Cornelius Silius attributed to the bad water in a wine jug. Marcus Pedius checked the water supply on hearing this but could find nothing wrong, though the servant who brought the jug into the room swore that it had been filled from the well in the outer courtyard.

Criton said, 'It may have been carelessness,' but Cornelius Silius shook his head and dismissed the man within the hour. Lucius Eggius, who sat up for two nights with the sick man, was inclined to agree with him. 'Another delay,' he said. 'But what a crude way to go about it.'

The news reached the palace and the King sent messages of sympathy. The Queen, more practical-minded, sent her own doctor, a Greek from Delos, who had formerly been in the employ of the Praefectus of Egypt. When the envoy was better the Queen sent another message, inviting him to stay at the palace. This Cornelius Silius insisted on his accepting. 'The residency is overcrowded and not a place in which to recover

187

from an illness.' Criton expressed his fears for his friend's safety. The tribune said bluntly, 'He will be quite safe. If anyone had wished otherwise he would be dead now, not standing on his feet like a young calf about to take its first steps.' Curtius Rufus, overhearing the conversation, said weakly, 'I agree with Silius. I can achieve nothing till I have seen the King and I must get fit as quickly as I can.'

On the day of his departure, Felicia came to see him. She had been ill too. 'Don't worry about me,' she said. 'I have survived much worse. Urracca wishes to speak to you. Something's upset the girl. She won't tell me what. Insists on seeing you.'

He said, 'Send her in. I owe her thanks for nursing me anyway, so I understand.'

Felicia said roughly, 'But for her you would have died. Ask Criton if you don't believe me.'

Urracca found him sitting in a chair by the window and wearing a loose robe. She looked pale and thin but her expression was as remote as ever.

He said, 'I am in your debt and I will do my best to repay it. Meanwhile, accept my thanks. I owe you my life it seems.'

She smiled faintly, 'You cannot be in debt to a slave,' she said. 'I did what I had to do. When I was a child I sat up once all night with a sick puppy and thought to save it. But it died.'

He said, 'I do not feel well enough to argue the matter,' and closed his eyes. 'What is it you wish to see me about?'

She clasped her hands in front of her. 'Don't go to the palace,' she said. 'I have heard stories about the Queen. We hear a great deal of gossip – there is little else to do – from those who call at the residency. The slaves pass it one to another and so to us. I think you will be in danger if you go.'

'Have you any proof of this?'

She shook her head.

'If they had wished to kill me I would be dead by now of that wine and water.'

'I know,' she said. 'It is a feeling that I have. Please, do not go. I am afraid for you.'

He opened his eyes. Her face was as composed as ever. He looked at her and grinned. It was not one of his best grins but it was the first she had received, and her hands tightened suddenly. 'Please,' she said again.

He shook his head. 'You mean well, and I thank you for it. But I cannot change my mind now.'

'I thought you might say that. I am sorry, master, that I have troubled you.' She bowed her head and went to the door. She turned and smiled. 'If a man will die from sugar why kill him with poison?' She went out and he heard the door close very gently behind her.

He took with him two of his slaves and was given a suite of rooms on the south side of the palace, overlooking the gardens. He had few visitors except the Chamberlain, who paid a formal call to ensure that he was comfortable and expressed polite regrets that his Excellency was still so unwell that he had not thought it necessary to bring his slave girls with him. Slowly he grew stronger and was able to walk without feeling the need to sit down every few minutes. He dictated letters, sent messages to Criton, and began to grow irritable with inaction. He learned that Juba was away from the city on a short visit to the interior – something to do with an animal hunt – but had left word that he looked forward to further talks with the envoy upon his return. Two days after the King's departure he received another visit from the Chamberlain. 'The Queen sends you greetings and is most happy to hear of your recovery.' The Numidian paused and cleared his throat. 'She invites you to dine with her tomorrow and promises you entertainment.'

'I accept the Queen's invitation with gratitude,' said Curtius Rufus gravely. 'May I ask if it is to be a formal banquet?'

'No, Excellency, a private dinner only. The Queen feels that in the interests of your health it would not be wise to tax your strength with the formalities of an official occasion.'

189

'I am the more honored. Please convey my thanks to the Queen for her concern.'

The Chamberlain bowed and departed. Alone again, Curtius Rufus went to the window and sat down in his chair. He took from his tunic the dice that he had not played with since Rome, and began to roll them upon the table. I am out of practice, he said to himself. I shall soon be staking all on a single throw. I pray to Fortune that she may favor me again. He remembered Maecenas's message, curt, brutal – and shivered. If he failed he knew that he would not see the seven hills again.

The dinner was served in the Queen's Reception Room, a blue and gold chamber with latticed windows, a painted ceiling, and a mosaic floor, partly covered by woven rugs. Torches flared in sockets on the walls, and the room was heated by braziers. He shared a cushioned couch with the Queen, and the ivory table before them was inlaid with gold leaf. They were attended by two of the ladies of her court, one of them, Naida, the raven-haired girl who was known to Cornelius Silius, while Nubian slaves in scarlet jackets and bell-like trousers stood sentinel around the walls. The meal was served by female slaves under the direction of a master of ceremonies, who was the only other man present apart from the Queen's secretary, an Egyptian, whom Curtius Rufus had met briefly on previous visits to the palace.

Cleopatra Selene wore a blue and gold sleeveless gown that fell in soft folds about her feet. Her dark hair, which she had worn piled on her head at their first meeting, had been dressed to fit her like a cap, and hung thick and straight in a gold net down to her bare shoulders. He noticed the intricately worked gold collar about her neck, the gold moon-shaped earrings that danced against the line of her jaw, and the gold belt, set with pearls, about her waist. In her finery, he thought, she was almost beautiful.

She was polite but formal, and they talked of commonplace matters once she had inquired after his health, the secretary joining in from time to time. The room grew warmer and the braziers gave off a smell of cedar wood that seemed to hang heavy in the air in a not unpleasant fashion. They drank from silver goblets such as he had never seen before, and there was always a smiling girl waiting to proffer a refill before he had emptied his cup.

She talked to him of Rome, of its architecture and its aqueducts, spoke of plays she had seen and of the books she had read. She touched on philosophy, mathematics, and science, and of her wish that she, with her husband, whose absence that evening she regretted more than she could say, might make of Iol Caesarea a new Alexandria, famed for its arts, its beauty and its civility. She talked well and she had the rare gift of making topics interesting that were almost unknown to the hearer. But she had had the best of teachers, he thought, as he tried desperately to make intelligent answers to the questions that she put to him.

'I am afraid, madam,' he said, 'that I know little of these matters. I am – an engineer and little else. I build things, but I cannot talk about them.'

He saw her smile slightly as she said gently, 'It takes an honest man to admit his ignorance before a woman. Perhaps an intelligent one, too. Tell me, does the statue of Cornelia still stand in the Portico of Octavia? There was talk of moving it before I left Rome.'

Between courses they were entertained by jugglers, a girl who sang to a harp, a pair of Negro tumblers, and a boy who did a dance with knives, walking upside down on the points as the climax to his act. The Queen watched them and he watched the Queen, catching her eye politely as she turned, now and again, to comment upon the performance, her every remark designed to encourage him to speak. He could smell her perfume, light and dry and pleasing; watched the gold and ivory clasp on

191

the shoulder of her gown shimmer in the light as she moved; and noted the smooth olive sheen of her skin, and the large amethyst ring that she wore on her left hand.

'You are very silent,' she said at length, and her voice, low and husky, sounded infinitely kind.

'If I am, madam,' he said politely, and his voice sounded strained and harsh in his ears, 'it is because I am dazzled by so much magnificence. To which,' he added frankly, 'I am not accustomed.' He grinned, feeling beads of sweat on his face.

'Oh, the room is quite ordinary and the entertainment is at best amusing.' She paused and looked at him under blue-painted eyelids, edged with kohl. 'If that is all? One may get accustomed to anything, as I know from experience.'

He felt suddenly as though he were on the edge of a high place. He saw the flash of light reflected from her ring as she moved her hand to her goblet. He said, 'It is not that at all. One should always walk softly in the presence of the gods.'

She continued to look at him. Her eyes grew luminous. She took the goblet and drank from it, watching him all the time. Then she let out a little sigh and said gently, 'Tell me why you say that. I command you.'

He said, and it was as though he had known all along the real truth about her, 'I have seen the amethyst on your finger and know the crescent moon when it moves before my eyes. It was not for nothing that at your birth you were named Cleopatra Selene.'

She said simply, 'It was ordained.' She called softly and one of her girls came and knelt beside her, a golden box in her hands. Never taking her eyes from him the Queen opened the box and took out a wrist clasp, made of silver and embossed with a patterned device he did not know. 'It is customary to exchange gifts,' she said. 'This is my gift to you. Let me put it on that the gift may be the more valued.' She touched his wrist with warm, impersonal fingers and snapped the clasp. 'Now you must give me a gift.'

192

He said, 'I did not know – I have not brought—'

'Will you give me your bracelet? It will be a fair exchange, and I will treasure it always in memory of the envoy of Augustus.'

He smiled. There was nothing else he could do, though the bracelet symbolized many things for him, and hope was only one of them.

'You may put it on my wrist.' She extended her arm and he did as she told him.

He drank his wine. It was quite late now and he wondered briefly whether he should make his excuses and retire. He did not know the etiquette in such matters. The flute players seemed to have retired; the slave girls had removed the discarded dishes; and the secretary had disappeared. The room seemed darker, but that might have been due to the fact that the braziers had been moved closer to the center of the floor. Some of the Nubians were no longer visible. Perhaps they had gone too.

The Queen said, 'It is still early. The entertainment I promised you is still to come. You will, I think, enjoy it. Only men of small desires experience small pleasures.'

He inclined his head at the compliment. He said, 'I am in your hands in this matter.'

She sat very still and her face was suddenly remote and without expression. Then she leaned a little toward him and he dropped his eyes to the swell of her breasts.

She smiled mockingly and said coolly, 'Look at me.' He raised his eyes and she nodded as though satisfied. 'Yes,' she said. 'You are indeed.'

Someone behind him clapped hands; a flute sounded in the shadows at the end of the chamber, to be joined presently by the low throbbing of a drum. A shape appeared out of the darkness and glided forward into the light, and the torches flickered suddenly as though startled, and then steadied, shining softly upon a blue and gold gown, dark hair held in a golden net, the

193

glint of crescent-shaped earrings, a golden torque, and long slim hands. He leaned forward and there was a sudden sweat on his forehead as he saw the eyes below the blue-painted lids. It was the face of the Queen.

He drew in his breath sharply and looked at the Queen by his side. She seemed amused and said in a low voice, 'Do you turn from the setting of the rising sun?'

He saw that his bracelet was not upon her wrist.

He turned again and the Queen was moving toward him. Ten paces away she paused, raising her hands and clasping them behind her head. The action, slow and infinitely graceful, stirred a chord of memory in his mind, but it was so faint that he could not pick out the tune. Her body began to undulate and she stretched her hand out to him with the gesture of a suppliant. At that moment he could see quite clearly the bracelet upon the fine-boned wrist. It was his own. The drumbeats increased in intensity as she began to dance.

He had seen the fashionable women of Rome perform upon the appointed day in honor of their Mystery, but their stylized and graceful movements owed more to art than to religious fervor. He had seen girls of another class who displayed themselves in smoky taverns or upon the stage, but their cold smiles and lascivious gestures could not reveal the warmth they did not possess. She was not like these others and he watched, entranced by the elusive smile on her lips, the enigmatic promise in her eyes, the subtle sway of her body.

There was a faint rustle of material as the Queen by his side leaned back against the cushions and watched his face, but he did not notice. He never took his eyes from the Queen, who danced in his honor. The torchlight flickered upon blue and gold, her beauty quickened dreams, and her shadow painted promises upon the wall.

He stirred as the music died, eased his cramped legs, and blinked once. The reception chamber was empty, the torches burned low upon the wall, and the Queen reclined gracefully by his side, turning a goblet round and round in her fingers. He passed a hand across his face and said hesitantly, 'I – I don't understand. My bracelet—' He looked at her in puzzled silence.

She said, 'It is mine now,' and held up her wrist. He shook his head in bewilderment.

The Queen said softly, 'How may I entertain you further?'

He did not speak but looked at the bracelet on her arm and then touched the clasp she had given him in exchange.

She said, 'I have called down the moon and still you are not content.' She rose to her feet. 'I will show you to your room or you may lose the way. It is late and the servants have retired.'

He followed her through a maze of corridors and anterooms, and was glad she guided him, for he could not remember the way. Outside the door at the end of a long passage she stopped. 'Your suite,' she said. She held out her hand and he bent and kissed her wrist. She smiled. 'I trust that you have all you desire. If you cannot sleep, then look upon the moon.' She turned away and seemed to melt into the darkness. He heard the faint rustle of her skirts die away as he opened the door and went inside.

The chamber was in darkness but the moon shone faintly through latticed windows set high in the walls, and it seemed to him that he stood in a strange place, ornate, larger, more luxuriously furnished than any he had yet seen. A huge divan, covered with embroidered material and scattered about with cushions, filled almost half the floor space and was hung, on three sides, by curtains of some fine stuff that trembled in the night air. The scent of a perfume came to him and he knew it: it was the Queen's. Puzzled, he turned and then stopped as something moved in the darkness. A shadow seemed to detach itself from the wall and floated toward him. He saw the moonlight shine upon blue and gold and heard the swish of a dress. His mouth felt dry. He said, 'But, madam—' and then the Queen put up her hands and touched his face. He looked down at her and then glanced back toward the closed door. The Queen put a hand on his mouth and said gently, 'She has gone. I am here. Look at me.'

He stared at her and she saw the expression on his face change. She smiled and said, 'I have danced for your pleasure. Do you wish to kiss me also?'

He said, 'A shoemaker should not raise his eyes above the sandals.'

She laughed softly. 'That depends, surely, who wears them. It is no answer to my question, Curtius Rufus.'

He stood motionless before her, his hands by his sides. He said hoarsely, 'I am the envoy of Rome.' She moved closer and he felt her arms round his neck, her hands in his hair.

He hesitated. He said, 'The – the kiss is the forerunner of adultery.'

She rubbed herself against him like a cat and said coolly, 'But we are not in Parthia now.'

Still he hesitated. He said, 'Today is the festival of Regifugium – the flight of the king.'

She laughed and he felt his mouth touched. After that he hesitated no longer.

In the morning when he awoke he was in his own chamber and it was long past daylight, and he could not recall how he had got there. He called out and his body slave came with the wine that he always drank upon rising. The slave looked at him curiously but said nothing, and then departed. Curtius Rufus looked at the neatness of the bed, at the tidy room and at the clothes folded upon a stool. He reached for the jug and it was then that he saw the bracelet upon his wrist. He remembered the words that Urracca had spoken to him; and he felt sick with fear.

Later that day he met the Queen at a formal ceremony: the leave-taking of an envoy on his way to Alexandria. Afterward she indicated that she wished to speak to him and he followed her into an anteroom, Naida standing by the door to see that they were not disturbed. For a while she talked of matters relating to his visit and he was grateful for the impersonal nature of their meeting. At its conclusion she paused, gave him a long look, and then said quietly, 'You have the bracelet still that I gave you?'

He touched his wrist. 'Yes, madam, I – I cannot find the catch.'

'Does that worry you?'

'When the King returns—?'

'He will not return for another two days. I have a large jewel chest. Even I cannot remember all that is in it.'

'It – it is not something I could have bought.' He broke off and licked his dry lips.

'No,' she said dryly. 'It is a piece out of the treasure that once belonged to my mother. That I possess it at all, I owe to the kindness of the Lady Octavia.' She smiled ironically. 'But the Lady Octavia has always a reputation for kindness. It is what she lives for.'

Curtius Rufus said, 'I do not understand.' He paused and said huskily, 'It might be best, madam, if I returned the bracelet.' He paused again and looked steadily at a point over her shoulder. 'Particularly, madam, since I have no memory of what has passed. None at all.'

She smiled. 'Maecenas has an excellent pupil. I understand you at least. Are you afraid?'

He nodded.

'There is no need to be.' She smiled again. 'Perhaps I do not choose that you should forget. The bracelet is yours. I cannot take back what I have given. As for the clasp, there is a trick to the opening of it.'

'May I know, madam?' He looked at her inquiringly.

'But of course. You may visit me in my apartments this evening and we can discuss the matter. I will send one of my attendants to fetch you.' The Queen paused and gave him a curious look. She said, 'One should never walk alone in the dark when the moon is up.'

Juba returned, looking relaxed and cheerful, expressed his pleasure at the envoy's recovery and readily agreed to the granting of an audience. 'I understand,' he said with a friendly smile. 'If I blow my nose in a closet there is a rumor across the city within the hour that I am dying.' He raised his voice slightly as a court official moved toward him. 'I would like to see the progress of work on the new cisterns. Perhaps you will ride out with me tomorrow? I understand that your engineer is making remarkable progress.'

'Yes, sir, but Fronto has some problems still and your advice would be appreciated.'

The cistern was half completed and a gang of men were on the site, working in groups under the direction of soldiers from the legionary escort. Some were mixing mortar while others sorted the piles of rubble stone that had been brought from the quarries. A great fire blazed, fed by sweating men who were burning stones to make lime; a surgeon was busy at the side of a cart, attending to the minor injuries of those who had suffered accidents; and the sound of hammers, the creak of pulleys, the shouts of men moving a crane into position increased in intensity as they picked their way through a litter of timber and scaffolding. Over all hung a thin cloud of dust.

Fronto explained his difficulties, received answers which partially satisfied him, and then led them on a conducted tour, pointing out the marked areas reserved for the cisterns yet to be built. 'And, of course, there will be covered galleries to protect the users from the sun in summer,' he said, at the end.

The King nodded silently and the engineer, at a signal from Curtius Rufus, withdrew. Juba frowned. 'Let us walk,' he said.

They strolled to the edge of the area. Behind was a scattering of buildings, and open country lay beyond. 'Well?'

Curtius Rufus said, 'I have been asked to inquire if you, sir, have any news of the legate's daughter? The girl who was kidnapped last autumn.'

The King turned his head. 'Should I have?'

'Sir, it is known she was taken by pirates from this coast. The reason was not ransom.'

The King frowned. 'I received inquiries about this matter at the time. I replied that I knew nothing. I still know nothing.'

Curtius Rufus twisted the rings on his fingers. 'The Africa flotilla has responsibility in this matter.'

Juba said, 'There are twelve hundred miles of coast, at least, between here and Tingis. A ship might beach anywhere at any time and not be seen.'

'I – I appreciate that, sir. You have heard nothing? No rumors, no stories?'

There was a perceptible pause while the King looked at a gang of men mixing slurry. 'Is my loyalty to Rome in question? I would have told all that I knew if I had known anything.'

'Yes, sir.' Curtius Rufus tried to moisten his lips. 'I only ask because you might have learned something, perhaps, that you did not wish put into a letter.'

The King said, in an expressionless voice, 'Do I suspect anything or anyone – is that what you really mean?'

Curtius Rufus nodded.

There was a long silence. Then the King turned fully and Curtius Rufus saw that his old-young face had become a mask. It bore no expression and the eyes had gone dead. The King said, 'This is why you really came. I half guessed at it from the first, but I pretended to myself that it was not so.'

Curtius Rufus said, 'Such a mission to aid you would still have come. You had requested it.'

'It is not quite the same.' Juba paused and then said bitterly, 'I

199

owe everything to Rome. My father chose the wrong side and died, fighting for Pompeius. It was a natural enough mistake to make. Others made it who opposed the deified Julius, and they had cause to know him better. After Thapsus, my father became a fugitive in his own country, an object of scorn and pity to his people. He found himself deserted in his house, abandoned by everyone except Marcus Petreius, the lieutenant of Pompeius, and a handful of servants. They dined together and then – and then they fought with swords, each to save the other the ignominy of capture. It requires great courage, great despair, great skill, to fall on your own sword. My father was the strongest and he slew Petreius, who thanked him before he died. Then he paid a slave to kill him in his turn.'

Curtius Rufus said, 'It is all past now.'

The King said, 'And still the memory eats me up when I think of it. I walked in a Roman triumph; I lived in Octavia's house; I was given Numidia back by Augustus; then he made changes and I was told I was to be a king of Mauretania instead. I am a king, and I have great wealth and a beautiful wife and power. But I have nothing that is mine. I have lived on gratitude all my life, and I shall do so until I die.'

Curtius Rufus said, 'No one can alter yesterday. Why tell me this? If I were a spiteful man—'

'You would still know that I hold my kingdom, as a drunken man holds a fragile goblet.' Juba blinked suddenly. A normal look returned to his face. He grinned. 'My people are not all lovers of Rome. I can say that without fear. It is known to all. I write regularly to Augustus on these matters. But for that reason I must go carefully. They think me too much a Romi already. I need time, patience, and peace.' He smiled suddenly. 'I am not a warrior. I was not allowed to be. My interests are elsewhere. If I acquire knowledge it is through my own efforts. That is something no one can take from me.'

Curtius Rufus wiped the dust from his face. He said, 'You know of no one who would wish to harm you?'

'Wherever there is a king there are people who wish to take his place.'

'You cannot help me then, sir?'

'No, I cannot help you.' He looked steadily at the envoy. 'Please do not forget that I am still the Ally and Friend of the Roman People.' He stood where he was, watching two men who were trying to break a large rock with iron bars. He said casually, 'Have you had any news from Rome recently? All is well, I trust.'

'I hope so, sir, but I have not had a letter in days.'

The King nodded. He said quietly, 'Those two men are wasting their time. If they were educated they would know that you cannot break a rock by such means. You must first build a fire.'

'And use vinegar,' said the envoy without thinking.

'Yes. If you have the means, any difficulty can be overcome.' The King turned to go back and Curtius Rufus followed him, stumbling a little over the rubble. He began to wonder if he had been given a warning, but if so the message was obscure and he did not understand it properly. He returned to the residency and called Criton to his room.

Criton said, 'Dear boy, I have been worried.' He stopped and looked at his friend's face. 'Well, you do look better. The palace was obviously good for you.'

Curtius Rufus grinned. 'I have missed you, too.'

'I must tell our honey-tongued Felicia to pass on the news. One of your slaves has had a face like Cassandra since you left.'

'Who is Cassandra?'

Criton shook his head. 'Never mind. I had forgotten you lack my education. And how was the Queen?'

Curtius Rufus said quickly, 'What have you heard?'

'Nothing, dear boy. That is why we worried about you. But Cornelius Silius has some interesting news; so, too, has Lucius Eggius.'

'It must wait. It is about the Queen I want to talk. I saw Juba this morning. He says he cannot help. The man is lying. He knows something and is afraid; but I shall never be able to persuade him to say what he knows.' He looked at Criton and added hopelessly, 'Well, what now?'

Criton said, 'What then of the Queen?'

Curtius Rufus said, 'I made a mistake.' His lips curled. 'No, that is not true. I betrayed us all.'

'Tell me, Curtius.'

Curtius Rufus told him. When he had finished he put his head in his hands. Presently he said, 'Can you explain it to me?'

Criton hesitated. 'No,' he said. The window shutter banged and he rose to close it. 'We shall get more rain; the wind has changed.' He sat down again on a stool by the fire. He said, 'Some things I do know. Her mother claimed to be the mystical daughter of Re, the bright god of the sun. She wore a ring, an amethyst, the stone of sobriety, which, I think, indicated that she was an initiate of Dionysius; but to her it meant more than that; it meant that she was beyond the weaknesses of the flesh. She might employ them for her own ends; but they were her servants, not her masters. They say she died by the bite of an asp. This I believe, for the asp was the servant of Re and made immortal whom it struck.'

'She said to me that evening – I remember, "One may be drunk without wine." That I knew, but I did not understand what she meant. She said many things I don't understand.'

Criton stared at the fire. He said, 'The princesses of the blood in the Macedonian line are known to have murdered, betrayed, and stolen, but no hint of scandal was ever attached to their name. None ever took a lover out of lust. They had too much pride. I do not think that Cleopatra Selene would have taken you – a man like myself of no birth.'

'It was a trick then. I thought so afterwards. She had a double.'

Criton said dryly, 'In this matter you know best. But I would have thought that no two women were so alike that you could not tell them apart in – in certain circumstances.' He added sharply, 'You do not sound so certain yourself.'

'If I were drunk I might say there was magic in it somewhere.'

Criton did not answer him.

Curtius Rufus said, 'Do you believe in such things?'

Criton said cautiously, 'If I believe in gods, why may I not believe in magic?' He smiled. 'And if I do not believe in magic, why then should I throw salt over my shoulder when I have spilt it? Why do I think it bad luck to remove a table while a guest is drinking? Why does Augustus, if the tale is true, always put the right shoe on first when he is dressing? Yet men do all these things.'

Curtius Rufus said, 'I do not know what to think.'

Criton said, 'She is her mother's daughter.' He did not look up from the fire as he spoke. He said, 'You and she exchanged bracelets, and hers you still have upon your wrist.'

'I don't know if what she said about its origin is true.'

'Cornelius Silius thinks it is very old. Because of that I prefer to choose my words carefully, lest her gods are listening. Those who worship in the wetlands beside the Nile believe that everyone born has a Ka, a second self which accompanies them into the world and never leaves them. Sometimes this being takes shape as the counterpart of the body.' He raised his eyes and looked at his friend. 'It is not necessarily evil,' he said gently.

Curtius Rufus said, 'I need some wine.' He rose to his feet and said, 'I still do not understand. Nor do I understand what the purpose of it all was.'

Criton nodded. 'At least, like me, you believe that what happened had a purpose. Cleopatra Selene was not just bored by her husband's absence. You did not win what you won by virtue of your reputation and your charm.'

'You are making fun of me.'

'No, I am not. As to understanding why; you will know the answer when next you see her. As to understanding how; that you may never know. The true magic is never wholly revealed.'

The lady-in-waiting arrived in a curtained litter and was led ceremoniously into the one room large enough to be used for receptions. Upon hearing the door open Naida turned, saw Curtius Rufus, and made her obeisance. 'I have come in answer to your message,' she said. 'I am not to be absent long, however, since the Queen needs me in a little while.' She saw the bracelet on his wrist and a smile flickered on her face. 'As my Lord will know, the Queen does not like to be kept waiting.' Her voice was pert and he realized that she knew.

He said, 'I wish to see the Queen if she will grant me an audience, but it must be in private and I wish no one else to know of the matter. It is for the Queen's safety, you understand?'

Naida said, 'I understand perfectly, and the Queen will appreciate your discretion.' She smiled. 'But – if my Lord will forgive me – it might be wiser to wait until the Queen sends for you.'

He said, 'You misunderstand me entirely. Tell your mistress I must see her as soon as possible. Tell her that the wreckage of a bireme has been found.'

Her face went pale. She said, 'I will do as you say,' and hurried from the room. She returned an hour later, looking less composed than she had on her first visit. She said, 'I have given your message and the Queen will see you. She has a private garden where she often walks in the early evening. It is quite secluded. I will come and fetch you. There is a gate in the wall to which I will be given the key, so there will be no need to enter through the palace buildings.'

He said, 'Let us be clear on one point. The Queen I wish to see is the Queen who gave me this bracelet.'

Her eyes widened and he saw shock, hate, and fear cross her

face. He said gently, 'I do not wish her any harm. It is her help I need.'

Naida said between her teeth, 'You Romi are all alike.'

The garden was on the west side of the palace, screened by trees and a high wall. He followed Naida along neatly dressed paths that led to a wide circle of grass, surrounding a fountain which splashed noisily; and there, in the shadow of a palm tree, the Queen awaited him. He glanced at the girl and Cleopatra Selene said, 'He cannot harm me. Wait on the other side of the pool, Naida. We shall not be long.'

When they were alone she said, 'So! I was right, your Excellency. The King has told me of what passed at your meeting. But I guessed from the first the reason for your coming. The State of Rome must be hard pressed to send a man of your quality. Still, you have all the right talents: the gifts of flattery and deception.' She paused and smiled, but only with her mouth. 'You are very silent. Well, I have done as you asked. Please explain what you meant by your extraordinary message.'

He said, 'If you did not understand it, madam, you would not have consented to see me.'

She said lightly, 'I have a woman's curiosity, Curtius Rufus.'

'True.' He paused. He said, 'I told a lie. The bireme has not been found. I do know, madam, that up to his death you were in almost constant communication with Primus, governor of Macedonia. I have a copy of one of the letters that you wrote. It says little, yet makes curious reading.'

She said coolly, 'We had obvious interests in common. Of his troubles I knew nothing. What of it? I have many friends at Rome who knew me from childhood. We write from time to time.'

He nodded. 'That I accept. I also know that you have in your household a man previously in the employ of Herod of—'

'He was a gift. He was a friend of my mother.'

'So I have been told. I have also been told, madam, that you

205

were not permitted to have those serve you who had served your mother.'

'No.'

'Your mother's Galatean bodyguard was given to Herod – afterwards. This man, this gift, was one of them.'

She said amused, 'I enjoy speaking different languages. He provides the opportunity.'

Curtius Rufus said, 'I envy you, madam.'

She relaxed and smiled. 'It helps to pass the time – amongst other amusements.'

He said, 'I can understand that. After the bustle and excitement of Rome, other cities, unfairly perhaps, often seem small and uneventful to live in. But you and your husband will make a new Alexandria out of your capital. It is only a question of time.'

'Yes,' she said, and her voice had softened a little. 'We owe you much and we are grateful.'

The sun was low in the west, shining like a blood-red ruby through torn strips of black velvet clouds. The palm trees swayed their tops as the first light wind of the evening hit them, and a surfacing fish spread tiny ripples across the pond. He felt the spray from the fountain on his face. He looked at her. She had grace and charm and youth, and, sometimes, beauty. She had a young and handsome husband, and great wealth and considerable power. She had everything that others, less fortunate but still ambitious, struggled all their lives to obtain. But even that was not enough.

He said casually, 'A curious thing occurred the other day. One of my officers saw a man he recognized, coming into the city. The man had come from Tingis; he was one of the Baquates, a tribe who live on the edge of the Middle Atlas, close to Vodubri in western Mauretania. He looked to be a poor man, but he asked for the palace. My officer was curious and took him to the residency and questioned him. He then had him searched. In a pouch round his neck the man carried what he claimed to be a

206

charm. My officer, who knows a little about Baquates, thinks otherwise. He thinks it is a message.'

'And is it?' The Queen looked at him under half-closed eyes.

'Perhaps you can tell me.' Curtius Rufus took from inside his tunic a long piece of coarse cloth to which had been stitched a number of tiny pockets. Each pocket held something different.

'The order in which they are arranged is important. First we have a fragment of jewelry, part of an earring, shaped like a crescent moon; next a pearl of good quality; after that an animal's eye, possibly that of a pig; now we come to a tooth – it could be from a lion; then a black pearl, not of good quality; next, a piece of material, a fragment of sail cloth; and, lastly, a small ruby. You will agree, madam, that it is a costly charm.'

'But you say it is a message.'

'My friend does. He knows about such things. He thinks it is a form of tally writing, each object representing an idea, a meaning or, perhaps, a word.'

'And do you know what the message says?'

'No, madam.' He saw relief in her eyes. 'But we have an idea. Let me explain. The earring shaped like a crescent represents the moon, and the moon is the person for whom the message is intended. Selene, I believe, means the moon. The white pearl is a girl of fair skin, with or without a name. The eye stands for a sign or signal of some kind. The lion's tooth – if it is a lion – stands for fighting or war. The black pearl is more difficult. But it could mean the opposite of a white pearl and stand for some kind of change. The sail cloth is the most difficult. It may represent a sail or a ship, but this does not make sense. But, as my friend said, ships make voyages, and voyages take time. Lastly, the ruby; the color of the sun when it sets.'

'Go on.'

'So we have what is for us a crude but possible message. It might run like this: to Cleopatra Selene; I have the girl still. If I do not receive the signal to make war I will exchange her, since time is running out; signed by one who lives in the west.' He grinned then and said with mock anxiety, 'I hope that that is the correct message. It took my secretary and the officer all night to make sense of it.'

The Queen rose to her feet. She said, 'Your friend has great imagination. Perhaps he is a poet.'

Curtius Rufus said, 'You have an answer, madam, for everything.'

The Queen said calmly, 'Let us have an end of these questions. They are tedious beyond belief. You would do well to remember that I have friends at Rome – still.'

He hesitated and she saw the disappointment on his face. She said coldly, 'I am going back. I have nothing more to say. I may see you again, when you are less inflamed with fantasies.'

She turned and signaled to the waiting girl.

Curtius Rufus bit his lip. He knew then that he had failed. He said, in anger and despair, 'Would that be your answer, madam, if you were ordered back to Rome to be questioned by Caesar's heir?'

She turned in a fury and her face became a mask of hate.

'Do not speak to me of Caesar's heir. He was my brother.'

He stared at her speechless. Very slowly she sank onto the seat and put her head in her hands. The waiting girl knelt by her side and put an arm round her shoulder. Very softly, she began to stroke the Queen's hair.

He could feel the breeze on his face and saw the light begin to fade. Presently he spoke. He said, 'Madam, I told your maid that I meant no harm. I only wish to know what has happened to the niece of Valerius Messalla. I want the Lady Valeria back, safe and unharmed.'

She did not speak. Nor did Naida look up.

He said, 'She is about your own age. But she has no husband. For six months she has been in their hands. Have you no pity?'

Cleopatra Selene raised her head and looked at him. Her face was quite calm. 'No,' she said. And then, as though in answer to a question he had not put, she said, 'I do not know how to cry. I was taught too well by the Lady Octavia.'

He said, 'I don't understand.'

'My brothers and I walked in his triumph. I was ten years old. We heard the cries of that rabble you call Rome, and we saw their faces. They would never have had the courage to face her living, but they were brave enough when she was dead.' She checked and then said in a quiet voice, 'I never heard my father's name spoken once in all those years, and if I asked about him I was beaten. They hated him so; and I lived on gratitude and patronage and favors till it made me want to vomit.'

He said, 'But the Lady Octavia – she was kind, surely?'

She laughed. 'It was meat and drink to her. She allowed no one to forget her magnanimity, her selfless devotion – her – kindness. It was all she lived for.'

He said, 'Does the victor ever have pity for the vanquished?'

'That is a question only a Romi would ask.'

He said, disconcerted, 'Your husband——?'

She took a deep breath. She said, 'My husband does not know.'

'That is what I have come to realize. Yet he suspects something. He is an unhappy man.' He paused and then said bluntly, 'Madam, do you care for him?'

The Queen smiled slightly. 'We have much in common and he is gentle and kind – much, much too gentle. They gave him back what was his by right and they made him marry me. I was getting too old to stay in Rome – there was a senator's son who liked me too well – and he thought we would make useful pieces on a draughts board.'

He said, 'We are all slaves of one kind or another.'

'But I have the blood of Alexander in my veins. I am the last of the Ptolemies. For three hundred and thirty-seven years my family ruled in Egypt. And now, for a kingdom I have a desert.'

'It is better to be a live queen than a dead one.'

She shivered. 'Will you send me a bowl of poison as Masinissa did to Sophonisba?'

He did not know the story but he gathered her meaning. He thought of Criton in the Lautumiae and shook his head. He said, 'It would serve no purpose.'

She stood up. 'That is what I think,' she said, and smiled.

He said, 'I came to help and to seek advice. The one deserves the other.'

'And if I remain silent?'

He said, 'Madam, I cannot pull you down without pulling down your husband too.'

'That is clever of you. Yes, we should be further proof of his failure to select the right people for his purpose.'

He did not pretend to understand her. He said stolidly, 'But I can tell your husband.' Her smile faded. 'He might have you put away if he knew that your presence threatened his throne. Unlike you he faces facts and, in facing them, has discovered interests that make his life worthwhile.'

She said, 'I do not threaten his throne.'

He said patiently, 'I do not suggest that you do. But you weaken his position even if it is unintentional.'

She lowered her eyelids. She realized that he understood very little. He was an ignorant man with but a single purpose, and the exchange of bracelets – a precaution only – had put his life into her hands.

She said, 'Very well. I will tell you what little I have learned. The girl from Hispania is in the western part of this kingdom. Where exactly I do not know. She may be in the Rif mountains or she may have been taken further inland to the Atlas.'

'How do you know this?'

'Those who took her wished me to assist them.' She paused and then looked at him with wide eyes. 'Do you not wish to ask me how?'

He shook his head. He felt obscurely that at some moment in the conversation he had lost the initiative.

She said coolly, 'You are wise not to ask.'

'Who has her, madam?'

'I do not know.'

He said, 'Do you expect me to believe that?'

Cleopatra Selene said scornfully, 'I am not interested in what you believe. I will help you because I care for my husband. But do not threaten me with journeys to Rome or I will pull you down in your turn. What do they say in Parthia? Who has not a bad name will not have mistresses. You have a reputation it would be difficult to escape from.' She smiled. 'You see, I know so much about you. And you will not do it, for you cannot while you carry my bracelet upon your wrist.'

Curtius Rufus swallowed hard. He said, 'Please go on, madam. I should not have interrupted you.'

She put up a hand and touched her hair into place. 'There is no guarantee that the girl will be returned. You see, I am being honest with you. I, at least, do not need to lie. Now, listen carefully. Once, King Bogud ruled in the west, from the Mulva to the Pillars of Hercules. He was a loyal ally of the divine Caesar. Later, he became my father's ally but that was when he had lost everything through foolishness; and he died at Agrippa's hands. The Romi, however, would not let his son, Manissa, play at kings. They gave his father's old kingdom to my husband, hoping to make one land out of what had formerly been two. Juba knows that Manissa is a proud, ambitious, and ruthless man; so to conciliate him a little, he made him governor in the west. Manissa has a palace at Vodubri and it is his aid you will have to seek. My husband's authority beyond the old Numidian border is in name only, though we and Manissa pretend otherwise. This is a game rulers play — but it is important — for it helps to keep the land and the tribes quiet. Ask your Lucius Eggius if I speak the truth.'

211

He said, 'I believe you but will Manissa use his influence to help me?'

'That is up to you.' She smiled. 'You will have to negotiate.'

Curtius Rufus nodded. 'I am sorry to have kept you so long, madam. It is good of you to give me so much of your time.' Her face was blurred in the dusk. He said, 'It is nearly dark. Will you help me once more? I shall need the King's permission to leave here. Could you persuade him?'

'See him first and I will do what I can.' Her face was almost lost in the shadows. She put on the cloak that her maid handed her and pulled the hood over her hair. 'You will need Manissa's permission also, your Excellency, to cross the Mulva, if you wish to stay alive.'

She turned and without a word of farewell disappeared along a path in the direction of the palace. He stood and watched her go, then said aloud to the trees, 'We have both lost from this encounter, but she knows what she has lost; I have still to find out.'

He walked slowly toward the gate in the wall.

CHAPTER XIII

The King laughed as the last of the dancers, trying wildly to maintain his balance, slipped and fell helplessly upon the greased hides. The court applauded, servants ran forward to clear the floor, and Juba, smiling, turned to the patient envoy. 'You have asked me twice and still I must say no.' He looked anxiously at Curtius Rufus. 'We need your men here. I value your advice too much and, besides, I fear for your safety. The tribes who live in the Rif and the Atlas are wild. They recognize no authority but their own customs.' This was the first time he had made such an admission and Curtius Rufus nodded politely.

The Queen glanced at the two men and then whispered in the King's ear. Juba shook his head; she touched his arm and spoke again; his face lost a little of its worry.

Curtius Rufus said calmly, 'I accept your decision, of course. I am sorry to have bothered you unduly.'

Juba said, 'Wait. I have been thinking.' He hesitated. 'It is true I would like to build a city at Vodubri. My governor deserves better than that poor place. It does not support his dignity as it should. Also' – he smiled shyly – 'I am anxious to have some details of the Phoenician settlements on the coast. It is for a monograph I have been thinking of writing. But—' He hesitated again.

Curtius Rufus said, 'My secretary is interested in history. He would be happy to gain information for you.'

'He would?' The King looked delighted and then perplexed. 'But there is still the risk.'

'I would inform the authorities in Rome that in the event of difficulties, sir, no blame could be attached to anyone.'

'Yes. Yes, of course.'

'An aqueduct, a proper water supply, is the first essential for a new city – that and roads.'

'The work here—?'

'Would not be stopped, sir.' Curtius Rufus smiled sympathetically. It was like throwing dice with one's tongue. 'Probus, the architect, and Fronto, the engineer, would remain, together with five of the craftsmen.' He smiled again, glancing from the King to the watchful girl. 'If, sir, you would be willing to take them into your service when I return to Rome I am sure I could persuade three or four of the craftsmen to remain. They enjoy the work and are happy to live in the city. It offers great opportunities.'

The King looked pleased. He said, 'Very well, I will give you a letter. But be careful not to upset Manissa. He is not easy to talk to and is a – proud man. I will write to him tomorrow to let him know you are coming.' The Queen whispered again. 'Yes, I accept that if the girl is held in my lands it reflects upon my honor.' A roar of laughter came from down the pillared hall where a conjuror entertained the diners with his tricks. He turned his head, saw the chamberlain watching him, and then said swiftly, 'Please be careful. Peace must be kept at all costs. My kingdom lies in your hands once you cross the Mulva.'

Curtius Rufus said gravely, 'I will remember that, sir, at all times.'

The Queen glanced down at her hands and smiled.

Lucius Eggius looked at the map while the others crowded round the table. The rumble of wheels sounded from the street.

'Market day,' said Attius. 'I've never stayed in such a noisy house.'

Cornelius Silius said, 'It is quiet enough when you are alone.

Strange as it may seem, I shall even miss the noise of our heavy-footed soldiers returning drunk from the brothels.'

Criton, his eyes dark with fatigue, said, 'I've checked the inventory. Here is a list of the stores we shall need.'

Curtius Rufus said, 'Well?'

Lucius Eggius frowned. 'The easiest and fastest journey is obviously by ship to Tingis, then overland to Vodubri.'

Cornelius Silius shook his head regretfully. 'I doubt if it is safe at the moment. I received a report from the garrison commander at Tingis – what an impressive title for a centurion with thirty men! – that the Mazices tribe are out. One of their periodic flare-ups with the hillmen in the Rif. I understand a caravan from Tingis was attacked ten days ago.'

Lucius Eggius laughed quietly. 'The campaigning season has begun.'

'Perhaps the troubles have died down,' suggested Vatinus hopefully.

'As to that I will find out. The dispatch boat sails tomorrow.'

'And if it hasn't, what do you suggest?' asked Curtius Rufus.

Lucius Eggius and the tribune exchanged glances.

The tribune said carefully, 'Well, there are a number of old Phoenician trading stations on the western coast. A sea voyage through the straits will be safer, so long as we do not meet pirates.'

Lucius Eggius said humorously, 'Safe till you make landfall anyway. Then you have the Baquates, west of Vodubri, to contend with. They are a tough and tenacious people, suspicious of strangers and jealous of their independence.'

Criton said nervously, 'Pirates!'

'Oh, yes,' said Lucius Eggius. 'The lucky travelers are the ones killed in the attack; the unlucky ones are those who live to be ransomed.'

Curtius Rufus said, 'We've still to get Manissa's agreement. How long it'll take to come—' He shrugged his shoulders.

215

'Meanwhile I suppose we must prepare to move. We'd better decide our route at the last moment.'

'That might be wise,' said Cornelius Silius. 'You can keep nothing secret in this city.'

Attius said, 'I'll be glad to get out of here. It's a dirty, smelly collection of muddy streets and crumbling houses. So will the men. They've tried all the wineshops and the brothels. They're getting restive. It's always the same when they're billeted too long in a civilian settlement.'

'There's not even a single public latrine that I've been able to find,' said Vatinus with feeling.

Marcus Pedius said callously, 'You should drink less,' at which there was a roar of laughter.

Curtius Rufus went to his room with a headache. He felt depressed and tired. Agrippa had warned him that the venture might prove a failure but still he had hoped. He had thought to find the solution to his problem in Juba's palace and that, by skill and diplomacy, he would be able to exert pressure on the King and so force him to help. But Juba, whatever he knew or feared, had denied all knowledge and escaped all pressures by admitting that a half of his kingdom was outside his control. Cleopatra Selene knew more and had admitted as much, but the extent of her involvement he could not determine. Now the solution to his problem – if there was a solution – lay in another place, in a town he had never heard of before, sited on a bleak plain he had never seen, five hundred miles beyond the effective influence of Roman law and Roman order. As a trader of horses he would have been happy to go there; he would have felt a youthful sense of excitement and adventure. As an envoy of Rome he felt none of these things. What he did feel he dared not admit even to Criton. Of one thing only was he certain: the folly of living had to be endured.

Juba said, 'I am very satisfied with the arrangements you have made. We can discuss my other plans when you return. Certainly we must attract people here. I want not only discharged veterans but people of culture and quality.'

'They will come in time, sir.'

'Of course. Meanwhile I have a surprise for myself. A shipment of statues and manuscripts that I ordered from Delos and which I thought would not arrive till the spring has just come through. I had a message this morning. Due to bad seas the navigator put in to Thabraca, where they discovered a leak. The governor has arranged to send the cargo on by road. He is a kind man.' Juba smiled delightedly. 'I am going to meet it at the border. I have no wish to lose it at the last.'

'Then, sir, you may be away when I depart.'

'Oh, yes, but you are coming back.' The King paused. 'Be careful of Manissa. Still, you have Lucius Eggius. He is a sound soldier. Take his advice and all will be well.' He smiled happily. 'Just think – those statues at last.'

'I wish you a pleasant journey, sir.'

'Thank you. The Queen will inform you when Manissa answers.' The King turned away and spoke to his secretary. Curtius Rufus, accustomed by now to the curious manner in which the occupants of thrones terminated conversations and audiences, went down to the workshops to see if Fronto had been successful in persuading the other craftsmen to enter Juba's service. The engineer had a silver tongue when he chose to exercise it.

Later he returned to the residency. Criton saw him coming across the outer courtyard and waved from the steps. 'Where have you been, dear boy? The dispatch boat has been in since midday. The captain told me the package was urgent.'

'Where is the letter?'

'In my tunic. I have another but it is not official.'

'Let's deal with business first. The other is probably from one of my creditors.'

He examined the seal and swore. 'Marcus Agrippa. If I get any more demands to hurry I will tell them to come and do the work themselves.'

Criton watched him read and saw his eyes widen.

Curtius Rufus said grimly, 'Look for yourself.'

'A conspiracy has been exposed through the vigilance of those authorized to watch over the safety of the state. This is known to have involved a number of high-placed persons whose loyalty had been supposed to be unquestionable. It was with the deepest regret, the profoundest horror and the greatest surprise that we learned the names of those responsible for an attempt proposed against the life of Augustus Caesar. Those who committed treason are now dead but their actions have gravely imperilled the security of all that we hold most sacred. As our envoy to a client kingdom you will do all in your power to allay the alarm of the faint-hearted, to reassure our citizens and to warn those who do not hold our friendship that law and order prevails and that the power of this State and the will of the Roman People remains unshaken.'

Criton said, 'Who?'

'The other letter?' Curtius Rufus took it in silence. It was from Gaius Maecenas. 'I enclose a note from one who is a friend of yours and who wished to send you greetings for the new year; but it is not of this that I wish to write. I am not by nature a man of action and I have all my life held to the view that violence may be restrained by reason, though events constantly demonstrate that it can only be restrained by force. You will have the news from travelers and merchants of which all Rome whispers in shock and horror. Fannius Caepio, noted for his Republican sympathies, fled the city just prior to the issue of the order for his arrest, as did his companions. The evidence as submitted was considered to be overwhelming and the Senate had no recourse but to condemn the criminals in their absence. Fannius Caepio was betrayed by a slave and taken as were the others. They were

218

then executed. You will understand my reluctance to discuss the matter further when I add that one of the accused and the executed was the new consul, Varro Murena, brother to the Lady Terentia and my own brother-in-law. I have now the unhappy duty of writing to his brother who is legate in Syria. What madness assails us when the gods destroy our reason! As to your own affairs, the important step is always the next step. Do not be slow in taking it. Life in the sun is better than life in the shade . . .'

Curtius Rufus read on to the end and then said quietly, 'I need a drink.' He was remembering what the Queen had said to him on the night of the banquet when they had dined alone and she had spoken of Murena.

Criton said, 'In that I will join you.'

Behind the closed doors of his room Curtius Rufus said, 'Why does he write at such length and how does this touch upon our affairs?'

Criton said carefully, 'He does not say that it does.'

Curtius Rufus said hurriedly, 'Do you remember the night we talked about that bag of gold?'

'I shall never forget it.'

'I feel now as I felt then.'

Criton's face took on its pointed look. 'Yes, Curtius, I do as well as you. His letter is carefully worded but to me it is clear from the way he writes that he has doubts of some kind.'

'I noticed that too.'

'Also, I get the impression that his own position is far from comfortable.'

'That is understandable.' Curtius Rufus remembered the Lady Terentia. How fond had she been of her brother? Was she the kind that cried or did she conceal her feelings behind a smile? There would be shame, embarrassment, anger, and bewilderment, surely, in that palace on the Esquiline? You needed pride and courage to outface the world at such a time.

Criton said, 'I mean more than that. His phrase about madness is supposed to refer to those others. Yet I feel he means to include himself.'

'You are being fanciful.'

'Perhaps I am.'

They looked at each other doubtfully. Then Curtius Rufus said grimly, 'Let me be fanciful now. Your patron was involved in the kidnapping of an influential senator's daughter. Why? He knew Murena and Fannius Caepio well, for they were all at his house that night. Primus, on whose behalf Murena spoke, was Proconsul of Macedonia; Murena's brother is Legate in Syria. What support did Murena hope for? The kidnapped girl was taken to Mauretania, where a king sits on a shaky throne, married to a woman who possesses all the qualities of kingship that he lacks. She is part Macedonian, daughter of a queen of Egypt, a province that practically borders Syria.' He hesitated and then said in a low voice, 'You could make a chain out of those links.'

Criton said, 'Did you know that as a child she was proclaimed a princess of Cyrenaica?'

'No.'

'The buffer state between Egypt and Africa Procunsularis.'

'But they would never let her have her inheritance back.'

Criton said sadly, 'Of course not, dear boy, but they, whoever they are or were, might have been only too willing to lead her into thinking so.'

Curtius Rufus said, 'It still does not explain why the girl was kidnapped. To me there seems no point in that at all.'

Criton smiled. 'I don't think we can make a chain that wouldn't snap the moment you tested it. In their world they all know each other.'

His friend poured out more wine. He said ruefully, 'Yes, I know. I never had the kind of mind that could concentrate long enough to make a beautiful patterned shape out of hundreds of fragments of colored stones.' He raised his cup and swirled the wine gently. Then he frowned and put down the cup with a crash.

'Dear boy!'

'I have just remembered something that the Proconsul told me.'

'Yes.'

Curtius Rufus took a deep breath. He said, 'If there was a successful revolt in Africa it would be possible to starve Rome into submission.'

Criton said, 'But Curtius, that was a weapon not even the Carthaginians possessed.'

'Precisely.' Curtius Rufus grinned. 'Never mind. I must be getting drunk as well as fanciful. P'rhaps I'd better remember why I'm here – as an envoy – to bring culture and – and civilization to the barbarians. Envoys are men of peace – and goodwill. Their only object is to – to reach agreement and make – friends.'

Criton said dryly, 'If one only had queens to deal with you would be a great ambassador.' His voice changed and sounded more urgent. 'Curtius, how much is she involved? I think we must be very careful.'

Curtius Rufus tried hard to be sober. He said thickly, 'That is something I don't ever want to know.' He sat down then on a stool and Criton saw him touch the bracelet upon his wrist.

The Numidian secretary led him into a small anteroom and said politely, 'One of the Queen's ladies will be here shortly, your Excellency. Your willingness to come at such short notice is much appreciated, particularly as the weather is bad.' He bowed and left the room. A monkey in a cage eyed him for a moment and then returned to its food tray. A parrot screeched in the garden outside, and he waited patiently. Presently he heard footsteps in the corridor and the swish of a woman's dress. Naida entered and smiled. 'I am sorry to keep your Excellency waiting. If you will be so kind as to follow me, my Lord.' He paced by her side down a marble corridor, across a wide terrace lined with trees, and then up a flight of stairs to another marble corridor that seemed endless.

He said politely, 'I had not realized the extent of the palace. I have not seen this part before.'

A smile flickered on her mouth and then vanished. She said politely, 'We are entering the Queen's apartments now.' She walked on, leading him through an endless series of small, windowless rooms, each one of which opened onto the next, and all of which appeared to be empty, though once or twice he thought he heard voices and the sound of laughter. Outside a pair of ivory doors ornamented with silver-colored handles she paused. 'This is the Queen's private audience chamber,' Naida said in a low voice. 'Next to one other it is her favorite room.'

He had an impression of a tessellated floor, covered with rugs, marble walls, etched with intricate designs, and, facing him, a long dais that ran the length of the room. On the wall at one end of the dais was a silver spout from which ran water into a marble basin. The Queen sat on the dais, her hair seeming darker than he had remembered it against the whiteness of her gown. She wore a diadem inlaid with precious stones, her earrings matched the diadem, and her armlets and necklace matched the earrings, so that when she moved her jewelry shimmered in the light.

He bowed and she gestured for him to take the chair that faced her. She said, 'You will be glad to learn that I sent the King's letter to Manissa by a fast ship. From Tingis it will go overland. You should have an answer soon.'

He said politely, 'Will it take long, madam?'

'Much depends on the weather. At this time of the year a river in full spate may damage a bridge or flood a track. But urgency was impressed on the messenger. He is quite reliable.'

'Is it possible the governor could refuse?'

She smiled. 'Everything is possible, your Excellency. But—'

She hesitated delicately. 'But who would dare to refuse the request of an envoy of Rome?'

He inclined his head in silence. The tone of her voice warned him that she did not wish for an answer. She looked pale, he thought, and wondered if she too had received letters from Rome. As though in answer to his thoughts she said gravely, 'Yes, I have heard the news. My husband asks that you convey to the Senate and the People of Rome his pleasure that the life of Augustus has been preserved, as also his horror at the outrage that was planned, yet, fortunately, so skilfully prevented.' Her voice was noncommittal but he thought he detected a flicker of amusement in her eyes. She looked at him calmly, 'It has been a great relief to us all, particularly in view of the known fact that he was so unwell earlier. He is now quite recovered, so I understand.' She was watching him intently as she spoke.

He said, 'I will convey the message of the King, your husband, to Rome. The Senate will be most appreciative.'

She picked up an amber ball and held it lightly in her hands as though to cool them. 'I met Murena several times when I was a child. He and the Lady Terentia were very close.'

Curtius Rufus said, 'I did not know him.' He coughed. 'You have lost a friend. Primus, too?'

'I shall write no more letters to Macedonia, certainly.' She paused. 'But if old friends die there are new ones yet to be made.'

He wondered what she felt. Her face told him nothing. He glanced at the silver spout. 'We always seem to meet now by running water, madam.'

'Yes, it drowns conversation and is a barrier to eavesdroppers.'

'You wish to say something that is private, madam?'

'I might.' She smiled. 'Would you know who the new consul will be?'

'I have no idea, madam. This is a matter on which I am not qualified to speak.'

'But you must have thoughts on the subject?'

He said cheerfully, 'I haven't the slightest idea, madam. All that is outside my understanding.'

'Did you hear any details I wonder? Murena spoke for Primus. Someone, surely, must have spoken for him.'

'I'm afraid I don't know,' he said bluntly. 'I've heard no particulars.'

She leaned back in her chair. 'Forgive these questions but we hear so much of our news only by letter.'

He said, 'I understand,' and wondered when she would come to the subject of the audience. The trickle from the tap seemed louder than before. He glanced upward and guessed from the gray light that it was raining.

The Queen played with the amber ball. She appeared more relaxed. She said, 'Tell me, if you are successful in this enterprise of yours, will it make your fortune? Will it be the first step in a great career?'

He grinned. 'I doubt it, madam. I was unemployed and in debt at the time of my engagement.'

'Now, that makes me curious but I, at least, will not ask questions that may offend.' She rested her head on the chair back and her eyelids drooped a little.

Curtius Rufus said, 'I may be offered a small post if I am very fortunate; no more than that.' He smiled. 'It seems that the poor are always poor; wealth is only given to the rich.'

'There are posts to be obtained elsewhere.' She gave him a look that was almost a caress. 'Men of talent are always in demand. Everyone has his star.'

'But not everyone can see it,' he said ruefully.

'It is up to you to make them see,' she said quietly. 'My husband admires very much what you have achieved here in so short a time.' She paused. 'Others will too, no doubt.' She paused again and said slowly, 'In the event of failure there will always be a post here. The climate is delightful and opportunities for advancement are great.' She lapsed into silence but it seemed to him that her relaxed manner was imposed.

He waited and watched her hands turn the amber ball round and round. Catching the light from the fire it gave off a deep yellow glow that seemed to increase in intensity as the room darkened. Points of flame danced in the jewels that she wore, and he relaxed a little, watching them with quiet pleasure. Her eyes were the eyes of the blind.

Presently she said in a low voice, 'You will cross the Mulva even though Manissa refuses permission?'

He did not know if she asked a question or stated a fact. He said quietly, 'Yes, madam.'

'You will find it easier to pull a snake out of the hole with your right hand. Yet you insist on going.'

He grinned but the sick feeling was in his stomach again. 'I must,' he said.

'Even though they who sent you do not expect you to succeed in your mission?'

He nodded. His mouth felt dry.

She opened her eyes wide then and very slowly they began to refocus. She said, 'Then I cannot help you. Be thankful that lightning does not strike where there is fire already.'

A rumble of thunder sounded overhead and the rain fell like a torrent against the roof. 'You have not read all your news from Rome,' she said with a smile. 'Perhaps it is best to walk alone in the dark after all.' She stood up and moved to a table upon which documents were lying. She picked up a pen and he saw that she was left-handed. Not looking at him she said, 'You will need a good cloak to protect you against the rain. Storms at this time of the year are rare but they may last several hours.'

The door opened and Naida appeared. With her back to him the Queen said, 'See that his Excellency is provided with a cloak against the night.'

He followed the girl back into the anteroom he had passed

through on his way to the private audience chamber. Then he checked, seeing in a niche in the wall a marble head he had not noticed when he arrived. It was the head of a woman with a veil covering all but a part of the intricately coiffured hair. The chin, the eyes, and the nose were unmistakable. If he had not seen its likeness in Rome he would still have known who it was: the only woman whom Rome had ever feared. Naida looked at him questioningly a moment, but he did not speak. She smiled slightly, opened the door, and stood aside to let him pass. He heard the door close behind him and stood in the half-light of a fading March day in a room that seemed familiar. Facing him was an immense divan, almost square in shape, hung with curtains and piled with richly embroidered cushions. Reclining against these lay a woman with dark hair, dressed in a white robe. On her arm she wore his bracelet.

She said, 'It is a dark night to walk alone in the rain.' She laughed softly, her earrings trembling like sparks of fire.

He stood motionless, as once before.

She said, 'I can read what is not written. We shall not meet again. Do you not wish to say goodbye?'

He took a step forward and she smiled at him. His face was tormented with desire. He said, 'Beyond what you have given me nothing is possible.'

'Come,' she said, and held out her arms.

CHAPTER XIV

The augur had stood with his back to the north and had pronounced the omens propitious for the journey; the sacrifice had been made before the assembled troops and their officers; and now Cornelius Silius, his cloak blowing about him, faced the altar that had been erected on the mole. The divine figure stood silhouetted against a broken sky, and the braziers that flanked it sent black smoke streaming toward the heavens. The beaked ships in the harbor stirred as the tide began to turn, while the seabirds, hunched along the wall, and whom many believed to be the souls of the dead, watched and waited in silence.

Cornelius Silius, his head cowled in his toga, raised his arms in supplication and cried, 'Immortal Vesta, guardian of the sacred flame; on you I call, to you I pray: make soft the waves and calm the sky; avert the evils of the night and the demons of the sun; grant a safe journey now to these thy people of Rome.'

The ceremony concluded, he turned to Curtius Rufus and said bluntly, 'Keep me informed and if you need help don't be too proud to ask for it.' To Criton he said, 'Look after him. He depends on you.' Criton smiled shyly, and the tribune said, 'I shall miss your company, all of you. It can be lonely here.'

They sailed on the dawn tide of the first day of the new month and, as the ships cleared harbor and stood out to sea, Curtius Rufus, looking back to the harbor, could still see the figure of a man standing alone upon the mole.

Criton, who had joined him, said anxiously, 'I wonder if she is watching from the palace roof. I am surprised she did not send for us to say goodbye.'

Curtius Rufus said, 'We are all still under one sky,' and then moved away and went below. For the rest of that day he was in a bad mood and spoke little.

The sea voyage was uneventful and with a wind to help them most of the way they reached Portus Sigensis in five days and four nights. Portus Sigensis was an imposing name for a mud-walled village of one street. 'It was a Phoenician trading post,' said Lucius Eggius sadly. 'They never bothered with harbors; just ran their boats up on the beach and left them there.' The village boasted a blacksmith, two elderly boat-builders, a handful of Greek and Jewish merchants, and little else. Behind lay a pattern of cultivated fields, a flock or two of sheep, the inevitable goats, and a great emptiness that stretched to the horizon.

'We shall do better at Siga,' said Lucius Eggius in answer to a question. 'It is a few miles inland and has a flourishing market once every eight days. You will be able to secure your mules there, Vatinus, as well as the last of our supplies.' He smiled at Marcus Pedius, who was looking worried.

The supply centurion said, 'How long will it take us to get there?'

'About nineteen days. There's plenty of water if one is careful but little to be bought in the way of food.'

'I hope the tribune was right about being able to buy mules,' said Vatinus as the legionaries, waist deep in water, offloaded the wagons and floated them ashore.

'Put the word out and you will get them all right. The Berber people here hire themselves in summer to the farmers at harvest time and then return to the Rif in the spring. The people of the Atlas do much the same, except that they're wilder and usually pass the winter on the edge of the great desert no one can cross.'

Curtius Rufus said curiously, 'How far south did you go?'

Lucius Eggius smiled. 'When we reach Vodubri I will tell you about it.'

They camped outside Siga, waited for market day, and then haggled for mules, horses, and food. Vatinus did the selection while Curtius Rufus, in a mixture of Punic and Berber, handled the actual bargaining. It was slow, tedious work and it took all day.

'I had hoped we might get some camels,' said Vatinus wistfully, scanning the great crowded space where booths full of goods, tents, penned animals, and men mixed in apparently inextricable confusion. 'I saw some exhibited in Rome once. They'd be better than mules. I'd like to ride one.'

Lucius Eggius said gravely, 'I am sorry. They are rarely seen this far north. The Gaetules of the desert use them constantly. They ride a trade route in the south all the way to Egypt.'

By sundown, when the market closed as families and cattle began to disperse, Curtius Rufus had bought sixty mules and hired four drivers. 'Not enough,' he said in a tired voice. 'We shall have to wait for the next market.'

Marcus Pedius said, 'Vatinus is overparticular. He turned away too many. We shall be short of supplies if we stay here too long.'

'Get your hired hunters to earn their keep,' said Attius insolently. 'Vatinus knows his job and it's a long way—'

'And I know my rank and yours. Watch your mouth.'

'Gently, gently,' said Lucius Eggius. 'It will all sort itself out in time.' But he looked worried as he spoke.

Eight days later they struck camp and marched. The convoy was led by Lucius Eggius and an escort of fifteen men. Behind were the civilian members of the mission and then the sixteen special freight and sleeping wagons that carried their effects, their personal baggage, the medical supplies, and the women of the party. Marcus Pedius followed the last of these with an escort of twenty men, and behind them were the remaining seventeen wagons that carried the personal effects of the escort and drivers, the rations for the entire convoy, and the firewood, oil, and feed for the animals. Vatinus marched at the tailgate of the final wagons, leading the spare animals, and with him was the cavalry groom and the personal slaves of the officers. The rearguard of fifteen was under the command of Attius.

For days they traveled across a vast plain that stretched out into the distance on every side and on which, it seemed, no living thing had ever grown. There were no trees and there were no rocks, and often they marched all day without seeing a living soul except the members of their own column. At night they made camp in military fashion and the sentries on duty would gaze out into the darkness of the night and hear the occasional howl of a jackal and the bark of a dog fox, calling to its mate. At such times, lost in the immensity of the silence, even the stars seemed like hostile eyes, and they would shiver in the cool air and hug themselves in their cloaks. By day the sky was clear, a pale blue in color, and the sun, though it was not yet the time of summer, made them sweat after the first three hours of marching.

'The Berbers call this "the anvil of the gods,"' said Lucius Eggius briefly at one midday halt. 'It is no place to cross at the time of the summer solstice. Then, at noon, the heat is almost unendurable.' On the ninth day they passed two gray stone pillars that bore faint traces of whitewash and which flanked the track like sentinels. 'The old Numidian border,' said the escort centurion. 'It was marked out the year after Scipio sacked Carthage.'

On the tenth day there came a change. The air seemed cooler, the flat plain less hostile. The advance guard reported movement ahead. The cavalry patrol went forward and returned an hour later to say that they had sighted great flocks of sheep grazing on the sparse grassland that lay before them. Presently they could see groups of men guarding the sheep. The herdsmen watched as the wagons rumbled by but made no sign, not even when the

230

soldiers waved to them. In the late afternoon they reached the Mulva. It was swift moving at this time of the year on account of the snows melting on the Middle Atlas, and there was difficulty over making a crossing. One wagon was hit by a piece of floating timber and overturned. The mules had to be loosened but one of the two soldiers cutting the traces lost his knife, and the wheel pair drowned before the other man could get to them. A second wagon broke its back axle coming out on the far bank, and there was a long delay while a length of ash was trimmed and shaped and fitted by the wheelwright.

They were moving at a steady twenty miles a day, and though the men were fit the length of the march was beginning to tell on all concerned. Crescens, the surveyor, who had long since begun to wish that he had remained with Probus and Fronto at Iol Caesarea, developed an infected foot and had to ride in a wagon with two of the praetorians. A mule died of a scorpion sting; a tired legionary of the Third let the ax slip cutting wood and gashed his leg; another was kicked in the chest by a mule (he died three days later); and Criton started a fever.

Then to the north appeared a smudge on the horizon, the eastern range of the Rif mountains. To the south the landscape softened, and the cavalry patrol reported tilled land, orchards of stunted bushes, streams that were in full spate, and an isolated village or two, guarded by mud walls and high towers. The ground began to slope and the column was forced to slow the pace of its march as it cautiously crossed another river, spanned by a wooden bridge, and then began the slow climb upward to the gap in the Berber mountain range that barred their way. Three hours past the bridge they reached the saddle and found the track obliterated by a landslide.

Lucius Eggius looked at the slopes to their right and left. 'We cannot move the wagons off the track,' he said calmly. 'We shall have to clear it. Vatinus, take twenty men and get up the slopes. Take the spare javelins and build a defensive position. Put scouts out in pairs to cover the flank and order them to withdraw on you the moment they see any hostile movement. Attius, cover the rear. We may expect trouble.'

Curtius Rufus said anxiously, 'It's not an accident?'

'I doubt it.'

'They could have broken the bridge.'

'If you were to go back you would find it broken now. It is a good thing for us that we have to go on.'

'It will take till nightfall to clear those rocks.'

Lucius Eggius smiled.

Marcus Pedius came up, red-faced and out of breath. 'We shall be short of water if we stay the night. I will put everyone on half rations.'

Lucius Eggius said, 'We have another twenty-six miles to go before we are out of this range. Two cups of water per man at sundown is all I will allow anyone. I shall want a good deal of the wine ration as well, though not for drinking.'

For the rest of the day the men worked at moving the loose debris that blocked the track, but when night came they had to stop, sleeping in their cloaks while double sentries kept watch.

Curtius Rufus, huddled against a wagon wheel, said, 'I am worried in case we find the road has been swept away.'

Crescens, his face smudged with dirt, shook his head. 'I climbed down. There is a lot of rock in the cliff. The cut road may have held.'

'Well, we shall know in the morning.'

There was no attack at dawn, as Lucius Eggius had feared, and by midday they had leveled a rubble-strewn track into the heart of the slide. Under Curtius Rufus's directions the soldiers built fires around the boulders they could not move, using all the spare firewood they carried. 'Be patient,' he said to Lucius Eggius. 'This cannot be done in a moment.' The fires were carefully tended and the men sweated in the additional heat as the smoke drove into their eyes, and the boulders began to warm.

232

Criton, shivering in the driver's seat of the front wagon, heard Curtius Rufus say 'Now!,' heard the sudden hiss as the vinegar was poured, and felt his face dampen as the steam obliterated the soldiers from his sight. The rocks cracked one by one as though a blacksmith had struck them in turn with a hammer, and Curtius Rufus said hoarsely, 'Try to move them now.'

By the ninth hour the column was on the move again. They spent the night camped uncomfortably again on the road, and reached the top of the pass the following day. 'From now on it will be easier,' said Lucius Eggius, looking tired but pleased.

Curtius Rufus, who had been walking his horse for the past hour, said quietly, 'Was I drunk back there or does the earth really change color like that? To the north it was nearly white and then, to the south, with barely six road widths in between, it was all reddish. That is a sight I have never seen before.'

Lucius Eggius laughed. 'Nor I, though an old shepherd I once met told me about it and I thought him a liar.'

They were short of water now and the streams they came to were too fouled to drink from. A patrol sent out reported dead sheep in the water. Lucius Eggius tried hard to laugh through cracked lips. 'An old trick. We shall have to find a well.' They found one outside an abandoned village but the first man who drank from it died.

They marched on through what seemed an endless range of hills, the wagon wheels throwing up a continuous scuffle of fine dust from the stone-strewn, twisting track they followed. Occasionally, through gaps in the landscape they could see the mountains to the south, the great range of the Middle Atlas, whose peaks were capped with snow and which glittered softly in the morning light. And then, moving northwest now, they marched right-handed to skirt another range of hills before them, and came out onto a dry, flat sweep of plain and could see in the center of it a huddle of buildings that might have been either a village, an encampment or a town. The cavalry patrol rode forward and then wheeled round and came cantering back to the column, waving their arms in their excitement.

Lucius Eggius turned round. 'Vodubri,' he said smiling. 'I prefer to call it Volubilis; it sounds better.'

Curtius Rufus wiped the sweat from his forehead. 'Are you certain?'

'Yes, it must be. I am sure of it.' The centurion glanced round the treeless plain and then grinned. 'If I am wrong you may crucify me on the next tree you find.'

Criton said, 'I never wish to see a wagon again.'

Curtius Rufus said, 'I hope you will change your mind about that. It will be easier to depart than to come. But how we depart is another matter.'

He stood outside the entrance to the camp and waited; beside him stood the officers of his mission, Lucius Eggius a little in advance of the rest. They had built their camp six hundred yards from the low, brown mud walls of the town. He saw the Tingis gate open and a cavalcade of horsemen, led by a man in white, trotted toward the camp. The horsemen stopped some thirty feet away, spreading out in a half circle. They wore brown robes and their heads were covered and their faces veiled from chin to nose. The man in white, who called himself the chief suffete, said brusquely, 'You wished to speak to me.'

Curtius Rufus looked up at him and said in Punic, 'Yes, and for the third time in as many days. We have camped here outside as you requested, yet still no invitation has been received to enter your fine town. I say again, I am the envoy of Rome. I have come at the wish of your king – Juba. I must ask you again to convey my respects to your lord. I wish to speak with him.'

The man in white said, 'I have told you already that our lord, Manissa, is hunting. When he will return I do not know. He enjoys the hunt and will return only at his pleasure.'

Curtius Rufus said, 'Is this the hospitality for which the Mauri are famous? I bring rich presents from those who have sent me.

234

They will not be pleased to know that I have been rudely treated.'

'Manissa rules,' said the chief suffete in a cold voice. It was a statement that Curtius Rufus had heard three times already and he knew that he would hear it again. 'Manissa rules, and it is his pleasure alone that concerns us.'

Curtius Rufus said patiently, 'That I understand. In two days' time I break camp and shall return across the Mulva.'

'You would be wise to stay.'

'I shall be wiser to go. An unwelcome guest should not knock too long or too loud on any door.'

The chief suffete leaned forward. 'I have told you—' He stopped suddenly as the envoy raised his arm, the sun shining upon the bracelet round his wrist.

Curtius Rufus said brusquely, 'In my camp it is I who rule. Do not tell me what I may or may not do. It is not your place.' He turned his back and walked swiftly into the camp, followed by his officers.

The chief suffete sat motionless for a moment. 'So,' he said. Then he raised his hand and wheeled his horse round. The cavalcade turned and swept back to the town and the gates closed behind them.

From the platform by the camp gate Lucius Eggius watched them go. 'You have made him angry. What did you say?'

Curtius Rufus told him.

'Was that wise?'

'They have been playing with us. It is a diplomatic hunt that has taken Manissa from the town. He will return now fast enough.'

Criton said, 'I hope you are right, dear boy. I do not like the look of these people at all.' He followed his friend back to the envoy's tent. When they were alone he said, 'What now?'

'We wait.'

'If Manissa is what I hear him to be—'

'He is. I have heard these stories too.'

'And you aren't afraid?'

Curtius Rufus grinned. 'Yes. But I think he is too.'

'Why?'

'A number of reasons. No caravan, no human being, not even a dog, has passed in or out of the town since we arrived. Yesterday I spoke to a shepherd, the day before that to a water carrier, who was with that party, scything grass. They both told me the same thing. The Mazices to the northwest are giving trouble, and the centurion commanding at Tingis has closed the town gates, withdrawn his outposts, and refused to allow any caravan to leave for the south. Why? Because the Mazices have broken the road.

'The Baquates, who occupy those hills overlooking this town, have also been causing difficulties. Volubilis is a vulnerable place. It depends for its existence on the caravan trade. These two tribes levy taxes on all caravans that enter the town; and without their goodwill not one can leave it. Manissa, apparently, has been big enough and strong enough up till now to keep them in check, but something has happened recently to undermine his authority.'

'And what is that, dear envoy?'

'I don't know. He has been losing control the last few months. We seem to have arrived at a difficult time.'

'Shall I tell the others what you've just told me?'

'Why not? We are all playing a game of chance.'

Twenty-four hours later a messenger came from the town and was admitted to the camp. 'The Lord Manissa is returning. He looks forward to meeting the friend of his cousin, the King.' He spoke in the singsong tone of one who has learned a message by heart. 'He regrets his absence at the time of your arrival. He will be here within two days. He asks you to wait until his coming.'

They waited. Fatigue parties were organized to cut grass as

fodder for the animals, while ditches were dug around the tents as a precaution against flooding in the event of further rain. Marcus Pedius, with the aid of an interpreter, a Greek merchant in the town, bargained for food and supplies at the city gate; Attius strengthened the camp defenses; and Lucius Eggius, under the pretext of exercising the horses, explored the plain and rode round the town at a respectable distance.

Curtius Rufus, walking through the camp after the midday break, saw Felicia and the three girls standing by the wall, looking across to the town. He thought they seemed tired and depressed, wondered if it would be a good thing to stop and speak, but decided against it, and walked on.

The messenger from the town returned. Their lord, Manissa, was in his palace, having ridden all night. He was happy at the prospect of meeting the envoy from Rome and would hold an audience the next day. Curtius Rufus dismissed the messenger with the customary gift and called a meeting of his staff. He said, 'Tomorrow we enter the town. I wish you all to come with me, except you, Attius, who must stay here in command of the camp. Now, I will tell you something you do not know.' Lucius Eggius smiled slightly. 'There are two reasons why we are here. I will touch on the lesser reason first.' He turned to Crescens. 'We have to repeat what we can of our performance at Iol Caesarea. We cannot achieve as much because we shall have to face opposition. The governor does not want us here at all. Let us be clear about that. Therefore we must achieve something that will win his approval and the support of the townspeople. In that way we may turn his flank.' He paused. He said, 'The governor is likely to use any excuse to ask us to leave. There must be no possibility of any complaints being lodged against us for our behavior. In this matter, whether envoy or water carrier, we are all ambassadors of Rome.'

Crescens rubbed his chin. 'What do you want us to undertake?'

'Something for the governor himself and something to please the people.'

Marcus Pedius said, 'What is the other reason we are here?' His voice was puzzled.

Lucius Eggius smiled again.

Curtius Rufus said, 'I will tell you that now.' And he did. When he had finished speaking there was a long silence. Then Vatinus said, 'The governor may not know.' His question echoed the thought in all their minds.

Curtius Rufus said, 'I have some information that suggests he does.'

Marcus Pedius said bluntly, 'And if he won't agree to her being handed over, what then? We can't get her by force. We would need a legion to do that – not fifty men.'

Attius said simply, 'She may be dead.'

Curtius Rufus said in exasperation, 'She was not kidnapped to be killed.'

Lucius Eggius coughed. He said, 'But she may have died. It is a rough country and they are a brutal people. You may crush an egg if you hold it in your hand so long that you forget what you are holding. Do you intend to ask him tomorrow?'

'Manissa? I am not sure. We might do best to wait as we did at Iol Caesarea. What do you think, Criton?'

The Macedonian said slowly, 'You have come here to trade. I do not think Manissa is the kind of man with whom it is wise to hold amusing conversations.'

Attius said, 'Is that why that slave is here – the beautiful one?'

Curtius Rufus hesitated. He said, 'She may be useful. I did not bring her for myself, if that is what you are thinking.'

Criton said, 'We all know what you have been thinking.'

Attius looked embarrassed and Vatinus laughed.

Curtius Rufus said coldly, 'No one would accuse you, Vatinus, of such thoughts.' The optio stared at him resentfully.

Marcus Pedius said, 'What a waste.' He was thinking of the girl.

Lucius Eggius looked at Curtius Rufus. He said quietly, 'The girl has lost her looks. I am not surprised after a journey such as we have had. I would not give ten denarii for her at the moment. You had best get that old woman to attend to her.' He glanced at Criton, who shook his head.

Curtius Rufus looked at them in turn. His face had a pinched look and his eyes were black with tiredness. He said, 'If anyone hears anything they are to let me know. I will have to decide what to say to Manissa when I meet him.'

They discussed other matters then and did not leave until the sun was beginning to set. Criton remained behind. He seemed nervous and worried. He said, 'Attius likes that girl. I have seen him watching her.'

'He will have to make do with that. He couldn't afford to buy her, not even on his praetorian pay.' Curtius Rufus bit his lip. 'How's the fever? Any better?'

'Yes, thank you.'

'You look tired out.'

'So do you.'

They looked at each other. Curtius Rufus said gently, 'What's wrong, Criton?'

'I – I'm just tired, I suppose. I lay awake last night, listening to the wind. It never stops blowing. You can hear it all night. I wish I was back in Rome. I wish I had never left it.'

'We shall be back soon enough. And if we haven't got the girl, or she's dead, we'll find ourselves back in that tenement block.' Curtius Rufus paused. He said, 'It's Vatinus, isn't it? He wants that Syrian boy of yours.'

Criton nodded miserably.

'And the boy?'

'They – they're good at pretending, but they only want

money. They're all whores at heart. Vatinus will get his staff soon. Marcus Pedius was saying as much the other day.'

'Has he been unfaithful?'

Criton nodded again. 'Yes,' he muttered. 'Vatinus has looks, an impressive uniform, good prospects and good pay. A Greek secretary is a nobody.'

'Sell him to the optio then and be rid of him. You can have one of my boys. The young one likes you.'

Criton looked at the walls of the tent. 'You don't understand,' he said. 'You never understand. I love him.' He put his head in his hands and began to cry.

The chief suffete, with an escort of horsemen, led them through the Tingis gate, two hours after sunrise. Close to, they could see the crudely made sun-baked walls of brown mud and plaster, scarcely fifteen feet high and less than a yard thick. There were no towers either side of the gate, and Lucius Eggius thought he had never seen a native town that could be stormed with such ease. The street was a dirt track that would turn to mud when the rain fell, and it wound in and out between narrow, flat-roofed houses that never rose above two stories in height and which seemed to have been erected – as Crescens remarked later – without thought as to how anyone was to pass between them. There was a bare eight feet between the walls. The window openings, mere slits heavily shuttered against the light, were all high up on the first floor, while the doorways were just wide enough to allow a man below medium height to enter or leave without difficulty. The side streets were even narrower, alleyways down which two women might just walk abreast. No one spoke except the escort, who cursed and shouted as they forced a way through the crowds ahead. Presently they reached the market square; this they crossed at an angle, making their way through another narrow lane that led toward a large white-faced building that stood on rising ground not far from the southeast wall. A flight of steps, crudely faced with stone, led up to a pair of double doors, blistered by the sun, outside which stood half a dozen men, carrying spears and wearing swords. Inside, the passages were high and narrow, the walls whitewashed, the ceilings painted blue. The floors were of brick, cemented over and painted in pattern designs that were strange even to Crescens. They came to a small chamber, the floor of which was strewn with rugs, but the only furniture was a low, round table of beaten gold. Around it were heaped a pile of cushions and, facing them, sitting cross-legged behind the table, was Manissa. He was quite alone.

Manissa was of medium height; smiling, dark-bearded, and handsome. He was dressed in white. On a plain leather belt he carried an ivory-handled knife held in a gold case, decorated with reliefs showing a fight between men and animals. The only jewelry he wore was a piece of amber set in gold, suspended over his chest by a gold chain. He glanced lazily at the group standing before him as though he were inspecting a herd of cattle. His stillness was frightening. At last he spoke. He had a deep voice, the kind that Curtius Rufus had always wished for, but in vain. He said, in Punic, 'The friends of my cousin are always welcome. I returned in a hurry from my hunting in order to meet you.' He paused and smiled with his mouth. 'I will be frank with you. You do not come at a good time. I have many problems, and the presence of Romi, like yourselves, can only add to them. I will be franker still. In my experience, envoys usually come not to negotiate but to spy, corrupt, betray.' Curtius Rufus, his hands behind his back, extended the palm of his left hand as a warning to his officers not to move or speak. He said politely, 'I visited your cousin to extend to him the friendship of Rome. Your brother and cousin asked me to visit you, my Lord, to offer my services to his most trusted governor and his right hand.'

'What services can you offer?'

'My Lord, I have skilled men with me. You have a fine town,

but it could be finer still. It could be made as beautiful as Alexandria and be a worthy residence for your magnificence.'

'I have seen Alexandria. I do not wish my town to be a Romi city. What do you propose?'

'We would propose, my Lord, but you would decide. For example, we could bring water to the town so that there would be fountains in the streets and baths in the houses.'

'Do you think we are a dirty people who never wash?' Manissa's voice was dangerously quiet.

'No, my Lord, but, as I have seen, it makes hard work for your people.'

'They are not afraid of work.'

'If, my Lord, they are saved time and effort in this respect, they can devote more time and effort to matters of greater concern – your interests.'

'I am not a poor man. This town is not empty of slaves. Their time, their effort is not important.'

Curtius Rufus felt the sweat on his forehead. He said steadily, 'I think, my Lord, that with a greater and more permanent water supply it would be more easily possible to irrigate the soil. Fine crops could be grown on the plain around the town. There would be better grazing for cattle and horses. Crops and cattle and horses can be sold. You would have more wealth.' He paused and looked unflinchingly at Manissa. 'No ruler ever had too much wealth. There would be less dependence upon the trade of caravans.'

Manissa said slowly, 'Very well, I give you leave to bring water to the town.'

Curtius Rufus said, 'I will be frank with you, my Lord. This can be done but it will take time.'

'How long?'

'Many months.'

Manissa said coolly, 'Guests and fresh meat stink after three days.' He smiled. 'I see this matter requires further talk. You must consult with my suffetes. They are my council. You would call them magistrates.'

Curtius Rufus said, 'I am asked to give you these presents as a token of the friendship that Augustus, the first citizen of Rome, bears to you.' He signed with his hand and Vatinus brought forward a silver-chased box. Manissa opened the box, looked at the contents a moment, and then closed the lid. He said, 'The jewels are magnificent. Convey my thanks to Augustus. But they are presents for a woman. I will pass them to where they will be most appreciated.'

Curtius Rufus heard movement behind him. The tone of Manissa's voice had been unmistakable. He said quickly, 'It is our custom to give jewels. If I have offended, I beg for forgiveness.'

Manissa smiled. 'It is nothing. An envoy is only the slave of his master.'

Curtius Rufus said, 'My Lord, there is one more matter. A Romi girl, the highborn daughter of a great family, was taken by Mauri pirates last year and is believed to be a prisoner in this land. I would ask your help in recovering the girl; if you would be kind enough to use your influence in this matter. She is very dear to her people.'

Manissa's face went blank. He said, 'I have heard of that raid on the Hispania coast. There are many lawless men in the Maghreb. I know nothing more of the matter. I regret that I cannot help you.'

Curtius Rufus bowed.

Manissa said, 'Your men may enter the town to buy food and supplies, but they must leave it by sundown when the gates are closed. Inside the town they must be obedient to my laws. Is that understood?'

'Yes, my Lord.'

'One more thing. No Romi may travel more than two miles from your camp in any direction without my authority. That is all for now. You have my permission to leave.'

They turned to leave. Curtius Rufus was the last to go. At the door he paused as Manissa spoke again. 'You speak Punic well for a Romi. Do you speak Berber also?'

'A very little, my Lord.'

Manissa smiled. 'It is not an easy language. We use the Phoenician alphabet. Few understand that. Well, should you wish to send messages back to Iol Caesarea, give them to the chief suffete. He will see that they are delivered safely.'

Curtius Rufus said, 'You are most generous.'

Manissa smiled. 'You may wish to write to the Queen. It would be a pity if any of your messages went astray.' He was still smiling as the door closed and the room was empty again, save for himself. But this time the smile extended to his eyes.

Crescens said wearily, 'It's very difficult to know what to do. The town, if you can call it that, needs pulling down. I swear by the gods there isn't an alleyway that runs straight for longer than thirty feet at a time.' He wiped his face and looked again at the rough plan he had made. 'The whole place is a cat's cradle of stinking streets. No sanitation; water brought in by slaves, women, or donkeys; no order, no method, nothing. It's one vast hovel. Pathetic, really.'

'I know all that,' said Curtius Rufus with patience. 'I've walked all morning. It'll take a month to get the smell out of my nostrils. Well, what about the water supply?'

Crescens said, 'There's a spring that rises in those hills to the southeast. We'd have to take it from there.'

'An aqueduct?' Curtius Rufus looked across the camp to where the wheelwright was shaping cornelwood spokes to repair a damaged wheel that lay by the smith's fire.

'It'd be a labor for Hercules. It's over six miles away. Further, if we tap it where we need to – what would we build it with, limestone? That means a source and a quarry to be dug. Brick?'

'Why not?' Curtius Rufus could see the slave girls returning from a walk. He watched them pass through the gates and saw the sentry speaking to them. One of the girls laughed and tossed her head.

'We'd need thousands.'

'It could be done.'

Crescens said, 'Oh, yes, it could be done.'

'Well, in my legion fifty men could make two hundred a day.'

'Yes, and we'd want a million at least. That would take a hundred working days and bring us to September, with nothing to show for our efforts. And where's the straw and the clay coming from?'

'We can recruit a labor force from the town.'

'Who will pay them, Manissa or us?'

Curtius Rufus hesitated. 'What do you suggest then?'

Crescens smiled savagely. 'Suggest the impossible. And watch his face when he refuses. Those Baquates won't let us come within a hundred yards of their precious foothills. He knows that but he won't admit to us that he's lost control over them — if he ever had it.'

'And then?'

'Oh, suggest we improve his five main streets by laying them with broken rubble. Even he might like that. He'd like his horse not to get its feet muddy every time he rides out.'

'Let's try that then. And we might offer to smarten up his palace.'

'I'll get the craftsmen to prepare some designs.' Crescens hesitated and then said bluntly, 'How long are we going to be here? A few months, or longer? I told my wife I'd be back by the June Kalends.'

'We may yet, if we're lucky.'

Crescens said, 'She depends on me. I don't like leaving her with only that brother of hers to turn to. He's about as honest as Mercury.'

'Don't worry. It won't be long.'

'I wrote her from Iol but I've had no reply.'

'We've all written and had no reply.'

A voice said sardonically, 'Some of us don't bother if we do get a letter.' It was Criton.

'What letter?'

'There was that other letter in that package from Rome. If Pero took the trouble to write, you might try taking the trouble to read it.'

'I'll come and get it.' Curtius Rufus turned to Crescens. 'We're meeting the suffetes tomorrow. We'll discuss the matter further then.' He followed Criton, who was walking ahead, and the surveyor heard him say, 'But she told me she couldn't write.' Crescens smiled sadly and bent over his plans.

Criton said, 'Here it is.' He handed it over without a word. Curtius Rufus, unaware that there was something wrong still, looked up. 'What is it?' he asked.

The Macedonian said, 'It is nothing. I am only a fool. I wish I were like you and that I could enjoy it without caring for the person I do it with. Perhaps that is the other difference between us.'

Curtius Rufus nodded. 'You may be right,' he said, and opened the letter. It was from her, all right. It began formally: 'to Curtius Rufus, the appointed envoy of Rome at the court of King Juba of Mauretania; he said I could write to you as he knew that I was your friend, and he would arrange for the letter to be sent with his official dispatches. So I am telling this to the letter writer who sits by the small fountain next to the jeweller's shop in the street of the silversmiths. You will have heard the news I am sure. My Lady goes about with a white face and does not smile. Lucia thinks it is because of her brother. She was fond of him as we all know, but I think she is worried about him, I mean her husband. The house has been quiet since it happened and there are no parties and few visitors. He is very kind but looks unhappy all the time, and the steward says that there is a cloud over him because of something that has happened. I had meant to tell you about the Saturnalia and our visits to the theatre before it happened, but now I can't. I was present with my Lady when Agrippa came, and there was nearly a quarrel, the way men do without raising their voices and smiling all the time. Agrippa said that he was very angry and could not forgive – he used a word, indiscretion, which I do not understand. I expect you do. The Master said that Valerius Messalla had approved, and Agrippa said that he would approve of anything. The Master said he had done what he did out of kindness for his wife, and that it was not his fault if her brother had not understood the reason for the message. He then said he might have known why the message went wrong, since her brother had never been a keen bather. I don't know what he meant, but Agrippa laughed and left the house. The steward, who has friends on the Palatine, says that Augustus is ill again. I asked my Lady and she said the news was correct. They are worried about that too. She said that if he died there would be civil war, so I went to the Pool of Curtius in the Forum and threw in a coin and said a prayer for him. Lots of people were doing the same. It rains all the time and we don't go out, so I am nursing a dove which has a damaged wing, and my friend, Felix, helps me. He knows a lot about birds. I did not mean to write, but I thought you might like to have a letter from Rome, although I expect you are working too hard to miss it much. The Master said your work was important and he was certain you would do it well. Don't drink too much; Your friend, Pero.'

Curtius Rufus read it aloud, and when he came to the end he put down the letter and sat in silence. He had not expected her to write after the quarrel that night in Rome. A great deal had happened since then, and he had very little time for thinking about the past. He did not dream at night of horses in the Circus, nor of the ships standing clear of Ostia harbor and setting their beaks toward the south, nor of the foreign places he had so much wanted to visit or see again. He did not dream because he was always too tired. He thought of her seldom, but when he did he knew that she had been right, as Criton had been right. They both knew him too well. He liked women for their company and for their charms, but he did not wish to marry and settle down, though he had talked about it enough. Like his father, he was a gambler and if, when things were bad, he wished for the respectable life he had never had, that too was only a wish, as long-lasting as the sight of a falling star, brief and insubstantial like a dream. He enjoyed living by his wits. He had no wish to change.

He said, 'Why did she write?'

Criton shrugged. 'You claim to know women. I don't, thank the gods. But I would say, my dear friend, that Pero wished to write – because she wished to write.'

Curtius Rufus said, 'The letter contains a warning of some kind.'

'Yes, even I can see that. The patrician class take baths for only two reasons; one of them is for personal comfort. The other—' He shivered suddenly.

'It was kind of her.'

Criton sighed. He said, 'I like Pero. She is a clever girl, but she is not that clever. What do you say when you write to some-one who has quarreled with you? If you have pride you don't mention the quarrel, nor do you say the things you want to say. You talk about other things, and it is this thing which is in her mind.' He paused. Then he said quickly, 'I think Maecenas encouraged her to write. He knew she might say what he could not himself.'

'How could he be certain?'

'No one can be, but he has a woman's subtlety. He has – as Pero says – committed an indiscretion. He needs a diplomatic success to wipe it out. He needs it quickly. And so do we, dear Curtius, if we are not to return and find all those patrons on whom we pin our hopes, living in the shade.'

Curtius Rufus rose and went to the door of the tent. He looked across the camp toward the mud walls of the town. Then he looked left to the brown and green hills. 'She might be anywhere,' he said. 'It all seems so hopeless.'

Criton sighed. 'I agree. I think that Attius was right and that she is dead. But we must still go on trying. That is the only reason we are here.'

The suffetes, at their morning meeting, approved the water plan and agreed to put it to Manissa when he held his public audience later in the day. 'This I regret you cannot attend,' said one of them in a friendly voice. 'For then the governor administers justice. The righteous who have grievances are rewarded and wrongdoers who are guilty are punished. The punishments you may watch. Thieves have their right hands cut off, women taken in adultery have their noses sliced so that they may no longer tempt men with their beauty, while their lovers are castrated. Murderers are exposed in a cage, hung from a tower, until they die. Lesser crimes are punished by a hundred lashes. The Lord Manissa is a merciful man. He does not like to shed blood except in battle.' He glanced slyly at the envoy, whose face had assumed an expression of bland interest. 'Our justice is swift and sure. That is as it should be when government is good.'

Later that day Manissa sent his answer. The water plan was a fine one but would take too long; there were reasons of state why it could not be implemented at this time. He approved the alternative schemes; work on these might commence immediately.

Under the direction of Lucius Eggius work was started on the street leading to the southwest gate, while the craftsmen opened a workshop in the shadow of the governor's palace and began to draw up their plans.

Each morning a ration party went into the town, and Marcus Pedius, conscious of his responsibilities, warned Lucius Eggius that some of the men were becoming friendly with the women they met, and that there might be trouble. Lucius Eggius, damp with sweat and covered with clay, went to see the envoy. Curtius Rufus, writing a long report, said irritably, 'Yes, yes, I agree. I think I had better speak to the suffetes. Let us hope that Manissa's generosity is as great as his justice is swift.' He saw the suffetes, who said they would speak with the governor, but after that he heard no more and concluded that the answer was in the negative. The waiting got on his nerves and he grew angry every time Criton said to him, 'Be patient. Wait till the street work is finished, then ask him again.'

One afternoon when the camp was almost empty except for a handful of men doing fatigues, and the only sound was the doleful clang of the blacksmith's hammer, the sentry on the north wall shouted suddenly. Curtius Rufus, lying on his bed, trying to rest, got up and hurried out. 'What is it?' he said.

'A caravan, sir,' said the sentry in an excited voice.

Curtius Rufus hurried to join him. Across the plain, far in the distance could be seen a faint smudge of gray and brown.

'They're from Tingis,' said the sentry. 'We may get some news at last.'

Curtius Rufus said, 'It's the first caravan in a month. They will be at the gates in an hour. Let me know when they get closer.'

News of the caravan's arrival spread rapidly, and when he walked from the camp to the Tingis Gate with Criton for company he found a crowd gathered there talking excitedly.

The caravan came nearer and the crowd's voice lost strength and faded into a frightened silence. Curtius Rufus touched Criton upon the arm. 'They've been attacked,' he said. 'Look at them.'

There were men sitting slumped on mules, their arms and heads roughly bandaged, but the bandages were caked with dried blood and covered with flies. A number of men on foot were limping, some with the aid of crutches, while others lay motionless in litters borne by their friends. They saw a mule without ears, and a horse with only one eye and a great gash across its cheek. There was a man lying across his horse's neck, who must have died within sight of the walls. There was a wagon, pushed by men because the mules had been slaughtered; pack horses that led themselves; and a foal that limped on three legs and which had been born soon after the caravan left Tingis.

Curtius Rufus said, 'I will get you to ask that Greek merchant of Marcus Pedius's what happened.'

He walked back to the camp and saw a figure that he knew, a little ahead of him. It was Urracca. 'Did you go down to watch?' he asked.

'Yes, Lord, it was something to do, though now I wish I had stayed in this camp.' She spoke in a listless voice and he saw that her face was very pale.

He said, 'They met some trouble, I'm afraid.'

She turned her head. 'Are you afraid?' she asked. 'You cannot be afraid, like me.'

'What is wrong?' he asked. He was worried by her looks and her voice. He was worried too about the way she walked. She seemed totally apathetic and listless. He remembered what Lucius Eggius had said, and wished he had paid more attention to her on the long journey from Iol Caesarea. She did not answer him until they reached the camp. Then she smiled wanly and said, 'I don't like this place. I hate the open spaces and the wind at night. I hate the soldiers who look at me all the time and lick their lips and smile and snigger as I walk by. Above all, I hate what is to come.'

He said, 'Even I do not know what is to come.'

She said, 'I know what you intend. Everyone talks about Manissa. To me he is a name. I wish that he would always be only a name.'

He smiled. 'No one has harmed you. What did you expect? Another Rome?'

Urracca shrugged her shoulders. 'I am sorry, my Lord. I should not have spoken so. It is not my place.' She looked at him then and her face set hard, the eyes remote and without expression. She said, 'My place is in your bed. It is because it is not that the soldiers snigger and make bets.'

She turned away to that part of the camp where the women's tents were erected, and he watched her go in silence.

Criton visited the Greek, who was pleased to see a man from his own lands. 'I have not spoken my own tongue to any except my wife, and she is dead, for many years. This we must celebrate. I have some wine I received eight caravans ago. It is Chian and I keep it for special occasions.'

Criton said, curiosity aroused, 'What occasions are special except religious ones, in a town like this? I cannot think why you stay here. I shall be glad to leave.'

The old man smiled. 'It would take too long to tell you the story of my life now, and you would not be interested. But I stay because of my family.'

'You have children?'

'I have a daughter. When she was fifteen the Lord Manissa sent for her.' He lowered his voice. 'It was a great honor, of course. I could not refuse. I had seen what happened to other men who refused his requests. For many years she has been his favorite and because of that I am allowed to visit her every year on her birthday. It is the day I live for in each year. But now—' He hesitated. 'I am not sure. It is said he has another interest.'

'Another girl?' asked Criton, but he spoke a shade too casually, and the old man took fright. 'It is not my business,' he said. 'Look, here is the wine. Taste it and tell me what you think.'

'It is excellent.' Criton put down his cup and the old man refilled it, asking questions of Rome and Greece, only some of which could Criton answer. Presently Criton said, 'What happened to the caravan? Did you have an interest in the goods that survived?'

'It was terrible. Terrible. The second caravan in two months the Mazices have attacked. This is unusual. It is customary for them to stop its passage, you understand, and ask for a tax before allowing it to proceed. That we expect. But this – this horror!' He looked round the darkened room as though expecting to be overheard. But the door was shut and nothing stirred in the hot, airless atmosphere of rugs, brassware, and spices. He said, 'They say the Baquates moved north to dominate the Tingis route and to take the Mazices' spoils from them. This has not happened before, but now, suddenly, there is bad blood. So the Mazices raided the caravan first in order that nothing might be left to their enemies.' He paused, and when he spoke again his lips scarcely moved, and Criton could barely hear what he said. 'They say the governor promised both tribes a great war, with plunder and rich lands as the prize. But the war has not come and the tribes say he has broken faith. They are fighting each other and share only one aim – to starve this town and destroy it.'

Lucius Eggius stood in the market square, the sweat streaking the dirt on his face, his armor coated with dust. Only his eyes flickered from side to side as he watched the activity about him. In one corner by the well a group of young men were gathered in a circle as a man with a stubble of white beard opened a wicker basket, trying to prod a sleepy snake into activity. A line of mules was being offloaded while their owner shouted instructions to his slaves about the laying out of his wares. Charcoal stoves were being set up as sweetmeat vendors prepared to cook the sticky cakes that were their speciality, while in the center of a flock of incurious goats stood a post from which a half-naked man was suspended. He had been flogged an hour previously for some offense, and if still alive at sundown would be cut down and allowed to go home, giving thanks to the gods in a loud voice for the mercy of the Lord Manissa. A donkey, led by a young boy, crossed the centurion's front, and the boy scowled and flung an insult in passing. Lucius Eggius saw a water carrier approaching. He shook his head and the man shrugged and moved off, shaking his bell, the wet goatskin bag on his back glistening in the light. Then Curtius Rufus appeared from behind a tent and Lucius Eggius smiled with his eyes. 'I'm glad you could come.'

'What is the problem?'

'The usual one. We are getting less popular every day. Work on the roads has slowed down. At first, Manissa's guard helped us by keeping the street clear of traffic, and they warned the inhabitants against throwing their refuse out of the windows.'

'Is that all?'

The centurion said dryly, 'This morning I had a chamber pot dropped on me – it was full at the time – and the crowd laughed, waiting to see what I would do.'

'And what did you do?'

'Tried to pretend it had not happened. They were disappointed.' Lucius Eggius sniffed. 'That's why I stink.'

'What else?' Curtius Rufus tried not to smile.

'The labor gangs have been cut by half. There are delays and accidents – too many to be genuine. You know the sort of thing I mean.'

'Yes, I saw it in Hispania when we used prisoners of war.'

Lucius Eggius said quietly, 'But that's not all. One of the soldiers was hurt when a poorly loaded wagon collapsed. It was quite deliberate. Another soldier was robbed yesterday in a shop, and when he complained the guards shrugged their shoulders and took no notice. The women spit, the men jeer, and the small boys throw stones and then run away. The men are getting restive.'

'Manissa's trying to provoke us. Wants us out of the way.'

'That is obvious. What do we do?' Lucius Eggius's voice was sharp. He had had a trying morning.

Curtius Rufus said, 'Have great patience. Avoid arguments, fights, and quarrels. I don't want one of your soldiers tied to that post.'

'Neither do I.'

'Well, tell 'em to stick it out. I'm still trying to get an audience again with the governor. He won't see me.'

'Another bad sign.'

'Of course. However, I'm hoping to rouse his curiosity. I and the five cavalry are going to excercise the horses again this afternoon.'

'So that explains the last three days. I thought perhaps you were training for the Circus.'

Curtius Rufus grinned. 'We had a good audience yesterday. Word will have got back. I think he'll come out to watch this afternoon. Would you care to bet on it?'

'Not with your dice. I saw you take a month's pay off Vatinus the other evening. Was that fair?'

'I wasn't cheating, my friend. Just giving Vatinus a lesson. It may teach him to leave other people's property alone.'

Lucius Eggius glanced at him sharply. 'Criton?'

'Yes.'

'I have heard something of that. Meanwhile, Attius makes cow's eyes at Urracca.' Lucius Eggius spoke idly and without picking his words as he usually did. 'It seems to have done her good. She is recovering her looks. He's giving her what she needs.'

Curtius Rufus grinned with his teeth. 'I hope, for his sake, that is all he is giving her.'

Lucius Eggius said, 'I'll join you after the midday meal. It should be interesting if he comes.'

'He'll come, all right.'

They rode on the plain outside the south wall of the camp, and the five Gauls, who prided themselves on their horsemanship, vied with Lucius Eggius and the envoy at throwing javelins while at full gallop at a target fixed to a post. Then, while the horses were being rested, Lucius Eggius said softly, 'There is a party coming out of the Tingis Gate.'

'Take no notice,' said Curtius Rufus. He wore breeches but was otherwise bare to the waist. His hair was tousled and he looked younger than the centurion had ever seen him look. 'Like cats and women, he will come if we ignore him. Get a trooper to fix an iron ring to the post.' He took a small bow that a slave handed him, and said with a grin, 'I am not very good, you understand, but this is how my father's countrymen fight.' Stooping, he put the bow between his legs, reversed the reflex curves, and strung it across his bent knees, apparently without effort of any kind. He remounted his horse, fitted an ivory ring on to his right thumb, took a short arrow from a quiver slung over his shoulder, waved, trotted in the direction of the post, and went on past it for two hundred yards.

Lucius Eggius watched him, listening to the sound of the horses coming up behind. When they were close by he raised his arm. There was a great cry in a strange tongue, the horse exploded into a gallop with Curtius Rufus lying flat along its back, his head against the animal's mane. As they drew level with the post he swung upright on the sheepskin covering and turned, the bow bent and the arrow drawn on the right of the bow ready to loose. The arrow flew and, with incredible speed, two other arrows followed it. Lucius Eggius and the cavalrymen were trained to watch the flight of an arrow, the throw of a spear, or the swing of a sword, and they saw quite clearly that each arrow, fired backward from the galloping pony, had gone through the iron ring, the last just grazing its shank. There was a roar of applause as Curtius Rufus wheeled his pony and trotted back with a grave face. He said cheerfully, 'A soldier in battle would have fired them faster. I am out of practice and did not care to miss, so I took my time.' He paused, looked past the centurion, and smiled a greeting. 'My Lord Manissa, this is an honor. We are amusing ourselves, for it is a fine day.'

Manissa said, 'I must congratulate you. That is not something I have seen before. May I see the bow?'

Curtius Rufus stretched out his hand and the governor examined the bow carefully. 'What is it made of? It is very powerful.'

'The string is of silk, knotted to loops of sinew. The bow is composite: strips of horn, laths of wood, and sinew from the neck of a stag, among other things.'

'How far do they shoot?' asked Lucius Eggius curiously.

'A trained archer can send a war arrow three hundred and fifty to four hundred yards. A flight arrow will go much further.'

The governor grunted. 'A fine weapon,' he said. 'I did not know you were a warrior.'

'I am not a warrior now. Though I was once. There was a time, long ago—' He broke off and smiled ruefully.

Manissa said, 'It is a good trick. But can a man ever win by retreating?'

Curtius Rufus said simply, 'There are more ways to win a battle or a war – even a war of words – than one would think.'

'And where do they fight like this?'

'In Parthia.'

'So! You were not born in Rome.'

'I was, my Lord.'

'Ah! I begin to understand.' The governor smiled suddenly. 'To each his own weapon. My people have their way.' He handed back the bow. 'You ride very well.'

'It is one of my few accomplishments.'

'I doubt that, for I have met few Romi who speak my tongue as you do.'

Curtius Rufus slid from the pony and looked up at the governor. It was diplomatic, he thought, to give Manissa the advantage of height.

'My Lord, the loss of the girl I spoke of when we first met is a matter to which the Senate of Rome cannot remain indifferent.

We view this matter with the gravest concern. Mauretania is our ally, yet the actions of those who commit acts of piracy cannot be ignored.' He paused. He said quietly, 'Nor, my Lord, can they be forgotten. This I have said to your cousin, the King, and this I must repeat to you. The ship and the people came from these shores – which you rule. The responsibility is yours.'

Manissa looked at him impassively. 'I have told you before that this small matter does not concern me.'

'It must concern you, my Lord. What touches Rome touches you.'

Manissa dropped his hands and his pony began to dance a little, at first in front and then to the side, as though he were trying to force Curtius Rufus to give way. The envoy stood quite still and did not move, even when Manissa reared the pony up on its hind legs so that Curtius Rufus looked up at the hooves poised above him. Lucius Eggius leaned forward in his anxiety.

Curtius Rufus grinned. 'My Lord, I should regard that as an unfriendly act to a man who has been granted the privilege of your hospitality. And so would those you rule.'

The pony sidled backwards. Manissa moved his hand, and the pony dropped, shaking its head and fretting at the bit. Manissa said, 'You have courage. When did that happen?' He pointed at the envoy's shoulders. They were covered in scar tissue as though at some time he had been in a terrible accident. The skin was puckered and ugly, all the way down to both elbows. Criton had seen him stripped many times but he had never asked that question. He was not a curious man and knew when to keep silent upon matters that did not concern him. Maecenas had seen him in the baths but had not asked. He was a man of tact and politeness. Lucius Eggius had seen him, too, on the day they poured vinegar over the rocks in the pass, and had held his tongue out of common courtesy. It was left to a violent and hostile man to breach the etiquette of behavior, and they waited to hear what the envoy would say.

Curtius Rufus smiled with his teeth. He said, 'No man has asked me that since it happened. Do I ask you, my Lord, what you do in bed with a woman? Then let me have peace in matters which are my concern and mine alone.'

Manissa said, 'So be it,' and turned his pony.

Curtius Rufus cried out, 'I have good reason to believe, my Lord, that you know where the girl is now hidden – whether she is alive or dead. You must know, or your rule is like that of the wind. It obeys no laws. It blows at any man's whim.'

Manissa said, over his shoulder, 'Have a care for your tongue, Romi. Stronger men than you have knelt in the town square and eaten their torn-out tongues at the bidding of my executioner.'

There was a murmur from the soldiers present and Criton put a shaking hand to his mouth. He looked as though he would like to be sick.

Curtius Rufus said, 'Then, my Lord, if I may, I will speak with you again on another day, and I will put the same question. And I must warn you now that if, on that day, you do not help me, then I shall decline to be responsible for the consequences.'

Manissa said over his shoulder – and he surprised them all by speaking in Latin – 'I had a message, a letter from Iol Caesarea, brought to me in the caravan that arrived yesterday. There was a letter for you also. Give it to him.' He spoke to a horseman, who threw a pouch at the envoy's feet. 'My message tells me that the news out of Rome is not good.' He had his back to Curtius Rufus as he spoke and his pony, dancing still, threw dust in the envoy's eyes. The Romans present looked at him expectantly, but in that moment all that Curtius Rufus noticed was not the dust but the afternoon breeze that touched his back.

Manissa's voice was harsh and exultant. He said, 'They tell me that Gaius Julius Caesar Octavianus, who was a sick man before you left Rome, has not left his house on the Palatine in days. Not even his fine titles – imperator, dux, princeps, consul – can save him now. He is a dying man.'

He drove his heels into his pony's sides and, followed by his escort, rode at a triumphant gallop toward the walls of Volubilis.

The news had the intended effect for, as Criton said, it was impossible that it should be otherwise. The message, written in haste by Cornelius Silius, who, in his agitation, made four mistakes encoding it, confirmed what Manissa had told them. It ended on a somber note of warning. 'There is unrest at Iol Caesarea and throughout the eastern half of the kingdom, as a result. King Juba, who has returned with his art treasures and who, until now, has behaved like a child given new toys, has expressed his sympathy and has advised that you return. The Queen sends messages of sympathy also, but does not enquire after you. I have been in touch with the Proconsul. I understand that Antonius Musa, Augustus' chief physician, is in attendance, but even he holds out little hope. This news is confirmed by a report from an officer on duty at the Palatine, and who may be trusted, that Augustus summoned Calpurnius Piso, the new consul, and Marcus Agrippa to his bedside. To the former he handed over state papers, to the latter his signet ring. I strongly advise you to make your way to the coast as quickly as possible. When he is dead your safe conduct cannot protect you. It should, but it will not. Nevertheless I offer prayers for your safety.'

They argued and discussed the matter far into the night but their discussions and their arguments got them nowhere. At the end of it all Criton said sadly, 'In moments of great crisis men always talk too much. It is such a waste of time.'

The news spread through the town and the fatigue party, engaged on building the road, encountered a hostile crowd when they began work the next day. Attius, escorting a forage party to cut grass, reported that there were campfires on the western horizon. The cavalry patrol was sent out to the limits allowed and, on their return, hazarded the opinion that it was a gathering of Mazices. Vatinus rode to the southwest gate of the town and reported that there was now a camp of Baquates four hundred yards across the plain, and that men of the tribe were going openly through the gate, some to buy supplies, others to talk to the suffetes, who spent their day gathered in council under a tree in the square. At sundown Marcus Pedius returned. He had tried to contact the Greek merchant, but the house was closed and he was told that the old man had gone away. 'They have arrested him,' he said. 'The governor, who is not a fool, has guessed where you gained your information. You should have told me to cut the old man's throat. It would have been a quicker death than the one he will suffer now.'

Lucius Eggius said calmly, 'It makes little difference. Our envoy had to try. That was the reason we came.'

Criton said, 'Well, what do we do now?'

They all turned and looked at their envoy.

Curtius Rufus said, 'I shall have to wait for further news. I cannot leave without trying once more.' He grinned. 'Moreover, I don't suppose we would get very far.'

'But he wouldn't dare attack us if we marched out,' said Attius. 'It would be an act of war.'

'We cannot leave without his permission.'

Lucius Eggius looked at the others and then said to the envoy, 'I think it dangerous to wait. We are agreed on this. The lives of all of us are in your hands. It would be best if you sought his leave for us to go. In the circumstances no blame can be attached to any of us for any failure on our part. We were ordered to avoid bloodshed at all costs. I like to think that that includes our own.'

Curtius Rufus sighed. 'Very well. I will send a request in the morning.'

He did so and a horseman returned an hour later with the governor's reply. He said, 'The Lord Manissa bids you stay to accomplish the purpose for which you came. There is unrest in the land and he cannot guarantee your safety out of sight of these walls. He will expect the work of improving the amenities of the town to continue.'

'And if I refuse, what then?'

The messenger said gravely, 'I was told to expect this question and instructed to reply to it as follows: the Lord Manissa bids you heed his words: Manissa rules and he rules alone. He says also: there are two ways of leaving the city of Volubilis – one of them is by dying.'

Curtius Rufus smiled. 'So be it,' he said. 'We will stay.'

That day was the Festival of Ceres, when lighted firebrands were tied to the tails of foxes let loose in the Circus Maximus, but it all seemed so much a part of a forgotten life that not even Curtius Rufus remembered, as they waited uneasily for what the next sun might bring.

The Kalends of May came and passed and the legionaries sweated under the sun as they worked eight hours a day in the fetid atmosphere of the crowded town, redigging the foundations of the streets, smoothing the layers of broken rubble with a gravel surface, and edging the whole with curbs of cut stone. Those who came from the land remembered that at home their friends and kinsmen would, by now, have begun the cutting of the hay. The Tarentine sheep had long since been washed ready for shearing, the cattle of autumn birth branded, and the vines trimmed in readiness for the second digging.

At odd moments Lucius Eggius thought of his aunt, whose affairs he could not handle; Crescens worried about his wife; and Marcus Pedius grew gloomy at thinking on the disasters that would befall his old cohort under the direction of a colleague whom he neither liked nor trusted. Criton, nervous of scorpions and suspicious of snakes since an adder had struck the second clerk in the ankle one morning, searched the floor of his tent each day and thought with longing of his old room in the tenement block by the Tiber. 'It wasn't fair,' he said angrily one hot day to an astonished and uncomprehending clerk. 'It wasn't fair to impose his friendship like that. He could have managed quite well without me. I am no use here to anyone, not even myself.' No one answered him. It was the season for childish tempers and angry scenes between reasonable men whose powers of restraint gradually slipped away as each unendurable day was succeeded by another. The heat haze began to shimmer upon the plain, the grass turned brown, and Volubilis trembled under the summer sun. And at night the sentries on the camp walls watched the fires of the Mazices move closer and closer to the town as the tribe increased in both fighting strength and boldness.

One morning a soldier was stoned by the crowd and brought back to camp on a stretcher, his face cut from chin to temple by a jagged rock. This incident was followed by another when the drivers, taking the mules down to the stream for their evening water, were set upon by a mob of Baquates armed with knives. One driver was wounded in the arm and the rest fled, but two of the mules were hamstrung and left to die on the bank. A cavalryman who could not stand the sound of the animals crying rode out alone and against orders to still their screaming. He said afterward, 'Funny brutes, them mules. They stopped making a noise the moment I dismounted. Just lay there and looked at me as though to say, "He's come now and everything'll be all right. He'll fix us up." I did it as quick as I could, while they stood around with their spears and their swords, laughing.'

One of his friends grinned. 'I didn't know you was soft-hearted.'

'I'm a farmer's son,' he replied. 'If you don't look after animals proper, you and them starve. It's all a matter of common sense.'

Lucius Eggius said to the envoy, 'It will get worse from now on. The men have almost taken enough. There's a limit to the floggings you can threaten them with.'

Curtius Rufus frowned and threw his dice from one hand to the other. 'Manissa won't make a move till he's certain. He's a frightened man. He's waiting for the next caravan from the coast, and with it news from Rome.'

'I would not have thought he was frightened,' said the centurion irritably. 'I never saw a man more sure of himself. But I agree that his people are getting out of hand. How he controls those nomads outside the town I cannot think.'

Criton, who had joined them at that moment, said in a hoarse voice, 'Though they worship different gods they all respect his, and he has promised them that Medaurus will give him a sign. That is why he goes to that broken-down temple each day. Isn't that right, Curtius?'

The envoy nodded.

Lucius Eggius said, curiously, 'How did you learn that?'

'I spoke to a number of merchants in the foreign quarter. There's a Jewish trader in rugs who lets things drop.'

The centurion said, 'Well, that may be, but I still don't see why he holds back. If he intends an uprising – why wait?'

Curtius Rufus said steadily, 'Whatever his gods promised him, I think he was waiting for some more tangible signal. His uprising was dependent upon support elsewhere.'

'But—'

'But he never received his signal. Remember the message we intercepted at Iol Caesarea? Things must have gone wrong elsewhere so he was compelled to wait.'

'And the girl was a pawn?'

'Yes,' said Criton angrily. 'A pawn. Proof to the Berbers that the Hispania coast was vulnerable; a prize to be displayed. Humiliate her and you humiliate Rome.'

Curtius Rufus looked at Criton. He said, 'She would make a fine sacrifice to a Mauri god. There are people here whose ancestors worshipped Moloch. His waiting, as Criton sees it, wasn't enough for the tribes. He had made promises and broken them. They hold Volubilis in their hand. They can starve the city if they choose. But they don't want to yet, because he's made them one last promise and they wait to see if he will keep it.'

Lucius Eggius stared. 'You mean that Augustus will die? That is the sign?'

Curtius Rufus said in a tired voice, 'I am sure of it. The jest is that he doesn't want an uprising at all now because he won't get the support he was promised. But he's on the wolf's back and he can't get off.'

Lucius Eggius said, 'What is this support that you talk of?' His eyes had narrowed and the patrician note had come back into his voice.

Curtius Rufus shrugged. 'Sometimes it is better to whisper than to shout. But there are times when silence is better still.'

'And meanwhile we must wait to be hacked to pieces,' said another voice. It was Marcus Pedius, red-eyed with fatigue.

'Oh, yes.' Curtius Rufus threw the dice into the air and caught them neatly. 'I don't understand the background to it. Criton, who has a better head than I, guesses at it.' He smiled at his friend. 'I trust his judgment.'

Marcus Pedius said, 'Can we trust yours?' His voice was harsh but not unfriendly.

'I live from one moment to the next. I manage as best as I can.'

'You may be right,' said Marcus Pedius suddenly. 'In the praetorian cohorts that provide details for escorts and guards for senior officials, you pick up quite a lot of curious news, and you learn after a time that behind every story there's almost always another story. People who play for power and influence behave a bit like two legionaries sitting down to draughts with their eyes blindfolded.' He paused to shout at a passing soldier who had failed to salute them, and then said, 'When we arrived I used to look forward to hearing the sentries cry out on sighting a caravan. It made the place seem less at the end of nowhere.

265

Now — now I dread the moment when the next one straggles into view.' He paused and said, 'I suppose there's no point in strengthening the camp?'

Curtius Rufus said curtly, 'They can overrun it in the space of an hour. Why prolong the matter? Are you afraid of dying?'

There was a long silence and they carefully avoided looking at each other.

Lucius Eggius said suddenly, 'When I was out here before, I went south with native guides and an armed escort. Did you know that the lower heights of the Atlas are covered with forests of cypress-type trees, and that their summits, even in summer, have snow on them? We crossed the Middle Atlas and so came to the desert. Parts of it were covered by great tracts of black sand and there were dark rocks, so hot at midday that you burnt your skin if you touched them. We met a caravan of the Gaetules who had made the journey down to a great river in the far south.' He smiled. 'We did not try to go that far.'

Curtius Rufus said, 'What was it like in that desert?'

Lucius Eggius shook his head. 'Bad, bad all the time. I do not see how you can live in it for long. We marched for twenty days across the rock and the sand before turning back, and each day we lived on one small cup of water. It was the most terrible journey I have ever made.'

'Why do you tell us this?' asked Marcus Pedius. He was envious that a man who earned less than himself seemed to have greater opportunities for enlarging his experience.

'Because, out there survival depends upon recognizing a tiny landmark that is a pebble turned over to show a different color; a footprint that has remained undisturbed for a month in the dry dust; the shape of a rock; or the smell of water in a well, half-choked with sand. You live by small things, and you survive by thinking like an animal; you eat leather if you are starving, or drink a camel's warm urine if you are dying of thirst.'

Curtius Rufus said, 'Well, I too, am relying on small signs.

266

Tell your men they will receive a bonus for good behaviour when they return to Rome. Tell them to trust me.'

Marcus Pedius glanced at the escort centurion and their eyes spoke. Lucius Eggius said, 'We will do our best, though it makes little difference to what will happen. We are prisoners in all but name. We are in Manissa's hands now, not yours.'

CHAPTER XV

Criton walked slowly through the alley and glanced toward the shop where the Greek merchant had lived. As he passed by, the door opened and a voice said, 'Buy something and come back as though you deliver merchandise. Knock three times.'

Criton did not answer but he heard the door close and knew that the old man was alive.

An hour later he was sitting inside a darkened room at the back of the shop and wondering, among other things, how he would explain the purchase of two expensive rugs when he made up the monthly accounts of their expenditure, and whether the officials in Rome would accept his story. He said, 'I am so relieved. I thought you were dead.'

The merchant said evasively, 'I shall be one day. This house is watched. I have been warned not to talk to the Romi.'

'Then I should not be here.'

'You will not come again. Now, listen to me.' The old man stirred in the half gloom and clasped his hands together. 'There is a citizen here, a Berber who makes swords. Once he served King Bogud when the king was an ally of Rome. This man had much to do with your soldiers. He was in the auxilia in Hispania for a time and he admired the Romi. He has a message of warning for your envoy. His information may be trusted, for he frequently goes to the governor's palace on business, and you should hear what he says. Go to the southwest gate at sundown tomorrow. There you will find a seller of dates. Ask him if the dates he sells are sweeter than those that may be bought at the Tingis Gate, and he will know that you have come from me and will give you the message.'

'How do I know this is not a trap?'

The old man said, 'You will know that when you walk out of here unharmed.'

Criton said doubtfully, 'Very well, I will do as you say. You are very kind.'

'No one in Volubilis is kind. We act only out of self-interest. I do this for the swordsmith, who in turn will expect favors from King Juba. It is not much to be a swordsmith when you have commanded an auxiliary of cavalry. Even I, who know nothing of soldiers, can understand that.'

Criton said gently, 'Your daughter – she is well?'

The old man laughed. 'Yes. The governor was very kind. He told me my daughter would be allowed to come back to look after me in my old age. He said he was sorry I should never see her again.'

Criton stared at him. Then he rose and went to the window and opened the shutters a little. The light from the sun fell upon the old man's face. Criton put a hand to his mouth and bit upon his fingers. The old man was blind. His eyes had been taken from him and the wounds were still unhealed. Criton closed the shutter and went quickly from the room. He paused by the door, listening, and thought he heard movement on an upper floor. He opened the door onto the street but no guards stood there, waiting to arrest him. He stepped out into the now empty alley and puckered his eyes against the glare of the light from the yellow walls opposite. Tomorrow, he thought, I will see the Dolphin rise in the evening sky, but he will see nothing. What did he do to offend the gods?

Two nights later Curtius Rufus and Lucius Eggius left the camp after dark and walked carefully across the plain to the stream where the men watered the mules. They waded the stream in silence and could see ahead of them the camp fires of the Baquates. A great fire on the steeply rising ground drew their attention. They scrambled up the slopes of a hill and saw that the fire burned on a ridge, and that it was surrounded by people, squatting in packed rows that stretched back into the darkness. In the center, a man in a dark robe was standing by the fire, making impassioned gestures, but they were too far to hear more than the murmur of his voice. Curtius Rufus said in a whisper, 'I am going closer. I want to hear what he says. If we are discovered, throw your javelins and run. Whatever happens, don't be taken alive.'

They crawled closer, making a wide detour and taking advantage of what cover they could find. Lying on the hill, sixty feet above the ridge, they could smell the wood smoke and hear the voice of the man by the fire. Curtius Rufus put his hand to his ear and prayed that he would not be speaking in a dialect he could not understand. Presently another rose to his feet and began to talk. He wore black robes, his head was covered, and his face veiled. He had a dagger in a sheath strapped to his left forearm. There came a murmur from the audience; questions were asked and answered. Lucius Eggius lay at the envoy's side, the sweat on his face, a javelin in his hand. Once he heard the name, Manissa, and it was followed by a roar from the gathering. It was the only word that he understood. The moon shifted across the sky, easily visible through light, moving clouds that would vanish before sunrise. Another man jumped to his feet and began to talk. Curtius Rufus listened for a moment or two and then turned his head. 'Let's go,' he said. 'Back the way we came. I have learned all that I need to know.' They returned without incident, taking three hours to cover a distance of a little under two miles, but their caution was justified, for as Lucius Eggius had suspected the camp was ringed at night by patrols of tribesmen. Manissa was taking no chances that the mission might try to withdraw and make its escape in the hours between sunset and dawn.

Curtius Rufus slept late and when he awoke Criton was by his bed, sitting patiently on a stool, writing his journal. He said anxiously, 'I was told by Lucius you wanted to see me. Well, did I waste time and government money on those wretched carpets?'

The envoy smiled cheerfully. 'No, you did not.' He got up then, splashed water over his face, and called for his body slave. When he had eaten a plate of dates and was pouring his second cup of wine, he said curiously, 'If he is blind, who called you from the doorway of his house? Don't tell me he knew your footsteps in the street.'

Criton said, 'I wondered at first. It was the swordsmith. He came out to the camp one day.' He put down his pen. 'Tell me, Curtius?'

'I'll tell you, but speak of it to no one else. There was a big tribal gathering of both the Mazices and the Baquates.' He paused. He said casually, 'There were also some others – Gaetules, I think, to judge by Lucius Eggius' description.'

'Oh!'

'Yes. That is what I felt. In five days' time Manissa is going to hold a great feast in the town square for the leaders and chief followers of the tribes. There will be music and dancing, and the envoy and officers of the mission will be invited to attend.' He put down his cup and looked at Criton. 'At this feast he will give them the sign they have been waiting for. We are to be killed as we leave the town. They will ambush us by the town wall. At dawn they will attack the camp and kill everyone in it. He will then lead them eastwards, razing the countryside as he goes.'

'Does Juba know this?'

Curtius Rufus said, 'I don't know. In this matter your judgment is as good as mine.'

Criton said, his face ashen, 'What do we do?'

The two men looked at each other for a long time and then Curtius Rufus moved and put his arm round the Macedonian's shoulder. He said gently, 'We were in a difficulty before. Do you remember that night in Rome? Somehow we got out of it. We must do so again.'

'Will you accept this invitation?'

'I must. How can I refuse?' He released Criton and stood back. 'I learned one other thing also, on that hillside. A tribesman asked: "What of the Romi girl?" and the Baquates' leader replied, "She is promised to the gods." That means she is either in the city or close by. But we had already guessed that.'

Criton said bitterly, 'I wish I had never let you persuade me into coming with you. This is a horrible place. Oh, Curtius, I feel so afraid.'

Curtius Rufus said grimly, 'I, too, am afraid. You know, Criton, I have one advantage over Manissa. I know that he does not want war.'

Criton's interest overcame his fear. He said eagerly, 'That is worth a great deal. The only purpose of negotiating is to reach agreement, and that means that both parties must make concessions. There was a speech made by King Archidamus at a conference held between Sparta and her allies that I seem to remember—' He broke off.

'What happened?'

Criton said gloomily, 'It ended in war with Athens.'

'This is not going to end in war.' Curtius Rufus paced up and down. 'We want Manissa as a friend and ally, not an enemy. I want to be certain that we walk into that town as honored guests, and that we leave the same way.'

Criton said sharply, 'Then we must make our effort at conciliation before the feast. We must give him the chance to reconsider before it is too late, and he must be able to do so with honor and dignity.'

'And how do we do that?'

'I will try to organize a meeting for you with the suffetes.' Criton rubbed his hands. 'I have an idea, but the suffetes will be the key to make it turn.'

'And if they will not be a key?'

'Then she will have won,' said Criton unsteadily, and his glance rested on the silver bracelet that the envoy wore upon his arm.

The chief suffete said, 'You are welcome.' His voice was hesitant, and Curtius Rufus knew that he was as uneasy and afraid as the rest of those who sat in the council chamber with him. He had heard their voices raised in discussion while he waited in an anteroom, and the arguments and recriminations of complaisant men who find themselves at last muddled and unprepared for a crisis that anyone with clear sight might have foreseen years before rang still inside his head. He saw them looking at him in a curious fashion and Criton, who was sensitive in such matters, said in a whisper, 'In their eyes we are already dead.'

The chief suffete gestured them to their seats. 'You have had difficulties, I know,' he said uncomfortably. 'These both the Lord Manissa and I regret.'

A counselor with a sharp face said ambiguously, 'They will be over soon. That we can promise you.'

There came a sudden silence, broken only by a nervous cough. Curtius Rufus looked round the table, smiling at each man in turn.

He said, 'Difficulties can always be overcome by men of goodwill.' He paused. 'I did not come to discuss my small concerns,' he said carefully. 'I came to discuss your larger ones and to offer any assistance that may – that may lie within my power.'

They stared at him, puzzled.

He said, 'Those of you who are old enough to remember will recall a time when this kingdom was divided. Both its kings at different times and for different reasons fought against Rome. Both were defeated honorably in battle. Each king, however,

273

made the same mistake. He chose the wrong side to support.' He paused, hoping that they would take the point. 'Since then Rome has become the mistress of Africa from Tingis in the west to the great deserts of Arabia in the east.'

One of the counselors said impatiently, 'Rome does not rule here.'

Another said, 'She rules only the fertile plains of the coast, not the interior.'

Curtius Rufus said, 'That I know. Nor does she wish to rule here.'

A middle-aged man, all lined face and gray hair, said 'No one can rule the Atlas, though many tried. Few even have crossed it.' His voice sounded a curious mixture of complacency and regret.

Curtius Rufus said, 'If you cross the Middle Atlas and travel south you will come to a desert of black sand where the Gaetules live; they trade down to the black river, making a journey through a land that burns with desolation by day and freezes with bitterness by night.'

There was a murmur of astonishment.

The chief suffete said, 'How do you know this? The Atlas is the abode of the gods, who veil the summits in snow throughout the year as a warning, lest men who climb should go too far and disturb their sleep.'

A voice cried contemptuously, 'Any man who knows the Veiled Ones could have told you.'

Curtius Rufus smiled. 'One man did – a Romi officer in my camp who crossed those mountains.' He glanced at Criton and then said gently, 'Where he goes others may follow.'

He looked at their faces. He said, 'Rome seeks friendship with Mauretania. The influence of a friend is better than the compulsion of a conqueror.'

'What – what assistance could you offer us?' asked a merchant curiously.

'A safe and secure trade with Hispania, for the many things

from that land which you covet. But more than that, we can help your land to become rich and fertile. If the land is properly irrigated – and this can be done – you will have better pasture for your animals, and may breed larger flocks. If a fertile soil, rich in water, is tilled you may grow crops where the land before was barren. Great farms may be developed and these will require goods from the cities. Thus you will increase your trade and your wealth.'

'And let the hillmen take all in taxes on our caravans?' said another counselor bitterly.

'At first, perhaps – as they do now – but if your city grows wealthy, it will also grow more influential. Influence and strength go hand in hand. You will have the funds to build better walls, have your city defended and your roads safeguarded. The hillmen, too, will benefit. Their herds and flocks will increase, and with wealth they may buy what poverty compels them to take now without payment.' Curtius Rufus paused. There was silence. No one moved, and he could not tell what effect his words were having.

The chief suffete said at length, 'Why do you say all this to us?'

'What is wrong with things as they are? What need for change?' muttered an elderly man with plump, soft hands.

'Because your city is held to ransom by the tribes. I saw the arrival of the caravan they attacked. Because I do not wish to see this city destroyed.'

'Why should they destroy it?'

'Why indeed, when a rich city may be of benefit to all? But you can answer that better than I.'

'Let us have plain speaking,' said an anxious voice.

Curtius Rufus said patiently, 'Very well. My government will be much concerned if there is unrest inside Mauretania, or even talk of war. This your king knows. Some of you may think him too foreign in his ways, but he has our friendship and our support, and he is a man of peace. His kingdom is not rich. This troubles him since he has your welfare at heart.' He glanced again at Criton, who nodded with his eyes. He had all their attention now.

The chief suffete said politely, 'The Lord Manissa rules, and there is no talk of war.'

'Then I have been misinformed. I am happy to hear it, for King Juba rules this land. Two heads cannot wear the same diadem at the same time; he does not intend to share it.'

'The governor——' began the chief suffete, anxiously, but Curtius Rufus cut him short. He said, 'He is loyal to his cousin, I know, and has many difficulties. In his peaceful endeavors the Lord Manissa has our support, as he has yours also. It is for this reason that we are prepared to offer him citizenship of Rome, an appointment in our army, and authority to raise an auxiliary, a regiment to serve with the legions. Thus do we honor those who have proved their loyalty and their friendship.'

A loud gasp ran round the room.

Curtius Rufus stood up. 'You have been patient with me, and I thank you. Remember this: you have everything to gain by peace, nothing by war.'

The chief suffete said in a low voice as he saw his guest to the door, 'All depends upon the Lord Manissa.'

'Does it?' Curtius Rufus smiled. 'Whom many fear must fear the many. That is a saying of my country. It is worth thinking on.'

Outside on the steps Curtius Rufus wiped the sweat from his forehead. 'I am exhausted,' he muttered.

Criton said in a low voice, 'You did not forget what I told you?'

'No. I remembered all your points. But has it occurred to you that we may have spoken too late? If he tries to hold back the tribes now he may not succeed. They will accuse him of breaking faith, of accepting bribes from the Romi. They may still turn on him and us, thinking they can do without him. Have you thought of that?'

Criton said, 'It is a question of who has the most influence.'

'You may be right. Well, it is up to them now. We cannot do more than wait, and pray.' He walked down the steps and Criton followed him. There was nothing more to say.

At midday Curtius Rufus sent for Felicia.

'I thought we'd been forgotten,' she said tartly, but her eyes were watchful. She was brown-faced and had lost weight. 'Well, I can guess what you want.'

Curtius Rufus said lightly, 'And what do I want?'

'You want me to tell you that the bird has been suitably fattened and is ready to be eaten.' She paused. 'Well, I can't. It was a bad journey. This is an uncomfortable place for women, and—' She sat down without being asked. 'That's better, the heat is terrible. You should have given her to Juba. She was looking her best then.'

He said coolly, 'I am giving her to Manissa. Has she practiced her dancing as I ordered?'

'Oh, yes, but she hasn't much heart for it. That secretary of yours is doing his best to cheer her up now. But what she needs is a man.' Felicia looked at him with calculating eyes. 'A love affair would have helped her keep her looks, of course. Didn't think of that, did you?' She paused and then said ironically, 'Why Manissa? To save him the trouble of taking her when we all get murdered?'

'How much do you know?'

'I can guess. Everyone talks. You can smell it in the air. Even the soldiers are making bets as to when we shall be attacked. The centurions try to pretend that nothing will happen, and you believe them till you look at their eyes.'

'You aren't frightened?'

'They don't usually kill women. What's all this about a Roman girl who was kidnapped? Why wasn't I—?'

'You talk too much. Tell Urracca she will dance at a feast three days from now.' He stood up and narrowed his eyes. 'Send her to me this evening at sundown.'

She smiled slyly. 'You've wasted your time, haven't you, my dear? Girls like that don't grow on trees. I should know.'

He drew in his breath sharply and his face changed. She knew then that she had gone too far. She flinched in her chair and waited for him to hit her.

He said, 'That heat must have addled what is left of your mind as well as your manners. Do you think I don't know?'

It was customary for the senior officers to dine late, usually toward the middle of the eleventh hour. It was an occasion of informality upon which Lucius Eggius set considerable value, for then they would recount the happenings of the day, and discuss any problems that might be a cause for concern. At dinner they normally drank sparingly for they were too tired to feel in the mood for celebration. Their world had shrunk to a level requiring bare existence: one in which work and sleep were the two activities that absorbed all their attention. But the strain was always there, and Criton's news of the impending feast had its effect. They ate in silence, scarcely saying a word, and it was not until the last dishes had been cleared that Marcus Pedius voiced their thoughts with terrifying clarity. 'I do not know what the rest of you intend,' he said jovially, 'But I am going to get drunk. We have more than enough wine in store. It would seem a pity to see it wasted on others.'

Lucius Eggius said calmly, 'For once the legions and the Praetorians are in agreement. We will all join you.' He shouted to a slave and it was then that he realized who was missing from the table. He turned to Criton inquiringly and the secretary shifted uncomfortably in his place. 'Curtius Rufus is dining alone. He has work to do,' Criton murmured.

The centurion stared, a faint smile on his face. 'Just so,' he said.

She came after dark, escorted by Felicia and two slaves whom he had sent to fetch her. She wore a traveling cloak, wrapped close about her, the cowl pulled over her hair, but he saw the twin flashes of fire as the stones danced beneath her ears, and knew that she had dressed in her finery for the occasion.

He said, 'We will dine first and talk afterwards. Would you like to remove your cloak? There is no one who will come in.'

She glanced at the slaves who were preparing to serve the meal. 'I think not, my Lord,' she said gravely. She smiled, watching his face carefully.

'You will find it very warm in here.'

She smiled again and pushed back the hood and then smoothed her hair. She was still very pale. 'No,' she said quietly. 'I shall not be too hot.'

He grinned in understanding.

He talked to her of Rome, and the dignity of an envoy, which he assumed each day with such difficulty, slipped from him as he told her about the Circus and the pressures that were exerted upon the charioteers to pull a race or cause an accident to a rival. He had a fund of scandalous stories about the greed of the landlords, who owned the great slum blocks in the poorer quarters, and of how the price of food could be artificially increased to the seller's advantage by a well-timed rumor about a disaster to the grain fleet from Alexandria. 'Never believe a merchant who says it is not in his interest to see an increase in shop prices. The only purpose of trade is to make the greatest profit for the least possible outlay. You don't do that by being generous or soft-headed. I know. I've sold horses and cargoes.' It was the voice of the freedman's son who had no need to pretend, and who saw life so much more clearly than those who ruled him. His eyes were bright and his voice carefree as he spoke of the successes and failures of his ramshackle existence, without

279

pride or pomposity. She thought that if she could keep him in that mood she might achieve the purpose she had in mind.

He told her of how he had tried to set up as an astrologer in Athens, until his venture failed as the result of a public disputation with a philosopher, who bested him and so ruined his business. 'Then I became assistant to an architect in Alexandria. We obtained the support of a speculator and built a tenement block. We took our patron and the officials of the council out to see the new building. They were impressed; they promised immediate payment of our fees and a contract. But then the gods took a hand.' He smiled. 'You will not believe it, but the building actually started to collapse as we walked back down the street. The architect blamed me for calculating my figures wrongly. I blamed the workmen, who were slovenly and had no pride in their job.' He shrugged. 'No matter; we both had to leave in a hurry. They ordered our arrest and I had to hide on a fishing boat that stank worse than a tanner's shop. Still, we had free living at our patron's expense while the building went up. That was something.'

She laughed at his telling of the tale, and the strained look left her eyes. He watched her face improve in color and smiled at the noise of singing coming from across the camp. She toyed with her cup and would have protested when he moved to refill it. 'I do not need it,' she said calmly. She looked him full in the eyes. 'Not unless you think I do, my Lord.'

He shook his head. 'A little madness is good for us all,' he said. 'Let us drink to Dionysius and do as the god commands.' His voice was kind but she could guess at what he did not say.

She bit her lip and stared at the table. 'So I go to Manissa,' she said tonelessly. 'I saw him when he came out to watch, the day you performed tricks on the horse. He is a fine-looking man. But—' She shivered. 'I have heard terrible things about him.'

He did not speak. She looked up but he avoided her eyes.

She said, 'I did not know we were coming to the interior. I

thought it was – Juba.' She paused and said, with an expression-less face, 'I liked Iol Caesarea. The town is poor, but one day it will be a fine place. And I liked standing on the mole. The sea was beautiful.' She twisted her hands in her lap and fell silent, waiting for him to speak. Still he said nothing. 'I have to go. I must do as my Lord tells me.'

He said then, 'You will dance for Manissa at the feast he is giving to entertain us. I do not want a dance of decorous modesty or stately pride. I want a dance of your own people, such as they dance near Gades. You understand me?' His voice had changed; it was the envoy speaking.

Under the chill of his tone she recovered her poise. She said, 'I have practiced hard. I will do my best.'

'Good. If he is pleased, and if he asks, I will give you to him. You will make a fitting present from one ruler in Rome to the Lord of the Atlas. He is a man of talent and ambition, the son of a king and the most powerful man in Mauretania after his cousin. You will do very well for yourself.'

She murmured with downcast eyes, 'I am only a slave.'

He grinned savagely. 'Oh, yes. That I know. But I know this also. You are not a girl that any man can forget easily. You will rule Manissa – in your own way and to your own advantage. And remember this: Mauretania is a client kingdom. Whatever may happen, Rome does not forget the loyalty of those who keep faith.'

She rose gracefully to her feet and undid the cloak. Beneath it she wore a gown he had not seen before and, with it, a selection of the jewels he had chosen from the shop in the Sacred Way.

She said, 'I had the dress made while in Iol Caesarea. As you can see I was not over-warm in the cloak.'

He said, 'Urracca.'

She smiled. 'It is customary to give a slave who has pleased you a gift when she leaves your service.'

'What would you like?'

281

'Something of yours that I may remember you by.' She recalled the urgency of Criton's words and knew that she must not fail him. She smiled. 'May I have your bracelet?'

Astonished, he said, 'That was given me by—'

'I know,' she said gently. 'But it is now yours and, for that reason, on my wrist can cause no harm.'

He stared at her, hesitating and puzzled.

'Please.'

'Very well, if you can find the clasp.'

'Let me try. There, it is not difficult if you know where to look.'

He rubbed his wrist. 'I am a little drunk. I'm not sure I understand you properly.'

She said, 'You must ask Criton, your secretary.'

He did not speak and she guessed that he was thinking of the bracelet upon her wrist. She shrugged her shoulders. She knew then that she had won for Criton, but in doing so she had lost for herself. She moved to pick up her cloak. 'Do you wish me to go?'

He nodded.

She said mockingly, 'I think you are wise, my Lord. For if I go you can only wonder at what you have lost, while if I stay you will remember.' She laughed softly.

He said coolly, 'Then you had better stay, for I have a great curiosity but a poor memory.'

She flushed and turned to the tent door. If Criton had been there at that moment she would have struck him.

'Wait.' He rose swiftly and caught at her wrist. 'Any man would desire you,' he said thickly, and his face had a look she knew well. 'Don't imagine, however, that I'll change my decision in the morning. You still go to Manissa. I will not lie to you about that.'

She said angrily, 'Then let me go. To you it can matter little what I do or think.'

'It matters a great deal,' he said, and his fingers hurt her wrist. 'You still belong to me, and at the moment—' He paused and said brutally, 'Your mind is of less service to the state than is your body. The last is sadly out of practice.'

Her face was shaded from the light and he did not see the expression in her eyes. If he had he would not have cared, for that was something he had always been able to change.

The two centurions, happily drunk, but not too drunk to walk, approached the envoy's tent on their way to their own, and saw the lights go out as the oil lamps were snuffed in turn.

Marcus Pedius said boisterously, 'I hope he made his mind up at last. I had a bet on it.'

Lucius Eggius chuckled. 'Collect your winnings tomorrow. The slave girl sleeps where it is warm.'

CHAPTER XVI

The invitation came, courteously worded, and was accepted, but no word arrived from the chief suffete and no answer was received to the message he had sent Manissa relating to the honors offered. He said to Criton, 'I must have failed. I suppose it was expecting too much.'

Criton said snappishly, 'Only a barbarian would fail to understand what you said. These people—' He broke off, almost crying with rage, frustration, and fear.

The officers' slaves were set to preparing their masters' best clothes, and though arms could not be worn Lucius Eggius insisted that each should carry a concealed knife. 'Our envoy would not approve,' he said to them at a meeting in his tent. 'But I do not intend to die like a sacrificial ox, not for any man's sake.' The carpenters and painters commenced furbishing the litter in which Urracca would travel, and it was decided that the two female slaves and Felicia would accompany her. 'It is more fitting,' said Criton. 'It will be best for them if they are not in the camp,' said Curtius Rufus, and Marcus Pedius agreed with him. The under-officer to Vatinus had asked for orders, desperately seeking reassurance, but all Lucius Eggius would say was of little help. 'When we leave, you are in sole command. You must do your best and no one will reproach you.' The man nodded, trying to appear calm. 'No one will take us alive,' he muttered hoarsely. 'Anything but that.'

It was late in the afternoon when the chief suffete rode to the camp with an escort of young men, dressed in their gayest clothing. The chief suffete bowed his head. 'The Lord Manissa bids me guide you to his feast. It will be enhanced by your presence.' The expression on his face was calm. Curtius Rufus could not ask and dared not guess at what the man had said to the governor.

The litter bearers stood waiting by the poles, the four officers were in a tight group behind the second litter, and Curtius Rufus, Criton, and Crescens stood a little to one side. The surveyor had the look of a man waiting to have a tooth drawn.

'You do not ride?' asked the suffete, his eyes flickering from the drawn curtains back to the envoy's face.

'No,' said Curtius Rufus. 'The exercise will do us good. We shall have enough of riding when we make our return to the coast.'

The chief suffete smiled, and Curtius Rufus glanced at his staff. He said in Latin, 'Many who dine at feasts as guests of honor have their appetites ruined because they worry unduly lest their speech be a failure. Yet usually all is well, and they find afterwards that they have worried over no cause at all.'

Marcus Pedius licked his lips, a muscle beat strongly in Lucius Eggius's cheek, and Vatinus held his hands behind his back to conceal their trembling. Criton said in Greek, 'I feel sick,' while Attius yawned uncontrollably.

The envoy smiled at the chief suffete. 'Let us delay pleasure no longer,' he said; and they moved out of the camp and toward the town.

The great market square had been cleared, fires lighted, carpets laid, tents set up, and a great pavilion erected on the southeast side. The sides of the square were packed with spectators, and in the pavilion, amid the flare of torches, the soft glow of cushions, and bronze and silver tables, Manissa awaited them, wearing a wonderful gold-embroidered gown with long sleeves and a high neck. Curtius Rufus saw that the pavilion was crowded; on one side there were the chief dignitaries of the town, the suffetes and the merchants, and on the other, the leaders of the fighting tribes from the Atlas and the desert, the Mazices, the Baquates, and the veiled men in black. These watched the arrival of the envoy and his staff with closed faces. As the litter bearers were directed to a small tent that stood between a disused well and two palm trees, Manissa rose to his feet. 'I bid you welcome,' he said in Latin. 'It is a good sign when the guest comes on foot. Be seated and take your pleasure.'

'I am honored,' said Curtius Rufus. 'I have messages to convey and a request to make.'

'Of course, but we will discuss serious matters later, when we have eaten and are in a good humor. I understand that you wish to entertain me. Is this customary? To entertain the host?'

'I do not know, my Lord. We bring you the gift of an entertainment and we pray that it may give you pleasure. We owe all to your kindness.'

Manissa smiled, and then a frown showed for a moment on his face. He seemed disconcerted. 'Come,' he said. 'I have other guests whom I wish you to meet.'

While they ate strange dishes, and Curtius Rufus made polite conversation, they were entertained by a man who, accompanied by a string instrument, half spoke and half sang. His voice, Criton thought, sounded like a cat in the night, but when Manissa explained that the poet was singing of the deeds of his people, the Macedonian grew interested and asked if the ballad was written down. 'No, indeed,' said the governor, 'for he can neither read nor write. These things are learned in the head and passed from father to son. It is a gift.' He was followed by a group of tribesmen who, forming a circle and standing shoulder to shoulder, stamped their feet and clapped hands in time to a man who led them, chanting monotonously as he did so. At this point Criton closed his eyes, and when asked if he felt unwell replied that he was momentarily overcome by the beauty of the performance.

As the meal came to a close, Manissa said, 'My people do not drink wine as do those of your race, though some of us have developed a taste for it. I have ordered some in your honor, however, and I hope it is to your liking.'

Criton asked, 'Do your women dance in public?' It was a problem that had been worrying him all day.

'Yes, for they enjoy it, and they have more grace than all but a minority of men.'

It was quite dark now and the moon was up. The square was filled with white-robed figures, standing with their backs to the fires, who kept up a rhythmic beat with their hands while the women danced in their heavy finery and their best jewelry. Then they began to chant and the sound swelled into a great throbbing noise as it was taken up by the packed crowds round the square.

Criton looked at the moon, then at the others. They were a little drunk by now, keyed up by the strangeness of the occasion. The wine had dulled the edge of fear, though not entirely, for he saw first Marcus Pedius and then Lucius Eggius glance at the moon as they, too, wondered how long it might be before the feast ended. Criton gazed at the blaze of color about him and thought of the walk through the dark streets that was still to come. He thought, too, of the silent horsemen outside the walls, waiting with terrible patience for the moment when the gates opened, and sword and dagger and lance would end it all in a thunder of hooves and a flash of blood. He turned to Curtius Rufus and said in a whisper, 'Don't wait too long. Some of the crowd begin to move already.'

The dance had come to an end.

Criton said in Latin, 'The men of my race come from the hills. Give them a sword and they will drink blood, a woman and they will drink pleasure. On their feast days they will drink till dawn. No wineskin brought to the feast may be left unopened. It is their custom.' He was a little drunk and he boasted to conceal his fear.

Manissa said, 'Of that I have heard. Did not a great warrior,

Iskander, come from your land, he who claimed to have conquered the world?'

Criton nodded, and Curtius Rufus, who saw that his friend had grown wide-eyed under Manissa's glance, said easily, 'That is correct, my Lord, but he made a greater conquest still.' He paused. 'He learned to conquer himself.'

Manissa said softly, 'So,' and the two men stared at each other without smiling for the length of a dozen heartbeats.

Manissa said, 'You talk in riddles that I do not read. Why should a warrior wish to conquer himself?'

The envoy said, 'A great one must do so or he is not great. Iskander, whom we call Alexander, was not one to allow himself to be moved by wrong actions, by the ambitions, greed, and folly of small minds. He never surrendered to the threats of such men. He had a great vision and he talked with the gods.'

Manissa touched his beard. 'Do you offer advice to your host?'

'No, my Lord. I offer assistance.'

The governor blinked.

'My Lord, it will soon be time to take our leave. I ask that I may express my thanks, so that all may hear, in the few words of Berber that I have learned.'

Manissa smiled, puzzlement showed in his eyes, and then was gone. Curtius Rufus glanced at his staff. They had paused in their conversation and were looking at him with expressions of appeal, fear, hope, and resignation, each according to his temperament.

Manissa nodded. 'They will appreciate your courtesy.' His voice was noncommittal.

Curtius Rufus stood up. He said in a loud voice, 'As the envoy of Rome to the court of King Juba, I am honored to be here as the friend of the King's cousin, the Lord Manissa, governor of the west and Lord of the Atlas mountains.' He spoke in fluent Berber and an astonished silence fell upon the pavilion and upon those in the square beyond. He raised his hands in the air and it was then that Manissa realized that he no longer wore the Queen's bracelet.

Curtius Rufus paused. He said, 'As further proof of friendship I am empowered by the Senate of Rome to offer Roman citizenship to the Lord Manissa, and this we give lightly to no man who is not born in that condition; second, I offer to the Lord Manissa the right to raise an auxiliary of cavalry which shall serve with the Roman legions that all men may know the worth of your warriors.'

One of the Veiled Men cried in a harsh voice, 'You do great honor to the Lord of the Atlas. Give us a sign that we may believe in the power and the influence of Rome.'

Curtius Rufus blinked; Lucius Eggius looked up at him, alarm in his eyes; Criton opened and shut his mouth, naked horror upon his face. Manissa smiled, and an absolute stillness fell upon the pavilion.

Curtius Rufus hesitated. He glanced at the sky and saw that the moon was on the wane. Then he spoke, arms uplifted, 'I swear by my gods that when the next caravan arrives it will bring me word that Augustus Caesar, who was believed to be dying, lives again. It will be a sign from the gods who have elevated Rome above all other cities that they offer protection to all its citizens – wherever they may be.' The crowd murmured as he fell silent.

Manissa's smile faded. He rose to his feet. He said, 'Why should you be believed?' and his voice sounded like thunder on a hot night.

Curtius Rufus said, between his teeth, 'Do you wait until the wolf gets his teeth into the moon before you will believe?'

Manissa said impassively, 'You cannot alter the future by words alone. What will come, will come.' He sat down and crooked a finger. A man on the far side of the pavilion rose to his feet, nodded, and went out into the night. It was the captain of his bodyguard. Manissa smiled. 'Let us see what Rome has to offer now.'

Curtius Rufus turned to Criton and said in a whisper, 'Tell your slave to warn the girl. It is time. We are in her hands now.'

A drum throbbed softly, the curtains of the tent between the palm trees opened, and Urracca appeared. She came forward gracefully and conversation died as she walked between the fires, keeping pace with the slow hand-beats of the drum. She knelt in the center of the performers' platform, her red and silver dancing skirt spread about her, hands crossed upon her breast. For a brief moment she looked at Manissa, and her eyes showed an interest that was either real or feigned. Two men with drums sat cross-legged before her, and all the time that she performed they did not take their eyes from her face. The girl's eyes, under darkened eyebrows, were now closed. The drums beat softly. She stretched out her arms and they trembled, as the fronds of a palm tree tremble in the dawn wind. So, very softly, she began her dance with subtle motions of her hands, her breast, and her hips. As the pace increased, the veil covering her upper body slipped from her head, and her jewelry chinked softly with every move and gesture of her body.

Curtius Rufus leaned back a little and watched those who sat beside him. He might have stabbed Manissa in the back at that moment, and they would not have noticed. She had all their attention.

The monotonous beat increased in intensity and the girl, as though in a self-induced trance, abandoned herself to its increasing pace until she seemed to be in a state of ecstasy.

The moon glowed upon the pavilion, sparks of flame were flung up into the darkness by the blazing fires, and the beat of the drums vibrated the very walls of the tent.

The drums suddenly ceased and there came an immense silence. The girl raised her hands above her head, the hands

290

moved, and Curtius Rufus heard the dry clack-clack of a castanet. She opened her eyes and smiled briefly, looking directly at Manissa. Then she rose to her feet and let the veil slip from her shoulders to the ground. The drums sounded again, she smiled brilliantly, tossed back her hair, and swayed joyfully into a dance around the edges of the platform that seemed an expression of pure pleasure. Her ankle bracelets hissed rhythmically beneath the snap of castanets, and Curtius Rufus heard Manissa's intake of breath. A murmur came from the others. Except for her swirling skirt, her dark hair flowing down her back, and her jewelry, she was naked above the hips.

Then the tempo of the dance changed and it seemed to Curtius Rufus, as he watched the lazy sway of her body, that she danced for Manissa alone. Now, as she moved before him, the joyousness was gone and in its place a half-awake quality seemed to veil her being. She was remote, mysterious and infinitely alluring. In the seductiveness of her smile and the provocative gesture of her hands she embodied all human desire. Wilful, destructive, and erotic, she belonged, like bronze, to the old order, and in her was incarnate all that men imagined only in their dreams.

The dance closed with a gesture of surrender that made the audience gasp. Curtius Rufus stepped forward and raised Urracca to her feet. Her body was covered with sweat, her face drained and exhausted, her eyes sleepy, and her feet coated in dust. He handed her to a slave and then turned to Manissa, who stood up while the pavilion and the square roared their applause. The two men looked at each other and Manissa's face was like carved stone. Curtius Rufus felt the sweat break out on his face.

Manissa said in a hoarse voice, 'I saw the bracelet on her wrist. You tell me she is a princess in her own land.'

Curtius Rufus said, 'She has been a slave in mine.' There was a meaning in his voice that Manissa understood.

The governor said, 'That is not important. What is her price?'

Curtius Rufus said, 'She is a gift, if you are pleased to accept her.'

'I am.' Manissa paused. Then he said, and his voice was still harsh, 'You are a clever man and you have put me in your debt.'

Curtius Rufus's hands began to shake. He said, 'I am also a sick man. The medicine for asking is giving.'

'So be it.'

The gates of the camp swung open and Lucius Eggius said incredulously, 'I never thought to stand here again.'

Curtius Rufus smiled through his exhaustion. 'Neither did I.' He walked on ahead without speaking, and Criton followed him, while the others, too tired to do more than nod, went to their tents.

He stood on the wall, looking out across the darkness of the plain, his hood over his head, and Criton watched him timidly. Presently the secretary said, in a tone of awe, 'He changed his mind. Why did he let us go? Did we dream our fears?'

'He kept it open till the last, though his allies may not have known that. I saw the marks in the sand outside the gates where his horsemen waited. We owe our lives to you.'

'It was your doing, Curtius. It was the way you spoke to the chief suffete, and again tonight, that made all the difference; not what was said.'

'We won't argue about it now. At least I managed to remember your lesson on Macedonian history.'

Criton looked at him. 'Do you mind about Urracca?'

There was a long silence, and then Curtius Rufus said in a whisper, 'No, I do not mind. I do not mind about anything anymore.'

'You should be pleased that we have succeeded.'

'Yes, I am pleased.'

He stood there, leaning against the wall, and Criton stayed

with him. Presently the stars faded, the sky turned pale and then pink; the dawn wind blew dust along the path behind their backs, and the sun rose for the commencement of another day.

CHAPTER XVII

At the fifth hour they met Manissa on the plain, halfway between the camp and the town. He was on horseback, accompanied by an escort and slaves bearing a litter. Curtius Rufus watched their coming, then turned to the litter, resting on the ground, and upon which Urracca reclined. He parted the curtains and said, 'If you lose the manumission, do not forget there will be a copy lodged in the archives in Rome. I shall leave a sum of money at Tingis, upon which you may draw if ever you need it.'

She said, 'You have been very kind.' She paused and then said ironically, 'I am grateful for my freedom. I do not think I shall lack protection, however.'

They looked into each other's eyes, and neither smiled.

He nodded. 'I will pray to the gods for your safety,' he said formally, and stepped back.

Manissa reined in his horse and dismounted. He said, 'I bring you, as promised, the Romi girl who was so barbarously kidnapped from her home in Hispania.' He lowered his voice. He said quietly, 'She is not well, and this I regret.'

The envoy said formally, 'I thank you for your assistance. My government will be most appreciative.' He paused and said in an expressionless voice, 'My government will expect the perpetrators of this unhappy outrage to be punished with all severity.'

Manissa said gravely, 'You may rely on my word that it will be done.' He touched the thumb ring on his right hand. 'Nothing will give me greater pleasure than to hand this to the executioner of the man responsible.'

An elderly woman of his household helped a girl out of the litter. Valeria was very young and wore a white day robe such as the Berber women wore, but the cowl over her head concealed her face. She walked forward very slowly, leaning on the elder woman's shoulder. She seemed very frail.

Curtius Rufus said to Lucius Eggius, 'You go to her. You are in uniform, and she belongs to your world more than mine. Tell Felicia to be gentle.' He watched Lucius Eggius approach, saw the girl flinch, and then heard the murmur of the centurion's voice. Manissa stepped back as she passed so that his shadow would not fall on her, and then stiffened as one of the envoy's slaves led the dancing girl to him.

Curtius Rufus said, 'Urracca, this is the Lord Manissa, governor of Volubilis.' The girl knelt and Manissa raised her up.

The Lord of the Atlas said, 'You have nothing to fear. I shall make you my wife. Presently we will talk together.' He nodded and a slave escorted her to the litter.

The two men faced each other. Manissa said, 'I would like you to stay for a while. There is much that you can do for us.'

'I had thought that guests stank after three days.'

Manissa chuckled. 'Guests, yes, but not friends.' He mounted his horse. 'Think it over and let me have your answer.' He wheeled his horse around and said, over his shoulder, 'You have the all-seeing eye. It is a great gift.' His horse wheeled again. 'The caravan from Tingis will be here before sundown. But I knew from the Queen's messenger last night that death had let him go. The bracelet told all. I will fight any man, but only a fool will meddle with the gods.' He turned his horse and rode toward the town.

While Lucius Eggius escorted Valeria to the quarters that had been prepared for her, Curtius Rufus walked thoughtfully back to his day tent. To Criton, he said, 'We have work to do. I must dictate letters, letting them know in Rome that she is safe. Tell Marcus Pedius that today is a rest day. We will discuss our future

... we dine, Everything depends on how fit the girl is to travel.'

But she was not fit. On this, all who had seen her were agreed. The senior medical orderly said she was much too thin, had no appetite, and could be persuaded to eat only with difficulty. Her feet, too, were badly scarred, though the wounds had healed. Lucius Eggius said she did not wish to see anyone, that she talked very little, could not bear to have Felicia out of her sight, and was, he thought, half out of her mind. Felicia said that it was not to be wondered at. She had been a prisoner for nearly nine months, had seen her parents killed before her eyes, could not speak the language of her captors, and must have lived daily in terror of being killed. She was fifteen years old.

'Yes,' said Curtius Rufus impatiently. 'I, too, have some imagination. Can she travel? It is only five days to the coast.'

'Ten, in that condition,' said the centurion in a worried voice. 'She is suffering from the heat amongst other things. Her breathing is bad.'

Curtius Rufus said, 'What do you advise?'

'That she remain here till she is strong enough to travel.'

'Very well. As soon as she can be moved, I want you to escort her direct to Tingis. I will see that a ship is waiting. From there you will take her to Rome, and you are not to let her out of your sight till she has been handed safely in to her uncle's care. The rest of us will follow in due course. The mules can be sold, and the drivers paid off in Tingis. From there, Attius can take the legionary detachment back by sea to Carthage. The rest of us will sail to Iol Caesarea. I must confer with Cornelius Silius and collect any technicians who wish to sail with us to Rome. Meanwhile, we must carry on with the work we started. There will be no difficulties now.'

The caravan arrived two hours before sundown, and a merchant brought to the camp a letter that Criton had difficulty in deciphering. Late that night he came to the envoy's tent and found Curtius Rufus drinking heavily.

Criton said, 'I have the message clear now. Augustus has recovered his health, and all Rome rejoices. We are to hurry if we wish to rejoice also. There is a rumor that he will resign the consulate.'

'That is all?'

'Yes.' Criton gave him a puzzled look. 'You do not seem surprised. It was a wonderful guess that you made.'

'I am the all-seeing eye.'

Criton frowned, perplexed.

'It is a joke, if only to me.'

Criton said, 'It will not be a joke if the girl dies.'

They constructed an awning for Valeria so that she might lie on a daybed, screened from the eyes of the curious, and gain the full advantage of the dawn breeze and the evening wind. There were times during the great heat that followed the summer solstice when they wondered how much she could endure. One of the two slave girls was always with her, and Felicia remained within call. Lucius Eggius sat with her in his off-duty time, sometimes saying nothing, sometimes talking gently of Rome and of the people she knew.

Crescens enlarged the workshop by the governor's palace where the craftsmen spent their days, making improvements and teaching their skills to local workmen. He also set about the rebuilding of a number of wells inside the town, and gave demonstrations to the elders of the neighboring villages on how to improve the irrigation of their plots of cultivated land.

The plain sweltered in the sun, the grass turned brown, and the earth cracked in the heat, for it was an exceptional summer. The troops continued their work of improving the main streets, and began also the rebuilding of the town gates, to demonstrate how the defenses might be strengthened. They worked from the second to the fifth hour, rested in the worst heat of the day, and then worked again from the ninth hour until sundown.

Once he had written a long dispatch to Maecenas, and another to Juba, and answered the letters he received, Curtius Rufus had little to do. He filled a part of his time demonstrating cavalry tactics, with the aid of his troopers, to Manissa's bodyguard; and accompanied the governor when he went to administer justice to the outlying villages. The lawsuits seemed trivial enough – one man complained against a neighbor, whose sheep had broken into a holding and grazed down all his young barley; two travelers complained of assault outside a village where they had stayed the night, one losing a tunic, the other a pig – but Manissa showed surprising patience. 'To administer justice one needs a clear and untroubled mind. You cannot be like your Iskander' – he smiled at Criton as he spoke – 'who cut that knot with a sword. You must unravel it, and for that you need the perseverance of a woman.' He added somberly, 'I am not always patient, as you know.'

The mission celebrated the birth of the Divius Julius with a religious ceremony and a public holiday, and an extra ration of wine was issued for the occasion. By the time the corn had been harvested and was ready for the threshing, Valeria's health had improved sufficiently for her to take short walks, though she flinched at the sight of strange faces, and those on duty about the camp had instructions to keep out of the way.

Lucius Eggius said, one evening, 'She would like to see you. I must warn you that she is afraid to return home, though I think she is well enough to travel now.'

They went into the tent where Valeria lay on a couch. She wore a gown made up from some of the material that Curtius Rufus had bought for Urracca. She had fair hair, tied in a knot at the nape of her neck, had been a pretty girl once, and might be so again in time. Now she was white-faced and looked strained and apprehensive. She kept twisting her fingers, and her eyes were dilated. His arrival was obviously a moment she had been dreading all day.

Lucius Eggius said, 'Lady Valeria, this is our envoy, Curtius Rufus, to whom we all owe so much.'

She said, 'I must – I must thank you for your help.' She smiled timidly. 'It is still a dream.'

Curtius Rufus grinned. He said, 'We all helped, no one more than another.' He sat down on a stool beside her. 'It was your uncle who was responsible for having us sent out. He is very fond of you.'

She said, 'I don't want to go back.'

He glanced at Lucius Eggius, who shrugged his shoulders. He said, 'You have nothing to be afraid of.'

'No, I cannot. Please.'

He looked up at the centurion and nodded to the tent door. Lucius Eggius hesitated. He nodded again and Lucius Eggius went out.

Realizing she was alone with him, she shrank back. 'Please, no.'

He said quietly, 'Tell me about it. You may tell me anything.'

She hesitated; he smiled; and then she poured it out, incoherently, the whole tale of her abduction, the long nightmare of her captivity. Then she cried for the first time since her release. 'So you see, I cannot; I could not bear it.'

He thought briefly of Urracca and frowned. 'Lucius Eggius will go with you, and your uncle will take you to his villa in the Campania. You may stay there as long as you wish.'

'Please!'

He smiled. 'You must.' He paused and said gently, 'The Valerii are noted for their courage. It takes more courage to live than to die. Your uncle needs you. You are the heart of his thoughts.'

She nodded and put a hand to her hair. 'Very well. I am sorry to have been so – so stupid.'

'Lucius.'

She turned her head and smiled shyly at the centurion.

He watched Lucius Eggius and saw the look on his face. It was enough. He nodded briefly and then left the tent.

Before they left, Lucius Eggius said hesitantly, 'May I offer a word of advice? The burden of ideals is always an impediment to success. That is something Marcus Tullius Cicero never understood.'

Curtius Rufus smiled. 'It is not the success I object to, but what such men must do to themselves in order to achieve it. There is a saying in my country: if you give a big stick to a small boy he is bound to hit you. It is always the small boys who want success.'

An hour later the tiny caravan, escorted by Manissa's men, left the camp and disappeared into the darkness, heading north across the open plain towards Tingis and the open sea.

CHAPTER XVIII

The vinage had been gathered when the mission broke camp and left Volubilis in late August. The town shimmered in the heat behind them, but no one looked back. They were all glad to be setting their faces toward home, and the troops sang as they marched. Curtius Rufus rode at the head of the column and spoke seldom during the seven days it took them to reach Tingis. Here they learned that Augustus had indeed resigned the consulate and that Sestius, a one-time quaestor to Marcus Junius Brutus, and an ardent Republican, had been appointed in his place.

At Iol Caesarea Curtius Rufus and Criton stayed two days at the residency with Cornelius Silius, who was anxious to learn the details of their stay in Volubilis.

'Tell the King,' said Curtius Rufus, 'that the Lord Manissa was always helpful and that, but for his aid, we should not have succeeded. He has a powerful ally in his cousin.'

The tribune said solemnly, 'He will be as glad to hear that as he is sorry to have been absent when you returned.'

That evening when they were alone on the roof and Curtius Rufus was looking in the direction of the palace, he said hesitantly, 'The Queen asked me to give you a message. She said, "Tell Curtius Rufus that once nine kings were the allies of my mother. I never had so many."'

'Was that all?'

'No. She said, "Tell him also that I shall not go to Egypt now, nor shall I dream upon the moon. I accept what the gods grant me and what they withhold." You understand all that?'

'Yes, I understand.' Curtius Rufus remained on the roof and thought of Cleopatra Selene. She sat alone in that palace in the midst of a bleak city; the wife of a man who had a desert for a kingdom, and all her fine dreams had blown to dust. She might touch that statue in the dark, with its blind eyes and its cold skin, and cry out, "Mother, why did you fail?" but when daylight came she would face reality. She would face it because she had courage and because she had no other choice. But Iol Caesarea was the one city to which he could not return. That too was a reality that had to be faced. He shivered as a breeze came in off the sea, lifted his hand in a salute of farewell and went below to the room where he had so nearly died.

They stayed three days and then slipped anchor and crossed the sea to Misenum. It was September, the sun blazed in a blue sky, the sea was smooth, and the oars splashed rhythmically as the ship moved steadily forward, twenty-five feet at every pull. Criton, standing on the stern castle, looked joyfully at the misted outline of the great volcano on shore to their right, and said happily, 'Oh, it is good to be back. Even the heat here is civilised.' There was a tedious delay on arrival while the wagons and animals were unloaded from the following ships, and Criton at least was thankful that Vatinus would not travel with them, but would remain to disperse the convoy and all the stores and equipment.

Another three days and the tombs that lined the Appian Way closed about them. They reached the outskirts of Rome, and the wheeled traffic was thick in both directions. Outside the Capena Gate they dismounted. Curtius Rufus shook hands with each man in the detachment and then faced the centurion.

Marcus Pedius said, 'Well, back to ordinary duty. It made a nice change.'

'That is what I thought,' said the envoy.

The two men smiled at each other and then Marcus Pedius saluted and led his men in the direction of the Campus Viminalis.

Curtius Rufus said to Criton, 'We must find somewhere to spend the night.'

'Oh, I had forgotten.'

'It has never been out of my thoughts.' He looked at the sun. 'It is now the fourth hour. Give my slaves your documents. I will go and report. You find somewhere to stay, and meet me by the Temple of the Dioscuri at – at the eighth hour.'

Criton looked suddenly anxious. 'Yes, Curtius.' He twisted his hands and then bit his lip.

Curtius Rufus said coolly, 'Well, you said you were glad to be back. Now be glad. We are on our own again. We have no one to command except ourselves.'

He strode off, winding his way rapidly between the crowds so that his slaves had occasionally to break into a run to catch up with him. At Agrippa's house on the Palatine he received a shock. The house was closed and shuttered. A passing soldier whom he accosted said cheerfully, 'You must be a stranger. He left Rome three days ago. He's been given special powers or something. Anyway he's gone to the east.'

'Gone?'

'That's right. If you want him so bad, you'll have to swim to Lesbos.'

'Thank you.' Curtius Rufus shook his head in bewilderment. He walked back across the hill and went down the steps that led to the back of the Shrine of Juturna. At the Temple of Saturn he saw an officer of the finance department and handed over the leather bag containing Criton's carefully recorded accounts. 'It is correct to the last sestercius. Here is a draft on the balance which I banked at Misenum. I thought it safer.'

The official nodded. 'Very wise of you. Here is a receipt. If I find any discrepancies I will let you know, so that you may explain them. Where will I find you?'

'Gaius Maecenas will know that. I have no residence as yet.'

'No, of course not. I will inform the quaestor that you have handed over the records.' The official frowned. 'Who authorized your mission?'

'Marcus Agrippa. I understand he is out of Rome.'

'He is. Have you a report for him? Good. Then you had best hand it in to the Senatorial Secretariat – to the left of the Curia, there! The Senate will be meeting later this month. You may be required to appear before them; it all depends. Anyway, they will inform you. But don't leave Rome until everything has been cleared up.' He paused again. 'One more thing. I am instructed to inform you that payment of a bounty to your escort is not approved. Since, however, you promised it, and the promise must be kept, the sum, which you may fix yourself, will be deducted from the balance of your salary. I am sorry.'

Curtius Rufus did not smile. He said politely, 'Do you know if Valerius Messalla is in Rome?'

'I doubt it. You had best try his house – the one on the Collis.'

Curtius Rufus turned to his slaves. 'Come on. We haven't finished walking yet. I want the Tabularium first. I have a manumission and a set of citizenship papers to lodge there.' At least no one can quarrel about my freeing Urracca, he thought angrily.

The senior slave said sensibly, 'It is a good walk. Let me get you a litter, sir. You look tired out.'

He was glad to rest. The crowded streets grew less crowded as shops and houses gave way to parks and gardens, with residences set well back from the road. The litter swayed gently and he dozed a little. He felt tired and sick with worry. What if Maecenas was out of Rome as well?

The litter stopped at last and a slave's voice said, 'We are here, sir.'

He knocked on the door and waited. Presently it opened.

'I wish to speak to the house steward.'

He went inside and waited again. The steward appeared, an

elderly man with an olive skin. 'Can I help you, sir? The master is away.'

Curtius Rufus said, 'I am a friend of – of his niece. I met her in – in Africa.'

The steward's eyes widened. Then he smiled. 'You are the envoy, sir. I have heard of you. We received a message from a centurion – I forget his name – that he had arrived with the Lady Valeria at Misenum. My master sent back a message that she was not to come to Rome, but to go to his villa in the Campania. He then closed the house and traveled south.'

'Was he——?'

'Oh, yes, sir. I have never seen him so happy. I understand that the centurion is staying at the villa.'

Curtius Rufus smiled. 'I only wished to know that she had come home safely.' He stood there for a moment, hesitating, but the steward only smiled at him. 'Well, thank you. That was the only reason for my calling.'

He left the house and gave his slaves instructions to take him to Maecenas's house on the Esquiline. That house, at least, was still open, and he reached it at the eighth hour, glad to be in the warm air on the heights above the dirt and noise and smell of Rome. He had forgotten how tiring that city was to be in and how long it took to do business on account of the sprawl of its hills.

He waited in an anteroom just off the atrium, and there came to him the Greek secretary, whom he had met on the night he dined at the house. The secretary smiled his welcome. 'I am sorry he is not here to see you but he will be back at the end of the month.' He saw the disappointed look on Curtius Rufus's face, and said in his soft voice, 'You will have heard of various troubles. My master thought it best to take the Lady Terentia into the country. They have gone to his villa at Tibur. He has left you this letter.'

Curtius Rufus took the letter and read it slowly.

'I regret that I cannot be the first to congratulate you on the success of your mission. I know the gratitude that the family of the Valerii feel towards you. I must inform you, however, that the honors and grant of citizenship, given by you to Manissa, under the general authority contained in an earlier letter, do not meet with approval and remain to be ratified by the Senate. You will be expected to account for your actions to that distinguished body. Give your dispatch to my secretary to be forwarded. I shall read it with interest. You will do well to remember that this is your official account of all that has occurred during your time as our envoy. No other will serve you so well. The question of future employment is best left to discussion when the Senate has met and I have returned to the city. Meanwhile, I am pleased to inform you that, through the kindness of the Lady Terentia, I have been persuaded to manumit one of my female slaves. This I have done in appreciation of your services. Something performed is always better than something merely promised.'

Curtius Rufus tucked the letter in his tunic and handed his dispatch to the secretary. 'Do you know where she has gone?'

'No, sir. The steward might know. But he is not here.'

'Did she give an oath to undertake household service for her patron?'

'Yes, sir. The Lady Terentia insisted. But it was agreed she should be free of the obligation when she married. As you know, sir, that is customary.'

'I know.'

He left the house, his head aching intolerably. She had no money except the little she had saved. It would not be enough to buy a share in a business, however small; and there was the burden of double employment, which so many freedmen found difficult. But then it was always harder for a woman unless she married or became a common-law wife. She would have done better to remain permanently with the household, as so many others had done – the secretary included.

Outside the Tullianum he paid off his litter bearers and walked through the thinning crowds in the Forum to where Criton was sitting on the steps of the Dioscuri, waiting for him.

Criton said anxiously, 'Dear boy, I have been waiting and waiting.' He peered at his friend's grinning face, bright with despair. 'Isn't everything all right? I have booked rooms in a small house on the Quirinal. The owner is a salt merchant who wishes to move. It is small but quiet, and has a tiny courtyard with a fountain. He – he might sell it to us. I mentioned your name.'

'That is kind of you. For how long could we afford it? We don't receive what is left of our salaries until the end of the month.'

Criton said simply, 'Tell me.'

Curtius Rufus handed him the letter and he read it aloud. Then he said quietly, 'It looks hopeful.'

'Do you think so? I lost one job because I exceeded my authority. Now, it seems I may lose the chance of another, for the same reason. Even if the Senate approves my report it only requires one false action by the governor of Volubilis to ruin me. And yet what else could I do? I am in Manissa's hands still.'

Criton said cheerfully, 'Don't worry about it. Send your slaves to the house. I'll give them money to buy food, and they can wait for us there.'

'I'm hungry.'

'So am I. Let's go to the baths and then dine in style.'

Curtius Rufus said grimly, 'Why not? We have earned a holiday. Let us spend the money I won off Vatinus and try to enjoy it.'

They walked idly past the shoemakers in the Argiletum, Criton pausing every now and then to read the advertisements pasted to the doorposts of the bookshops, and sniffing happily at the mingled smells of fresh leather and glue.

It was late when they left the baths, the rooms were already filling up with workers who had come off duty, and there was a cool breeze blowing. Curtius Rufus smiled. His head felt better.

Criton said, 'It will be sundown in a couple of hours. Where shall we eat?'

Curtius Rufus said suddenly, 'I know. Let's go to the Winged Mercury. The food at least is good.'

The eating house was half full, and at one long table a jovial group of racing enthusiasts were rowdily entertaining their favorite charioteer, a thin man with a humorous face and light blue eyes. Criton raised an eyebrow but Curtius Rufus shrugged and found a table in a corner away from the serving counter. He was not in the mood for gossip about the Circus. Soon, under the influence of wine, he felt more cheerful. Criton said after his sixth cup, 'It really is good to be back. I will go and see Pylades in the morning.'

'To get work?'

Criton shrugged. 'Perhaps. At least I will hear the scandal. Lucius Eggius and the others — we did not have very much in common. I missed the conversation of my friends. And you?'

Curtius Rufus said slowly, 'When I was out there I found it a great strain. It was difficult trying to be respectable. I wanted only one thing' — he took the dice from his tunic and rolled them on the table — 'to be back in Rome and living on my wits.' He paused. 'Now that I'm back, I'm not so sure. It was good to have a position and be somebody.' He laughed. 'I'm a little drunk. I feel cold here.' He touched his stomach. 'I still don't really understand why it was so important to get her back.' He paused again. He said, 'You know they raped her. Not Manissa, but the men who took her on the ship. She had a miscarriage too. That's why she didn't want to come back. I swore her to silence. But that's not in my report. Let's have another drink.'

Criton said, 'I don't believe it. You're making it up. You're drunk.'

Curtius Rufus did not answer. He played with the dice on the wet table. Criton signaled to the bar and said in a low voice, 'You should have killed Manissa.'

Curtius Rufus said in a slurred voice, 'I did better. I made a friend of him. We were successful. Remember?'

A cool voice said suddenly, 'Your wine, if you are not too drunk to drink it.'

Curtius Rufus raised his head. He saw a gold bracelet that he dimly recognized and a silver chain around a blue waist. He looked up into the ironic gaze of a tall girl with auburn hair. He said, 'Pero,' and grasped her wrist. 'What are you doing here?'

'Working,' she said calmly. 'I was told when you might reach Rome. He – he is very kind. I guessed you might come here to celebrate. I have been here seven nights now. I would have stayed ten.'

'And then?'

'And then I would have gone.' She glanced at Criton, who rose to his feet. 'Tell me where he is lodged and I will bring him. He is not safe alone. He gets drunk. In another hour he will be cheating at dice and become involved in a brawl. He is incapable of looking after himself.'

Criton thought of Manissa. 'You are probably right, Pero,' he said, and gave her the direction for which she asked.

Pero sat down. 'You were successful. I am glad for your sake. They will give you a fine job and you will go up in the world.'

'I doubt it.' Curtius Rufus thought of what Lucius Eggius had last said. Well, he might deserve it but the gold ring of the lower nobility was hardly likely to come his way. He laughed. 'If I am very lucky I might get a job with the Circus, but the senior post usually goes to an officer of the equestrian order. I doubt it. There would have to be a vacancy on the staff, and I am in trouble over exceeding my authority. I have very little money. I am back where I was.'

She said, 'You must tell me all about it when you are less tired. I should like to hear it all.'

Criton said, 'I will see you later. I feel inspiration coming over me.' He walked unsteadily toward the door.

Curtius Rufus thought of Urracca and of all that had happened and knew that there were things he would never tell anyone; things he himself still did not understand, never would understand.

He said, 'I have a small present for you. Here, take it. It is very old, and if I told you where it came from you would not believe me.'

She opened the pouch and looked at it, turning it in her hand so that the triple ring, each shank of which was set with an oval emerald in a gold frame, blazed in the light. 'It is beautiful,' she said, and gave him a smile that brought him a moment's pain. She would never know that he had intended it for someone else.

Her smile faded. She said quietly, 'Don't send me away. I could not bear it.'

They looked at each other. Then Curtius Rufus smiled. He said, 'I won't do that.' He took hold of both her hands. 'I am not a good choice. I shall make you miserable, just as you said.'

She smiled. 'What happened to your bracelet? Did you lose it or give it away? It doesn't matter. I will buy you a new one when I have saved some money, and am rich.'

He said, 'That's right; when we are rich.'

They held hands for a long time and then he paid the bill and they left the noise and the smoke and the smell of wine behind them, and walked through the dark streets to the small house on the Quirinal where Criton, writing poetry by the light of a single lamp, sat in his room and awaited their coming.